Nora Roberts is the number one New York Times bestselling author of more than one hundred novels. With more than 300 million copies of her books in print, and over 150 New York Times bestsellers to date, Nora Roberts is indisputably the most celebrated women's fiction writer today.

Visit her website at www.nora-roberts.co.uk

The Hollow

Nora Roberts

piatkus

PIATKUS

First published in the US in 2008 by Jove Books, The Berkley Publishing Group,
a division of Penguin Group (USA) Inc.
First published in Great Britain in 2008 by Piatkus Books
This paperback edition published in 2008 by Piatkus Books
Reprinted 2008, 2009, 2010

A CIP catalogue record for this book
is available from the British Library.

ISBN 978-0-7499-3885-7

Data manipulation by Phoenix Photosetting, Chatham, Kent
Printed in the UK by CPI Mackays, Chatham ME5 8TD

Papers used by Piatkus are natural, renewable and
recyclable products sourced from well-managed forests and certified
in accordance with the rules of the Forest Stewardship Council.

Mixed Sources
Product group from well-managed
forests and other controlled sources
www.fsc.org Cert no. SGS-COC-004081
© 1996 Forest Stewardship Council

Piatkus
An imprint of
Little, Brown Book Group
100 Victoria Embankment
London EC4Y 0DY

An Hachette UK Company
www.hachette.co.uk

www.piatkus.co.uk

In memory of my parents

Keep the home fires burning.

— LENA GUILBERT FORD

The natural flights of the human mind are not from pleasure to pleasure, but from hope to hope.

— SAMUEL JOHNSON

Prologue

∿

ON A BRIGHT SUMMER MORNING, A TEACUP POO-
dle drowned in the Bestlers' backyard swimming pool. At
first Lynne Bestler, who'd gone out to sneak in a solitary
swim before her kids woke, thought it was a dead squirrel.
Which would've been bad enough. But when she steeled
herself to scoop out the tangle of fur with the net, she recognized her neighbor's beloved Marcell.

Squirrels generally didn't wear rhinestone collars.

Her shouts, and the splash as Lynne tossed the hapless
dog, net and all, back into the pool, brought Lynne's husband rushing out in his boxers. Their mother's sobs and their
father's curses as he jumped in to grab the pole and tow the
body to the side, woke the Bestler twins, who stood screaming in their matching My Little Pony nightgowns. Within
moments, the backyard hysteria had neighbors hurrying to
fences just as Bestler dragged himself and his burden out
of the water. As, like many men, Bestler had developed an

attachment to ancient underwear, the weight of the water was too much for the worn elastic.

So Bestler came out of his pool with a dead dog, and no boxers.

The bright summer morning in the little town of Hawkins Hollow began with shock, grief, farce, and drama.

Fox learned of Marcell's untimely death minutes after he stepped into Ma's Pantry to pick up a sixteen-ounce bottle of Coke and a couple of Slim Jims.

He'd copped a quick break from working with his father on a kitchen remodel down Main Street. Mrs. Larson wanted new countertops, cabinet doors, new floors, new paint. She called it freshening things up, and Fox called it a way to earn enough money to take Allyson Brendon out for pizza and the movies on Saturday night. He hoped to use that gateway to talk her into the backseat of his ancient VW Bug.

He didn't mind working with his dad. He hoped to hell he wouldn't spend the rest of his life swinging a hammer or running a power saw, but he didn't mind it. His father's company was always easy, and the job got Fox out of gardening and animal duty on their little farm. It also provided easy access to Cokes and Slim Jims—two items that would never, never be found in the O'Dell-Barry household.

His mother ruled there.

So he heard about the dog from Susan Keefaffer, who rang up his purchases while a few people with nothing better to do on a June afternoon sat at the counter over coffee and gossip.

He didn't know Marcell, but Fox had a soft spot for animals, so he suffered a twist of grief for the unfortunate poodle. That was leavened somewhat by the idea of Mr. Bestler, whom he *did* know, standing "naked as a jaybird," in Susan Keefaffer's words, beside his backyard pool.

While it made Fox sad to imagine some poor dog drowning in a swimming pool, he didn't connect it—not then—to the nightmare he and his two closest friends had lived through seven years before.

He'd had a dream the night before, a dream of blood and fire, of voices chanting in a language he didn't understand. But then he'd watched a double feature of videos—the *Night of the Living Dead* and *The Texas Chainsaw Massacre*—with his friends Cal and Gage.

He didn't connect a dead French poodle with the dream, or with what had burned through Hawkins Hollow for a week after his tenth birthday. After the night he and Cal and Gage had spent at the Pagan Stone in Hawkins Wood—and everything had changed for them, and for the Hollow.

In a few weeks he and Cal and Gage would all turn seventeen, and that was on his mind. Baltimore had a damn good chance at a pennant this year, so that was on his mind. He'd be going back to high school as a senior, which meant top of the food chain at last, and planning for college.

What occupied a sixteen-year-old boy was considerably different from what occupied a ten-year-old. Including rounding third and heading for home with Allyson Brendon.

So when he walked back down the street, a lean boy not quite beyond the gangly stage of adolescence, his dense brown hair tied back in a stubby tail, golden brown eyes shaded with Oakleys, it was, for him, just another ordinary day.

The town looked as it always did. Tidy, a little old-timey, with the old stone townhouses or shops, the painted porches, the high curbs. He glanced back over his shoulder toward the Bowl-a-Rama on the Square. It was the biggest building in town, and where Cal and Gage were both working.

When he and his father knocked off for the day, he thought he'd head on up, see what was happening.

He crossed over to the Larson place, walked into the unlocked house where Bonnie Raitt's smooth Delta blues slid smoothly out of the kitchen. His father sang along with her in his clear and easy voice as he checked the level on the shelves Mrs. Larson wanted in her utility closet. Though the windows and back door were open to their screens, the room smelled of sawdust, sweat, and the glue they'd used that morning to install the new Formica.

His father worked in old Levi's and his Give Peace a Chance T-shirt. His hair was six inches longer than Fox's, worn in a tail under a blue bandanna. He'd shaved off the beard and mustache he'd had as long as Fox remembered. Fox still wasn't quite used to seeing so much of his father's face—or so much of himself in it.

"A dog drowned in the Bestlers' swimming pool over on Laurel Lane," Fox told him, and Brian stopped working to turn.

"That's a damn shame. Anybody know how it happened?"

"Not really. It was one of those little poodles, so they think it must've fallen in, then it couldn't get out again."

"You'd think somebody would've heard it barking. That's a lousy way to go." Brian set down his tools, smiled at his boy. "Gimme one of those Slim Jims."

"What Slim Jims?"

"The ones you've got in your back pocket. You're not carrying a bag, and you weren't gone long enough to scarf down Hostess Pies or Twinkies. I'm betting you're packing the Jims. I get one, and your mom never has to know we ate chemicals and meat by-products. It's called blackmail, kid of mine."

Fox snorted, pulled them out. He'd bought two for just this purpose. Father and son unwrapped, bit off, chewed in perfect harmony. "The counter looks good, Dad."

"Yeah, it does." Brian ran a hand over the smooth eggshell surface. "Mrs. Larson's not much for color, but it's good work. I don't know who I'm going to get to be my lapdog when you head off to college."

"Ridge is next in line," Fox said, thinking of his younger brother.

"Ridge wouldn't keep measurements in his head for two minutes running, and he'd probably cut off a finger dreaming while he was using a band saw. No." Brian smiled, shrugged. "This kind of work isn't for Ridge, or for you, for that matter. Or either of your sisters. I guess I'm going to have to rent a kid to get one who wants to work with wood."

"I never said I didn't want to." Not out loud.

His father looked at him the way he sometimes did, as if he saw more than what was there. "You've got a good eye, you've got good hands. You'll be handy around your own house once you get one. But you won't be strapping on a tool belt to make a living. Until you figure out just what it is you want, you can haul these scraps on out to the Dumpster."

"Sure." Fox gathered up scraps, trash, began to cart them out the back, across the narrow yard to the Dumpster the Larsons had rented for the duration of the remodel.

He glanced toward the adjoining yard and the sound of kids playing. And the armload he carried thumped and bounced on the ground as his body went numb.

The little boys played with trucks and shovels and pails in a bright blue sandbox. But it wasn't filled with sand. Blood covered their bare arms as they pushed their Tonka trucks through the muck inside the box. He stumbled back as the boys made engine sounds, as red lapped over the bright blue sides and dripped onto the green grass.

On the fence between the yards, where hydrangeas headed up toward bloom, crouched a boy that wasn't a boy. It bared its teeth in a grin as Fox backed toward the house.

"Dad! Dad!"

The tone, the breathless fear had Brian rushing outside. "What? What is it?"

"Don't you—can't you see?" But even as he said it, as he pointed, something inside Fox knew. It wasn't real.

"What?" Firmly now, Brian took his son's shoulders. "What do you see?"

The boy that wasn't a boy danced along the top of the chain-link fence while flames spurted up below and burned the hydrangeas to cinders.

"I have to go. I have to go see Cal and Gage. Right now, Dad. I have to—"

"Go." Brian released his hold on Fox, stepped back. He didn't question. "Go."

He all but flew through the house and out again, up the sidewalk to the Square. The town no longer looked as it usually did to him. In his mind's eye Fox could see it as it had been that horrible week in July seven years before.

Fire and blood, he remembered, thinking of the dream.

He burst into the Bowl-a-Rama where the summer afternoon leagues were in full swing. The thunder of balls, the crash of pins pounded in his head as he ran straight to the front desk where Cal worked.

"Where's Gage?" Fox demanded.

"Jesus, what's up with you?"

"Where's Gage?" Fox repeated, and Cal's amused gray eyes sobered. "Working the arcade. He's . . . he's coming out now."

At Cal's quick signal, Gage sauntered over. "Hello, ladies. What . . ." The smirk died after one look at Fox's face. "What happened?"

"It's back," Fox said. "It's come back."

One

~JL~

FOX REMEMBERED MANY DETAILS OF THAT LONG-ago day in June. The tear in the left knee in his father's Levi's, the smell of coffee and onions in Ma's Pantry, the crackle of the wrappers as he and his father opened Slim Jims in Mrs. Larson's kitchen.

But what he remembered most, even beyond the shock and the fear of what he'd seen in the yard, was that his father had trusted him.

He'd trusted him on the morning of Fox's tenth birthday, too, when Fox had come home, bringing Gage with him, both of them filthy, exhausted, and terrified, with a story no adult would believe.

There'd been worry, Fox reflected. He could still see the way his parents had looked at each other as he told them the story of something black and powerful and *wrong* erupting out of the clearing where the Pagan Stone stood.

They hadn't brushed it off as overactive imagination, hadn't even come down on him for lying about spending the night at Cal's and instead trooping off with his friends to spend the night of their tenth birthday in the woods west of town.

Instead they'd listened. And when Cal's parents had come over, they'd listened, too.

Fox glanced down at the thin scar across his wrist. That mark, one made when Cal had used his Boy Scout knife nearly twenty-one years before to make him, Cal, and Gage blood brothers, was the only scar on his body. He'd had others before that night, before that ritual—what active boy of ten didn't? Yet all of them but this one had healed smooth— as he'd healed from any injury since. Without a trace.

It was that mark, that mixing of blood, that had freed the thing trapped centuries before. For seven nights it had stormed through Hawkins Hollow.

They thought they'd beaten it, three ten-year-old boys against the unholy that infected the town. But it came back, seven years later, for seven more nights of hell. Then returned again, the week they'd turned twenty-four.

It would come back again this summer. It was already making itself known.

But things were different now. They were better prepared, had more knowledge. Only it wasn't just him, Cal, and Gage this time. They were six with the three women who'd come to the Hollow, who were connected by ancestry to the demon, just as he, Cal, and Gage were connected to the force that had trapped it.

Not kids anymore, Fox thought as he pulled up to park in front of the townhouse on Main Street that held his office and his apartment. And if what their little band of six had been able to pull off a couple weeks before at the Pagan Stone was any indication, the demon who'd once called himself Lazarus Twisse was in for a few surprises.

After grabbing his briefcase, he crossed the sidewalk. It had taken a lot of sweat and considerable financial juggling for Fox to buy the old stone townhouse. The first couple of years had been lean—hell, they'd been emaciated, he thought now. But they'd been worth the struggle, the endless meals of PB and J, because every inch of the place was his—and the Hawkins Hollow Bank and Trust's.

The plaque at the door read FOX B. O'DELL, ATTORNEY AT LAW. It could still surprise him that it had been the law he'd wanted—more that it had been small-town law.

He supposed it shouldn't. The law wasn't just about right and wrong, but all the shades between. He liked figuring out which shade worked best in each situation.

He stepped inside, and got a jolt when he saw Layla Darnell, one of that little band of six, behind the desk in his reception area. His mind went blank for a moment, as it often did if he saw her unexpectedly. He said, "Um . . ."

"Hi." Her smile was cautious. "You're back sooner than expected."

Was he? He couldn't remember. How was he supposed to concentrate with the hot-looking brunette and her mermaid green eyes behind the desk instead of his grandmotherly Mrs. Hawbaker? "I—we—won. The jury deliberated less than an hour."

"That's great." Her smile boosted up several degrees. "Congratulations. That was the personal injury case? The car accident. Mr. and Mrs. Pullman?"

"Yeah." He shifted his briefcase to his other shoulder and kept most of the pretty parlorlike reception area between them. "Where's Mrs. H?"

"Dentist appointment. It's on your calendar."

Of course it was. "Right. I'll just be in my office."

"Shelley Kholer called. Twice. She's decided she wants to sue her sister for alienation of affection and for . . . Wait." Layla picked up a message pad. "For being a 'skanky, no-good ho'—she actually said 'ho.' And the second call involved her wanting to know if, as part of her divorce settlement, she'd get her cheating, butt-monkey of a soon-to-be-ex-husband's points for some sort of online NASCAR contest because she picked the jerkwad's drivers for him. I honestly don't know what that last part means except for jerkwad."

"Uh-huh. Well, interesting. I'll call her."

"Then she cried."

"Shit." He still had a soft spot for animals, and had a spot equally soft for unhappy women. "I'll call her now."

"No, you'll want to wait about an hour," Layla said with a glance at her watch. "Right about now she's getting hair therapy. She's going red. She can't actually sue her skanky, no-good ho of a sister for alienation of affection, can she?"

"You can sue for any damn thing, but I'll talk her down from it. Maybe you could remind me in an hour to call her. Are you okay out here?" he added. "Do you need anything?"

"I'm good. Alice—Mrs. Hawbaker—she's a good teacher. And she's very protective of you. If she didn't think I was ready to fly solo, I wouldn't be. Besides, as office manager in training, I should be asking you if you need anything."

An office manager who didn't jump-start his libido would be a good start, but it was too late for that. "I'm good, too. I'll just be . . ." He gestured toward his office, then walked away.

He was tempted to shut the pocket doors, but it felt rude. He never closed the doors of his office unless he was with a client who needed or wanted privacy.

Because he never felt quite real in a suit, Fox pulled off the jacket, tossed it over the grinning pig that served as one of the hooks. With relief, he dragged off his tie and draped it over a happy cow. That left a chicken, a goat, and a duck, all carved by his father, whose opinion had been that no law office could be stuffy when it was home to a bunch of lunatic farm animals.

So far, Fox figured that ran true.

It was exactly what he'd wanted in an office, something part of a house rather than a *building*, with a view of neighborhood rather than urban streets. Shelves held the law books and supplies he needed most often, but mingled with them were bits and pieces of him. A baseball signed by the one and only Cal Ripken, the stained-glass kaleidoscope his mother had made him, framed snapshots, a scale model of the Millennium Falcon, laboriously and precisely built when he'd been twelve.

And, in a place of prominence sat the big glass jar, and its complement of dollar bills. One for every time he forgot and said fuck in the office. It was Alice Hawbaker's decree.

He got a Coke out of the minifridge he kept stocked with them and wondered what the hell he was going to do when Mrs. Hawbaker deserted him for Minneapolis and he had to deal with the lovely Layla not only as part of the defeat-the-damn-demon team, but five days a week in his office.

"Fox?"

"Huh?" He spun around from his window, and there she was again. "What? Is something wrong?"

"No. Well, other than Big Evil, no. You don't have any appointments for a couple of hours, and since Alice isn't here, I thought we could talk about that. I know you've got other work, but—"

"It's okay." Big Evil would give him focus on something other than gorgeous green eyes and soft, glossy pink lips. "Do you want a Coke?"

"No, thanks. Do you know how many calories are in that can?"

"It's worth it. Sit down."

"I'm too jumpy." As if to prove it, Layla rubbed her hands together as she wandered the office. "I get jumpier every day that nothing happens, which is stupid, because it should be a relief. But nothing's happened, nothing at all since we were all at the Pagan Stone."

"Throwing sticks and stones and really harsh words at a demon from hell."

"That, and Gage shooting at it. Or Cal . . ." She stopped, faced Fox now. "I still get shaky when I remember how Cal stepped right up to that writhing mass of black and shoved a knife into it. And now nothing, in almost two weeks. Before, it was nearly every day we saw it, felt it, dreamed of it."

"We hurt it," Fox reminded her. "It's off wherever demons go to lick their wounds."

"Cybil calls it a lull, and she thinks it's going to come back harder the next time. She's researching for hours every day, and Quinn, well, she's writing. That's what they do, and they've done this before—this kind of thing if not this precise thing. First-timer here, and what I'm noticing is they're not getting anywhere." She pushed a hand through her dark hair, then shook her head so the sexy, jagged ends of it swung. "What I mean is . . . A couple of weeks ago, Cybil had what she thought were really strong leads toward where Ann Hawkins might have gone to have her babies."

His ancestors, Fox thought. Giles Dent, Ann Hawkins, and the sons they'd made together. "And they haven't panned out, I know. We've all talked about this."

"But I think—I feel—it's one of the keys. They're your ancestors, yours, Cal's, Gage's. Where they were born may matter, and more since we have some of Ann's journals, we're all agreed there must be others. And the others may explain more about her sons' father. About Giles Dent. What was he, Fox? A man, a witch, a good demon, if there are such things? How did he trap what called itself Lazarus Twisse from that night in sixteen fifty-two until the night the three of you—"

"Let it out," Fox finished, and Layla shook her head again.

"You were meant to—that much we agree on, too. It was part of Dent's plan or his spell. But we don't seem to know any more than we did two weeks ago. We're stalled."

"Maybe Twisse isn't the only one who needs to recharge.

We hurt it," he repeated. "We've never been able to do that before. We scared it." And the memory of that was enough to turn his gilded brown eyes cool with satisfaction. "Every seven years all we've been able to do is try to get people out of the way, to mop up the mess afterward. Now we know we can hurt it."

"Hurting it isn't enough."

"No, it's not." If they were stalled, he admitted, part of the reason was his fault. He'd pulled back. He'd made excuses not to push Layla on honing the skill—the one that matched his own—that had been passed down to her.

"What am I thinking now?"

She blinked at him. "Sorry?"

"What am I thinking?" he repeated, and deliberately recited the alphabet in his head.

"I told you before I can't read minds, and I don't want—"

"And I told you it's not exactly like that, but close enough." He eased a hip onto the corner of his sturdy old desk, and brought their gazes more level. His conservative oxford-cloth shirt was open at the throat, and his dark brown hair waved around his sharp-featured face and brushed the back of his collar. "You can and do get impressions, get a sense, even an image in your head. Try again."

"Having good instincts isn't the same as—"

"That's bullshit. You're letting yourself be afraid of what's inside you because of where it came from, and because it makes you other than—"

"Human?"

"No. Makes you 'other.' " He understood the complexity of her feelings on this issue. There was something in him that was other as well. At times it was more difficult to wear than a suit and tie. But to Fox's mind, doing the difficult was just part of living. "It doesn't matter where it came from, Layla. You have what you have and are what you are for a reason."

"Easy to say when you can put your ancestry back to some bright, shining light, and mine goes back to a demon who raped some poor sixteen-year-old girl."

"Thinking that's only letting him score points off you. Try again," Fox insisted, and this time grabbed her hand before she could evade him.

"I don't—stop pushing it at me," she snapped. Her free hand pressed against her temple.

It was a jolt, he knew, to have something pop in there when you weren't prepared. But it couldn't be helped. "What am I thinking?"

"I don't know. I just see a bunch of letters in my head."

"Exactly." Approval spread in his smile, and reached his eyes. "Because I was thinking of a bunch of letters. You can't go back." He spoke gently now. "And you wouldn't if you could. You wouldn't just pack up, go back to New York, and beg your boss at the boutique to give you your job back."

Layla snatched her hand away as color flooded her cheeks. "I don't want you prying into my thoughts and feelings."

"No, you're right. And I don't make a habit of it. But, Layla, if you can't or won't trust me with what's barely under the surface, you and I are going to be next to useless. Cal and Quinn, they flash back to things that happened before, and Gage and Cybil get images, or even just possibilities of what's coming next. We're the now, you and me. And the now is pretty damn important. You said we're stalled. Okay then, let's get moving."

"It's easier for you, easier for you to accept because you've had this thing . . ." She waved a finger beside her temple. "You've had this for twenty years."

"Haven't you?" he countered. "It's more likely you've had it since you were born."

"Because of the demon hanging on my family tree?"

"That's right. That's an established fact. What you do

about it's up to you. You used what you have a couple of weeks ago when we were on our way to the Pagan Stone. You made that choice. I told you once before, Layla, you've got to commit."

"I have. I lost my job over this. I've sublet my apartment because I'm not going back to New York until this is over. I'm working here to pay the rent, and spending most of the time I'm *not* working here working with Cybil and Quinn on background, research, theories, solutions."

"And you're frustrated because you haven't found the solution. Commitment's more than putting the time in. And I don't have to be a mind reader to know hearing that pisses you off."

"I was in that clearing, too, Fox. I faced that thing, too."

"That's right. Why is that easier for you than facing what you've got inside you? It's a tool, Layla. If you let tools get dull or rusty, they don't work. If you don't pick them up and use them, you forget how."

"And if that tool's sharp and shiny and you don't know what the hell to do with it, you can do a lot of damage."

"I'll help you." He held out his hand.

She hesitated. When the phone in the outer office began to ring, she stepped back.

"Let it go," he told her. "They'll call back."

But she shook her head and hurried out. "Don't forget to call Shelley."

That went well, he thought in disgust. Opening his briefcase, he pulled out the file on the personal injury case he'd just won. Win some, lose some, Fox decided.

As he figured it was the way she wanted it, he stayed out of her way for the rest of the afternoon. It was simple enough to instruct her through interoffice e-mail to generate the standard power-of-attorney document with the specific names his client required. Or to ask her to prepare and send out a bill or pay one. He made what calls he needed to make himself rather than asking Layla to place them first.

That kind of thing had always struck him as stupid in any case.

He knew how to use the damn phone.

He managed to calm Shelley down, catch up on paperwork, and win a game of online chess. But when he considered sending Layla another e-mail to tell her to go ahead and knock off for the day, he realized that came under the heading of avoidance, not just keeping the peace.

When he walked out to reception, Mrs. Hawbaker was manning the desk. "I didn't know you were back," he began.

"I've been back awhile. I've just finished proofing the papers Layla took care of for you. Need your signature on these letters."

"Okay." He took the pen she handed him, signed. "Where is she? Layla?"

"Gone for the day. She did fine on her own."

Understanding it was a question as much as an opinion, Fox nodded. "Yeah, she did fine."

In her brisk way, Mrs. Hawbaker folded the letters Fox had signed. "You don't need both of us here full-time and can't afford to be paying double either."

"Mrs. H—"

"I'm going to come in half days the rest of the week." She spoke quickly now, tucking letters into envelopes, sealing them. "Just to make sure everything runs smoothly for you, and for her. Any problems, I can come in, help handle them. But I don't expect there to be. If there aren't problems, I won't be coming in after Friday next. We've got a lot of packing and sorting to do. Shipping things up to Minneapolis, showing the house."

"Goddamn it."

She merely pointed her finger at him, narrowed her eyes. "When I'm gone you can turn the air blue around here, but until I am, you'll watch your language."

"Yes, ma'am. Mrs. H—"

"And don't give me those puppy dog eyes, Fox O'Dell. We've been through all this."

They had, and he could feel her sorrow, and her fear. Dumping his own on her wouldn't help. "I'll keep the F-word jar in my office, in memory of you."

That made her smile. "The way you toss it around, you'll be able to retire a rich man on the proceeds of that jar. Even so, you're a good boy. You're a good lawyer, Fox. Now, you go on. You're clear for the rest of the day— what's left of it. I'm just going to finish up a couple things, then I'll lock up."

"Okay." But he stopped at the door, looked back at her. Her snowy hair was perfectly groomed; her blue suit dignified. "Mrs. H? I miss you already."

He closed the door behind him, and stuck his hands in his pockets as he walked down to the brick sidewalk. At the toot of a horn, he glanced over and waved as Denny Moser drove by. Denny Moser, whose family owned the local hardware store. Denny, who'd been a balletic third baseman for the Hawkins Hollow Bucks in high school.

Denny Moser, who during the last Seven had come after Fox with a pipe wrench and murder on his mind.

It would happen again, Fox thought. It would happen again in a matter of months if they didn't stop it. Denny had a wife and a kid now—and maybe this time during that week in July, he'd go after his wife or his little girl with a pipe wrench. Or his wife, former cheerleader and current licensed day-care provider, might slit her husband's throat in his sleep.

It had happened before, the mass insanity of ordinary and decent people. And it would happen again. Unless.

He walked along the wide brick sidewalk on a windy March evening, and knew he couldn't let it happen again.

Cal was probably still at the bowling alley, Fox thought.

He'd go there, have a beer, maybe an early dinner. And maybe the two of them could figure out which direction to try next.

As he approached the Square, he saw Layla come out of Ma's Pantry across the street, carrying a plastic bag. She hesitated when she spotted him, and that planted a sharp seed of irritation in his gut. After she sent him a casual wave, they walked to the light at the Square on opposite sides of the street.

It might have been that irritation, or the frustration of trying to decide to do what would be natural for him—to wait on his side of the corner for her to cross and speak to her. Or to do what he felt, even with the distance, she'd prefer. For him to simply keep going up Main so they didn't intersect. Either way, he was nearly at the corner when he felt the fear—sudden and bright. It stopped him in his tracks, had his head jerking up.

There, on the wires crossing above Main and Locust, were the crows.

Dozens of them crowded together in absolute stillness along the thin wire. Hulking there, wings tucked—and, he knew—watching. When he glanced across the street, he saw that Layla had seen them, too, either sensing them herself or following the direction of his stare.

He didn't run, though there was an urgent need to do just that. Instead he walked in long, brisk strides across the street to where she stood gripping her white plastic bag.

"They're real." She only whispered it. "I thought, at first, they were just another . . . but they're real."

"Yeah." He took her arm. "We're going inside. We're going to turn around, and get inside. Then—"

He broke off as he heard the first stir behind him, just a flutter on the air. And in her eyes, wide now, huge now, he saw it was too late.

The rush of wings was a tornado of sound and speed. Fox shoved her back against the building, and down. Pushing her face against his chest, he wrapped his arms around her and used his body to shield hers.

Glass shattered beside him, behind him. Brakes squealed through the crash and thuds of metal. He heard screams, rushing feet, felt the jarring force as birds thumped into his back, the quick sting as beaks stabbed and tore. He knew the rough, wet sounds were those flying bodies smashing into walls and windows, falling lifeless to street and sidewalk.

It was over quickly, in no more than a minute. A child shrieked, over and over—one long, sharp note after another. "Stay here." A little out of breath, he leaned back so that Layla could see his face. "Stay right here."

"You're bleeding. Fox—"

"Just stay here."

He shoved to his feet. In the intersection three cars were slammed together. Spiderwebs cracked the safety glass of windshields where the birds had flown into them. Crunched bumpers, he noted as he rushed toward the accident, shaken nerves, dented fenders.

It could have been much worse.

"Everybody all right?"

He didn't listen to the words: *Did you see that? They flew right into my car!* Instead he listened with his senses. Bumps and bruises, frayed nerves, minor cuts, but no serious injuries. He left others to sort things out, turned back to Layla.

She stood with a group of people who'd poured out of Ma's Pantry and the businesses on either side. "The damnedest thing," Meg, the counter cook at Ma's, said as she stared at the shattered glass of the little restaurant. "The damnedest thing."

Because he'd seen it all before, and much, much worse, Fox grabbed Layla's hand. "Let's go."

"Shouldn't we do something?"

"There's nothing to do. I'm getting you home, then we'll call Cal and Gage."

"Your hand." Her voice was awe and nerves. "The back of your hand's already healing."

"Part of the perks," he said grimly, and pulled her back across Main.

"I don't have that perk." She spoke quietly and jogged to keep up with his long, fast stride. "If you hadn't blocked me, I'd be bleeding." She lifted a hand to the cut on his face that was slowly closing. "It hurts though. When it happens, then when it heals, it hurts you." Layla glanced down at their clasped hands. "I can feel it."

But when he started to let her go, she tightened her grip. "No, I want to feel it. You were right before." She glanced back at the corpses of crows scattered over the Square, at the little girl who wept wildly now in the arms of her shocked mother. "I hate that you were right and I'll have to work on that. But you were. I'm not any real help if I don't accept what I've got in me, and learn how to use it."

She looked back at him, took a bracing breath. "The lull's over."

Two

~∿~

HE HAD A BEER SITTING AT THE LITTLE TABLE with its fancy iron chairs that made the kitchen in the rental house distinctly female. At least to Fox's mind. The brightly colored minipots holding herbs arranged on the windowsill added to that tone, he supposed, and the skinny vase of white-faced daisies one of the women must have picked up at the flower shop in town finished it off.

The women, Quinn, Cybil, and Layla, had managed to make a home out of the place in a matter of weeks with flea market furniture, scraps of fabric, and generous splashes of color.

They'd managed it while devoting the bulk of their time to researching and outlining the root of the nightmare that infected the Hollow for seven days every seven years.

A nightmare that had begun twenty one years before, on the birthday he shared with Cal and Gage. That night had changed him, and his friends—his blood brothers. Things had changed again when Quinn had come to town to lay the groundwork for her book on the Hollow and its legend.

It was more than a book to her now, the curvy blonde who enjoyed the spookier side of life, and who had fallen for Cal. It was more than a project for Quinn's college pal Cybil Kinski, the exotic researcher. And he thought it was more of a problem for Layla Darnell.

He and Cal and Gage went back to babyhood—even before, as their mothers had taken the same childbirth class. Quinn and Cybil had been college roommates, and had remained friends since. But Layla had come to the Hollow, come into this situation, alone.

He reminded himself of that whenever his patience ran a bit thin. However tightly the friendship was that had formed between her and the other two women, however much she was connected to the whole, she'd come into this alone.

Cybil walked in carrying a legal pad. She tossed it on the table, then picked up a bottle of wine. Her long, curling hair was pinned back from her face with clips that glinted silver against the black. She wore slim black pants and an untucked shirt of candy pink. Her feet were bare, with toenails painted to match the shirt.

Fox always found such details particularly fascinating. He could barely remember to match up a pair of socks.

"So . . ." Her deep brown eyes tracked over to his. "I'm here to get your statement."

"Aren't you going to read me my rights?" When she smiled, he shrugged. "We gave you the gist when we came in."

"Details, counselor." Her voice was smooth as top cream. "Quinn particularly likes details in the notes for her books and we all need them to keep painting the picture. Quinn's getting Layla's take upstairs while Layla changes. She had blood on her shirt. Yours, I'm assuming, as she didn't have a scratch on her."

"Neither do I, now."

"Yes, your super-duper healing power. That's handy. Run it through for me, will you, cutie? I know it's a pain, because when the others get here, they'll want to hear it, too. But isn't that what they say on the cop shows? Keep going over it, and maybe you'll remember something more?"

Since she had a point, he began at the moment he'd looked up and had seen the crows.

"What were you doing right before you looked up?"

"Walking up Main. I was going to drop in and see Cal. Buy a beer." Lips curved in a half smile, he lifted the bottle. "Came here and got one free."

"You bought them, as I recall. It just seems if you were walking toward the Square, and these birds were doing their Hitchcock thing above the intersection, you'd have noticed before you said you did."

"I was distracted, thinking about . . . work, and stuff." He raked his fingers through hair still damp from being stuck under the faucet to wash the bird gunk out. "I guess I was looking across the street more than up the street. Layla came out of Ma's."

"She walked over to get some of Quinn's revolting two percent milk. Was it luck—good or bad—that both of you were there, right on the spot?" Her head cocked to the side; her eyebrow lifted. "Or was that the point?"

He liked that she was quick, that she was sharp. "I lean toward it being the point. If the Big Evil Bastard wanted to announce it was back to play, it makes a bigger impact if at least one of us was on the scene. It wouldn't be as much fun if we'd just heard about it."

"I lean the same way. We agreed before that it's able to influence animals or people under some kind of impairment easier, quicker. So, crows. That's happened before."

"Yeah. Crows or other birds flying into windows, into people, buildings. When it does start, even people who were here when it happened before are surprised. Like it was the first time they'd seen anything like it. That's part of the symptoms, we'll call it."

"There were other people out—pedestrians, people driving by."

"Sure."

"And none of them stopped and said: Holy crap, look at all those crows up there."

"No." He nodded, following her. "No. No one saw them, or no one who did found them remarkable. That's happened before, too. People seeing things that aren't there, and people not seeing things that are. It's just never happened this far out from the Seven."

"What did you do after you saw Layla?"

"I kept walking." Curious, he angled his head in an attempt to read her notes upside down. What he saw were squiggles of letters and signs he didn't understand how anyone could decipher right-side up. "I guess I stopped for a second the way you do, then I kept walking. And that's when I . . . I felt it first, that's what *I* do. It's a kind of awareness. Like the hair standing up on the back of your neck, or that tingle between the shoulder blades. I saw them, in my head, then I looked up, and saw them with my eyes. Layla saw them, too."

"And still, no one else did?"

"No." Again, he scooped a hand through his hair. "I don't think so. I wanted to get her inside, but there wasn't time."

She didn't interrupt or question when he ran through the rest of it. When he was done, she set down her pencil, smiled at him. "You're a sweetheart, Fox."

"True. Very true. Why?"

She continued to smile as she rose, skirted the little table. She took his face in her hands and kissed him lightly on the mouth. "I saw your jacket. It's torn, and it's covered with bird blood and God knows what else. That could've been Layla."

"I can get another jacket."

"Like I said, you're a sweetheart." She kissed him again.

"Sorry to interrupt this touching moment." Gage strode in, his dark hair windblown, his eyes green and cynical. He stored the six-pack he carried in the fridge, then pulled out a beer.

"Moment's over," Cybil announced. "Too bad you missed all the excitement."

He popped the top. "There'll be plenty more before it's over. Doing okay?" he asked Fox.

"Yeah. I won't be pulling out my DVD of *The Birds* anytime soon, but other than that."

"Cal said Layla wasn't hurt."

"No, she's good. She's upstairs changing. Things got a little messy."

At Fox's glance, Cybil shrugged. "Which is my cue to go up and check on her and leave you two to man talk."

As she walked out, Gage followed her with his eyes. "Looks good coming or going." Taking a long pull on the beer, he sat across from Fox. "You looking in that direction?"

"What? Oh, Cybil? No." She'd left a scent in the air, Fox realized, that was both mysterious and appealing. But . . . "No. Are you?"

"Looking's free. How bad was it today?"

"We've seen a lot worse. Property damage mostly. Maybe some cuts and bruises." Everything about him hardened, inside and out. "They'd've messed her up, Gage, if I hadn't been there. She couldn't have gotten inside in time. They weren't just flying at cars and buildings. They were heading right for her."

"It could've been any one of us." Gage pondered on it a moment. "Last month, it went after Quinn when she was alone in the gym."

"Targeting the women," Fox said with a nod, "most specifically when one of them is alone. From the viewpoint—the faulty viewpoint—that a woman alone is more vulnerable."

"Not entirely faulty. We heal, they don't." Gage kicked back in his chair. "There's no way to keep three women under wraps while we try to come up with how to kill a centuries-old and very pissed-off demon. Besides that, we need them."

He heard the front door open and close, then shifted in his chair to watch Cal come in with an armload of take-out bags. "Burgers, subs," Cal announced. He dumped them on the counter as he studied Fox. "You're okay? Layla's okay?"

"The only casualty was my leather jacket. What's it like out there?"

Getting out his own beer, Cal sat with his friends. His eyes were a cold and angry gray. "About a dozen broken windows on Main Street, and the three-car pile-up at the Square. No serious injuries, this time. The mayor and my father got some people together to clean up the mess. Chief Larson's taking statements."

"And if it goes as it usually does, in a couple of days, nobody will think any more about it. Maybe it's better that way. If things like this stuck in people's minds, the Hollow'd be a ghost town."

"Maybe it should be. Don't give me the old hometown cheer," Gage said to Cal before Cal could speak. "It's a place. A dot on the map."

"It's people," Cal corrected, though this argument had gone around before. "It's families, it's businesses and homes. And it's ours, goddamn it. Twisse, or whatever name we want to call it, isn't going to take it."

"Doesn't it occur to you that it would be a hell of a lot easier to take him down if we didn't have to worry about the three thousand people in the Hollow?" Gage tossed back. "What do we end up doing through most of the Seven, Cal? Trying to keep people from killing themselves or each other, getting people medical help. How do we fight it when we're busy fighting what it causes?"

"He's got a point." Fox lifted a hand for peace. "I know I've wished we could just clear everybody the hell out, have a showdown. Fucking get it done. But you can't tell three thousand people to leave their homes and businesses for a week. You can't empty out an entire town."

"The Anasazi did it." Quinn stepped in from the doorway. She went to Cal first. Her long blonde hair swung forward as she leaned over his chair to kiss him. "Hi."

When she straightened, her hands stayed on his shoulders. Fox wasn't sure the gesture was purely out of affection or to soothe. But he knew when Cal's hand came up to cover one of hers, it meant they were united.

"Towns and villages have emptied out before, for mysterious and unexplained reasons," she continued. "The ancient Anasazi, who built complex communities in the canyons of Arizona and New Mexico, the colonial village of Roanoke. Causes might have been warfare, sickness, or something else. I've been wondering if some of those cases might be the something else we're dealing with."

"You think Lazarus Twisse wiped out the Anasazi, the settlers of Roanoke?" Cal asked.

"Maybe, in the case of the Anasazi, before he took any name we know. Roanoke happened after sixteen fifty-two, so we can't hang that on our particular Big Evil Bastard. Just a theory I've been kicking around." She turned to poke into the bags on the counter. "In any case, we should eat."

While food and plates were transferred to the dining room, Fox managed to get Layla aside. "Are you okay?"

"Yeah." She took his hand, turned it over to study the unbroken skin. "I guess you are, too."

"Listen, if you want to take a couple of days off, from the office, I mean, it's fine."

She released his hand, angled her head as she took a

long study of his face. "Do you really think I'm that . . . lily-livered?"

"No. I just meant—"

"Yes, you do. You think because I'm not sold on this idea of the—the Vulcan Mind Meld, I'm a coward."

"I don't. I figured you'd be shaken up—anyone would be. Points for the Spock reference, by the way, even though it's inaccurate."

"Is it?" She brushed past him to take her seat at the table.

"Okay." Quinn gave Cal's burger one wistful glance before she started on her grilled chicken. "We're all up to date on what happened at the Square. Bad birds. We'll log it and chart it, and I'm planning on talking to bystanders tomorrow. I wondered if it might be helpful to get one of the bird corpses and send it off for analysis. Maybe there'd be a sign of some physical change, some infection, something *off* that would come out in an autopsy."

"We'll just leave that to you." Cybil made a face as she nibbled on the portion of the turkey sub she'd cut into quarters. "And let's not discuss autopsies over dinner. Here's what I found interesting about today's event. Both Layla and Fox sensed and saw the birds, as far as I can tell, simultaneously. Or near enough to amount to the same. Now, is that simply because all six of us have some connection to the dark and the light sides of what happened, and continues to happen in Hawkins Hollow? Or is this because of the specific ability they share?"

"I'd say both," was Cal's opinion. "With the extra click going to shared ability."

"I tend to agree. So," Cybil continued, "how do we use it?"

"We don't." Fox scooped up fries. "Not as long as Layla pulls back from learning how to use what she's got. That's the way it is," he continued when Layla stared at him. "You don't have to like it, but that's how it is. What you have isn't any good to you, or to the team, if you won't use it, or learn how to use it."

"I didn't say I wouldn't, but I'm not going to have you shove it down my throat. And trying to shame me into it isn't going to work either."

"What will?" Fox countered. "I'm open to suggestions."

Cybil held up a hand. "Since I opened this can of worms, let me try. You've got reservations about this, Layla. Why don't you tell us what they are?"

"I feel like I'm losing pieces of myself, or who I thought I was. Adding this in, I'm never going to be who I was again."

"That may be," Gage said easily. "But you're probably not going to live past July anyway."

"Of course." On a half laugh, Layla picked up her glass of wine. "I should look on the bright side."

"Let's try this." Cal shook his head at Gage. "The odds are you'd have been hurt today if something hadn't clicked between you and Fox. And it clicked without either one of you purposely trying. What?" he asked as Quinn started to speak, then stopped herself.

"No. Nothing." Quinn exchanged a quick look with Cybil. "Let's just say I think I understand where everyone's coming from, and everyone makes a point. So I want to say, Layla, that maybe you could consider looking at it another way. Not that you're losing something with this, but you could be gaining something. Meanwhile, we're still going through Ann Hawkins's journals, and the other books Cal's great-grandmother gave us. And Cybil's working on finding where Ann might have gone the night Giles Dent faced down Lazarus Twisse at the Pagan Stone, where she stayed to have her sons, where she lived until she came back here when they were about two. We're still hopeful that if we find the place, we may find more of her journals. And Cybil also verified her branch of the family tree."

"A younger branch than all of yours, so far as I can tell," Cybil continued. "One of my ancestors, a Nadia Sytarskyi, traveled here with her family, and with others in the mid-nineteenth century. She married Jonah Adams, a descendent of Hester Deale. I actually get two branches, as about fifty years later, one of my other ancestors—Kinski side, also came here, and hooked up with Nadia and Jonah's grandchild. So, like Quinn and Layla, I'm a descendent of Hester Deale, and the demon who raped her and got her with child."

"Making us all one big happy family," Gage put in.

"Making us something. It doesn't sit well with me," Cybil added, speaking directly to Layla, "to know that part of what I have, part of what I am, comes down from something evil, something neither human or humane. In fact, it pisses me off. Enough that I intend to use everything I have, everything I am, to kick its ass."

"Does it worry you that it may be able to use what you have and are?"

Cybil lifted her glass again, her dark eyes cool as she sipped. "It can try."

"It worries me." Layla scanned the table, the faces of the people she'd come to care for. "It worries me that I have something in me I can't fully understand or control. It worries me that at some point, at any point, it may control me." She shook her head before Quinn could speak. "Even now I don't know if I chose to come here or if I was directed here. More disturbing to me is not being sure anymore if anything I've done has been a choice, or just some part of a master plan created by these forces—the dark and the light. That's what's under it for me. That's the sticking point."

"Nobody's chaining you to that chair," Gage pointed out.

"Ease off," Fox told him, but Gage only shrugged.

"I don't think so. She's got a problem, we've all got a

problem. So let's deal with it. Why don't you just pack up and go back to New York? Get your job back selling—what is it—overpriced shoes to bored women with too much money?"

"Step back, Gage."

"No." Layla put a hand on Fox's arm as he started to rise. "I don't need to be rescued, or protected. Why don't I leave? Because it would make me a coward, and up until now I've never been one. I don't leave because what raped Hester Deale, what put its half-demon bastard in that girl, drove her mad, drove her to suicide, would like nothing better than for me to cut and run. I know better than anyone here what it did to her, because it made me experience it. Maybe that makes me more afraid than the rest of you; maybe that was part of the plan. I'm not going anywhere, but I'm not ashamed to admit that I'm afraid. Of what's out there, and of what's inside me. Inside all of us."

"If you weren't afraid you'd be stupid." Gage lifted his glass in a half toast. "Smart and self-aware are harder to manipulate than stupid."

"Every seven years good people in this town, ordinary people, smart, self-aware people hurt each other, and themselves. They do things they'd never consider doing at any other time."

"You think you could be infected?" Fox asked her. "That you could turn, hurt someone? One of us?"

"How can we be sure I'm immune? That Cybil and Quinn are? Shouldn't we consider that because of our line of descent we could be even more vulnerable?"

"That's a good question. Disturbing," Quinn added, "but good."

"Doesn't fly." Fox shifted so Layla met his eyes. "Things didn't go the way Twisse planned or expected, because Giles Dent was ready for him. He stopped him from being around when Hester delivered, stopped him from potentially siring more offspring, so the line's been diluted.

You're not what he was after, and in fact, according to what we know, what we can speculate, you are part of what's going to give me, Cal, and Gage the advantage this time around. You're afraid of him, of what's in you? Consider Twisse is afraid of you, of what's in you. Why else has he tried to scare you off?"

"Good answer." Quinn rubbed her hand over Cal's.

"Part two," Fox continued. "It's not just a matter of immunity to the power he has to cause people to commit violent, abnormal acts. It's a matter of having some aspect of that power, however diluted, that when pooled together is going to end him, once and for all."

Layla studied Fox's face. "You believe that?"

He started to answer, then took her hand, tightening his grip when she started to pull it free. "You tell me."

She struggled—he could see it, and he could feel it— that initial and instinctive shying away from accepting the link with him. He had to resist the urge to push, and simply left himself open. And even when he felt the click, he waited.

"You believe it," Layla said slowly. "You . . . you see us as six strands braided together into one rope."

"And we're going to hang Twisse with it."

"You love them so much. It's—"

"Ah . . ." It was Fox who pulled away, flustered and embarrassed that she'd seen more, gone deeper than he'd expected. "So, now that we've got that settled, I want another beer."

He headed into the kitchen, and as he turned from the refrigerator with a beer in his hand, Layla stepped in.

"I'm so sorry. I didn't mean to—"

"It's nothing. No big."

"It *is*. I just . . . It was like being inside your head, or your heart, and I saw—or felt—this wave of love, that connection you have for Gage and Cal. It wasn't what you asked me to do, and it was so intrusive."

"Okay, look, it's a tricky process. I was a little more open than I should've been because I figured you needed me to be. The fact is, you don't need as much help as I thought. As you thought."

"No, you're wrong. I do need help. I need you to teach me." She walked to the window to look out at the dark. "Because Gage was right. If I keep letting this be a problem for me, it's a problem for all of us. And if I'm going to use this ability, I have to be able to control it so I'm not walking into people's heads right and left."

"We'll start working on it tomorrow."

She nodded. "I'll be ready." And turned. "Would you tell the others I went on up? It's been a very strange day."

"Sure."

For a moment, she just stood, looking at him. "I want to say, and I'm sorry if it embarrasses you, but there's something exceptional about a man who has the capacity to love as deeply as you do. Cal and Gage are lucky to have a friend like you. Anyone would be."

"I'm your friend, Layla."

"I hope so. Good night."

He stayed where he was after she'd gone, reminding himself to stay her friend. To stay what she needed, when she needed it.

Three

IN THE DREAM IT WAS SUMMER. THE HEAT GRIPPED with sweaty hands, squeezing and wringing out energy like water out of a rag. In Hawkins Wood, leaves spread thick and green overhead, but the sun forced its way through in laser beams to flash into his eyes. Berries ripened on the thorny brambles, and the wild lilies bloomed in unearthly orange.

He knew his way. It seemed Fox had always known his way through these trees, down these paths. His mother would have called it sensory memory, he thought. Or past-life flashes.

He liked the quiet that was country woods—the low hum of insects, the faint rustle of squirrels or rabbits, the melodic chorus of birds with little more to do on a hot summer day but sing and wing.

Yes, he knew his way here, knew the sounds here, knew even the feel of the air in every season, for he had walked here in every season. Melting summers, burgeoning springs, brisk autumns, brutal winters. So he recognized the chill in the air when it crawled up his spine, and the sudden change of light, the gray tinge that wasn't the simplicity of a stray cloud over the sun. He knew the soft growl that came from behind, from in front, and choked off the music of the chickadees and jays.

He continued to walk the path to Hester's Pool.

Fear walked with him. It trickled along his skin like sweat, urged him to run. He had no weapon, and in the dream didn't question why he would come here alone, unarmed. When the trees—denuded now—began to bleed, he kept on. The blood was a lie; the blood was fear.

He stopped only when he saw the woman. She stood at the small dark pond, her back to him. She bent, gathering stones, filling her pockets with them.

Hester. Hester Deale. In the dream he called out to her, though he knew she was doomed. He couldn't go back hundreds of years and stop her from drowning herself. Nor could he stop himself from trying.

So he called out to her as he hurried forward, as the growling turned to a wet snicker of horrible amusement.

Don't. Don't. It wasn't your fault. None of it was your fault.

When she turned, when she looked into his eyes, it wasn't Hester, but Layla. Tears streaked her face like bitter rain, and her face was white as bone.

I can't stop. I don't want to die. Help me. Can't you help me?

Now he began to run, to run toward her, but the path stretched longer and longer, the snickering grew louder and louder. She held out her hands to him, a final plea before she fell into the pool, and vanished.

He leaped. The water was viciously, brutally cold. He dove down, searching until his burning lungs sent him up to gulp in air. A storm raged in the woods now, wild red lightning, cracking thunder, sparking fires that engulfed entire trees. He dove again, calling for Layla with his mind.

When he saw her, he plunged deeper.

Once again their eyes met, once again she reached for him.

She embraced him. Her mouth took his in a kiss that was as cold as the water. And she dragged him down to drown.

HE WOKE GASPING FOR AIR, HIS THROAT RAW AND burning. His chest pounded with pain as he fumbled for the light, as he shoved up and over to sit on the side of the bed and catch his laboring breath.

Not in the woods, not in the pond, he told himself, but in his own bed, in his own apartment. As he pressed the heels of his hands to his eyes he reminded himself he should be used to the nightmares. He and Cal and Gage had been plagued by them every seven years since they'd turned ten. He should be used, too, to pulling aspects of the dream back with him.

He was still chilled, his skin shivering spasmodically over frigid bones. The iron taste of the pool's water still coated his throat. Not real, he thought. No more real than bleeding trees or fires that didn't burn. Just another nasty jab by a demon from hell. No permanent damage.

He rose, left the bedroom, crossed his living room, and went into the kitchen. He pulled a cold bottle of water out of the fridge and drank half of it down as he stood.

When the phone rang, he felt a fresh spurt of alarm. Layla's number was displayed on the caller ID. "What's wrong?"

"You're okay." Her breath came out in a long, jerky whoosh. "You're okay."

"Why wouldn't I be?"

"I . . . God, it's three in the morning. I'm sorry. Panic attack. I woke you up. Sorry."

"You didn't wake me up. Why wouldn't I be okay, Layla?"

"It was just a dream. I shouldn't have called you."

"We were at Hester's Pool."

There was a moment of silence. "I killed you."

"As attorney for the defense, I have to advise that's going to be a hard case to prosecute, as the victim is currently alive and well and standing in his own kitchen."

"Fox—"

"It was a dream. A bad one, but still a dream. He's playing on your weakness, Layla." And mine, Fox realized, because I want to save the girl. "I can come over. We'll—"

"No, no, I feel stupid enough calling you. It was just so real, you know?"

"Yeah, I do."

"I didn't think, I just grabbed the phone. All right, calmer now. We'll need to talk about this tomorrow."

"We will. Try to get some sleep."

"You, too. And Fox, I'm glad I didn't drown you in Hester's Pool."

"I'm pretty happy about that myself. Good night."

Fox carried the bottle of water back to the bedroom. There, he stood looking out the window that faced the street. The Hollow was quiet, and still as a photograph. Nothing stirred. The people he loved, the people he knew, were safe in their beds.

But he stood there, watchful in the dark and thought about a kiss that had been cold as the grave. And still seductive.

"CAN YOU REMEMBER ANY OTHER DETAILS?" CYBIL wrote notes on Layla's dream as Layla finished off her coffee.

"I think I gave you everything."

"Okay." Cybil leaned back in the kitchen chair, tapped

her pencil. "The way it sounds, you and Fox had the same dream. It'll be interesting to see if they were exact, or how the details vary."

"Interesting."

"And informative. You could've woke me, Layla. We all know what it's like to have these nightmares."

"I felt steadier after I'd spoken to Fox, and he wasn't dead." She managed a small smile. "Plus, I don't need to be shrink-wrapped to figure out that part of the dream was rooted in what we talked about last night. My fear of hurting one of you."

"Especially Fox."

"Maybe especially. I'm working for him, for now. And I need to work with him. You and I and Quinn, we're, well, fish in the same pool. I'm not as worried about the two of you. You'll tell Quinn about the dream."

"As soon as she's back from her workout. Since I assume she dragged Cal to the gym with her, she'll probably talk him into coming back here for coffee. I can tell them both, and someone will fill Gage in. Gage was a little rough on you last night."

"He was."

"You needed it."

"Maybe I did." No point in whining about it, Layla thought. "Let me ask you something. You and Gage are going to have to work together, too, at some point. How's that going to work?"

"I'll cross that bridge when. And I think we'll figure out a way to handle it without shedding each other's blood."

"If you say so. I'm going to go up and get dressed, get to work."

"Do you want a ride in?"

"No, thanks. The walk'll do me good."

Layla took her time. Alice Hawbaker would be manning the office, and there would be little to do. With Alice there, Layla didn't think it would be wise to huddle with Fox over a shared dream. Nor would it be the best time to have a lesson on honing, and more important to her, controlling her ability.

She'd handle busywork for a couple of hours, run whatever errands Alice might have on tap. It had only taken her a few days to understand the rhythm of the office. If she had any interest or aspirations toward managing a law office, Fox's practice would have been just fine.

As it was, it would bore her senseless within weeks.

Which wasn't the point, Layla reminded herself as she deliberately headed to the Square. The point was to help Fox, to earn a paycheck, and to keep busy.

She stopped at the Square. And that was another point. She could stand here, she thought, she could look at the broken or boarded windows straight-on. She could tell herself to face what had happened to her the evening before, promise herself she would do all she could to stop it.

She turned, started down Main Street to cover the few blocks to Fox's office.

It was a nice town if you just overlooked what happened to it, in it, every seven years. There were lovely old houses along Main, pretty little shops. It was busy in the way small towns were busy. Steady, with familiar faces running the errands and making the change at the cash registers. There was a comfort in that, she supposed.

She liked the wide porches, the awnings, the tidy front yards and bricked sidewalks. It was a pleasant, quaint place, at least on the surface, and not quite postcardy enough to make it annoying.

The town's rhythm was another she'd tuned to quickly. People walked here, stopped to have a word with a neighbor or a friend. If she crossed the street to Ma's Pantry, she'd be greeted by name, asked how she was doing.

Halfway down the block she stopped in front of the little gift shop where she'd picked up some odds and ends for the house. The owner stood out front, staring up at her broken windows. When she turned, Layla saw the tears.

"I'm sorry." Layla walked to her. "Is there something—"

The woman shook her head. "It's just glass, isn't it? Just glass and things. A lot of broken things. A couple of those damn birds got through, wrecked half my stock. It was like they wanted to, like they were drunks at a party. I don't know."

"I'm so sorry."

"I tell myself, well, you've got insurance. And Mr. Hawkins'll fix the windows. He's a good landlord, and those windows will be fixed right away. But it doesn't seem to matter."

"I'd be heartbroken, too," Layla told her, and laid a hand on her arm for comfort. "You had really pretty things."

"Broken now. Seven years back a bunch of kids—we think—busted in and tore the place up. Broke everything they could, wrote obscenities on the walls. It was hard coming back from that, but we did it. I don't know if I've got the heart to do it again. I don't know if I have the heart." The woman walked back to her shop, went inside behind the broken glass.

Not just broken glass and broken things, Layla thought as she walked on. Broken dreams, too. One vicious act could shatter so much.

Her own heart was heavy when she walked into the reception area. Mrs. Hawbaker sat at the desk, fingers clicking away at the keyboard. "Morning!" She stopped and gave Layla a smile. "Don't you look nice."

"Thanks." Layla slipped off her jacket, hung it in the foyer closet. "A friend of mine in New York packed up my clothes, shipped them down for me. Can I get you some coffee, or is there anything you want me to get started on?"

"Fox said to ask you to go on back when you got in. He's got about thirty minutes before an appointment, so you go ahead."

"All right."

"I'll be leaving at one today. Be sure to remind Fox he's

in court in the morning. It's on his calendar, and I sent him a memo, but it's best to remind him at the end of the day, too."

"No problem."

From her observations, Layla thought as she walked down the hall, Fox wasn't nearly as forgetful or absent-minded as he and Alice liked to think. Since the pocket doors to his office were open, she started to knock on the edge as she entered. Then she just stopped and stared.

He stood in back of his desk in front of the window in his no-court-today jeans and untucked shirt, juggling three red balls. His legs were spread, his face absolutely relaxed, and those tiger eyes of his following the circle as his hands caught and tossed, caught and tossed.

"You can juggle."

She broke his rhythm, but he managed to catch two balls in one hand, one in the other before they went flying around the room. "Yeah. It helps me think."

"You can juggle," she repeated, dazed and delighted.

Because it was rare to see her smile just that way, he sent the balls circling again. "It's all timing." When she laughed, he shot them high, began to walk and turn as he tossed the balls. "Three objects, even four, same size and weight, not really a challenge. If I'm looking for a challenge I mix it up. This is just think juggling."

"Think juggling," she repeated as he caught the balls again.

"Yeah." He opened his desk drawer, dropped them in. "Helps clear my head when I'm . . ." He got a good look at her. "Wow. You look . . . good."

"Thanks." She'd worn a skirt and a short, cinched jacket and now wondered if it was too upscale for her current po-sition. "I got the rest of my clothes, and I thought since I had them . . . Anyway, you wanted to see me."

"I did? I did," he remembered. "Wait." He crossed to the doors, slid them closed. "Do you want anything?"

"No."

"Okay." His juggling-clear head was fogged up again thanks to her legs, so he went to his minifridge and took out a Coke. "I thought, since there's some time this morning, we should compare notes about the dream. Let's sit down."

She took one of the visitors' chairs, and Fox took the other. "You go first," she told him.

When he'd finished, he got up, opened his little fridge, and took out a bottle of Diet Pepsi. When he put it into her hand and she just stared at it, he sat again. "That's what you drink, right? That's what's stocked in the fridge at your place."

"Yes. Thanks."

"Do you want a glass?"

She shook her head. The simple consideration shouldn't have surprised her, and yet it did. "Do you keep Diet Sprite in there for Alice?"

"Sure. Why not?"

"Why not," she murmured, then drank. "I was in the woods, too," Layla began. "But it wasn't just me. She was in my head, or I was in hers. It's hard to tell. I felt her despair, her fear, like they were mine. I . . . I've never been pregnant, never had a child, but my body felt different." She hesitated, then told herself she'd been able to give Cybil the details. She could give them to Fox. "My breasts were heavy, and I understood, I *knew*, I'd nursed. In the same way I'd experienced her rape. It was that same kind of awareness. I knew where I was going."

She paused again, shifted so she could look at his face. He had a way of listening, she thought, so that she knew he not only heard every word, but also understood what came behind them. "I don't know those woods, have only been in them that one time, but I knew where I was, and I knew I was going to the pond. I knew why. I didn't want to go. I didn't want to go there, but I couldn't stop myself. I couldn't stop her. I was screaming inside because I didn't want to die, but she did. She couldn't stand it anymore."

"Couldn't stand what?"

"She remembered. She remembered the rape, how it felt, what was in her. She remembered, Fox, the night in the clearing. He—it—controlled her so that she accused Giles Dent of her rape, denounced him and Ann Hawkins as witches, and she assumed they were dead. She couldn't live with the guilt. He told her to run."

"Who?"

"Dent. In the clearing, just before the fire, he looked at her—he pitied her, he forgave her. He told her to run. She ran. She was only sixteen. Everyone thought the child was Dent's, and pitied her for that. She knew, but was afraid to recant. Afraid to speak."

It pierced her as she spoke of it. That fear, that horror and despair. "She was afraid all the time, Fox, and mad with that fear, that guilt, those memories by the time she delivered the child. I felt it all, it was all swimming inside her—and me. She wanted to end it. She wanted to take the child with her, and end that, too, but she couldn't bring herself to do it."

Those alert and compassionate eyes narrowed on Layla's face. "She thought about killing the baby?"

As she nodded, Layla drew air in slowly. "She feared it, and hated it, and still she loved it. It, not she. I mean—"

"Hester thought of the baby as 'it.' "

"Yes. Yes. But still, she couldn't kill the baby. If she had—I thought, when I understood that, if she had, I wouldn't be here. She gave me life by sparing the child, and now she was going to kill me because I was trapped with her. We walked, and if she heard me she must've thought I was one of the voices driving her mad. I couldn't make her listen, couldn't make her understand. Then I saw you."

She paused to drink again, to steady herself. "I saw you, and I thought, Thank God. Thank God, he's here. I could feel the stones in my hand when she picked them up, feel the weight of them dragging down the pockets of the dress we wore. There was nothing I could do, but I thought—"

"You thought I'd stop her." So had he, Fox mused. Save the girl.

"You were calling out, telling her it wasn't her fault. You ran to her—to me. And for an instant, I think she heard you. I think, I felt, she wanted to believe you. Then we were in the water, going down. I couldn't tell if she fell or jumped, but we were under the water. I told myself not to panic. Don't panic. I'm a good swimmer."

"Captain of the swim team."

"I told you that?" She managed a small laugh, wet her throat again. "I told myself I could get to the surface, even with the weight, I'm a strong swimmer. But I couldn't. Worse, I couldn't even try. It wasn't just the stones weighing me down."

"It was Hester."

"Yes. I saw you in the water, diving down, and then . . ." She closed her eyes, pressed her lips hard together.

"It's okay." Reaching over, he closed a hand over hers. "We're okay."

"Fox, I don't know if it was her, or if I . . . I don't know. We grabbed on to you."

"You kissed me."

"We killed you."

"We all came to a bad end, but it didn't actually happen. However vivid and sensory, it wasn't real. It was a hard way for you to get inside Hester Deale's head, but now we know more about her."

"Why were you there?"

"Best guess? We've got this link, you and me. I've shared dreams with Cal and Gage before. Same thing. But there was more this time, another level of connection. In the dream, I saw you, Layla. Not Hester. I heard you. That's interesting. Something to think about."

"When you juggle."

He grinned. "Couldn't hurt. We need to—"

His intercom buzzed. "Mr. Edwards is here."

Fox rose, flipped the switch on his desk. "Okay, give me a minute." He turned back to Layla as she rose. "We need some more time on this. My last appointment today's at—"

"Four. Mrs. Halliday."

"Right. You're good. If you're not booked, we could go upstairs after my last appointment, do some work on this."

It was time, Layla thought, to suit up. "All right."

He walked to the doors with her, slid them open. "We could have some dinner," he began.

"I don't want you to go to any trouble."

"I have every delivery place within a five-mile radius on speed dial."

She smiled a little. "Good plan."

He walked out with her to where two hundred and twenty pounds of Edwards filled a chair in reception. His belly, covered in a white T-shirt, pillowed over the waistband of his jeans. His scrubby gray hair was topped by a John Deere gimme cap. He pushed to his feet, held out a hand to clasp the one Fox offered.

"How you doing?" Fox asked.

"You tell me."

"Come on back, Mr. Edwards. We'll talk about it."

Works outside, Layla decided as Fox led his client back. A farmer maybe, or a builder, a landscaper. A couple clicks over sixty, and discouraged.

"What's his story, Alice? Can you tell me?"

"Property dispute," Alice said as she gathered up envelopes. "Tim Edwards has a farm a few miles south of town. Developers bought some of the land that runs with it. Survey puts some eight acres of Tim's land over the line. Developer wants it, so does Tim. I'm going to run to the post office."

"I can do that."

Alice wagged a finger. "Then I wouldn't get the walk or the gossip. I've got notes here on a trust Fox is putting together. Why don't you draft that out while I'm gone?"

Alone, Layla sat, got to work. Within ten minutes, she wondered why people needed such complicated, convoluted language to say the straightforward. She picked her way through it, answered the phone, made appointments. When Alice came back, she had questions. She noted that Edwards walked out looking considerably less discouraged.

By one o'clock, she was on her own and pleased to print out the trust Alice had proofed for her. By page two, the printer signaled its cartridge was out of ink. She went to the supply closet across from the pretty little law library hoping Fox stocked back-ups. She spotted the box on the top shelf.

Why was it always the top shelf? she wondered. Why were there top shelves anyway when not everyone in the world was six feet tall? She rose to her toes, stretched up and managed to nudge a corner of the carton over the edge of the shelf. With one hand braced on a lower shelf, she wiggled it out another inch.

"I'm going out to grab some lunch," Fox said from behind her. "If you want anything— Here, let me get that."

"I've almost got the damn thing now."

"Yeah, and it's going to fall on your head."

He leaned in, reached up, just as she turned.

Their bodies brushed, bumped. Her face tipped up, filled his vision as her scent slid around him like satin ribbons. Those sea-siren eyes made him feel a little drunk and a lot needy. He thought: Step back, O'Dell. Then he made the mistake of letting his gaze drop down to her mouth. And he was done.

He angled down, another inch, heard her breath draw in. Her lips parted, and he closed that last whisper of distance. A small, soft taste, then another, both feather light. Then her lashes swept down over those seductive eyes; her mouth brushed his.

The kiss went deeper, a slow slide into heat that tangled

his senses, that filled them with her until all he wanted was to sink and sink and sink. And drown.

She made some sound, pleasure, distress, he couldn't tell with the blood roaring in his ears. But it reminded him where they were. How they were. He broke the kiss, realized he was essentially shoving her into the storage closet.

"Sorry. I'm sorry." She was working for him, for God's sake. "I shouldn't have. That was inappropriate. It was—" Amazing. "It was . . ."

"Fox?"

He jerked back an entire foot at the voice behind him. When he whirled around, he could feel his stomach drop straight to his knees. "Mom."

"Sorry to interrupt." She gave Fox a sunny smile, then turned it on Layla. "Hi. I'm Joanne Barry. Fox's mother."

Why was there never a handy hole in the floor when you needed one? Layla thought. "It's nice to meet you, Ms. Barry. I'm Layla Darnell."

"I told you Layla's helping me out in the office. We were just . . ."

"Yes, you were."

Still smiling, she left it at that.

She was the kind of woman you'd probably stare at even if you weren't stunned stupid, Layla thought. There was all that rich brown hair waving wild around a strong-boned face with its full, unpainted mouth, and long hazel eyes that managed to look amused, curious, and patient all at once. Joann had the tall, willowy build that carried the low-slung jeans, boots, and skinny sweater look perfectly.

Since it appeared Fox had been struck dumb, Layla managed to clear her throat. "I, ah, needed a new cartridge. For the printer? It's on the top shelf."

"Right. Right. I was getting that." Fox turned, managed to collide with Layla again. "Sorry." Jesus Christ. He'd no more than pulled the box down when Layla snatched it away, and fled.

"Thanks!"

"Do you have a minute for me?" Jo asked sweetly. "Or do you need to get back to what you were doing when I came in?"

"Cut it out." Fox hunched his shoulders, led the way back to his office.

"She's very pretty. Who could blame you for playing a little boss and secretary?"

"Mom." Now he dragged his hands through his hair. "It wasn't like that. It was . . . Never mind." He dropped into a chair. "What's up?"

"I had some things to do in town. One of which was to drop by your sister's for lunch. Sparrow tells me she hasn't seen you in there for two weeks."

"I've been meaning to."

Jo leaned back against his desk. "Eating something that isn't fried, processed, and full of chemicals once a week won't kill you, Fox. And you should be supporting your sister."

"Okay. I'll go in today."

"Good. Second, I had some pottery to take into Lorrie's. You must've seen what happened to her shop."

"Not specifically." He thought of the smashed windows, the corpses of crows on Main Street. "How bad's the damage?"

"It's bad." Jo lifted a hand to the trio of crystals that hung from a chain around her neck. "Fox, she's talking about closing. Moving away. It breaks my heart. And it scares me. I'm scared for you."

He rose, put his arms around her, rubbed his cheek against hers. "It's going to be okay. We're working on it."

"I want to do something. Your dad and I, all of us, we want to do something."

"You've done something every day of my entire life." He gave her a squeeze. "You've been my mom."

She eased back to take his face in her hands. "You get

that charm from your father. Look right at me and reassure me it's going to be okay."

Without hesitation or guile, his eyes met hers. "It's going to be okay. Trust me."

"I do. She kissed his forehead, his cheek, then the other, then gave him a light peck on the lips. "But you're still my baby. I expect you to take good care of my baby. Now go have lunch at your sister's. Her eggplant salad's on special today."

"Yummy."

Tolerant, she gave him a light poke in the belly. "You ought to close the office for an hour and take that pretty girl to lunch with you."

"The pretty girl works for me."

"How did I manage to raise such a rule follower? It's disheartening." She gave him another poke before starting for the door. "I love you, Fox."

"I love you, Mom. And I'll walk out with you," he added quickly, realizing his mother would have no compunction about stopping by Layla's desk and pumping the pretty girl for information.

"I'll have another chance to get her alone and grill her," Jo said casually.

"Yeah. But not today."

THE SALAD WASN'T BAD, AND SINCE HE'D EATEN at the counter he'd had a little time to hang with his baby sister. Since she never failed to put him in a good mood, he walked back to his office appreciating the sunny, blustery day. He'd have appreciated it more if he hadn't run into Derrick Napper, his childhood nemesis, as the now Deputy Napper came out of the barbershop.

"Well, hell, it's O'Dell." Napper slipped on his dark glasses, looked up, then down the street. "Funny, I don't see any ambulances to chase."

"Did you get that buzz cut on the town nickel? Somebody overpaid."

Napper's smile spread thin on his tough, square face. "I heard you were at the scene yesterday when there was trouble at the Square. Didn't stand by and give a statement, or come in to file a witness report. Being the town shyster, you ought to know better."

"You'd be wrong on that, nothing new there. I stopped by and spoke to the chief this morning. I guess he doesn't tell his bootlickers everything."

"You ought to remember how many times my boot kicked your ass in the past, O'Dell."

"I remember a lot of things." Fox walked by. Once a bully, he thought, always an asshole. Before the Seven was over, he imagined he and Napper would tangle again. But for now, he put it out of his mind.

He had work to do, and as he opened the door of his office, admitted he had a road to smooth out. Might as well get it done.

As he came in, Layla walked toward reception holding a vase of the flowers Alice Hawbaker liked having in the offices. Layla stopped dead.

"I was just giving these fresh water. There weren't any calls while you were gone, but I finished the trust and printed it out. It's on your desk."

"Good. Listen, Layla—"

"I wasn't sure if there was anything to type up regarding Mr. Edwards, or—"

"Okay, okay, put those down." He settled it by taking the vase out of her hands and setting it on a table.

"They actually go over—"

"Stop. I was out of line, and I apologize."

"You already did."

"I'm apologizing again. I don't want you to feel weirded out because in the office we've got the employer-employee thing going on, and I made a move on you. I didn't intend . . . Your mouth was just there."

"My mouth was just there?" Her tone changed from flustered to dangerously sweet. "As in on my face, under my nose, and above my chin?"

"No." He rubbed his fingers in the center of his forehead. "Yes, but no. Your mouth was . . . I forgot not to do what I did, which was completely inappropriate under the circumstances. And I'm going to start pleading the Fifth in a minute, or maybe just temporary insanity."

"You can plead whatever you want, but you may want to consider that my mouth, which was just there, wasn't forming words like *no*, or *stop*, or *get the hell away from me*. Which it's perfectly capable of doing."

"Okay." He said nothing for a moment. "This is very awkward."

"Before or after we add your mother into it?"

"That moves it from awkward to farce." He slipped his hands into his pockets. "Should I assume you're not going to engage counsel and sue me for sexual harassment?"

She angled her head. "Should I assume you're not going to fire me?"

"I'm voting yes to both questions. So we're good here?"

"Dandy."

She picked up the vase and carried it to the right table. "By the way, I ordered another replacement cartridge for the printer." She slid a glance his way, lips just curved.

"Good thinking. I'll be—" He gestured toward his office.

"And I'll be—" She pointed to her desk.

"Okay." He started back. "Okay," he repeated, then looked at the supply closet. "Oh boy."

Four

~∿~

AT FOUR FORTY-FIVE, FOX WALKED HIS LAST
client of the day to the door. Outside, March was kicking
thin brown leaves along the sidewalk, and a couple of kids
in hoodies walked straight into the whooshing wind. Probably going up to the arcade at the bowling center, he
mused. Squeeze in a couple of games before dinner.

There'd been a day he'd have walked through the wind
for a couple of games of Galaxia. In fact, he thought, he'd
done that last week. If that made him twelve on some level,
he could live with it. Some things shouldn't change.

He heard Layla speaking on the phone, telling the caller
that Mr. O'Dell was in court tomorrow, but she could make
an appointment for later in the week.

When he turned she was keying it into the computer,
into the calendar, he supposed, in her efficient way. From
his angle he could see her legs in the opening of the desk,
the way she tapped a foot as she worked. The silver she
wore at her ears glinted as she swiveled to hang up the

phone, then her gaze shifted to meet his. And the muscles of his belly quivered.

He definitely wasn't twelve on this particular level. Thank God some things did change.

It must've been the goofy smile on his face that had her cocking her head at him. "What?"

"Nothing. Just a little internal philosophy. Anything important on that call?"

"Not urgent. It was only regarding a partnership agreement—a couple of women writing a series of cookbooks they believe are going to be bestsellers. Rachael Ray, step back, I'm told. They want to formalize their collaboration before they hit the big time. You have a busy schedule this week."

"Then I should be able to afford Chinese for dinner, if you're still up for it."

"I just need to shut down for the day."

"Go ahead. I'll do the same. We can go up through the kitchen."

In his office, Fox shut down his computer, shouldered his briefcase, then tried to remember exactly what state his apartment might be in.

Uh-oh. He realized he'd just hit another area at which he remained twelve.

Best not to think about it, he decided, since it was too late to do anything about it. Anyway, how bad could it be?

He walked into the kitchen where Mrs. Hawbaker kept the coffeemaker, the microwave, the dishes she'd deemed appropriate for serving clients. He knew she kept cookies in there, because he raided them routinely. And her vases, boxes of fancy teas.

Who'd stock cookies when Mrs. H deserted him? Wistfully, he turned when Layla came in.

"She buys the supplies with the proceeds from the F-word jar in my office. I tend to keep that pretty well funded. I guess she's told you."

"A dollar for every F-word, honor system. Since I've seen your jar, I'd say you're pretty free with the F-word, and honorable about it." He's so sad, she thought, and it made her want to cuddle him, to stroke the messy, waving hair. "I know you're going to miss her."

"Maybe she'll come back. Either way, life moves on." He opened the door to the stairway. "I might as well tell you since Mrs. H doesn't deal with my apartment, and in fact, refuses to go up here since an unfortunate incident involving oversleeping and neglected laundry, it's probably a mess."

"I've seen messes before."

But when she stepped up from the tidy office kitchen into Fox's personal one, Layla understood she'd underestimated the definition of mess.

There were dishes in the sink, on the counter, and on the small table that was also covered with what appeared to be several days of newspapers. A couple boxes of cereal (did grown men actually eat Cocoa Puffs?), bags of chips, a bottle of red wine, some bottles of condiments, and an empty jug of Gatorade fought for position on the short counter beside a refrigerator all but wallpapered with sticky notes and snapshots.

There were three pairs of shoes on the floor, a battered jacket slung over one of the two kitchen chairs, and a stack of magazines towered on the other.

"Maybe you want to go away for an hour, or possibly a week, while I deal with this."

"No. No. Is the rest this bad?"

"I don't remember. I can go check before—"

But she was already stepping over shoes and into the living room.

It wasn't as bad, he thought. Not really. Deciding to be proactive, he moved by her and began to grab up the debris. "I live like a pig, I know, I know. I've heard it all before." He stuffed an armload of discarded clothes into the neglected hall closet.

Sheer bafflement covered her face, coated her voice. "Why don't you hire a housekeeper, someone to come in once a week and deal with this?"

"Because they run away and never come back. Look, we'll go out." It wasn't embarrassment—hey, his place—as much as fear of a lecture that had him snatching up an empty beer bottle and a nearly empty bowl of popcorn from the coffee table. "We'll find a nice, sanitary restaurant."

"I roomed with two girls in college. I had to call in the Hazmat team at the end of the semester." She picked up a pair of socks from a chair before he could get there, then handed them to him. "But if there's a clean glass I could use some of that wine."

"I'll put one in an autoclave."

He grabbed more on his way back to the kitchen. Curious, Layla looked around the room, tried to see beyond the disarray. The walls were actually a very nice sagey shade of green, a warm tone that set off the wide oak trim around the windows. A gorgeous woven rug that might have been vacuumed sometime in the last decade, spread across a wide-planked floor of deep, dark wood. The art on the walls was lovely—watercolors, pen-and-ink sketches, photographs. The room might've been dominated by a big, flat-screen TV, and a flurry of components, but there was some beautiful pottery.

His brother's, she imagined, or his mother's. He'd shown her his younger brother's pottery business from the road once. She turned when she sensed Fox come in again.

"I love the art, and the pottery. This piece." She trailed a finger along a long, slender bottle in dreamy shades of blue. "It's so fluid."

"My mother's work. My brother, Ridge, did that bowl on the table under the window."

She walked to it. "It's gorgeous." She traced the gentle curve of its lip. "And the colors, the shapes of them. It's like a forest in a wide cup."

She turned back to take the glass of wine. "How about the art?"

"My mother, my brother, my sister-in-law. The photographs are Sparrow's, my younger sister."

"A lot of talent in one family."

"Then there are the lawyers, my older sister and me."

"Practicing law doesn't take talent?"

"It takes something."

She sipped her wine. "Your father's a carpenter, isn't he?"

"Carpentry, cabinetmaking. He made the table Ridge's bowl's on."

"Made the table." Now she crouched to get a closer look. "Imagine that."

"No nails, no screws. Tongue and groove. He's got magic hands."

She swiped a finger over the surface, through the dust. "The finish is like satin. Beautiful things." Eyebrows lifted, she rubbed her finger clean on the sleeve of Fox's shirt. "I'm forced to say you should take better care of them, and their environment."

"You wouldn't be the first. Why don't I distract you with food?" He held out a paper menu. "Han Lee's China Kitchen."

"It's a little early for dinner."

"I'll call ahead, tell them to deliver at seven. That way we can get some work done."

"Sweet and sour pork," she decided after a glance at the menu.

"That's it?" he asked when she handed it back to him. "Pitiful. Sweet and sour pork. I'll take care of the rest."

He left her again to make the call. A few minutes later she heard the sound of water running, dishes clinking. Rolling her eyes, she walked into the kitchen where he was attacking the dishes.

"Okay." Layla took off her jacket.

"No. Really."

"Yes." Rolled up her sleeves. "Really. One-time deal, since you're buying dinner."

"Should I apologize again?"

"Not this time." Her eyebrows lifted. "No dishwasher?"

"See, that's the problem. I keep thinking I should take out that bottom cabinet there, have one installed, but then I think, hey, it's just me, and I use paper plates a lot."

"Not often enough. Is there a clean dish towel some-where?"

"Oh. Well." He gave her a befuddled frown. "Be right back."

Shaking her head, Layla stepped up to the sink he'd de-serted and took over. She didn't mind. It was a mindless chore, oddly relaxing and satisfying. Plus there was a nice view from the window over the sink, one that stretched out to the mountains where the sunlight sprinkled over the steely peaks.

The wind was still kicking at the trees, and it billowed the white sheets hanging on a line in the yard below. She imagined the sheets would smell like the wind and the mountains when they were tucked onto their bed.

A little boy and a big black dog ran around a fenced yard with such joy and energy in the gallop she could al-most feel the wind on her own cheeks, rushing through her hair. When the boy in his bright blue coat leaped up to stand on his swing, his fingers tight on the chains, the thrill of height and speed pitched into Layla's belly.

Is his mother in the kitchen making dinner? she wondered dreamily. Or maybe it's the dad's turn to cook. Better, they're cooking together, stirring, chopping, talking about their day while the little boy lifts his face to the wind and flies.

"Who knew washing dishes could be so sexy?"

She laughed, glanced over her shoulder at Fox. "Don't think that's going to convince me to repeat the favor."

He stood where he was, a badly wrinkled dishcloth in his hand. "What?"

"Washing dishes is only sexy when you're not the one with your hands in the soapy water."

He came forward, put a hand on her arm. His eyes locked on hers. "I didn't say that out loud."

"I heard you."

"Apparently, but I was thinking, not talking. I was distracted," he continued when she took a step away from him, "by the way you looked, the way the light hit your hair, the line of your back, the curve of your arms. I was distracted," he repeated. "And open. What were you, Layla? Don't think, don't analyze. Just tell me what you were feeling when you 'heard' me."

"Relaxed. I was watching the little boy on the swing in the yard. I was relaxed."

"Now you're not." He picked up a plate, began to dry it. "So we'll wait until you are."

"You can do that, with me? Hear what I'm thinking?"

"Emotions come easier than words. But I wouldn't, unless you let me."

"You can do it with anyone."

He looked into her eyes. "But I wouldn't."

"Because you're the kind of man who puts a dollar in a jar, even if no one's around to hear you swear."

"If I give my word, I keep my word."

She washed another dish. The charm of sheets flapping in the wind, of a little boy and his big dog dissolved. "Did you always control it? Resist the temptation?"

"No. I was ten when I started tapping in. During the first Seven, it was scary, and I could barely keep a handle on it. But it helped. When it was over, that first time, I figured it would be gone."

"It wasn't."

"No. It was very cool to be ten and be able to sense what people were thinking, or feeling. It was big, and not just in the wow, I've got a superpower kind of thing. It was big because maybe I wanted to ace a history test, and the smartest kid in history was right there in the next row. Why not reach in, get the answers?"

Since he was drying dishes, he decided to take the extra step and actually put them away. She'd be calmer if they continued with the chore, if all hands were busy. "After a few times, a few aces, I started feeling guilty about it. And weird because I might take a peek into a random teacher's head to see what they were planning to toss at us. And I'd get stuff I shouldn't have known about. Problems at home, that kind of thing. I was raised to respect privacy, and I was invading it right and left. So I stopped." He smiled a little. "Mostly."

"It helps that you're not perfect."

"It took time to figure out how to deal. Sometimes if I wasn't paying enough attention, things would slip through—sometimes if I was paying too much attention, ditto. And sometimes it was deliberate. There were a couple of events with this asshole who liked to razz me. And . . . when I got a little older, there was the girl thing. Take a quick sweep through and maybe I'd see if I had a shot at getting her shirt off."

"Did it work?"

He only smiled, and slid a plate into its cabinet. "Then a couple weeks before we turned seventeen, things started happening again. I knew—we knew—it wasn't finished after all. It came home to me that what I had wasn't something to play around with. I stopped."

"Mostly?"

"Almost entirely. It's there, Layla, it's part of us. I can't control the fact that I might get a sense from someone. I can control pushing in, pulling out more."

"That's what I have to learn."

"And you may have to learn to push. If it comes down to someone's privacy or their life, or the lives of others, you have to push in."

"But how do you know when—when, if, who?"

"We'll work on it."

"I'm not relaxed around you, most of the time."

"I've noticed. Why is that?"

She turned away to get more dishes, then slid a bowl into the sink. The little boy had gone inside, she noted. In to eat dinner. His dog curled on the porch by the back door and slept off playtime.

"Because I'm aware you can, or could, sense what I think or feel. Or I worry that you can, so it makes me nervous. But you don't, because you hold back, or because I'm nervous enough to stop you. Maybe both. You didn't know what I was thinking, or feeling earlier today when you kissed me."

"My circuits were crossed at the time."

"We're attracted to each other. Would that be an accurate reading?"

"It's dead-on from my end."

"And that makes me nervous. It's also confusing, because I don't know how much we're picking up from each other, how much is just basic chemistry." Layla rinsed the bowl, passed it to Fox. "I don't know if this is something we should be dealing with, with everything else we have to worry about."

"Let's back up, just a little. Are you nervous because I'm attracted to you, or because we're attracted to each other?"

"Door number two, and I don't have to see inside your head when I can see by your face you like that idea."

"Best damn idea I've heard in weeks. Possibly years."

She planted a wet, soapy hand on his shirt as he started to lean in. "I can't relax if I'm thinking about going to bed with you. The idea of sex generally stirs me up."

"We could relax later. In fact, I can guarantee we'll be a lot more relaxed later if we finish the stirring-up part first."

She not only left her hand planted, but nudged him a full step back with it. "No doubt. But I compartmentalize things. It's how I'm built, it's how I work. This, between us, I have to put it in another compartment for a while. I have to think about it, worry about it, wonder about it. If I'm going to learn from you, if I'm going to help end what wants to end us, I need to focus on that."

His expression sober and attentive, he nodded. "I like to juggle."

"I know."

"And I like to negotiate. And," he dried her hand, then brought it to his lips, "I know when to let the opposing party consider all the options. I want you. Naked. In bed, in a room filled with shadows and quiet music. I want to feel your heart pound against my hand while I do things to you. So put that in your compartment, Layla."

He tossed aside his dishcloth as she stared at him. "I'm going to go get your wine. It should help you relax some before we get to work."

She was still staring when he strolled out. She managed to press a hand to her heart, and yes, it was pounding.

Obviously, she had a lot to learn if he'd had that in him and she hadn't sensed it.

It was going to take more than a glass of red wine to help her relax now.

SHE DRANK THE WINE; HE CLEARED OFF THE kitchen table. Then he poured her another glass. She didn't say a word, and he gave her room for silence, room for her thoughts until he sat.

"Okay, do you know how to meditate?"

"I know the concept." There was a thin edge of irritation in her tone. He didn't mind it.

"You ought to sit down so we can get started. The thing about meditating," he began when she joined him, "is most people can't really reach that level where they turn their minds off, where there's not something in there about work or their dentist appointment, the ache in their lower back.

Whatever. But we can get close. Yoga breathing, using the breath. Closing your eyes, picturing a blank white wall—"

"And chanting 'ummm.' How is that going to help me tap in to this thing? I can't walk around in a meditative state."

"It's to help clear yourself out after. To help you—I sound like my mother—cleanse your mind, your aura, balance your chi."

"Please."

"It's a process, Layla. So far, you've only skimmed the surface of it, or dipped your toe in. The deeper you go, the more it takes out of you."

"Such as?"

"Too deep for too long? Headaches, nausea, nosebleeds. It can hurt. It can drain you."

She frowned, then ran her finger down the bowl of her glass. "When we were in the attic of the old library, Quinn had a flashback to Ann Hawkins. And she came out of it pretty shaken up. Severe headache, queasy, clammy." Layla puffed out her cheeks. "All right. I'm crappy at meditating. When we end with the corpse position in yoga class, I'm relaxed, but I'm going to be thinking of what I'm doing next, or if I should buy this great leather jacket that came in. I'll practice. I can practice with Cybil."

Because she's safer than I am, Fox thought, and let that go. "All right, let's just skim along the surface for right now. Relax, clear the clutter out of the front of your mind. Like when you were doing the dishes."

"It's harder when it's deliberate. Things want to pop in."

"That's right. So compartmentalize," he suggested with an easy smile. "Put them in their slot. Tuck them away. Look at me." His hand moved to rest on hers. "Just look at me. Focus on me. You know me."

She felt a little strange, as if the wine had gone straight to her head. "I don't understand you."

"That'll come. Look at me. It's like opening a door.

Turn the knob, Layla. Put your hand on the knob and turn it, ease the door open, just a couple inches. Look at me. What am I thinking?"

"You hope I don't eat all the pot stickers." She *felt* his humor, like a warm blue light. "You did that."

"We did that. Stay at the door. Stay focused. Open it just a little wider and tell me what I'm feeling."

"I . . . calm. You're so calm. I don't know how you manage it. I don't think I'm ever that calm, and now, with what's happened, what's happening, I don't know if I'll ever be really calm again. And . . . You're a little hungry."

"I pretended to eat most of an eggplant salad at lunch. Which is why I ordered . . ."

"Kung Pao beef, snow peas, cold noodles, a dozen egg rolls, pot stickers. A *dozen* egg rolls?"

"If there are any leftovers, they're good for breakfast."

"That's disgusting. And now you're thinking I'd be good for breakfast," she added and drew her hand from under his.

"Sorry, that slipped through. Doing okay?"

"A little light-headed, a lot dazed, but yeah, okay. It's going to be easier with you though, isn't it? Because you know how to work it. Work me."

Picking up his neglected beer, he tipped back in his chair. "A woman comes into the shop you managed in New York. She's just browsing around. How do you know where to direct her, how to work her?"

"Satisfy her," Layla corrected, "not work her. Some of it would be the way she looks—her age, how she's dressed, what kind of bag, what kind of shoes. Those are surface things, and can lead in the wrong direction, but they're a start. And I grew up in the business, so I have a sense of customer types."

"But I'm betting nine times out of ten you knew when to get the flashy leather purse out of the stockroom or steer her toward the conservative black one. If she said she wanted a business suit, but really had a yen for a sexy little dress and fuck-me shoes."

"I had a lot of experience reading . . . Yes." She let out a hiss of breath, the annoyance self-directed. "I don't know why I keep resisting it. Yes, I'd often tune in. The owner called it my magic touch. I guess she wasn't far off."

"How did you do it?"

"If I'm assisting a customer, I'm, well, I'm focused on them, on what they want, what they like—and yeah, what I can sell them. You have to listen to what they say, and there's body language, and also my own sense of what would look great on them. And sometimes, I always thought it was instinct, I'd get a picture in my head of the dress or the shoes. I'd think it was reading between the lines of what they said when I chatted them up, but I might hear this little voice. Maybe it was their thoughts. I'm not sure."

She was easing into it, he thought, into acceptance of what she held inside her. "You were confident in what you were doing, sure of your ground, which is another kind of relaxation. And you cared. You wanted to get them what they really wanted or would work for them, make them happy. And make a sale. Right?"

"I guess so."

"Same program, different channel." He dug into his pocket, pulled out change. Cupping his palm away from her, he counted it out. "How much am I holding?"

"I—"

"The amount's in my head. Open the door."

"God. Wait." She took another sip of wine first. Too much running through her own head, Layla realized. Put it away. "Don't help me!" she snapped when he reached for her hand. "Just . . . don't."

Put it away, she repeated to herself. Clean it out. Relax. Focus. Why did he think she could do this? Why was he so sure? Why did so many men have such wonderful eyelashes? Oops. No side trips. She closed her eyes, visualized the door. "A dollar thirty-eight." Her eyes popped open. "Wow."

"Good job."

She jolted at the knock on the door.

"Delivery guy. Do him."

"What?"

"While I'm talking to him, paying him, read him."

"But that's—"

"Rude and intrusive, sure. We're going to sacrifice courtesy in the name of progress. Read him," Fox commanded as he rose and walked to the door. "Hey, Kaz, how's it going?"

The kid was about sixteen, Layla estimated. Jeans, sweatshirt, high-top Nikes that looked fairly new. Shaggy brown hair, small silver hoop in his right ear. His eyes were brown, and passed over her—lingered briefly—as bags and money changed hands.

She took a deep breath, nudged at the door.

Fox heard her make a sound behind him, something between a gasp and a snort. He kept on talking as he added the tip, made a comment about basketball.

After he closed the door, Fox set the bags on the table. "Well?"

"He thinks you're chill."

"I am."

"He thinks I'm hot."

"You are."

"He wondered if you're going to be getting any of that tonight and he wouldn't mind getting some of that himself. He didn't mean the egg rolls."

Fox opened the bags. "Kaz is seventeen. A guy that age is pretty much always thinking about getting some. Any headache?"

"No. He was easy. Easier than you."

He smiled at her. "Guys my age think about getting

some, too. But we usually know when it's just going to be egg rolls. Let's eat."

HE DIDN'T TRY TO KISS HER AGAIN, NOT EVEN when he drove her home. Layla couldn't tell if he thought about it, and decided that was for the best. Her own thoughts and feelings were a tangle of frayed knots, which told her she'd need to take Fox's advice and go for the meditation.

She found Cybil on the living room sofa with a book and a cup of tea.

"Hi. How'd it go?"

"It went well." Layla dropped into a chair. "Surprisingly well. I'm feeling a little buzzed, actually. Like I knocked back a couple of scotches."

"Want tea? There's more in the pot."

"Maybe."

"I'll get you a cup," Cybil said when Layla started to rise. "You look beat."

"Thanks." Closing her eyes, Layla tried the yoga breathing, tried to envision relaxing from the toes up. She made it to her ankles when she gave it up. "Fox says I should meditate," she told Cybil when Cybil came back with a fancy cup and saucer. "Meditation bores me."

"Then you're not doing it right. Try the tea first," she said as she poured some out. "And say what's on your mind, it's the best way to get it out of your mind so you can meditate."

"He kissed me."

"I'm shocked and amazed." Cybil handed Layla the cup, returned to the couch to curl her legs up. She gave a careless laugh when Layla frowned at her. "Sweetie, the guy's got those foxy Fox eyes on you all the time. He watches you leave the room, watches you come back in. Boy's got it bad."

"He said— Where's Quinn?"

"With Cal. Maverick found himself a card game, so Cal's house is empty for a change. They're taking advantage."

"Oh. Good for them. They're great together, aren't they? Just click, click."

"He's the one for her, no question. All the others she tried out were like O'Doul's."

"O'Doul's?"

"Near-love. Cal's the real deal. Easier to talk about them than you?"

Layla sighed. "It's confusing to feel this way. To feel him feeling this way, and to try not to feel him feeling it. Because that's only more confusing. Add in we're working together on multiple levels, and that creates a kind of intimacy, and that intimacy has to be respected, even protected because the stakes are so damn high. If you mix it up with the separate physical or emotional intimacy of personal relationship and sex, how do you maintain the basic order needed to do what we're all here to do?"

"Wow." Lips curved, Cybil sipped her tea. "That's a lot of thinking."

"I know."

"Try this. Simple and direct. Are you hot for him?"

"Oh God, yes. But—"

"No, no qualifiers. Don't analyze. Lust is an elemental thing, potent, energizing. Enjoy it. Whether you act on it or not, it gets the blood moving. You'll layer the rest onto it eventually. You'll have to. You're human and you're female. We have to layer on emotions and concerns, consequences. But take the opportunity to appreciate the right now." Cybil's dark eyes sparkled with humor. "Enjoy the lust."

Layla considered as she sampled her tea. "When you put it that way. It feels pretty good."

"When you finish your tea, we'll use your lust as your focus point to move into a meditation exercise." Cybil smiled over the rim of her cup. "I don't think you'll be bored."

Five

~⌇~

CYBIL'S LUST-AS-SPRINGBOARD MEDITATION MIGHT'VE given Layla a fit of giggles initially, but then she thought she'd done pretty well. Better, certainly, than her usual faking-it method at yoga class. She'd breathed in the lust, as instructed—navel to spine—breathed out the tension, the stress. Focused on that "tickle in the belly" as Cybil had described it. Owned it.

Somewhere around the laughter, the breathing, and the tickle, she'd relaxed so fully she'd heard her own pulse beating. And that was a first.

She slept deep and dreamless, and woke refreshed. And, Layla had to admit, energized. Apparently, meditation didn't have to bore her senseless.

With Fox in court and Alice at the helm, there was no reason to go into the office until the afternoon. Time, she thought as she showered, to dive into research mode with Cybil and Quinn. To put her energy into finding more answers. She still hadn't added the incident at the Square to her chart, or catalogued the dream both she and Fox had shared.

She dressed for the morning in jeans and a sweater before earmarking the afternoon wardrobe change for Secretary Layla. And that, she had to admit, was fun. It felt good to need to dress for work, to plan and consider the outfit, the accessories. In the weeks between leaving New York and starting at Fox's office, she'd been busy, certainly. She'd had enormous adjustments to make, monumental obstacles to face. But she'd missed working, missed knowing someone expected her to be in a certain place at a certain time to do specific tasks.

And, shallow or not, she'd missed having a reason to wear a great pair of boots.

As she headed out, intending to hit the kitchen for coffee, she heard the clacking of the keyboard from the office they'd set up in the fourth bedroom.

Quinn sat cross-legged in the chair, typing away. Her long blonde hair swayed in its sleek tail as she bopped her head to some internal music.

"I didn't know you were back."

"Back." Quinn hammered a few more keys, then paused to look over. "Swung by the gym, worked off a few hundred calories, screwed that with an enormous blueberry muffin from the bakery, but I figure I'm still ahead considering the stupendous and energetic sex I enjoyed last night. Got coffee, got showered, and am now typing up Cybil's notes on your dream." Quinn stretched up her arms. "And I still feel like I could run the Boston Marathon."

"That must've been some sex."

"Oh boy, oh boy." Wiggling her butt in the chair, Quinn let out her big, bawdy laugh. "I always thought it was romance novel hype that sex was better when you're in love. But I'm living, and extraordinarily satisfied, proof. But that's nearly enough about me. How are you?"

If she hadn't woken feeling energized, Layla mused,

two minutes around Quinn would have perked her right up. "While not extraordinarily satisfied, I'm feeling pretty peppy myself. Is Cybil up?"

"In the kitchen, doing her morning coffee and newspaper thing. We passed briefly, and she grunted something along the lines that you made progress with Fox yesterday."

"Did she mention that we happened to find our lips colliding in the storage closet at his office when his mother came in?"

Quinn's bright blue eyes popped wide. "She wasn't coherent enough. You tell me."

"I just did."

"I require details."

"I require coffee. I'll be back."

Another thing she'd been missing, Layla realized. Having fun and personal details to share with girlfriends.

In the kitchen Cybil nibbled on half a bagel as she read the newspaper spread over the table. "Not a single mention of the crows in today's paper," she announced when Layla walked in. "It's extraordinary, really. Yesterday, a brief article, stingy on the details, and no follow-up."

"It's typical, isn't it?" Thoughtful, Layla poured coffee. "Nobody pays a lot of attention to what happens here. And when there are reports or questions, interest, it doesn't stick, or it comes across as lore."

"Even the people who've lived through it, who live here, gloss it over. Or it glosses over on them."

"Some that remember it too well leave." Layla decided on yogurt, took out a carton. "Like Alice Hawbaker."

"It's fascinating. Still, there aren't any other reports on animal attacks, or unexplained occurrences. Not today, anyway. Well." With a lazy shrug, Cybil started to fold the paper. "I'm going to go tug on a couple of very thin threads toward finding where Ann Hawkins lived for our missing two years. It's damned irritating," Cybil added as she rose.

"There weren't that many people around here in sixteen fifty-two. Why the hell can't I find the right ones?"

BY NOON, LAYLA HAD DONE ALL SHE COULD DO with her housemates. She changed into gray trousers and heeled boots for her afternoon in the office.

On her walk she noticed that the windows on the gift shop had been replaced. Cal's father was a conscientious landlord, one she knew had a lot of pride in his town. And she noticed the large, hand-printed Going Out of Business Sale sign that hung in the display window.

That was a damn shame, she thought as she walked on. The lives people built, or tried to build, tumbling down around them, through no fault of their own. Some let it lie in ruins, unable to find the hope and the will to rebuild, and others shoved up their sleeves and put it back together.

There was new glass at Ma's Pantry, too, and on other shops and houses. People, jackets buttoned or zipped against the chill, came and went, in and out. People stayed. She saw a man in a faded denim jacket, a tool belt slung at his hips, replacing a door on the bookstore. Yesterday, she thought, that door had been scarred, its windows broken. Now it would be fresh and new.

People stayed, she thought again, and others strapped on their tool belts and helped them rebuild.

When the man turned, caught her gaze, he smiled. Layla's heart took a jump, a little bump that was both pleasure and surprise. It was Fox's smile. For a moment she thought she was hallucinating, then she remembered. His father was a carpenter. Fox's father was replacing the door of the bookstore, and smiling at her across Main Street.

She lifted her hand in a wave and continued to walk. Wasn't it interesting to get a glimpse of what Fox B. O'Dell might look like in twenty years?

Pretty damn good.

She was still laughing to herself when she went inside Fox's office and relieved Alice for the day.

Since she had the offices to herself, she slid in a CD and started the work Alice had left her to Michelle Grant on low volume, muting it whenever the phone rang.

Within an hour, she'd cleared the desk, updated Fox's calendar. Since she still considered it Alice's domain, she resisted killing another hour reorganizing the storage room and the desk drawers to her personal specifications.

Instead, she pulled out one of the books in her satchel that covered a local's version of the legend of the Pagan Stone.

She could see it in her mind's eye, ruling the clearing in Hawkins Wood. Rising altarlike out of the scorched ground, somber and gray. Solid, she thought now as she paged through the book. Sturdy and ancient. Small wonder how it had come by its name, she decided, as it had struck her as something forged by gods for whatever, whomever, they might worship.

A center of power, she supposed, not on some soaring mountaintop, but in the quiet, sleepy woods.

There was nothing new in the book she scanned—the small Puritan settlement rocked by accusations of witch-craft, a tragic fire, a sudden storm. She wished she'd brought one of Ann Hawkins's journals instead, but she didn't feel comfortable taking them out of the house.

She put the book away and tried the Internet. But that, too, was old news. She'd read and searched and read again, and there was no question both Quinn and Cybil were better at this end than she was. Her strength was in or-ganizing, in connecting the dots in a logical manner. At the moment, there were simply no new dots to connect.

Restless, she rose to walk to the front windows. She needed something to do, a defined task, something to keep her hands and her mind busy. She needed to do something. Now.

She turned back with the intention of calling Quinn and begging for an assignment, no matter how menial.

The woman stood in front of the desk, her hands folded at her waist. Her dress was a quiet gray, long skirt, long sleeves, high at the neck. She wore her sunny blonde hair in a simple roll at the nape.

"I know what it is to be impatient, to be restless," she said. "I could never sit long without an occupation. He would tell me there was purpose in rest, but I found it so hard to wait."

Ghosts, Layla thought. Why should a ghost trip her heartbeat when only moments ago she'd been thinking of gods? "Are you Ann?"

"You know. You are still learning to trust yourself, and what was given to you. But you know."

"Tell me what to do, tell *us* what to do to stop it. To destroy it."

"It is beyond my power. It is even beyond his, my beloved's. It is for you to discover, you who are part of it, you who are part of me and mine."

"Is it evil in me?" Oh, how the possibility of that burned in Layla's belly. "Can you tell me that?"

"It is what you make of it. Do you know the beauty of now? Of holding it?" Both grief and joy radiated in Ann's face, in her voice. "Moment to moment, it moves and it changes. So must you. If you can see into others, into heart and mind, if you can look and know what is real and what is false, can you not look into yourself for the answers?"

"This is now, but you're only giving me more questions. Tell me where you went before the night of the fire at the Pagan Stone."

"To live, as he asked of me. To give life that was precious. They were my faith, my hope, my truth, and it was love that conceived them. Now you are my hope. You must not lose yours. He never has."

"Who? Giles Dent? Fox." Layla realized. "You mean Fox."

"He believes in the justice of things, in the right of them." She smiled now, with absolute love. "This is his great strength, and his vulnerability. Remember, it seeks weakness."

"What can I— Damn it!" Ann was gone, and the phone was ringing.

She'd write it down, Layla thought as she hurried back to the desk. Every word, every detail. She damn well had something to do now.

She reached for the phone. And picked up a hissing snake.

The scream tore out of her as she flung the writhing black mass away. Stumbling back, more screams bubbling up in her throat, she watched it coil like a cobra with its long, slanted eyes latched on hers. Then it lowered its head and began to slither across the floor toward her. Prayers and pleas jostled in her head as she backed toward the door. Its eyes glowed red as it surged, lightning fast, to coil again between her and the exit.

She heard her breath, coming too fast, in quick pants now that hitched and clogged in her throat. She wanted to turn and run, but the fear of turning her back on it was too great. It began to uncoil, inch by sinuous inch, began to wind toward her.

Was it longer now? Oh God, dear God. Its skin glistened an oily black, and it undulated as it slunk its way across the floor. Its hissing intensified when her back hit the wall. When there was nowhere left to run.

"You're not real." But the doubt in her voice was clear even to her, and it continued to come. "Not real," she repeated, struggling to draw in her breath. Look at it! she ordered herself. Look at it and see. Know. "You're not real. Not yet, you bastard."

Gritting her teeth, she shoved away from the wall. "Go

ahead. Slither, strike, you're not *real*." On the last word she slammed her foot down, stabbing the heel of her boot through the oily black body. For an instant, she felt substance, she saw blood ooze out of the wound and was both horrified and revolted. As she ground down with all of her might, she *felt* its fury and, more satisfying, its pain.

"Yeah, that's right, that's right. We hurt you before, and we'll hurt you again. Go to hell, you—"

It struck. For an instant, one blinding instant, the pain was her own. It sent her pitching forward. Before she could scramble up to fight, to defend, it was gone.

Frantic, she yanked up her pants leg, searching for a wound. Her skin was unbroken, unmarred. The pain, she thought as she crawled toward her purse, was an illusion. It made me feel pain, it had that much in it. But not enough to wound. Her hands shook as she fumbled her phone out of her bag.

In court, she remembered, Fox was in court. Can't come, can't help. She hit speed dial for Quinn. "Come," she managed when Quinn answered. "You have to come. Quick."

"WE WERE ON OUR WAY OUT THE DOOR WHEN you called," Quinn told her. "You didn't answer the phone, your cell or the office number."

"It rang." Layla sat on the sofa in reception. She'd gotten her breath back, and had nearly stopped shaking. "It rang, but when I picked it up . . ." She took the bottle of water Cybil brought her from the kitchen. "I threw it over there."

When she gestured, Cybil walked over to the desk. "It's still here." She lifted the phone off its charger.

"Because I never picked it up," Layla said slowly. "I never picked anything up. It just made me think I did."

"But you felt it."

"I don't know. I heard it. I saw it. I thought I felt it." She looked down at her hand, and couldn't quite suppress a shudder.

"Cal's here," Cybil said with a glance out the window.

"We called him." Quinn rubbed Layla's arm. "We figured we might as well bring in the whole cavalry.

"Fox is in court."

"Okay." Quinn rose from her crouch in front of Layla when Cal came in.

"Is everyone all right? Nobody's hurt?"

"Nobody's hurt." With her eyes on Cal, Quinn laid a hand on Layla's shoulder. "Just freaked."

"What happened?"

"We were just getting to that. Fox is in court."

"I tried to reach him, got his voice mail. I didn't leave a message. I figured if he was out he didn't need to hear something was wrong when he'd be driving. Gage is on the way." Cal walked over, running a hand down Quinn's arm before he sat down beside Layla.

"What happened here? What happened to you?"

"I had visitors from both teams."

She told them about Ann Hawkins, pausing first when Quinn pulled out her recorder, then again when Gage came in.

"You said you heard her speak?" Cal asked.

"We had a conversation right here. Just me and a woman who's been dead for three hundred years."

"But did she actually speak?"

"I just said . . . Oh. Oh. How stupid am I?" Layla set the water aside, pressed her fingers to her eyes. "I'm supposed to stay in the moment, pay attention to the now, and I didn't. I wasn't."

"It was probably a fairly big surprise to turn around and see a dead woman standing at your desk," Cybil pointed out.

"I was wishing I had something to do, something to

keep me busy, and, well, be careful what you wish for. Let me think." She closed her eyes now, tried to picture the episode. "In my head," she murmured. "I heard her in my head, I'm almost sure. So I had, what, a telepathic conversation with a dead woman. It gets better and better."

"Sounds more like a pep talk from her end," Gage pointed out. "No real information, just get out there and give your all for the team."

"Maybe it's what I needed to hear. Because I can tell you the pep talk might have turned the tide when the other visitor showed up. The phone rang. It was probably you," she said to Quinn. "Then—"

She broke off when the door opened. Fox breezed in. "Somebody's having a party and didn't . . . Layla." He rushed across the room so quickly Quinn had to jump back or be bowled over. "What happened?" He gripped both her hands. "Snake? For fuck's sake. You're not hurt." He yanked up her trouser leg before she could answer.

"Stop. Don't do that. I'm not hurt. Let me tell it. Don't read me that way."

"Sorry, it didn't feel like the moment for protocol. You were alone. You could've—"

"Stop," she commanded, and deliberately pulled her hands from his, just as she deliberately tried to block him out of her mind. "Stop. I can't trust you if you push into my head that way. I won't trust you."

He drew back, on every level. "Fine. Fine. Let's hear it."

"Ann Hawkins came first," Quinn began, "but we'll go back to that if it's okay with you. She's just run that one."

"Then keep going."

"The phone rang," Layla said again, and told them.

"You hurt it," Quinn said. "On your own, by yourself. This is good news. And I like the boots."

"They've recently become my favorite footwear."

"But you felt pain." Cal gestured to her calf. "And that's not good."

"It was only for a second, and I don't know—honestly don't—how much of it was panic or the expectation of pain. I was so scared, for obvious reasons, then add in the snake. I was hyperventilating, and couldn't stop at first. I'd have passed out, I think, if I hadn't been more afraid of having a snake slithering all over me while I was unconscious. I have a thing."

Cybil cocked her head. "A snake thing? You have ophidiophobia? Snake phobia," she explained when Layla simply looked blank.

"She knows all kinds of stuff like that," Quinn said proudly.

"I don't know if it's an actual phobia. I just don't like—okay, I'm afraid of snakes. Things that slither."

Cybil looked at Quinn. "The giant slug you and Layla saw in the hotel dining room the day she checked in."

"Tapping in to her fears. Good one, Cyb."

"It was spiders when the four of you were together at the Sweetheart dance." Cybil cocked her eyebrow. "You've got a spider thing, Q."

"Yeah, but it's an ick rather than an eek."

"Which is why I didn't say you have arachnophobia."

"That would be Fox," Cal volunteered.

"No. I don't like spiders, but—"

"Who wouldn't go see *Arachnophobia*? The movie? Who screamed like a girl when a wolf spider crawled over his sleeping bag when we—"

"I was twelve, for Christ's sake." With the appearance of a man stuck between embarrassment and impatience, Fox jammed his hands in his pockets. "I don't like spiders, which is different from being phobic. They have too many legs, as opposed to snakes, who don't have any, and which I find kind of cool. I'm only somewhat freaked by spiders that are bigger than my goddamn hand."

"They were," Layla agreed.

Fox blew out a breath. "Yeah, I guess they were."

"She said, Ann said that it seeks out our weaknesses."

"Spiders and snakes," Cal offered.

"That ain't what it takes," Gage finished and got a ghost of a smile from Cybil.

"What scares you?" she asked him.

"The IRS, and women who can rattle off words like *ophidiophobia*."

"Everyone has fears, weak spots." Wearily, Layla rubbed the back of her neck. "It'll use them against us."

"We should take a break, get you home." Fox studied Layla's face. "You've got a headache. I see it in your eyes," he said stiffly when her back went rigid. "I'll close up for the day."

"Good idea." Quinn spoke up before Layla could object. "We'll go back to our place. Layla can take some aspirin, maybe a hot bath. Cyb'll cook."

"Will she?" Cybil said dryly, then rolled her eyes as Quinn smiled. "All right, all right, I'll cook."

When the women left, Fox stood in the center of the room, scanning it.

"Nothing here, son," Gage pointed out.

"But there was. We all felt it." Fox looked at Cal, got a nod.

"Yeah. But then none of us thought she imagined it."

"She didn't imagine it," Gage agreed, "and she handled it. There's not a weak spine among the three of them. That's an advantage."

"She was alone." Fox swung back. "She had to *handle* it alone."

"There are six of us, Fox." Cal's voice was calm, reasoned. "We can't be together or even buddied up twenty-four hours out of the day. We have to work, sleep, live, that's just the way it is. The way it's always been."

"She knows the score." Gage spread his hands. "Just like the rest of us."

"It's not a fucking hockey game."

"And she's not Carly."

At Cal's statement, the room went silent.

"She's not Carly," he repeated, quietly now. "What happened here today isn't your fault any more than what happened seven years ago was your fault. If you drag that around with you, you're not doing yourself, or Layla, any favors."

"Neither of you ever lost anyone you loved in this," Fox shot back. "So you don't know."

"We were there," Gage corrected. "So we damn well know. We know." He slid up his sleeve and held out the wrist scored with a thin white scar. "Because we've always been there."

Because it was pure truth, Fox let out a breath. And let go of the anger. "We need to come up with a system, a contact system. So if any of us are threatened while we're alone, all of us get the signal."

"We'll have to come up with something," Fox added. "But right now I need to close up, and get out of this suit. Then I want a beer."

BY THE TIME THEY ARRIVED AT THE RENTAL house, dinner preparations were already under way, with Quinn dragooned into serving as Cybil's line chef.

"What's cooking?" Cal leaned down, tipped Quinn's chin up, and kissed her mouth.

"All I know is I'm ordered to peel these carrots and potatoes."

"It was your idea to have dinner for six," Cybil reminded her, but smiled at Cal. "What's cooking is delicious. You'll like it. Now go away."

"He can peel carrots," Quinn objected.

"Fox can peel carrots," Cal volunteered. "He can handle vegetables because that's about all they ate at his house."

"Which is why you should practice," Fox shot back. "I want to talk to Layla. Where is she?"

"Upstairs. She . . . hmm," Quinn finished when Fox simply turned and walked out. "This ought to be interesting. Sorry I'm missing it."

He headed straight up. Fox knew the layout of the second floor, as he'd been drafted into carting up bits and pieces of furniture when the women were settling in. He turned straight into her bedroom, through the open door, where she was wearing nothing but a bra and a pair of low-cut briefs.

"I need to talk to you."

"Out. Get out. Jesus." She grabbed a shirt from the bed, whipped it in front of her.

"It won't take that long."

"I don't care how long it takes, I'm not dressed."

"For Christ's sake, I've seen women in their underwear before." But since she merely lifted her arm, pointed at the door, he compromised by turning around. "If you've got modesty issues, you should close your door."

"This is a houseful of women, and I . . . never mind."

He heard the rustling of clothes, slamming of drawers. "How's the headache?"

"It's fine—gone, I mean. I'm fine, so if that's all—"

"You might as well dismount."

"Excuse me?"

"From your high horse. And you can toss out the idea of me apologizing for reading you before. You were pumping off fear, and it rammed right into me. What happened after was instinctive, and doesn't make me a psychic Peeping Tom."

"You can curb your instincts, and do it all the time. You told me."

"It's a little tougher when it's someone I care about in crisis. So deal. Meanwhile you might want to start thinking about another job."

"You're *firing* me?"

He figured she'd had enough time to pull something on, so he turned around. He still had a crystal-clear picture of her wearing only bra and panties in his head, but had to admit she made an equally impressive picture wearing jeans, a sweater, and outrage.

"I'm suggesting you think about finding a job where you work around people, so you're not left alone. I'm in and out of the office, and once Mrs. H—"

"You're suggesting I need a babysitter?"

"No, and right now I'm saying you have a big overreact button, and your finger's stuck on it. I'm suggesting you shouldn't feel obligated to come back to the office, that if it makes you uneasy, I get it, and I'll make other arrangements."

"I'm living and working in a town where a demon comes to play every seven years. I have a lot more to be uneasy about than doing your damn filing."

"There are other jobs where you wouldn't be doing anyone's damn filing alone in an office on a regular basis. Alone in an office where you were singled out and attacked."

"In an office where I fought back and did some damage."

"I'm not discounting that, Layla."

"Sounds like it to me."

"I don't want to feel responsible for something happening to you. Don't say it." He held up a hand. "My office, my schedule, my feelings."

She angled her head, the gesture both acknowledgment and challenge. "Then you'll have to fire me or, to toss back your own advice, deal."

"Then I will—deal. We're going to try to come up with some sort of alarm or signal that can reach everyone at the same time. No more phone trees."

"What, like the Bat Signal?"

He had to smile. "That'd be cool. We'll talk about it."

When they walked out together, he asked, "Are we smooth now?"

"Smooth enough."

Despite Cybil's edict, the rest gathered in the kitchen. Whatever was on the menu already scented the air. Cal's dog, Lump, sprawled under the little cafe table, snoring.

"There's a perfectly good living room in the house," Cybil pointed out. "Well-suited for men and dogs, considering its current decor."

"Cyb still objects to the flea-market-special ambiance." Quinn grinned and crunched into a stalk of celery. "Feeling better, Layla?"

"Much. I'm just going to grab a glass of wine then go up and chart this latest business. By the way, why were you calling me? You said you'd tried to call me on the office phone and my cell."

"Oh God, with all the excitement, we forgot." Quinn looked over at Cybil. "Our top researcher's come up with another lead to where Ann Hawkins might have lived after the night at the Pagan Stone."

"A family by the name of Ellsworth, a few miles outside of the settlement here in sixteen fifty-two. They arrived shortly after Hawkins, about three months after from what I've dug up."

"Is there a connection?" Cal asked.

"They both came over from England. Fletcher Ellsworth. Ann named one of her sons Fletcher. And Ellsworth's wife, Honor, was third cousin to Hawkins's wife."

"I define that as connection," Quinn stated.

"Have you pinpointed the location?"

"Working on it," Cybil told Cal. "I got as much as I got because one of Ellsworth's descendents was at Valley Forge with George, and one of *his* descendents wrote a book about the family. I got in touch—chatty guy."

"They always talk to Cyb." Quinn took another bite of celery.

"Yes, they do. He was able to verify that the Ellsworths we're interested in had a farm west of town, in a place that was called Hollow Creek."

"So we just have to—" Quinn broke off, catching Cal's expression. "What?" Because he was staring at Fox, she turned, repeated. "What?"

"Some of the locals still call it that," Fox explained. "Or did, when my parents bought the land thirty-three years ago. That's my family's farm."

Six

IT WAS FULL DARK BY THE TIME FOX PULLED UP
behind his father's truck. The lateness of the hour had been
one of the reasons his parents weren't going to be invaded
by six people on a kind of scavenger hunt.

They'd have handled it, he knew. The house had always
been open to anyone, anytime. Relatives, old friends, new
friends, the occasional stranger could count on a bed, a
meal, a refuge at the Barry-O'Dells'. Payment for the hos-
pitality might be feeding chickens, milking goats, weeding
a garden, splitting wood.

Throughout his childhood the house had been noisy,
busy, and often still was. It was a house where those who
lived in it were encouraged to pursue and explore their own
paths, where the rules were flexible and individualized, and
where everyone had been expected to contribute to the
whole.

It was still home, he thought, the rambling house of stone

and wood with its wide front porch, its interesting juts and painted shutters (currently a sassy red). He supposed even if he ever got the chance to make his own, to build his own family, this farm, this house, this place would always be home.

There was music when he stepped into the big living room with its eccentric mix of art, its bold use of color and texture. Every piece of furniture was handcrafted, most by his father. Lamps, paintings, vases, bowls, throws, pillows, candles, all original work—family or friends.

Had he appreciated that as a child? he wondered. Probably not. It was just home.

A pair of dogs rushed from the rear of the house to greet him with welcoming barks and swinging tails. There'd always been dogs here. These, Mick and Dylan, were mutts—as they always were—rescued from the pound. Fox crouched to give them both a rub when his father followed them out.

"Hey." Brian's grin flashed, that instant sign of pleasure. "How's it going? You eat?"

"Yeah."

"Come on back. We're still at it, and there's a rumor about apple cobbler." Brian swung an arm over Fox's shoulders as they walked back to the kitchen.

"I was going to drop by today while I was working in town," Brian continued, "but I got hung up. Look what I found," he said to Jo. "He must've heard about the cobbler."

"It's all over town." Fox went around the big butcher-block table to kiss his mother. The kitchen smelled of his mother's herbs and candles, and the thick soup from the pot on the stove. "And before you ask, I've had dinner."

He sat in a chair he helped make when he'd been thirteen. "I came by to talk to you guys about the house—the farm."

"Moving back in?" Brian asked and picked up his spoon to dig back into what Fox recognized as his mother's lentil and brown rice soup.

"No." Though that door would always be open, he knew. "The main part of the house is pre–Civil War, right?"

"Eighteen fifties," Jo confirmed. "You know that."

"Yeah, but I wondered if you knew if it was built on any earlier structure."

"Possible," his father answered. "The stone shed out back's earlier. It stands to reason there was more here at one time."

"Right. You looked into the history. I remember."

"That's right." Jo studied his face. "There were people farming here before the white man came over to run them out."

"I'm not talking about the indigenous, or their exploitation by invaders." He did *not* want to get her started on that one. "I'm more interested in what you might know about after the settlers came here."

"When the Hollow was settled," Jo said. "When Lazarus Twisse arrived."

"Yeah."

"I know the land was farmed then, that the area was known as Hollow Creek. I have some paperwork on it. Why, Fox? We're not close to the Pagan Stone, we're outside of town."

"We think Ann Hawkins might have stayed here, had her sons here."

"On this farm?" Brian mused. "How about that?"

"She wrote journals, I told you about that, and how there are gaps in them. We haven't found any from the time she left—or supposedly left—the Hollow until she came back a couple years later. If we could find them. . . ."

"That was three hundred years ago," Jo pointed out.

"I know, but we have to try. If we could come by in the morning, first thing in the morning before I have any clients coming in—"

"You know you don't have to ask," Brian said. "We'll be here."

Jo said nothing for a moment. "I'll get the famous cobbler." She rose, stroking a hand over her son's shoulder on her way to the cupboard.

HE'D WANTED TO KEEP ALL OF IT AWAY FROM HIS family, away from home. When he drove the familiar roads back to the farm at the first break of dawn, Fox told himself this search didn't, wouldn't, pull his family in any further. Even if they proved Ann had stayed there on their land, even if they found her journals, it didn't change the fact the farm was one of the safe zones.

None of their families had ever been infected, none of them had ever been threatened. That wasn't going to change. He simply wouldn't allow it to change. The threat was coming sooner, and harder, that was fact. But his family remained safe.

He pulled in front of the farmhouse just ahead of Cal and Gage.

"I've got two hours," he told them as they got out. "If we need more, I can try to shuffle some stuff. Otherwise, it has to wait until tomorrow. Saturday's clear."

"We'll work it out." Cal stepped aside so that Lump and the two host dogs could sniff each other and get reacquainted.

"Here comes the estrogen." Gage lifted his chin toward the road. "Is your lady ready to ante up, Hawkins?"

"She said she is, so she is." But Cal walked to the car, drew Quinn aside when the women piled out. "I don't know if I can help you with this."

"Cal—"

"I know we went over this last night, but I'm allowed to be obsessive about the woman I love."

"Absolutely." She linked her hands around his neck so that her bright blue eyes smiled into his. "Obsess me."

He took the offered mouth, let himself sink in. "I'll do

what I can, you know that. But the fact is, I've been coming here all my life, slept in this house, ate in it, played in it, ran the fields, helped with chores. It was my second home, and I never got a single flash of the past, of Ann, of anything."

"Giles Dent wasn't here, neither were the ones—the guardians that came before him. Not so far as we know. If Ann came here to stay, she came here without him, and stayed on after Dent was already gone. This one's on me, Cal."

"I know." He touched her lips with his again. "Just take it easy on yourself, Blondie."

"It's a wonderful house," Layla said to Fox. "Just a wonderful spot. Isn't it, Cybil?"

"Like a Pissarro painting. What kind of farming, Fox?"

"Organic family farming, you could say. They'll be around back this time of morning, dealing with the animals."

"Cows?" Layla fell into step behind him.

"No. Goats, for the milk. Chickens, for the eggs. Bees for the honey. Vegetables, herbs, flowers. Everything gets used, and what's surplus we—they—sell or barter."

The scent of animals wound through the morning air, exotic to her city-girl senses. She spotted a tire swing hanging from the thick, gnarled branch of what she thought might be a sycamore. "It must've been great growing up here."

"It was. I might not have thought so when I was shoveling chicken manure or hacking at bindweed, but it was great."

Chickens clucked in their busy and urgent voices. As they rounded the house Fox saw his mother casting feed for them. She wore jeans, her ancient Wellingtons, a frayed plaid shirt over a thermal pullover. Her hair was down her back, a long, thick braid.

Now it was his turn for a flash from the past. He saw her in his mind, doing the same chore on a bright summer morning, but she'd worn a long blue dress, with a sling around her, and his baby sister tucked into it.

Singing, he remembered. She so often sang while she worked. He heard her now, as he'd heard her then.

"I'll fly away, O glory, I'll fly away—in the morning."

In the near paddock, his father milked one of the nannies, and sang with her.

And Fox's love for them was almost impossible to hold.

She saw him, smiled at him. "Timed it to miss the chores, I see."

"I was always good at it."

She cast the rest of the seed before setting her bucket down to come to him. She kissed him—forehead, one cheek, the other, the lips. "Morning." Then turned to Cal and did exactly the same. "Caleb. I heard you had news."

"I do. Here she is. Quinn, this is Joanne Barry, my childhood sweetheart."

"Apparently I have quite an act to follow. It's nice to meet you."

"Nice meeting you." She gave Quinn's arm a pat, then turned to Gage. "Where have you been, and why haven't you come to see me?"

She kissed him, then wrapped her arms around him in a hard hug.

He hugged back—that's what Cybil noted. He held on, closed his eyes and held tight. "Missed you," he murmured.

"Then don't stay away so long." She eased back. "Hello, Layla, it's good to see you again. And this must be Cybil."

"It must be. You have a very handsome farm, Ms. Barry."

"Thanks. Here comes my man."

"LaMancha goats?" Cybil commented and had Jo giving her another, longer look.

"That's right. You don't look like a goatherd."

"I saw some a couple of years ago in Oregon. The way the tips of the ears turn up is distinctive. High butterfat content in the milk, isn't that right?"

"It is. Would you like to try some?"

"I have. It's excellent, and fabulous for baking."

"It certainly is. Bri, Cybil, Quinn, and Layla."

"Nice to—hey, we've met." He grinned at Layla. "Sort of. I saw you yesterday, walking down Main."

"You were replacing a door at the bookstore. I thought how comforting it was that there are people who know how to fix what's broken."

"Our specialty. Nice job with the blonde, Cal," he added, giving Cal a one-armed hug and a wink. "About damn time," he said to Gage, and hugged him in turn. "You guys want breakfast?"

"We don't have a lot of time," Fox told him. "Sorry."

"No problem. I'll take the milk in, Jo."

"I'll get the eggs. Go ahead and put tea on, Bri. It's cold this morning." She turned back to Fox. "Let us know if you need anything, or if we can help."

"Thanks." Fox gestured the group aside while his mother began gathering eggs into a basket. "How do you want to start? Inside?"

"We know the house wasn't here then?" Quinn looked at Fox for confirmation.

"About a hundred years later, but it could have been built on another's foundation. I just don't know. That shed? Well, what's left of that shed, the one covered with vines? That was here."

"It's too small." Layla studied the remaining walls. "Would be, even for the time period for a house. If we're talking about a small family taking in a woman and her three babies, that couldn't have been big enough."

"A smokehouse maybe," Cybil mused. "Or an animal shelter. But it's interesting that most of it's still here. There could be a reason for that."

"Let me try the house first." Quinn studied the shed, the land, the big stone house. "Maybe walking around the house out here. I might get something. If not, we'll do a walk through, since it's okay with Fox's parents. If nothing then . . . there's the land, that grove of trees, the fields, certainly the little ruin there. Fingers crossed, okay?"

She crossed the fingers of her left hand, held the right out for Cal. "The clearing in the woods, that's sacred ground—magic spot. And the stone, it pushed those flashes right in. The attic in the library, that grabbed hold, too. I didn't have to do anything. I'm not sure what I should do."

"Think about Ann," Cal told her. "You've seen her, you've heard her. Think about her."

Quinn pictured Ann Hawkins as she'd seen her the first time, with her hair loose, carrying pails of water from the stream, her belly huge with her sons, and her face alight with love for the man who waited for her. She pictured her as she'd seen her the second time, slim again, dressed demurely. Older, sadder.

She walked over the tough winter grass, the thick gravel, over stepping stones. The air was cool and brisk on her cheeks, and was tinged with the scent of animal and earth. She held firm to Cal's hand, knowing—feeling—he gave her whatever he had so that their abilities linked as their fingers did.

"I'm just not going there. I'm getting glimpses of you," she said to Cal with a quick laugh. "A little guy, when you still needed your glasses. Fairly adorable. I can get zips of the three of you running around, and a younger boy, a girl. A toddler—another girl. She's so cute."

"You have to go deeper." Cal squeezed her hand. "I'm right with you."

"That might be the problem. I think I may be picking up on things you remember, your pictures." She squeezed his hand in turn, then drew hers free. "I think I have to try it alone. Give me a little space. Okay, everybody? A little room."

She turned, reached the corner of the house, then followed its line. It was so sturdy, she thought, and as Cybil had said, so handsome. The stone, the wood, the glass. There were flower beds sleeping, and in others sweet and hopeful shoots that must have been daffodils and tulips, hyacinths, and the summer lilies that would follow the spring.

Strong old trees offered shade, so she imagined—or maybe she saw—the flowers that shied from sunlight blooming there.

She smelled smoke, she realized. There must be wood fireplaces inside. Of course there would be. What wonderful old farmhouse didn't have fireplaces? Somewhere to curl up on a cold evening. Flames sending dancing shadow and light, and the warmth so welcome.

She sat in a room lit by firelight and the glow of a single tallow candle. She did not weep though her heart was flooded with tears. With quill and ink, Ann wrote in her careful hand in the pages of her journal.

Our sons are eight months old. They are beautiful, and they are healthy. I see you in them, beloved. I see you in their eyes and it both comforts and grieves me. I am well. The kindness of my cousin and her husband are beyond measure. Surely we are a burden on them, but we are never treated as such. In the weeks before, and some weeks after the birth of our sons there was little I could do to help my cousin. Yet she never complained. Even now with the boys to look after, I cannot do as much as I wish to repay her and cousin Fletcher.

Mending I do. Honor and I made soap and candles, enough for Fletcher to barter.

This is not what I wish to write, but I find it so hard to subscribe these words to this paper. My cousin has told me that young Hester Deale was drowned in the pool of Hawkins Wood, and leaves her infant daughter orphaned. She condemned you that night, as you had foreseen. She condemned me. We know it was not by her will she did so, as it was not by her will the motherless child was conceived.

The beast is in the child, Giles. You told me again and again that what you would do would change the order, clean the blood. This sacrifice you made, and I and our children with you, was necessary. On nights like this, when I am so alone, when I find my heart full of sorrow for a girl I knew who is lost, I fear what was done, what will be done so long from this night will not be enough. I mourn that you gave yourself for nothing, and our children will never see their father's face, or feel his kiss.

I will pray for the strength and the courage you believed lived inside me. I will pray to find them again when the sun rises. Tonight, with the darkness so close, I can only be a woman who longs for her love.

She closed the book as one of the babies began to cry, and his brothers woke to join him. Rising, she went to the pallet beside her own to soothe, to sing, to offer her breast.

You are my hope, she whispered, offering one a sugar teat for comfort while his brothers suckled.

WHEN QUINN'S EYES ROLLED BACK, CAL LIFTED her off her feet. "We need to get her inside." His long, fast strides carried her to the steps leading to the side porch. Fox rushed ahead, getting the door, then going straight into the family's music room.

"I'll get some water."

"She'll need more." Cybil hurried after him. "Which way's the kitchen?"

He pointed, turned in the opposite direction.

Because Quinn was shivering, Layla whipped a throw from the back of a small couch as Cal laid Quinn down.

"My head," Quinn managed. "God, my head. It's off the

Richter scale. I may be sick. I need to . . ." She swung her legs over, dropped her head between her knees. "Okay." She breathed in, breathed out as Cal massaged her shoulders. "Okay."

"Here, try some water. Fox got you some water." Layla took the glass he'd brought back, knelt to urge it on Quinn.

"Take it easy," Cal advised. "Don't sit up until you're ready. Slow breaths."

"Believe me." She eyed the brass bucket Gage set next to her, then shifted her gaze to the kindling now scattered over the hearth. "Good thinking, but I'm pretty sure I'm not going to need that."

She eased up until she could rest her throbbing head on Cal's shoulder. "Intense."

"I know." He pressed his lips lightly to the side of her head.

"Did I say anything? It was Ann. She was writing in her journal."

"You said plenty," Cal told her.

"Why didn't I think to turn on my recorder?"

"Got that." Gage held up her minirecorder. "I pulled it out of your purse when the show started."

She took a slow sip of water, glanced at Fox out of eyes still blurry in a pale, pale face. "Your parents wouldn't happen to have any morphine around here?"

"Sorry."

"It'll pass." Cal kissed her again, rubbed gently at the back of her neck. "Promise."

"How long was I gone?"

"Nearly twenty minutes." Cal glanced over when Cybil came back in carrying a tall pottery mug.

"Here." Cybil stroked Quinn's cheek. "This'll help."

"What is it?"

"Tea. That's all you have to know. Come on, be a good girl." She held the mug to Quinn's lips. "Your mother has an amazing collection of homemade teas, Fox."

"Maybe, but this tastes like—" Quinn broke off when Joanne walked in. "Ms. Barry."

"That blend tastes pretty crappy, but it'll help. Let me have her, Cal." Brushing Cal aside, Joanne took his place, then pressed and rubbed at two points at the base of Quinn's neck. "Try not to tense. That's better. Breathe through it. Breathe the oxygen in, exhale the tension and discomfort. That's good. Are you pregnant?"

"What? No. Um, no."

"There's a point here." She took Quinn's left hand, pressed on the webbing between her thumb and forefinger. "It's effective, but traditionally forbidden for pregnant women."

"The Adjoining Valley," Cybil said.

"You know accupressure?"

"She knows everything," Quinn claimed, and took her first easy breath. "It's better. It's a lot better. Down from blinding to annoying. Thank you."

"You should rest awhile. Cal can take you upstairs if you want."

"Thanks, but—"

"Cal, you ought to take her home." Layla stepped forward to pat a hand on Cal's arm. "I can ride into the office with Fox. Cybil, you can get Gage back to Cal's, right?"

"I could do that."

"We haven't finished," Quinn objected. "We need to move on to part two and find out where she put the journal."

"Not today."

"She's right, Blondie. You haven't got another round in you." To settle the matter, Cal picked her up off the couch.

"Well, hard to argue. I guess I'm going. Thanks, Ms. Barry."

"Jo."

"Thanks, Jo, for letting us screw up your morning."

"Anytime. Fox, give Cal a hand with the door. Gage,

why don't you take Cybil back, let Brian know every-thing's all right? Layla." Jo put a hand on Layla's arm, holding her in place while the others left the room. "That was smoothly done."

"I'm sorry?"

"You maneuvered that so Quinn and Cal would have time alone, which is exactly what they both need. I'm go-ing to ask you a favor."

"Of course."

"If there's anything we can or should do, will you tell me? Fox may not. He's protective of those he loves. Some-times too protective."

"I'll do what I can."

"Can't ask for more than that."

Fox waited for Layla to join him outside. "You don't have to go into the office."

"Cal and Quinn need some space, and I'd just as soon be busy."

"Borrow Quinn's car, or Cybil's. Go shopping. Do something normal."

"Work is normal. Are you trying to get rid of me?"

"I'm trying to give you a break."

"I don't need a break. Quinn does." She turned as Cybil and Gage came out. "I'm going to go into the office for the day, unless you need me back at home."

"I've got it covered," Cybil told her. "Other than log-ging in this morning's fun and games, there isn't much else to do until we find the journal."

"We're putting a lot of stock in a diary," Gage com-mented.

"It's the next step." Cybil shrugged.

"I can't find it." Fox spread his hands. "Maybe she wrote them, maybe she wrote them here—it seems clear she did. But I lived in this house and never got a glimmer. I went through it again last night, wide open. Walked around inside, out, the old shed, the woods. I got nothing."

"Maybe you need me."

His eyes latched on to Layla.

"Maybe it's something we need to do together. We could try that. We've still got a little time now. We could—"

"Not now. Now while my parents are here in case . . . of anything. They'll both be away tomorrow, all morning." Out of harm's way, if there is any harm to be had. "At the pottery, at the stand. We'll come back tomorrow."

"Fine with me. Well, cowboy." Cybil gestured to Quinn's car. "Let's ride." She said nothing else until she and Gage were inside, pulling out ahead of Fox's truck. "What does he think might happen that he doesn't want his parents exposed to?"

"Nothing's ever happened here, or at Cal's parents' place. But, as far as we know, they've never been connected before. So who the hell knows?"

She considered as she drove. "They're nice people."

"About the best."

"You spent a lot of time here as a boy."

"Yeah."

"God, do you ever shut up?" she demanded after a moment. "It's all talk, talk, talk with you."

"I love the sound of my own voice."

She gave it another ten seconds of silence. "Let's try another avenue. How'd you do in the poker game?"

"Did okay. You play?"

"I've known to."

"Are you any good?"

"I make it a policy to be good, or learn to be good, at everything I do. In fact—"

As she rounded the curve, she saw the huge black dog hunched in the middle of the road a few yards ahead. Meeting its eyes, Cybil checked the instinct to slam the brakes. "Better hang on," she said coolly, then punched the gas instead.

It leaped. A mass of black, the glint of fang and claw. The car shuddered at impact, and she fought to control it with her heart slammed in her throat. The windshield exploded; the hood erupted in flame. Again, she fought the instinct to hit the brakes, spun the car hard into a tight one-eighty. She prepared to ram the dog again, but it was gone.

The windshield was intact; the hood unmarred.

"Son of a bitch, son of a bitch," she said, over and over.

"Turn around, and keep going, Cybil." Gage closed a hand over the one that clamped the steering wheel. It was cold, he noted, but rock steady. "Turn the car around, and drive."

"Yeah, okay." She shuddered once, hard, then turned the car around. "So . . . What was I saying before we were interrupted?"

Sheer admiration for her chutzpah had a laugh rolling out of him. "You got nerve, sister. You got nerves of fucking steel."

"I don't know. I wanted to kill it. I just wanted to kill it. And, well, it's not my car, so if I wrecked it running over a damn devil dog, it's Q's problem." And at the moment, her stomach was a quivering mess. "It was probably stupid. I couldn't see anything for a minute, when the windshield . . . I could've run us into a tree, or off the road into the creek."

"People who are afraid to try something stupid never get anywhere."

"I wanted to pay it back, for what it did to Layla yesterday. And that's not the sort of thing that's going to work."

"It didn't suck," Gage said after a minute.

She laughed a little, then shot him a glance and laughed some more. "No, now that you mention it, it really didn't."

Seven

~✦~

FOX'S FRIDAY SCHEDULE DIDN'T GIVE HIM MUCH time to think, or to brood. He went from appointment to meeting, back to appointment and into phone conference. At midafternoon, he saw a clear hour and decided to use it to take a walk around town to give his brain a rest.

Better yet, he thought, he'd walk up to the Bowl-a-Rama, grab a few minutes with Cal. He'd get a better sense of how Quinn was doing, how they were all doing if he talked with Cal.

When he stepped into reception to tell Layla, he found her talking with Cal's great-grandmother Estelle Hawkins.

"I thought we were meeting at our usual clandestine rendezvous." He walked over to kiss her soft, thin-skinned cheek. "How are we going to keep our secret affair secret?"

"It's all over town." Essie's eyes twinkled through the thick lenses of her glasses. "We might as well start living in sin openly."

"I'll go up and pack."

She laughed, swatted at him. "Before you do, I was hoping you'd have a few minutes for me. Professionally."

"I've always got time for you, in any way. Come on back. Layla's going to hold my calls." He winked at her as he took Essie's arm. "In case our passions overwhelm us."

"Should I just lock the outside door?" Layla called out as he led Essie away.

"It's a wonder you can keep your mind on your work," Essie told him as they moved into his office, "with a pretty girl like that around."

"I have Herculean power of will. Want a Coke?"

"You know, I believe I do."

"Two seconds."

He got a glass, ice, poured. She was one of Fox's favorite people, and he made sure she was comfortable before he sat with her in the sitting area of his office. "Where's Ginger?" he asked, referring to Cal's cousin who lived with Essie.

"She went on to the bank before it closes. She'll be coming back for me. This won't take long."

"What can I do for you? Want to sue somebody?"

She smiled at him. "Can't think of anything I'd like less. I wonder why people are forever suing each other."

"Blame the lawyers. Still, it's a better alternative to beating the hell out of each other. Mostly."

"People do that, too. But I'm not here for either. It's about my will, Fox."

It gave him a little pang. She was ninety-three, and he certainly understood and appreciated the value of having your affairs well in order long before you approached Essie's age. But it still gave him a little pang to think of his world without her in it.

"I updated your will and your trust a few years ago. Do you want changes?"

"Nothing big. I have a couple pieces of jewelry I wanted to earmark for Quinn. Right now, my pearls and my aquamarine earrings are going to Frannie. She understands I want to leave them to her future daughter-in-law. I've talked to her about it. And I know I can leave it like that, I can trust her to give them to Quinn. But, as I recall, you told me it's easier on those left behind if everything's spelled out."

"It generally is. I can take care of that for you." Though he trusted his memory when it came to Essie's business, Fox rose to get a legal pad and note it all down. "It won't take long to draft the change. I can bring it by for your signature on Monday if that works for you."

"That's just fine, but I don't mind coming in."

He knew she continued to go into the library nearly every day, but if he could save her a trip he'd rather. "Tell you what, when it's ready, I'll give you a call. Then we'll see which way it works best. Is there anything else you want to change, add, take out?"

"No, just those two pieces. You have everything spelled out so clearly. It gives me peace of mind, Fox."

"And if any of my grandchildren turn out to be lawyers, they can handle it for you."

Her lips curved, but her eyes stayed somber as she reached out to pat his hand. "I'd like to live to see Cal married next fall. I'd like to live through this next Seven and dance with my boy at his wedding."

"Miss Essie—"

"Wouldn't mind dancing with you at yours. And I can be greedy and say I'd like to hold Cal's firstborn in my arms. But I know that may not be. What's coming this time is worse than all the rest."

"We won't let anything happen to you."

She let out a sigh that was full of affection. "You've seen to this town since you were ten years old. You and Cal and Gage. I'd like to live to see the day you didn't have to see to it. I'm holding out for that." She gave his hand another pat. "Now I expect Ginger will be coming along to fetch me."

He rose to help her to her feet. "I'll walk you out, wait for her."

"You just go about your business. I hope you've got something fun planned for the weekend."

"I would if you'd go out with me."

She laughed, leaning on his arm as he walked her out. "There was a day."

He stood at the window, watching as Ginger eased Essie into the car.

"She's a remarkable woman," Layla commented.

"Yeah, she's something. I need you to pull her estate file. She wants a couple of changes."

"All right."

"Do you ever think we'll lose this? That we'll lose the town, ourselves, the whole damn ball?"

She hesitated. "Don't you?"

"No." He glanced back at her. "No, I know we'll win this. But we won't all make it. Not everyone who's out there going about their business today is going to come through it."

Instead of taking his walk, Fox went back into his office. He took a copy of his own will out of the desk drawer to review it.

JUST AFTER FIVE HE WALKED HIS LAST CLIENT TO the door, then turned to Layla. "We're out of here. Grab your things. We're going bowling."

"I really don't think so, but that's a nice thought. I want to check in with Quinn."

"She's meeting us there. The whole gang's hitting the Bowl-a-Rama. It's Friday night. Pizza, beer, and duckpins."

She thought of the quiet bowl of soup she'd planned, a glass of wine and a book. "You like to bowl."

"I hate it, which is problematic seeing as one of my closest friends owns a bowling alley." He got her coat as he spoke. "But the pizza's good, and there are pinball machines. I love me some pinball. Regardless, we earned a break. From everything."

"I guess we did."

He held out her coat. "Friday night in the Hollow? The Bowl-a-Rama's the place to be."

She smiled. "Then I guess we'd better get there. Can we walk?"

"Read my mind. Figuratively speaking. I've been antsy all day." He paused after they'd stepped outside. "Pansies in the tub outside the Flower Pot and see there? That's Eric Moore, clean-shaven. He shaves off his winter beard every March. Spring's coming."

He took her hand as they hit the sidewalk. "Do you know what I love as much as pinball and pizza?"

"What?"

"Taking a walk with a pretty girl."

She aimed a look at him. "Your mood's improved."

"Anticipation of pizza does that for me."

"No, I mean it."

He shot a wave at someone across the street. "I wallowed some. I need a good wallow once in a while, then I scrape it off."

"How?"

"By remembering we all do what we do. By reminding myself I believe good mostly wins out in the long run. Sometimes the long run's a bitch, but good mostly wins out."

"You're cheering me up."

"Good. That was the plan."

"I wasn't exactly wallowing. I think I got jammed up at worrying. Pansies in the tub, that's a good sign, but I hate that it's offset by ones like this." She gestured toward the gift shop. "I want to believe good mostly wins out, too, but it's hard knowing it costs so much, that some people have to lose."

"Maybe it's not a loss. Maybe they'll relocate to Iowa and hit the lottery, or double their business. Or they'll just be happier there, for whatever reason. The wheel's got to turn before you get anywhere."

"So says the man practicing law in the town where he was born."

"I turned the wheel." They crossed at the Square. "It brought me right back here. Brought you here, too."

He pulled open the door, and led her into the noise of the Bowl-a-Rama.

"To pizza and pinball."

"And pansies, to continue the alliteration. Then there's bowling and bonhomie."

"Bonhomie. Triple word score."

"Play your cards right." He turned her and, letting the mood carry him, laid his lips on hers before she could prepare herself. "There could be sex and satisfaction."

"I'm not playing cards just yet."

"So we settle for friends and frivolity. And boy, am I done with that." He led her to lane six, where Cal sat along with Quinn and Cybil, changing shoes. "Where's Turner?"

"Deserted us for the arcade," Cybil told him.

"And the pinball rivalry continues. Catch you later."

"No problem. I'll have three beautiful women to myself." Cal held out a pair of bowling shoes. "Size seven?"

"That would be me." Layla slid onto the booth as Fox gestured Cal a few steps away.

"How'd you get Gage to come in?"

"It's his father's night off. Bill's not around, so . . ."

"Got it. I'm going to go whip his ass at Tomcat. He'll be buying the beer."

"Tomcat?" Cybil's eyebrows rose dramatically. "Isn't that a war game?"

"Maybe." Fox eyed her narrowly. "What are you, my

mother? And you don't have to mention me whipping Gage's ass at a war game to my mother if you should happen to run into her."

An hour with the lights, the bells, the patter of antiaircraft cut away even the fading edges of Fox's pensive mood. It didn't hurt to stand and watch a trio of attractive women bend and stretch while he drank a victory beer. Gage had *never* been able to beat him at Tomcat.

"Best view in the house," Gage commented as they stood back, studying Quinn's posterior as she approached the line.

"Hard to beat. Friday night leagues are coming in." Fox glanced over where men and women in bowling shirts passed by the front desk. "Cal's going to have a full house tonight."

"There's Napper." Gage sipped his beer while he studied the man in the maroon and cream team shirt. "Is he still—"

"Yeah. Had some words with him just a couple days ago. He's just an older asshole now, with a badge."

"A fifty-eight." Layla plopped down to change her shoes after her last frame. "I don't think I've discovered my newest passion."

"I like it," Cybil said as she sat beside her. "I'd vote for more attractive footwear, but I like the game, the destruct, reconstruct of it."

"Meaning?"

"Deliver the ball, destroy the pins. Hit them right, you can make them destroy each other. Then, wait a minute, they're all back again, like ten soldiers. After all those war games," she said with a teasing smile for Fox, "I'm starving." She tipped her head back, looked at Gage. "How'd your battle fare?"

"I do better with cards and women."

"I kicked his ass, as promised. Beer's on Gage."

They didn't discuss the morning as they sat around a table with pizza and beer. They didn't talk about their plans for the next day. For the moment, they were simply a group of friends enjoying one another and the entertainment offered in a small, rural town.

"My game next time," Gage announced. "A nice friendly game of poker." He sneered at Fox. "We'll see who's buying the beer then."

"Anytime, anywhere." Fox grinned as he grabbed a slice of pizza. "I've been practicing."

"Strip poker doesn't count."

"Does if you win," he said with his mouth full.

"Look who's back!" Shelley Kholer wiggled her way over in jeans designed to bruise internal organs and a shirt sized for an undeveloped twelve-year-old. She grabbed Gage's face with both hands and gave him a long, greedy and slightly drunken kiss.

"Hey, Shell," he said when he had his tongue back.

"I heard you were back, but haven't seen hide or hair. Aren't you just as yummy as ever? Why don't we—"

"What's new?" he interrupted, and picked up a beer to shield his mouth from another assault.

"I'm getting a divorce."

"Sorry to hear it."

"I'm not. Block's a worthless, two-timing bastard with a dick the size of a pickle. One of those little ones, you know?"

"I didn't know that."

"Shoulda run away with you," she said and sent everyone at the table a blurry smile. "Hi, y'all. Hey, Fox! I want to talk to you about my divorce."

She wanted to talk about her divorce twenty hours out of every twenty-four, Fox thought. The other four were reserved for talking about her sister who'd gotten a little too friendly with Shelley's husband. "Why don't you come into the office next week?"

"I can talk freely here. I got no secrets. I got no secrets in the whole damn town. Every sumbitch in it knows my husband got caught with his hand on my sister's tit. I wanna add that thing, that loss of consortium—that loss of nookie thing to the complaint."

"We'll talk about that. Why don't I buy you a cup of coffee up at the counter, and we can—"

"Don't want coffee. I got a nice buzz on to celebrate my upcoming divorce. I want another beer, and I want to make out with Gage. Like the old days."

"Why don't we have one anyway?"

"I could make out with you," she said to Fox as he rose to lead her away. "Did we ever make out?"

"I was fifteen in the old days," Gage announced when Fox steered Shelley to the counter. "I just want that on record."

"She's so unhappy. Sorry," Layla murmured. "It's one of those things I can't help but pick up on. She's so miserable."

"Fox'll help her through it. It's what he does." Cal nodded toward the counter where Shelley sat, listening to Fox, her head resting on his shoulder. "He's the sort of lawyer who takes the term *counselor* to heart."

"If my sister played squeeze the melons with my husband, I'd want to skin him in a divorce, too." Cybil broke off a tiny corner of a nacho. "That's if I were married. And after I'd beaten them both to bloody pulps. Is her husband really named Block?"

"Unfortunately," Cal confirmed.

At the counter, Shelley ignored the coffee, but she listened.

"It'd be better if you didn't badmouth Block in public. Say whatever you want about him to me, okay? But it's not good for you to go off on him, especially about the size of his dick, in public."

"He doesn't really have a little pickle dick," Shelley muttered. "But he should. He shouldn't have any dick at all."

"I know. Are you here by yourself?"

"No." She sighed now. "I came with my girlfriends. We're in the arcade. We're having a Fuck Men night. In the bad way."

"That's fine. You're not driving, are you, Shelley?"

"No, we walked from Arlene's. We're going back there after. She's pissed at her boyfriend."

"If you're ready to go while I'm still here, and you want someone to drive you, or walk you, come and get me."

"You're the sweetest damn thing in the whole world."

"Do you want to go back to the arcade?"

"Yeah. We're going home soon anyway to make apple martinis and watch *Thelma and Louise*."

"Sounds great." He took her arm, steered her clear of Gage and the table, and walked her to the arcade.

Deciding he'd earned another beer, he swung back by the counter, ordered one on Gage's tab.

"So, you're sticking it to Shelley in more ways than one."

Fox didn't turn at Napper's voice. "Slow night for crime, Deputy Take-a-Nap?"

"People with real jobs take nights off. What's your excuse?"

"I like watching people without balls throw them."

"I wonder what'll happen to yours when Block finds out you're doing his wife."

"Here you go, Fox." Behind the counter, Holly set down Fox's drink, gave him a quick, understanding look. She'd worked the counter for enough years to know when trouble was brewing. "Get you something, Deputy?"

"Pitcher of Bud. I bet Block's going to kick your pansy ass into next week."

"You're going to want to stay out of that." Fox turned now, faced Napper. "Block and Shelley have enough problems without you screwing with them."

"You telling me what to do?" He jabbed a finger into Fox's chest, bared his teeth in a fierce "dare you" grin.

"I'm telling you Block and Shelley are going through a tough time and don't need you making it worse because you want to fuck with me." Fox picked up his beer. "You need to move."

"I don't need to do a goddamn thing. It's my night off."

"Yeah? Mine, too." Fox, who'd never been able to walk away from a dare, tipped the beer down Napper's shirt. "Oops. Butterfingers."

"You stupid fuck." He shoved, and the force of it would've knocked Fox on his ass, if he hadn't anticipated it.

He danced lightly to the side, so that Napper's forward motion sent the deputy careening into one of the counter stools. When he righted himself, spun to retaliate, he wasn't just facing Fox, but Gage and Cal as well.

"That's a damn shame," Gage drawled. "All that beer wasted. Looks good on you though, Napper."

"We run your kind out of town these days, Turner."

Gage spread his arms in invitation. "Run me."

"None of us are looking for trouble here, Derrick." Cal took a step forward, his eyes hard on Napper's. "This is a family place. Lots of kids in here. Lots of witnesses. I'll take you over to our gift shop, get you a new shirt. No charge."

"I don't want a damn thing from you." He sneered at Fox. "Your friends won't always be around to protect you, O'Dell."

"You keep forgetting the rules." Now Gage stepped forward, effectively blocking Fox before his friend rose to the bait. "You mess with one of us, you mess with all of us. But Cal and I? We'll be happy to hold Fox's coat while he kicks the shit out of you. Wouldn't be the first time."

"Times change." Napper shoved his way past them.

"Not so much," Gage murmured. "He's as big a dick as ever."

"Told you." With apparent ease, Fox stepped back up to the counter. "I'm going to need another beer, Holly."

When he walked back to the table, Quinn gave him a sunny smile. "Dinner and a show. This place has it all."

"That show's been running about twenty-five years."

"He hates you," Layla said quietly. "He doesn't even know why."

"There doesn't have to be a why for some people." Fox laid a hand over hers. "Forget him. How about a round of pinball—any machine. And you get a thousand-point handicap."

"I think that may be an insult, but . . . Don't! Don't drink that. God. Look."

The beer glass in Fox's hand foamed with blood. He set it down slowly. "Two wasted beers in one night. I guess the party's over."

WHEN QUINN OPTED TO STAY AT THE BOWLING center with Cal until closing, Fox walked Layla and Cybil home. It was only a couple of blocks, and he knew they were far from defenseless. But he didn't like the idea of them being out at night on their own.

"What's the back story on the jerk currently wearing your beer?" Cybil asked him.

"Just a bully who's needled me since we were kids. Deputy Bully now."

"No particular reason?"

"I was skinny, smaller than him—smarter, too—and came from tree-hugger stock."

"More than enough. Well . . ." Her fingers gave his biceps a testing pinch. "You're not skinny now. And you're still smarter than him." She sent Fox an approving smirk. "Quicker, too."

"He wants to hurt you. It's on his top ten list of things to accomplish." Layla studied Fox's profile as they crossed the street. "He won't stop. His kind doesn't."

"Napper's top ten list isn't my biggest concern. He has to get in line."

"Ah, home again." Cybil climbed the first step, turned, looked around the quiet street. "We managed bowling, dinner, a minor brawl, and a memo from evil, and it's still shy of eleven. The fun never ends in Hawkins Hollow." She laid her hands on Fox's shoulders. "Thanks for walking us home, cutie." She gave him a light kiss. "See you in the morning. Layla, why don't you work out the logistics—timing, transportation—with Fox and let me know. I'll be upstairs."

"My parents should be out of the house by eight," he told Layla when Cybil strolled away. "I can come by and pick you all up if you need."

"That's all right. We'll take Quinn's car, I imagine. Who's going to walk you home, Fox?"

"I remember the way."

"You know what I mean. You should come in, stay here."

He smiled, eased in a little closer. "Where here?"

"On the couch, for now anyway." She put a fingertip to his chest, eased him right back.

"Your couch is lumpy, and you only have basic cable. You need to work on your strategy. If you'd asked me to stay because you were worried about it just being you and Cybil in the house, I'd be trying to sleep on your couch with a rerun of *Law and Order* while I was thinking about you upstairs in bed. Kiss me good night, Layla."

"Maybe I am worried about being in the house, just me and Cybil."

"No, you're not. Kiss me good night."

She sighed. She really was going to have to work on her strategy. Deliberately, she tipped her face up, and gave him the light, friendly kiss Cybil had. "Good night. Be careful."

"Careful doesn't always get the job done. Case in point."

He caught her face in his hands, lowered his lips to hers.

Though the kiss was soft, though it was slow, she felt the impact from the top of her head to the soles of her feet. The glide of his tongue, the brush of his thumbs at her temples, the solid line of his body dissolved her bones.

He held her face even as he lifted his head, looked into her eyes. "That was a kiss good night."

"It was. No question about it."

He kissed her again with the same silky confidence until she had to grip his forearms for balance.

"Now neither one of us will get any sleep." He stepped back. "So my work here is done. Unfortunately. I'll see you tomorrow."

"Okay." She made it to the door before she turned, looked back at him from what she considered a safe distance. "I have a careful nature, especially when it's important. I think sex is important, or should be."

"It's on my top ten list of personal priorities."

She laughed, opened the door. "Good night, Fox."

Inside, Layla went straight upstairs where Cybil came out of the office, eyebrow lifted. "Alone?"

"Yeah."

"Can I ask why you're not about to get a good taste of adorable lawyer?"

"I think he might matter too much."

"Ah." With a knowing nod, Cybil leaned on the door-jamb. "That always tangles things up. Want to work off some sexual frustration with research and logs?"

"I'm not sure charts and graphs have that kind of power, but I'll give it a shot." She shrugged out of her jacket as she stepped into the office. "What do you do when they might matter too much?"

"Generally, I run—either straight into it or away. It's had mixed results." Cybil walked over to study the map of the town Layla had generated and pinned to the wall.

"I tend to circle around and around, weigh and think entirely too much. I'm wondering now if it was because I tuned in." She tapped her head. "Without really knowing I was tuning in."

"That may be." Cybil picked up a red pushpin—representing blood—stuck it into the bowling center on the map to signal another incident. "But Fox would be a lot to think about under normal circumstances. Add in the abnormal, and it's a lot to consider. Take your time if time's what you need."

"Under normal circumstances that would be reasonable." At the desk, Layla chose a red index card, wrote: *Bloody Beer, Fox, Bowl-a-Rama*, and the time and date. "But time is one of the issues, isn't it? And how much we may actually have."

"You sound like Gage. It's a good thing you two didn't hook up or you'd never look beyond the dark side."

"That may be, but . . ." Frowning, Layla studied the map. "There's another pin, a black pin on the road between Fox's house and Cal's."

"Standing for the big, ugly dog. Didn't I tell you? No, that's right, you went straight from work to the center. Sorry."

"Tell me now."

Once she had, Layla selected a dark blue card, the color she'd chosen for any demon in animal form sighting, filled it in.

"I hate to say this, but while my mind is now occupied and my hands busy, I'm still sexually frustrated."

"There, there." Cybil patted Layla's shoulder. "I'm going to go make some tea. We'll add some chocolate. That always helps."

Layla doubted if candy was going to satisfy her appetite for adorable lawyer, but she'd take what she could get.

Eight

~◡~

A CHILLY TRICKLE OF RAIN DAMPENED THE morning. It was the sort, Fox knew, that tended to hang around all day like a sick headache. Nothing to do but tolerate it.

He dug out a hooded sweatshirt from a basket of laundry he'd managed to wash, but hadn't yet put away. At least he was ninety percent sure he'd washed it. Maybe seventy-five. So he sniffed it, then bumped that up to a hundred percent.

He found jeans, underwear, socks—though the socks took longer as he actually wanted them to match. As he dressed, glanced around his bedroom, he vowed he'd find the time and the willpower to put the stupid laundry away, even though it would eventually be in need of washing and putting away again. He'd make the bed sometime in this decade, and shovel out the rest of the junk.

If he could get it to that point, maybe he could find a cleaning lady who'd stick it out. Maybe a cleaning guy, he considered over his first Coke of the day. A guy would get it better, probably.

He'd look into it.

He laced on his old workboots, and because house-keeping was on his mind, tossed discarded shoes in the closet and, inspired, shoved the laundry basket in after them.

He grabbed his keys, another Coke and a Devil Dog that would serve as his while-driving breakfast. Halfway down the outside steps, he spotted Layla standing at the base.

"Hey."

"I was just coming up. We saw your truck was still here, so I had Quinn drop me off. I thought I'd ride with you."

"Great." He held up the snack cake. "Devil Dog?"

"Actually, I've had enough of devil dogs on four legs."

"Oh yeah." He ripped the wrapper as he joined her. "Strangely, that's never put me off the joy of the Devil Dog."

"That is not your breakfast," she said as he bit in. He only smiled, kept walking.

"My stomach stopped maturing at twelve." He pulled open the passenger door of his truck. "How'd you sleep?"

She shot a look at him over her shoulder as she climbed in. "Well enough." She waited until he'd rounded the hood and slid behind the wheel. "Even after Cybil told me about her and Gage's run-in—literally—with a devil dog. It happened when they were driving to Cal's from your place."

"Yeah, Gage filled me in while I was skinning him at pinball." He set his Coke in the drink holder, took another bite of the cake. After a quick check, he pulled away from the curb.

"I wanted to ride with you because I had some ideas on how to approach this thing today."

"And I thought it was because you can't keep away from me."

"I'm trying not to react with my hormones."

"Damn shame."

"That may be, but . . . It took so much out of Quinn yesterday. I'm hoping we could try, you and me, and take her out of the mix. The whole point is to find the journals, if they're there. If they are, they're in the now. If not, then we'd have to fall back to Quinn. But—"

"You'd like to spare her the migraine. We can try it. I'm also assuming you didn't mention this idea to her."

"I figured, if you agreed, we could bring it up as something we came up with on the drive over." She smiled over at him. "There, I'm working on my strategy. Did you dream last night?"

"Only about you. We were in my office, and you were wearing this really, really little red dress and those high heels with the ankle straps? Those kill me. You sat on my desk, facing me. I was in the chair. And you said, after you'd licked your lips: 'I'm ready to take dictation, Mr. O'Dell.' "

She listened, head cocked. "You just made that up."

He shot her a quick and charming grin. "Maybe, but I guarantee I'll have that dream tonight. Maybe we should go out. There's this bar over the river? A nice bar. They have live music on Saturday nights. They get some pretty decent musicians in."

"It sounds so normal. I keep trying to keep a grip on normal with one hand while I'm digging into the impossible with the other. It's . . ."

"Surreal. I forget about it—between the Sevens, I can forget about it for weeks, even months sometimes. Then something reminds me. That's surreal, too. Going along, doing the work, having fun, whatever and *zap*, it's right back in my head. The closer it gets, the more it's in my head." His fingers danced against the steering wheel to the beat of Snow Patrol. "So a nice bar with good music is a way to remember it's a lot, but it's not everything."

"That's a smart way to look at it. I'm not sure I can get

to that point, but I'd like to listen to some music across the river. What time?"

"Ah . . . nine? Is nine good for you?"

"All right." She drew in a breath when he turned in the lane to the farmhouse. She was making a date with a man she was about to link with psychically. Surreal didn't quite cover it.

It also felt rude, she discovered, to go inside the house without invitation. It was Fox's childhood home, true enough, but he no longer lived there. She thought about going into her parents' condo when they weren't there, deliberately choosing a time they weren't there, and simply couldn't.

"This feels wrong," she said as they stood in the living room. "It feels wrong and intrusive. I understand why we want to do this while they're not home, but it feels . . ." At a loss, she settled for the standby. "Rude."

"My parents don't mind people coming in. Otherwise, they'd lock the doors."

"Still—"

"We have to prioritize, Layla." Quinn spread her hands. "The reason we're here is more important than standard guidelines of courtesy. I got so much outside the house yesterday. I'm bound to get more inside."

"About that. I had this idea, talked it over with Layla on the drive. If you don't mind us cutting in line, Quinn, I'd like to try something with Layla first. We may be able to visualize where the journals are, if they're here. Or at least get a sense of them."

"That's good thinking. And not just because I'd rather you didn't go through it again," Cal added when Quinn narrowed her eyes at him. "It could work, and better yet, with Fox and Layla linked, it downscales the side effects."

"And if it doesn't work," Fox added, "back to you."

"All right, that makes sense. Believe me, it's not as if I look forward to having my head explode."

"Okay, then we're up. This is the oldest part of the house. Actually, this room and the ones directly above *were* the house as far as anyone can tell. So, logically, if there was a cabin or a house here before this one was built, it could be over the same spot. Maybe, especially given Quinn's trip yesterday, they used some of the same materials."

"Like the fireplace." Quinn crossed to it, stepped over Lump, who'd already stretched out in front of the low fire, to run her hand over the stones. "I'm big on the idea of hiding stuff behind bricks and stones."

"And if we hack at that mortar, start pulling out stones without being a hundred percent, my father will kill me. Ready?" Fox asked Layla.

"As I'll ever be."

"Look at me." He took her hands. "Just look at me. Don't think. Imagine. A small book, the writing inside. The ink's faded. Imagine her handwriting. You've seen it in her other journals."

His eyes were so rich. That old gold color so fascinating. His hands weren't lawyer-smooth. Not like the hands of a man who carried a briefcase, who worked at a desk. There was labor on them, strength and capability in them. He smelled of the rain, just a little of rain.

He would taste like cake.

He wanted her. Imagined touching her, gliding his hands over bare skin, sliding them over her breasts, her belly. Laying his lips there, his tongue, tasting the heat, the flesh . . .

In bed, when there's only us.

She gasped, jerked back. His voice had been clear inside her head.

"What did you see?" Cal demanded. "Did you see it?"

With his eyes still locked on Layla's, Fox shook his head. "We had to get something out of the way first. One more time?" he said to Layla. "Use your compartments."

Her skin felt hot, inside and out, but she nodded. And she did her best to set her own desires, and his, aside.

Everything drew together into a narrow point. In it she heard the jumbled thoughts of her companions, like background chatter at a cocktail party. There was concern, doubt, anticipation, a mix of feelings. These, too, she set aside.

The book was in her head. Brown leather cover, dried from age. Yellowed pages and faded ink.

With the dark so close outside, I long for my love.

"It's not here." Fox spoke first as he carefully let the connection between him and Layla fade. "It's not in this room."

"No."

"Then I need to try again." Quinn squared her shoulders. "I can try to home in on her, on the journal. See when she packed it away, maybe to take back to her father's house in town. The old library."

"No, they're not in the old library," Layla said slowly. "They're not in this room."

"But they're here," Fox finished. "It was too clear. They have to be here."

Gage tapped a foot on the floor. "Could be under. She might have hidden them under floorboards, if there were floorboards."

"Or buried them," Cybil continued.

"If they're under the house, we're pretty well screwed," Gage pointed out. "If Brian would be unhappy with us taking some stones out of the fireplace, he'd be pretty well crazed if we suggested razing the damn house to get under it for some diaries."

"You don't have enough respect for diaries," Cybil commented. "But you're right about the first part."

"We need to try again. We can go room to room," Layla suggested. "The basement? Is there a basement? If she did bury them, we might get a better signal from there. Because I can't believe they're inaccessible. Giles told her what would happen, told her about us—about you."

"She may have hidden them to keep them from being lost or destroyed." Cal paced as he tried to think it through. "From being found too soon, or by the wrong people. But she'd want us to find them, she'd have wanted that. Even if just for sentiment."

"I agree with that. I know what I felt from her. She loved Giles. She loved her sons. And everything in her hoped for what those who came after her would do. We're her chance to be with Giles again, to free him."

"Let's take it outside. Yeah, there's a basement," Fox told Layla. "But we could focus on the whole house from outside. And the shed. The shed was here, most likely, when Ann was here. We should try the shed."

As Fox had expected, the rain continued, slow and thin. He put his parents' dogs in the house with Lump to keep them out of the way. And with the others, stepped out in the stubborn drizzle.

"Before we do this, I had an idea—came to me in there—about the Bat Signal?"

"The what?" Quinn interrupted.

"Alarm system," Fox explained. "I can get it, the way I could get all the mental chatter in there. It's just like tuning a radio, really. If you push toward me, I should pick it up. If I push toward any of you, same goes. We'll want to run it a few times, but it should work faster than phone tag."

"Psychic team alert." Cybil adjusted her black bucket hat. "Unlimited minutes, and fewer dropped calls. I like it."

"What if you're the one in trouble?" Under her light jacket, Layla wore a hoodie in what she supposed should be called an orchid color. She drew the hood up and over her hair as they crossed the yard.

"Then I push to Cal or Gage. We've done that during the Seven before. Or to you," he added, "once you've gotten a better handle on it. We used to play in there. Remember?" Fox called out to Cal and Gage. "We used it for a fort for a while, only we didn't call it a fort—too warlike for the Barry-O'Dells. So we said it was our clubhouse."

"We murdered thousands from in there." Gage stopped, hands tucked in his pockets. "Died a million deaths."

"We made our plans for the birthday hike to the Pagan Stone while we were in there." Cal stopped. "Do you remember? I'd forgotten that. A couple weeks before our birthday, we got the idea."

"Gage's idea."

"Yeah, blame me."

"We were—what the hell, let me think. School was out. Just out. It was the first full day of freedom, and my mom let me come over and hang all day."

"No chores," Fox continued. "I remember now. I got a pass on chores, one-day pass. First day after school let out. We were playing in there."

"Vice cops against drug lords," Gage put in.

"A change from cowboys and Indians," Cybil commented.

"Hippie boy wouldn't play greedy invaders against indigenous peoples. And if you'd ever gotten one of Joanne Barry's lectures on same, you wouldn't either." The memory had a smile ghosting around Gage's mouth. "We were so juiced up, September was a lifetime off. Everything was hot and bright, green and blue. I didn't want that to end, I remember that, too. Yeah, it was my idea. Major adventure, total freedom."

"We all jumped on it," Cal reminded him. "Plotted the whole thing out right in there." He gestured toward the vine-wrapped stones. "I'm damned if that's a coincidence."

They stood there a moment, side by side. Remembering, Layla supposed. Three men of the same age, who'd come from the same place. Gage in his black leather jacket, Cal in his flannel overshirt and watch cap, Fox in his hooded sweatshirt. Odd, she thought, how something as basic as their choice in outerwear spoke to their individuality even while their stance spoke of their absolute unity.

"Layla." Fox reached out. Her hands were wet and cool. Rain sparkled on her lashes. Even without the psychic link, her anxiety and eagerness flowed toward him.

"Just let it come," he told her. "Don't push, don't even reach for it. Relax, look at me."

"I have a hard time doing both of those things at the same time."

His grin was pure male pleasure. "We'll see what we can do about that later. For right now, bring the book into your head. Just the book. Here we go."

He was both bridge and anchor. She would realize that later, that he had the skill, had the understanding to offer her both. As she crossed the bridge, he was with her. She felt the rain on her face, the ground under her feet. She smelled the earth, the wet grass, even the wet stone. There was a hum, low and steady. She understood with a stab of awe that it was the growing. Grass, leaves, flowers. All humming toward spring and sunlight. Toward the green.

She heard the faint whoosh of air that was a bird winging by, and the scrape that was a squirrel scampering across a branch.

Amazing, she thought, to understand that she was a part of it, and always had been. Always would be. What grew, what breathed, what slept. What lived and died.

There was the smell of earth, of smoke, of wet, of skin. She heard the sigh of rain leaving a cloud, and the murmur of the clouds drifting.

So she drifted, across the bridge.

The pain was sudden and shocking, like a vicious and violent rip inside her. Head, belly, heart. Even as she cried out, she saw the book—just a flash. Then the flash was gone, and so was the pain, leaving her weak and dizzy.

"Sorry. I lost it."

Gage's hands hooked under her armpits as she toppled. "Steady, baby. Easy does it. Cybil."

"Yes, I've got her. Lean on me a minute. You had quite a ride."

"I could hear the clouds moving, and the garden grow. It hums. The flowers hum under the ground. God, I feel . . ."

"Stoned?" Quinn suggested. "You look stoned."

"That's about right. Wow. Fox, did you—" She broke off when she managed to focus. He was on his knees on the wet gravel, his friends crouched on either side of him. And there was blood on his shirt.

"Oh my God, what happened?" She pushed instinctively with her mind, but rammed into a wall. She stumbled, went down on her hands and knees in front of him. "You're hurt. Your nose is bleeding."

"Wouldn't be the first time. Damn it, I just washed this stupid sweatshirt. Just give me some room. Give me room." He dragged a bandanna out of his pocket, pressing it to his nose as he sat back on his heels.

"Let's get him inside," Quinn began, but Fox shook his head, then pressed his free hand to it as if the movement threatened to break it away from his shoulders. "Need a minute."

"Cal, go get him some water. Let's try your mother's trick, Fox." Cybil moved behind him. "Just breathe." She found the points, pressed. "Should I ask if you're pregnant?"

"Not a good time to make me laugh. Little sick here."

"Why was it worse for him than for Quinn?" Layla demanded. "It was supposed to be less, because we were linked. But it's worse. You know." She aimed a fierce look at Gage. "Why?"

"Being O'Dell, he stepped in front of you and took the full punch. That'd be my guess. And because of the link, it was a hell of a punch."

"Is that it?" Furious, Layla turned on Fox. "I'm listening to clouds and you're getting kicked in the face."

"Your face is prettier than mine. Marginally. Quiet a minute, okay? Have a little pity for the wounded."

"Don't ever do it again. You look at me, you listen to me. Don't ever do it again. You promise that, or I'm done with this."

"I don't like ultimatums." Even through the glaze of pain in his eyes, the temper sparked. "In fact, they piss me off."

"You know what pisses me off? You didn't trust me to carry my share."

"It has nothing to do with trust or shares. Thanks, Cybil, it's better." He got carefully to his feet, took the water Cal offered and drank it straight down. "They're wrapped in oilcloth, behind the south wall. I couldn't tell how many. Two, maybe three. You know where the tools are, Cal. I'll be back out to help in a minute."

He made it into the house, into the bathroom off the kitchen before he was as sick as a man after a two-day drunk. With his stomach raw and his head a misery, he rinsed his face, his mouth. Then just leaned on the sink until he had his breath back.

When he came out, Layla stood in the kitchen. "We're not finished."

"You want to fight? We'll fight later. Right now we've got a job to do."

"I'm not doing anything until you give me your word you won't shield me again."

"Can't do it. I only give my word when I'm sure I can keep it." He turned, started rooting through cupboards. "Nothing but holistic shit in this house. Why is there never any damn Excedrin?"

"You had no right—"

"Sue me. I know some good lawyers. We do what we do, Layla. That's the way it is. That's the way I am. I took

a shot because I knew it was a good one. I got there because of you, because of us. I wasn't going to let you get
hurt if I could stop it, and I'm not going to promise not to
do what I can to stop you from being hurt down the road."

"If you think because I'm a woman I'm weaker, less capable, less—"

His face was sheet pale as he rounded on her. Even temper couldn't push the color back into his face. "Christ,
don't start waving the feminist flag. Did you meet my
mother? Your sex has nothing to do with it—other than the
fact that I'm gone on you, which, being straight, I wouldn't
be if you were a guy. I survived. I got a headache, a nose-
bleed, and I lost my breakfast—and dinner, and possibly a
couple of internal organs. But other than wishing to goddamn hell and back there was some aspirin and a can of
Coke around this house, I'm fine. You want to be pissed, be
pissed. But be pissed correctly."

As he drilled his fingers into his forehead, she opened
the purse she'd left on the kitchen table. From it she took a
little box with a crescent moon on the top.

"Here." She handed him two pills. "It's Advil."

"Praise the Lord. Don't be stingy. Give me a couple
more."

"I'm still pissed, correctly or incorrectly." She handed
him two more pills, inwardly wincing when he dry-
swallowed the lot. "But I'm going out to help do the job because I'm part of this team. Let me say this first, if you're so
gone over me, consider how I feel seeing you on the ground,
bleeding and in pain. There are lots of ways to be hurt. Think
about that."

When she stalked out he stayed where he was. She
might've had a point, but he was too worn out to think
about it. Instead, he got the pitcher of his mother's cold tea
out of the fridge and downed a glass to wash the dregs of
annoyance and sickness from his throat.

Because he still felt shaky, he left the chiseling to Gage

and Cal. Eventually, he'd have to tell his parents, he thought. Especially if they weren't able to replace the stone in such a way the removal didn't show.

No, he thought, he'd have to tell them either way or he'd feel guilty.

In any case, they'd understand—a lot better than a certain brunette—why he'd wanted to try this when they were away from home. They may not like it, but they wouldn't start shoveling the you-don't-trust-me crap over his head. Not their style.

"Try not to chip it."

"It's a fucking stone, O'Dell." Gage slammed the hammer on the knob of the chisel. "Not a damn diamond."

"Tell that to my parents," he muttered, then jammed his hands in his pockets.

"You'd better be sure this is the one." Cal struck from the other side. "Or else we're going to be doing a lot more than chipping one rock."

"That's the one. The wall's four deep, one of the reasons it's still standing. That one was probably loose or she worked it loose. The past shit's your milieu."

"Milicu, my ass." Wet, his knuckles scraped, Cal struck again. By the next strike, the knuckles had already healed, but he was still soaked to the skin. "It's coming."

He and Gage worked it loose by hand as Fox fought the image of the whole wall crumbling like a game of Jenga.

"Sucker weighs a ton," Gage complained. "More like a damn boulder. Watch the fingers." He cursed as the movement pinched his fingers between rocks, then let the weight of the stone carry it to the ground. Sitting back on his heels, he sucked at his bleeding hand as Cal reached into the opening.

"Son of a bitch. I've got it." Cal drew out a package wrapped in oilcloth. "Score one for O'Dell." Carefully, hunching over to protect the contents from the rain, he unwrapped the cloth.

"Don't open them," Quinn warned from behind them. "It's too wet out here. The ink might run. Ann Hawkins's journals. We found them."

"We'll take them back to my place. Get out of these wet clothes, then—"

The blast shook the ground. It knocked Fox off his feet, smashing him into the stone wall with his hip and shoulder taking the brunt. Head ringing, he turned to see the house burning. Flames shot through the roof, clawed through broken windows with the roaring belch of black smoke behind them. He ran toward home, through a blistering wall of heat.

When Gage tackled him, he slammed hard into the ground and swung out with blind fury. "The dogs are inside. Goddamn it."

"Pull yourself together." Gage shouted over the bellow of fire. "Is it real? Pull it together, Fox. Is it real?"

He could feel the burn. He swore he could feel it, and the smoke stinging his eyes, scoring his throat as he choked in air. He had to fight back the image of his home going up in flames, of three helpless dogs trapped and panicked.

He gripped Gage's shoulder as an anchor, then Cal's forearm as his friends pulled him to his feet. They stood linked for a moment, and a moment was all he needed.

"It's a lie. Damn. Just another lie." He heard Cal's breath shudder out. "Lump's fine. The dogs are fine. It's just more bullshit."

The fire wavered, spurted, died, so the old stone house stood whole under the thin and steady rain.

Fox let out a breath of his own. "Sorry about the fist in the face," he said to Gage.

"You hit like a girl."

"Your mouth's bleeding."

Gage swiped at it, grinned. "Not for long."

Cal strode to the house, threw open the door to let the

dogs out. Then simply sat on the floor of the back porch with his arms full of Lump.

"It's not supposed to come here." Fox walked forward, too, set a hand on the porch rail he'd helped build. "It's never been able to come here. Not to our families."

"Things are different now." Cybil crouched down and rubbed the other two dogs as they wagged tails. "These dogs aren't scared. It didn't happen for them. Just us."

"And if my parents had been in there?"

"It wouldn't have happened for them either." Quinn dropped down beside Cal. "How many times have the three of you seen things no one else has?"

"Sometimes they're real," Fox pointed out.

"This wasn't. It just wanted to shake us up, scare us. It—Oh God, the journals."

"I have them."

Fox turned, saw Layla standing in the rain, clutching the wrapped package against her breasts. "It wanted to hurt you. Couldn't you feel it? Because you found them. Couldn't you feel the hate?"

He'd felt nothing, Fox realized, but panic—and that was a mistake. "So he scored one, too." He crossed to Layla, drew up the hood that had fallen away. "But we're still ahead."

Nine

~⌐~

THERE WAS COFFEE FOR THOSE WHO WANTED IT, and a fire burning bright in Cal's living room to warm chilled bones. There were enough dry clothes to go around, though Layla wasn't sure what sort of a fashion statement she made in a pair of Cal's jogging shorts bagging well past her knees and a shirt several sizes too big. But Cybil had snagged the spare jeans Quinn had left at Cal's, and beggars couldn't be choosers.

While the washer and dryer churned away, she topped off her coffee. Her feet swished over the kitchen floor in enormous wool socks.

"Nice outfit," Fox said from the doorway.

"Could start a trend." She turned to face him. Cal's clothes fit him a great deal better than they did her. "Are you all right now?"

"Yeah." He got a Coke out of the fridge. "I'm going to ask you to put whatever mad you've still got on aside for a while. We'll deal with that later, if we have to."

"That's the problem, isn't it? Personal feelings, reactions, relationships. They get in the way, knot things up."

"Maybe. Can't do much about it as *person*'s the root of personal. We can't stop being people, or it wins."

"What would have happened if Gage hadn't stopped you, if you'd gotten inside the house?"

"I don't know."

"You do, or you can speculate. Here's what I speculate. At that moment, the fire was real to you, you believed it, so it was real. You felt the heat, the smoke. And if you'd gotten in, despite how quickly you heal, you could've died because you believed."

"I let the son of a bitch scam me. My mistake."

"Not the point. It could kill you. I never really considered that before. It could use your mind to end your life."

"So we have to be smarter." He shrugged, but the gesture was an irritable jerk that told her temper was still lurking inside him. "It got one over on me today because nothing's ever happened at the farm, or at Cal's parents' house. They've always been out-of-bounds. Safe zones. So I didn't think, I just reacted. That's never smart."

"If it had been real, you'd have gone in. You'd have risked your life to save three dogs. I don't know what to think of you," she said after a moment. "I don't know what to feel. So I guess, like my mad, I need to put that aside and deal with it later."

"Sorry." Quinn stood in the doorway of the adjoining dining room. "We're ready in here."

"Just coming." Layla walked out. A few seconds later, Fox followed.

"I guess we should just dive in." Quinn took a seat beside Cal at the table. She glanced over to where Cybil sat with a notepad, ready to write down thoughts, impressions. "So, who wants to do the honors?"

Six people studied the wrapped package on the table. Six people said nothing.

"Oh, hell, this is silly." Quinn picked up the books, carefully unwrapped them. "Even considering they were protected, they're awfully well preserved."

"We can assume, under the circumstances, she had some power, some knowledge of magicks," Cybil pointed out. "Pick one, read an entry aloud."

"Okay, here goes." There were three, so she took the top one, opened it to the first entry. The ink was faded, but legible, the handwriting—familiar now—careful and clear.

There must be a record, I think, of what was, what is, what will be. I am Ann. My father, Jonathan Hawkins, brought my mother, my sister, brother, and me to this place we call the Hollow. It is a new world where he believes we will be happy. So we have been. It is a green place, a rough place, a quiet place. He and my uncle cleared land for shelter, for crops. The water is cold and clear in the spring. More came, and the Hollow became Hawkins Hollow. My father has built a small and pretty stone house, and we have been comfortable there.

There is work, as there should be work, to keep the mind and hands busy, to provide and to build. Those who settle here have built a stone chapel for worship. I have attended the services, as is expected. But I do not find God there. I have found him in the wood. It is there I feel at peace. It is there I first met Giles.

Perhaps love does not come in an instant, but takes lifetimes. Is this how I knew, in that instant, such love? Is this how I felt, even saw in my mind's eye lifetime by lifetime with this man who lived alone in a stone cabin in the green shadowed wood that held the altar stone?

He waited for me. This I knew as well. He waited for me to come to him, to see him, to know him. When we met we spoke of simple things, as is proper. We spoke of the sun and the wild berries I picked, of my father, of the hide Giles tanned.

We did not speak of gods and demons, of magic and destiny, not then. That would come.

I walked the wood, wandered my way to the stone cabin and the altar at every opportunity. He was always waiting for me. So the love of lifetimes bloomed again, in the green wood, in secret. I was his again, as I ever was, as I ever will be.

Quinn paused, sighed. "That's the first entry. It's lovely."

"Pretty words don't make much of a weapon," Gage commented. "They don't provide answers."

"I disagree with that," Cybil said. "And I think she deserves to have those words read as she wrote them. Lifetimes," she continued, tapping her notes. "That indicates her understanding that she and Dent were reincarnations of the guardian and his mate. Time and again. And he waited for her to accept it. He didn't launch right into, 'Hey, guess what, you and I are going to get cozy. You'll get knocked up with triplets, we'll hassle with some Big Evil Bastard, and a few hundred years from now our ancestors are going to fight the fight.' "

"Boy, a guy hits me with a line like that, I'm naked in a heartbeat." Quinn traced a finger down the page. "I'm with Cyb on this. There's value in every word because she wrote it. It's hard not to be impatient, just skim over looking for some magic formula for destroying demons."

Layla shook her head. "It won't be like that anyway."

"No, I don't think so either. Should I read on, in order?"

"I think we should see how it evolved, from her eyes." Fox glanced at Gage, at Cal. "Keep going, Quinn."

She read of love, of changes of seasons, of chores and quiet moments. She wrote of death, of life, of new faces. She wrote of the people who came to the stone cabin for healing. She wrote of her first kiss beside a stream where the water sparkled in the sun. She wrote of sitting with Giles in the stone cabin, in front of a fire that flamed red and gold as he told her of what had come before.

He said to me that the world is old, older than any man can know. It is not as we have been taught, nor what we are told to believe in the faith of my father and my mother. Or that is not all of it. For, he said, in this old, old time before man came to be, there were others. Of the others there were the dark and the light. This was their choice, for there is always the freedom to choose. Those who chose the light were called gods, and the dark ones demons.

There was death and blood, battles and war. Many of both were destroyed as man came to be. It was man who would spread over the world, who would rule it and be ruled by it. It was coming to, he said, the time of man, as was right. Demons hated man even more than they hated gods. They despised and envied their minds and hearts, their vulnerable bodies, their needs and weaknesses. Man became prey for the demons who survived. It came to be that those gods who survived as well became guardians. Battle after battle raged until there were only two, one light, one dark. One demon, one guardian. The light pursued the dark over the world, but the demon was clever and cunning. In this last battle, the guardian was wounded mortally, and left to die. There came upon this dying god a young boy, innocent and pure of heart. Dying, the god passed his power and his burden to the boy. So the boy, a mortal with the power of gods, became guardian. The boy became a man, hunting the dark. The boy became a man who loved a woman with the power of magic, and they had a son. At his death, the guardian passed his power and his burden to his son, and so it was done over all the years. Lifetime by lifetime, until this time, until this place. Now, he said, it is for us.

I knew he spoke truth, for I saw it in the fire as he spoke. I understood the dreams I have had all of my life that I never dared speak of to any living soul. There, in the firelight, I pledged myself to him. There, in the firelight, I gave myself to him. I would not go back to the house of

my father but live with my beloved in the wood, in the
stone cabin near the altar Giles called the Pagan Stone.

Quinn leaned back. "Sorry, my eyes are blurring."

"It's enough for now." Cal handed her the glass of water he'd poured. "It's a lot for now."

"It jibes with some versions of the lore that trickled down." Shifting, Cybil studied her notes. "The battles, the passing of power. The way I'm reading this is there's only this single demon left. I'm not sure if I buy that, I'm a little too superstitious. But it could be interpreted that this is the only demon known to walk the world freely, at least every seven years. Why didn't he mate before Hester Deale? That's curious, isn't it?"

"Maybe he couldn't get it up." Gage smiled thinly.

"I don't think that's far off. I think, however sarcastic, it's a viable theory." Cybil held up a finger. "Maybe they couldn't mate with humans, it couldn't. But as Giles apparently discovered a way to imprison the thing, at least for a time, it discovered a way to procreate. Each side evolving, so to speak. Every living thing evolves."

"Good thought," Fox agreed. "Or it might be that up until Hester, it was shooting blanks, so to speak. Or the women it violated never came to term for one reason or another. We should take a break. Quinn's been at it a couple hours now, and I don't know about anyone else, but I could use some fuel."

"Don't look at me," Cybil said firmly. "I cooked last time."

"I'll do it." Layla pushed to her feet. "Can I root around in the kitchen, Cal, until I come up with something?"

"Have at it."

She was bent over, head in the refrigerator when Fox walked in. When a man thought how good a woman's ass looked in baggy, drooping shorts, he decided, that man had it bad.

"Thought I could give you a hand."

She straightened, turned with her hands full of a pack of American cheese slices, a pound of bacon, and a couple of hothouse tomatoes. "I thought grilled cheese, bacon, and tomato sandwiches. Maybe a quick pasta salad on the side if he's got something I can throw together for that. I can handle it."

"Because you want me out of here."

"No." She dumped the armload on the counter. "I'm not mad. It's too much trouble to stay mad. You could see if the clothes are dry so I could get out of these shorts and into my own clothes."

"Sure. But you look kind of cute."

"No, I don't."

"You're not looking at you." Gauging her mood, he stepped forward. "I can slice tomatoes. In fact, it's one of my more amazing skills. Plus." He kept moving in until she was backed against the counter with his hands planted on either side of her. "I know where Cal keeps the pasta."

"Making you invaluable in the kitchen?"

"I hope not. Layla." His eyes roamed her face. "I'm not going to tell you what to think or how to feel, or when to take those thoughts and feelings out of whatever box you need to keep them in. But I think about you. I feel for you. Unlike slicing tomatoes, packing away thoughts and feelings isn't one of my finer skills."

"I'm afraid of you."

Instant and complete shock ran over his face. "What? Of me? Nobody's afraid of me."

"That's absolutely not true. Deputy Napper is afraid of you. It's part of the reason he keeps after you. But that's a different kind of thing anyway. I'm afraid because you make me feel things I'm not sure I'm ready to feel, want things I'm not sure I'm ready to want. It would probably be easier if you rushed me, just did the sweep-off-the-feet routine because then I wouldn't have to feel responsible for my own choices."

"I could try that."

"No." She shook her head. "You won't. You're not built that way. Relationships are partnerships, sex is a mutual act and decision. That's how you were raised from the ground up, that's who you are. And it's part of what attracts me and makes it harder at the same time."

She put a hand on his chest, nudged slightly. When he eased back, she smiled as the basic action and reaction proved her point.

"I'm afraid of you," she continued, "because you'd run into a burning building to save a dog. Because you'd take what was my share of pain and trauma. You were right before. It's your nature. It wasn't just because it was me. You'd have done the same if it had been Cal or Gage, Quinn or Cybil. A complete stranger. I'm afraid of what you are because I've never known anyone like you. And I'm afraid that I'll take the chance, I'll reach out and take hold, then I'll lose you because, exactly because of who you are."

"All this time, I never knew I was such a scary guy."

She turned away, took a knife from the block, set it on the cutting board. "Slice the tomatoes."

She opened a cupboard, found the pasta herself. As she hunted up pan and skillet, his phone rang. She glanced over as he read the caller ID. "Hey, Mom and/or Dad. Yeah. Really?" He set the knife down again, leaned on the counter. "When? No kidding. Sure, sure." He tipped the phone away, murmured to Layla. "My sister and her partner are flying in. What?" he said into the phone. "No, not a problem. Ah, listen, while I've got you . . . We were out at the farm today, me and the rest. Early this morning. The thing is . . ." He trailed off, walked away into the adjoining laundry room.

Layla smiled as she heard the murmur of his voice. Yes, it was his nature, she thought as she put on water for the pasta. To save dogs, to be honest. And to explain to Mom and/or Dad just why he'd chiseled a stone out of their old shed.

It was hardly a wonder she was half in love with him.

The rain continued into the damp and dreary afternoon. They ate before moving into the living room by mutual consent where Quinn continued to read by the fire.

It was almost dreamy now, Layla thought. The patter of rain, the crackle of flame and wood, the sound of Quinn's voice speaking Ann's words. She curled in her chair, cozy again in her own warm clothes, drinking tea while Fox and Lump stretched out on the floor nearby.

If she were to take a picture, it would look like a group of friends, gathered together on a rainy day, in that chilly window between winter and spring. Quinn with her book, Cal beside her on the couch. Cybil curled like a lazy cat on the other end, and Gage sprawled in a chair drinking yet another cup of coffee.

But she had only to listen to the words for the picture to change. She had only to listen to see a young woman building another fire in a hearth, her bright hair sweeping down her back. To feel the ache in the heart that had stopped beating so long ago.

I am with child. There is such joy in me, and there is such grief.

Joy for the lives inside her, Layla thought. Grief as those lives signaled the beginning of the end of Ann's time with Giles. She imagined Ann preparing meals, fetching water from the stream, writing in the first journal with the cover Giles had made her from the leather he'd tanned himself. She wrote of ordinary things, of ordinary days. Pages and pages of the simple and the human.

"I'm tapped," Quinn said at length. "Somebody else can take over, but the fact is, my brain's just plain tired. I don't think I can take any more in right now even if someone else reads."

Cal shifted her to rub at her shoulders, while Quinn stretched in obvious relief. "If we try to take in too much at once, we'll probably miss something anyway."

"Lots of daily minutia in that section." Cybil flexed her

writing hand. "He's tutoring her, showing her simple magicks. Herbs, candles, drawing out what she already had.
She's very open to it. It seems obvious he didn't want to
leave her without weapons, tools, defenses."

"Pioneer days," Fox commented. "Hard life."

"I think life was part of the point," Layla added. "The
ordinary. We've all felt that, mentioned it at one time or another through this. The ordinary matters, it's very much
what we're fighting for. I think she wrote about it, often,
because she understood that. Or maybe because she needed
to remind herself of it so she could face whatever was
coming."

"We're more than halfway through the first journal."
Quinn marked the page before setting the book down. "She
still hasn't mentioned specifics on what's coming. Either
he hasn't told her yet, specifically, or she hasn't wanted to
write of it." She yawned hugely. "I vote we get out of here
awhile or take a nap."

"They can all get out of here." Cal lowered his head to
nip at her neck. "We'll take a nap."

"That's a lame euphemism for rainy-day sex, and you
guys already get enough sex." Cybil uncurled a leg to give
Cal a light kick. "Option two, another form of entertainment. That isn't poker," she added before Gage could speak.

"Sex and poker are the top two forms of entertainment,"
he told her.

"While I have no objection to either, there must be
something a group of young, attractive people can find to
do around here. No offense to the Bowl-a-Rama, Cal, but
there must be somewhere we can get adult beverages,
noise, maybe music, bad bar food."

"Actually— Ow!" Layla glared down at Fox when he
pinched her foot. "Actually," she began again, "Fox mentioned a place that seemed to fit that bill. A bar across the
river with live music on Saturday nights."

"We're so going there." Cybil pushed to her feet. "Who's

stuck being designated drivers? I nominate Quinn from our side."

"Seconded," Layla called out.

"Aw."

"You're getting sex," Cybil reminded her. "No complaints will be registered."

"Gage." Fox mimed a gun with his thumb and forefinger.

"Always is," Gage said.

Even with the agreement it took thirty minutes for such vital matters as redoing makeup, dealing with hair. Then there was the debate over who was riding with whom, complicated by the fact that Cal remained adamant over not leaving Lump unattended.

"That thing came after my dog once, it could come after him again. Where I go, so goes the Lump. Plus, I ride with my woman."

Which left Fox squeezing into Cal's truck with Gage behind the wheel and Lump riding shotgun.

"Why can't he ride in the middle?" Fox demanded.

"Because he'll slobber on me, shed on me, and I'll smell like dog."

"I'm going to."

"Your problem, son." Gage slid a glance over. "And I guess it might be, as the pretty brunette may object to being slobbered on by you scented with eau de Lump."

"She hasn't complained yet." Fox reached over to let the window down a few inches for Lump's sniffing nose.

"I can't blame you for moving in that direction. She's got that classy waif with brains and an underlayer of valor you'd go for."

"Is that what I go for?" Amused, Fox leaned against the bulk of Lump to study Gage's profile.

"She's right up your alley, with the unexpected addition of urban polish. Just don't let it screw you up."

"Why would it?"

When Gage didn't answer, Fox shifted. "That was seven years ago, and Carly didn't screw me up. What happened did, for a while. Layla's part of this, Carly wasn't. Or shouldn't have been."

"Does the fact that she's part of this worry you at all? You two have the connection, like Cal and Quinn. Now Cal's picking out china patterns."

"Is he?"

"Metaphorically speaking. Now here you are moving on Layla, and getting that cocker spaniel look in your eye when she's within sniffing distance."

"If I have to be a dog I want a Great Dane. They have dignity. And no, it doesn't worry me. I feel what I feel." He caught a glimmer. He couldn't help it; it was just there. And it made him smile as only brothers smile at each other. "But it worries you. Cal and Quinn, me and Layla. That leaves you and Cybil. You afraid fate's going to take a hand? Destiny's about to kick your ass? Should I order the monogrammed towels?"

"I'm not worried. I factor the odds in any game I play, make the players."

"The third female player is extremely hot."

"I've had hotter."

Fox snorted, turned to Lump. "He's had hotter."

"Plus, she's not my type."

"I didn't know there was any woman who wasn't your type."

"Complicated women aren't my type. You tangle in the sheets with a complicated woman, you're going to pay a price for it in the morning. I like them simple." He grinned over at Fox. "And plenty of them."

"A complicated woman will give you more play. And you like play."

"Not that kind. Simple gets you through. And plenty of simple gets you through a lot. I figure going for quantity, seeing as we might not live past our next birthday."

Reaching over, Fox gave Gage a friendly punch on the arm. "You always cheer me up with that sunny, optimistic nature of yours."

"What are you bitching about? You're going to eat, drink, and possibly make Layla, while I settle for club soda and bad music in a crowded West Virginia bar."

"You could get lucky. I bet there's at least one simple woman inside."

Gage considered as he pulled to the curb near the bar. "There is that."

IT WASN'T WHAT HE'D PLANNED, FOX THOUGHT. He'd had the idea of sitting with Layla at a corner table, well in the back where the music wasn't loud enough to hamper conversation. A little get-to-know-each-other-better-as-regular-people interlude, maybe followed by a little low-key necking. Which, if done right, might have led to some fooling around in his truck, and ended with her in his bed.

He'd considered it a pretty damn good plan, with room for flexible options.

He'd ended up crammed with five other people at a table for four, drinking beer and eating nachos while the juke blasted out twangy country.

And laughing, a lot.

The live music wasn't bad when it started. The five guys stuffed in the stage corner managed to pump it out pretty well. He knew them and, feeling generous, bought them a round on their break.

"Whose idea was this?" Quinn demanded. "This was a *great* idea. And I'm not even drinking."

"Mine, technically." Fox clinked his beer to her glass of diet something. "I routinely have great ideas."

"It was your general concept," Layla corrected. "My ex-ecution. But you were right. It's a nice bar."

"I particularly like the Bettie Page wall clock." Cybil gestured toward it.

"You know Bettie Page?" Gage wanted to know.

"Know of, certainly. The fifties pinup sensation who became a cult icon, partially due to being the target of a Senate investigation—read witch hunt in my opinion—on porn."

"Cybil met her." Quinn lifted her soda, sipped.

Gage peered over his drink. "Get out."

"I helped research the script for the biopic that came out a couple of years ago. She was lovely, inside and out. Are you a fan, Mr. Turner?"

"Yeah, actually, I am." He took a sip of club soda as he studied Cybil. "You've got a lot of unusual avenues in there."

She smiled her slow, feline smile. "I love to travel."

When the band came back, two of its members stopped by the table. "Want to jam one, O'Dell?"

"You guys are doing fine without me."

"You play?" Cybil poked him in the shoulder.

"Family requirement."

"Then go jam one, O'Dell." Now she gave him a push. "We insist."

"I'm drinking here."

"Don't make us cause a scene. We're capable. Q?"

"Oh yeah. Fox," she said. "Fox. Fox. Fox." Letting her voice rise a bit on each repetition.

"Okay. Okay."

When he rose, Quinn put her fingers between her lips and whistled.

"Control your girl."

"Can't." Cal only grinned. "I like 'em wild."

Shaking his head, Fox lifted a guitar from its stand, held a brief conference with the band as he slung the strap over his shoulder.

Cybil leaned over to Layla. "Why are guitar players so sexy?"

"I think it's the hands."

His certainly seemed to know what they were doing as he turned, tapped out the time, then led with a complex riff.

"Show-off," Gage muttered, and made Cybil laugh.

He went with "Lay Down Sally," an obvious crowd pleaser. Layla had to admit it had a tingle working in her when he leaned into the mike and added vocals.

He looked the part, didn't he? she thought. Faded jeans over narrow hips, feet planted in run-down work boots, shaggy hair around a handsome face. And when those tiger eyes, full of fun, latched on hers, the tingle went right up to the top of the scale.

Cybil scooted over until her lips were a half inch from Layla's ear. "He's really good."

"Yeah, damn it. I think I'm in trouble."

"Right this minute? I wish I was." With another laugh, she leaned back while the song ended, and the bar erupted with applause.

Fox was already shaking his head, taking off the strap.

"Come on," Cybil called out. "Encore."

He kept shaking his head as he came back to the table. "I do more than one in a row, they have to pry the guitar out of my greedy hands."

"Why aren't you a rock star instead of a lawyer?" Layla asked him.

"Rock starring's too much work." The music pumped out again as he leaned close to her. "I resisted the more obvious Clapton. How many guys have hit you with "Layla" over the years?"

"Pretty much all of them."

"That's what I figured. I've got this individualist streak. Never go for the obvious."

Oh yeah, she thought when he grinned at her. She was definitely in trouble.

Ten

~✍~

THE RAIN HUNG AROUND, IRRITATINGLY, INTO the kind of gloomy, windswept morning where sleeping in was mandatory. Or would've been, Fox thought as he shut his apartment door behind him, if a guy didn't have demon research on his Sunday morning schedule.

Despite the damp, he opted to walk the handful of blocks to Layla's. Like juggling, walking was thinking time. Apparently the other residents of the Hollow didn't share his view or had nothing much to think about. Cars crammed nose to ass at the curb outside Ma's Pantry and Coffee Talk, windshields running, bumpers dripping. And inside, he mused, people would be tucking into the breakfast special, getting their coffee topped off, complaining about the windy rain.

From across the street, he eyeballed the new door on the bookstore and thought, Nice job, Dad. As Layla had done, he studied the Going Out of Business sign on the gift shop. Nothing to be done about that. Another business would move in. Jim Hawkins would find another tenant who'd slap fresh paint on the walls and fill the place with whatevers. A Grand Opening sign would go up; customers would wander in to check it all out. Through the transition, people would still be eating the breakfast special, sleeping in on a rainy Sunday morning, or nagging their kids to get dressed for church.

But things would change. This time, when the Seven came around, they'd be more than ready for the Big Evil Bastard. They'd do more than mop up the blood, put out the fires, lock up the deranged until the madness passed.

They had to do more.

Meanwhile, they'd do the work, look for answers. They'd had fun the night before, he mused. Hanging out, letting music and conversation wash away a long, hard day. Progress had been made during that day. He could feel all of them taking a step toward something.

So while he might not be sleeping in or tucking into the breakfast special at Ma's, he'd spend the day with friends, and the woman he wanted for his lover, working toward making sure others in the Hollow could keep right on doing the everyday, even during the week of July seventh, every seventh year.

He made the turn at the Square, hands in the kangaroo pockets of his hooded sweatshirt, head ducked down in the rain.

He glanced up idly as he heard the squeal of brakes on wet pavement. Fox recognized Block Kholer's truck, and thought, Shit, even before Block slammed out of it.

"You little son of a bitch."

Now, as Block strode forward, ham-sized hands fisted, size fourteen Wolverines slapping the pavement, Fox thought: Shit.

"You're going to want to step back, Block, and calm down." They'd known each other since high school, so Fox's hopes of Block doing either were slim. As tempers went, Block's was fairly mild—but once Block worked up a head of steam, somebody was going to get pounded.

Since he sincerely didn't want it to be him, Fox tuned in and managed to evade the first swing.

"Cut it out, Block. I'm Shelley's lawyer, that's reality. If I wasn't, somebody else would be."

"I heard that's not all you are." He swung again, missed again when Fox ducked. "How long you been doing my wife, you cocksucker?"

"I've never been with Shelley that way. You know me, goddamn it. If you got that tune from Napper, consider who was whistling it."

"I got kicked out of my own goddamn house." Block's blue eyes were bright with rage in a wide face stained red with more. "I gotta go into Ma's to get a decent breakfast because of you."

"I wasn't the one with my hand down my sister-in-law's shirt." Talk was his business, Fox reminded himself. Talk him down. So he kept his voice cool and even as he danced back from another punch. "Don't hang this on me, Block, and don't do something now you're going to have to pay for."

"You're going to fucking pay."

Fox was fast, but Block hadn't lost all the skill he'd owned on the football field back in his day. He didn't punch Fox as much as mow him down. Fox hit the ivy-covered slope of a lawn—and the rocks underneath the drenched ivy—and slid painfully down to the sidewalk with the enraged former defensive tackle on top of him.

Block outweighed him by a good fifty pounds, and most of that was muscle. Pinned, he couldn't avoid the short-armed, bare-knuckled punch to the face, or the punishing rabbit jabs in his kidneys. Through the vicious pain, the blurred vision, he could see a kind of madness on Block's face that had panic snaking in.

And the thoughts sparking out were every bit as mad and murderous.

Fox did the only thing left to him. He fought dirty. He clawed, going for those mad eyes. At Block's howl, he rammed his fist into the exposed throat. Block gagged, choked, and Fox had room to maneuver, to jam his knee between Block's legs. He got in a few punches, aiming for the face and throat.

Run. That single thought bloomed like blood in Fox's mind. But when he tried to roll, crawl, fight his way clear and gain his feet, Block slammed Fox's head against the sidewalk. He felt something inside him break as the steel-toed boot kicked viciously at his side. Then he fought for air as meaty hands closed around his throat.

Die here.

He didn't know if it was Block's thoughts or his own circling in his screaming head. But he knew he was slipping away. His burning lungs couldn't draw air, and his vision was dimmed and doubled. He struggled to push what he had into this man he knew, a man who loved the Redskins and NASCAR, who was always good for a bad, dirty joke and was a genius with engines. A man stupid enough to cheat on his wife with her sister.

But he couldn't find it. He couldn't find himself or the man who was killing him on the sidewalk a few steps from the Town Square on a rainy Sunday morning.

Then all he could see was red, like a field of blood. All he could see was his own death.

The pressure on his throat released, and the horrible weight on his chest lifted. As he rolled, retching, he thought he heard shouting. But his ears rang like Klaxons, and he spat blood.

"Fox! Fox! O'Dell!"

A face swam in front of his. Fox lay across the sidewalk, the rain blessedly cool on his battered face. He saw a blurred triple image of Chief of Police Wayne Hawbaker.

"Better not move," Wayne told him. "I'll call an ambulance."

Not dead, Fox thought, though the red still swam at the edges of his vision. "No, wait." It croaked out of him, but he managed to sit up. "No ambulance."

"You're hurt pretty bad."

He knew his one eye was swollen shut, but he managed to focus the other on Wayne. "I'll be okay. Where the fuck is Block?"

"Cuffed and locked in the back of my car. Christ, Fox, I had to damn near knock him cold to get him off you. What the hell was going on here?"

Fox wiped blood from his mouth. "Ask Napper."

"What does he have to do with it?"

"He'd be the one who got Block worked up, making him think I'd been screwing around with Shelley." Fox wheezed in another breath that felt like broken glass inside his throat. "Never mind, doesn't matter. No law against lying to an idiot, is there?"

Wayne said nothing for a moment. "I'll call down to the firehouse, get the paramedics here to look you over at least."

"I don't need them." As helpless anger, helpless pain churned inside him, Fox braced a bleeding hand on the sidewalk. "I don't want them."

"I'll be taking Block in. I'll need you to come in when you're able, file formal assault charges."

Fox nodded. Attempted murder was closer to the mark, but assault would do.

"Let me help you into the front of the car. I'll take you where you want to go."

"Just go on. I can get where I'm going."

Wayne dragged a hand through his wet, graying hair. "Chrissakes, Fox, you want me to leave you on the sidewalk, bleeding?"

Once again, Fox focused his good eye. "You know me, Chief. I heal quick."

Acknowledgment and worry clouded Wayne's eyes. "Let

me see you get to your feet. I'm not driving off until I know you can stand and walk."

He managed it, every inch of him screaming. Three broken ribs, Fox thought. He could already feel them trying to heal, and the pain was hideous. "Lock him up. I'll be in when I can."

He limped off, didn't stop until he heard Hawbaker drive away. Then he turned, and stared at the grinning boy standing across the street.

"I'll heal, you fucker, and when the time comes, I'll do a lot worse to you."

The demon in a child's form laughed. Then it opened its mouth, wide as a cave, and swallowed itself.

By the time Fox made it to the rental house, one of his ribs had healed, and the second was working on it. His loosened teeth were solid again; the most minor of the scrapes and cuts had closed.

Should've gone home to finish this up, he realized. But the beating and the agony of the healing left him exhausted and fuzzy-headed. The women would just have to deal with it, he told himself. They'd probably have to deal with worse before it was over.

"We're up here!" Quinn called down at the sound of the door opening, closing again. "Be down in a minute. Coffee's on the stove, Coke's in the fridge, depending on who you are."

The bruising on his windpipe was still too severe. He didn't have it in him to call back, so made his way painfully to the kitchen.

He started to reach for the refrigerator, frowned at his broken wrist. "Come on, you bastard, finish it up." While the bones knit, he used his left hand to get out a Coke, then fought bitterly with the tab of the can.

"We're getting a late start. I guess we were— Oh my God." Layla rushed forward. "Fox! God. Quinn, Cybil, Cal! Get down here. Fox is hurt!"

She tried to get an arm around him, take his weight. "Just open this, will you? Open the stupid can."

"Sit down. You need to sit down. Your face. Your poor face. Here, sit down here."

"Just open the goddamn can." He snapped it out, but she only pulled out a chair. The fact that she could ease him down on it with little effort told him he was still in bad shape.

She opened the can, started to cup his hands around it. Her voice was thin, but steady when she spoke. "Your wrist is broken."

"Not for long."

He took his first long, desperate sip as Cal ran in. One look had Cal cursing. "Layla, get some water, some towels to clean him up some." He crouched, put a hand on Fox's thigh. "How bad?"

"Worst in a long time."

"Napper?"

"Indirectly."

"Quinn," Cal said with his eyes still on Fox. "Call Gage. If he isn't on his way, tell him to get here."

"I'm getting ice." She dragged the ice bin out of the freezer. "Cybil."

"I'll call." But first she bent over, laid her lips gently on Fox's bloody cheek. "We'll take care of you, baby."

Layla brought a basin and cloth. "It hurts. Can we give him anything for the pain?"

"You have to go through it, even use it. It helps if the three of us are together." Cal's eyes never left Fox's face. "Give me something."

"Ribs, left side. He got three, one's finished, one's working."

"Okay."

"They should go." He hissed on a fresh flood of pain. "Tell them to go."

"We're not going anywhere." Gently, efficiently, Layla began to stroke the cold damp cloth over Fox's face.

"Here, honey." Quinn held the ice bag to Fox's swollen eye.

"I got him on his cell." Cybil hurried back in. "He was already in town. He'll be here any second." She stopped, and despite her horror at Fox's condition, watched in fascination as the raw bruises on his throat began to fade.

"He messed me up inside," Fox managed. "Can't focus, can't find it, but something's bleeding. Concussion. Can't think clear through it."

Cal kept his gaze steady on Fox's face. "Focus on that first, the concussion. You have to push the rest of it back."

"Trying."

"Let me." Layla shoved the bloodied cloths at Cybil before kneeling at Fox's feet. "I can see if you let me in. But I need you to let me. Let me see the pain, Fox, so I can help you focus on it, heal it. We're connected. I can help."

"You can't help if you freak. Remember that." He closed his eyes, and opened for her. "Just the head. I can handle the rest once I clear that."

He felt her shock, her horror, then her compassion. That was warm, soft. She guided him to where he needed to go just as she'd guided him to the chair.

And there, the pain was fierce and full, a monster with jagged teeth and stiletto claws. They bit, and mauled. They tore. For an instant he shied from it, started to struggle back. But she nudged him on.

A hand gripped his sweaty fist, and he knew it was Gage.

So he opened to himself, to them, rode on the pain, on the hot, bucking back of it, as he knew he must. When it ebbed enough for him to speak again, perspiration soaked him.

"Ease back now," he said to Layla. "Ease back. It's a little too much, a little too fast."

He kept riding the pain. Bones, muscles, organs. And clung unashamed to Gage's hand, to Cal's. When the worst had passed, and he could take his first easy breath, he stopped. His own nature would do the rest.

"Okay. It's okay."

"You don't look okay."

He looked at Cybil, saw there were tears running down her cheeks. "The rest is just surface. It'll take care of itself."

When she nodded, turned away, he looked down at Layla. Her eyes were swimming, but to his relief, no tears fell. "Thanks."

"Who did this to you?"

"That's the question." His voice raw, Gage straightened, then walked to the stove for coffee. "The second being, and when are we going to go kick the shit out of him?"

"I'd like to help with that." Cybil got a mug for Gage herself, then laid a hand over his, squeezed hard.

"It was Block," Fox told them as Quinn brought fresh water to clean the healing cuts and scrapes on his face.

"Block Kholer?" Gage tore his gaze from his hand, still warm from Cybil's though she now stood two feet away. "What the hell for?"

"Napper convinced him I'd screwed his wife."

Cal shook his head. "Block might be stupid enough to believe that asshole, which makes him monumentally stupid. And if he did, I could see him looking for some pushy-shovey, maybe even taking a swing at you. But, bro, he damn near killed you. That's just not . . ."

Fox managed a small, slow sip of the Coke when he saw Cal understood. "It was there. The little fucker. Across the street. I had my attention on Block, since I sensed he wanted to pound me to pulp, so I missed it. I saw it in Block's face though, in his eyes. The infection. If Wayne Hawbaker hadn't come by, he wouldn't have damn near killed me. I'd be dead."

"It's stronger." Quinn gripped Cal's shoulder. "It's gotten stronger."

"We had to figure it would. Everything's accelerated this time. You said Wayne came by. What did he do?"

"I was out of it at first. When I got it together, he had Block cuffed, locked in the car. He said he had to just about knock him cold to get him there. He was fine—Wayne—he was fine. Himself. Concerned, a little pissed, a lot confused. It didn't affect him."

"Maybe it couldn't." Layla pushed to her feet. She took the bloodied water to dump because if her hands were in the sink, no one could see them shake. "I think if it could have, it would have. You said Block meant to kill you. It wouldn't want the police, wouldn't want anyone to stop that from happening."

"One at a time." Composed again, Cybil pursed her lips. "Not good news, but not all bad." She brushed at Fox's wet, tangled hair. "Your eye's healing. You're almost back to full handsome again."

"What are you going to do about Block?" Quinn asked.

"I'll go over and talk to him, and Wayne later. Right now, I could really use a shower, if you ladies don't mind."

"I'll take you up." Layla held out a hand.

"You need to sleep," Cal said.

"A shower's probably enough."

"That kind of healing empties you out. You know that."

"I'll start with the shower." He walked out with Layla. The pain still nipped, but its teeth were dull, its claws stunted.

"I'll wash your clothes while you're in there," she told him. "There are a few things of Cal's around here you can use. Those jeans are toast now anyway."

He glanced down at his torn, ripped, and bloody Levi's. "Toast? They're just broken in."

She tried for a smile as they climbed the stairs, but couldn't quite pull it off. "Does it still hurt?"

"Mostly just sore now."

"Then . . ." She turned at the top of the stairs, put her arms around him and held close.

"It's all right now."

"Of course it's not all right now. None of it's all right. So I'm just going to hold on to you until I can handle it again."

"You handled it just fine." He lifted a hand, stroked it down her hair. "Right down the line."

Needing to be steady for him, Layla eased back to take his face carefully in her hands. His left eye looked red and painful, but the swelling was nearly gone. She kissed it, then his cheeks, his temples. "I was scared to death."

"I know. That's what heroism is, isn't it? Doing what has to be done when you're scared to death."

"Fox." She kissed his lips now, gently. "Take off your clothes."

"I've been waiting to hear you say that for weeks."

Now she was able to smile. "And get in the shower."

"Better and better."

"If you need someone to wash your back . . . I'll send Cal."

"And my dreams are crushed."

In the end, she untied his shoes while he sat on the side of the tub. She helped him out of his shirt and jeans with a depressingly sisterly affection. When he stood in his boxers, and she said, "Oh, Fox," he knew by the tone it wasn't due to delight in his manly physique, but to the bruises that covered it.

"When so much is internal, it just takes longer for the outside to heal."

She only nodded, and carrying his clothes, left him to shower.

It felt like glory—the hot water, the soft spray. It felt like glory to be alive. He stayed under the water, his hands braced on the shower wall, until it ran cool, until the pain circled the drain and slid away like the water. Jeans and a sweatshirt sat neatly folded on the counter when he stepped out. He managed to get them on, forced to pause several times to rest, to wait until nasty little bouts of dizziness passed. Once he'd wiped the steam from the mirror over the sink and taken stock of his face, the still fading bruises, the raw look of his eye, the cuts not quite healed, he had to admit Cal was right, as usual.

He needed to sleep.

So he walked—felt like floating—into Layla's room. He crawled onto her bed and fell asleep with the comforting scent of her all around him.

When he woke, there was a throw tucked around him, the shades were drawn and the door shut. He sat up carefully to take fresh stock. No pain, he thought, no aches. Not even when he poked his fingers around his left eye. The dragging fatigue no longer weighed on him. And he was starving. All good signs.

He stepped out, found Layla in the office with Quinn. "I dropped out awhile."

"Five hours." Layla moved to him immediately, searched his face. "You look perfect. The sleep did you good."

"*Five* hours?"

"And change," Quinn added. "It's good to have you back."

"Somebody should've shoved me out of bed. We were supposed to go through the rest of the first journal, at least."

"We did. And we're putting the notes together." Layla gestured to Quinn's laptop. "We'll have the CliffsNotes version for you later. It's enough for now, Fox."

"I guess it has to be."

"Give yourself a break. Isn't that what you tell me? Cybil made some amazing leek and potato soup."

"Please tell me there's some left."

"Plenty, even for you. Come on, I'll fix you a bowl."

Downstairs, Gage stood at the living room window. He glanced over. "Rain stopped. I see you're back to your ugly self."

"Still prettier than you. Where's Cal?"

"He headed over to the bowling alley a few minutes ago. He wants us to let him know when you decide to join the living again."

"I'll get the soup."

Gage waited until he was alone with Fox. "Fuel up, then we'll call Cal. He'll meet us at the police station. Quinn's putting the main points of today's reading session down for you."

"Anything major?"

"It didn't answer anything for me, but you need to read it for yourself."

He wolfed down two bowls of soup and a hunk of olive bread. By the time he finished, Quinn came down with a folder, and the journal. "I think you'll get the gist from the synopsis, but since the rest of us have read this one, you should take it for tonight. In case you want to look anything over."

"Thanks, for the notes, the soup, the TLC." He cupped Layla's chin, pressed his lips firmly to hers. "Thanks for the bed. I'll see you tomorrow."

When the men left, Cybil cocked her head. "He's got very nice lips."

"He does," Layla agreed.

"And I think what I saw in the kitchen, when I watched him fight to heal, suffer to heal . . . I think it was the bravest thing I've ever witnessed. You're a very lucky woman. And . . ." She drew a piece of paper out of her pocket. "You're also the lucky winner of today's whose turn is it to go to the market sweepstakes."

Layla took the list and sighed. "Woo hoo."

CHIEF HAWBAKER STARED AT FOX'S UNMARRED face when the three of them walked into the station house. Wayne had seen that sort of thing before, Fox thought. But he supposed it wasn't something most people got used to.

The fact was, in the Hollow, most people just didn't notice, or pretended not to.

"I guess you're doing all right. I came by the house Ms. Black rented, seeing as you were hobbling off in that direction. A certain Ms. Kinski answered the door. Gave me quite a piece of her mind. But she said you were taken care of."

"That's right. How's Block?"

"Had the paramedics come clean him up some." Wayne scratched at his jaw. "Even so, he looks a lot worse than you. In fact, if I hadn't seen what went down, I'd tend to think you went after him instead of the other way around. I think he must have hit his head." Hawbaker kept his eyes steady, and his voice just casual enough to let them know he was going to let Fox decide how to handle it. "He doesn't remember it all very clearly. He did admit he went for you, went hard for you, but he's a little confused as to why."

"I'd like to talk to him."

"I can arrange that. Should I be talking to Derrick?"

"He's your deputy. But I'd advise you to keep him clear of me. To keep him way clear."

Wayne said nothing, only got the keys and led Fox through the offices, and into the detention area. "He hasn't asked for a lawyer, hasn't asked to make a phone call. Block? Fox wants a word with you."

Block sat on the cot in one of the three cells, with his head in his big, raw-knuckled hands. He sat up quickly, shoved to his feet. As Block strode to the bars, Fox saw the nasty cuts where he'd clawed him. He didn't consider it petty to feel satisfaction over Block's two black eyes and split lip.

"Jesus, Fox." Block's black-and-blue eyes were as wide and pitiful as a kid's on time-out. "I mean, Jesus H. Christ."

"Can we have a minute, Chief?"

"That all right with you, Block?"

"Sure, yeah, sure. Jesus H. Christ, Fox, I thought I beat hell out of you. You're not hurt."

"You hurt me, Block. You damn near killed me, and that's what you were trying to do."

"But—"

"You remember when I was playing second base back in our junior year, and the ball took a bad hop? It smashed right into my face. Bottom of the third, two out, runner on first. They thought maybe it broke my cheekbone. You remember how I was back on second in the bottom of the fourth?"

As both a little fear and a lot of confusion ran over his battered face, Block licked his swollen lip. "I guess I sort of do. I was thinking maybe this was a dream. I was sitting here thinking that, and that it never really happened. But I guess it did. I swear to God Almighty, Fox, I don't know what came over me. I never went at anybody like that before."

"Did Napper tell you I'd been at Shelley?"

"Yeah." In obvious disgust, Block kicked lightly at the bottom of the bars. "Asshole. I didn't believe him. He hates your ever-fucking guts, and always has. 'Sides, I knew Shelley hadn't been running around. But . . ."

"The idea of it gnawed at you."

"It did. I mean, shit, Fox, she kicked me out, and she's done served me with papers, and she won't talk to me." His fingers clamped around the bars as he hung his head. "I got to thinking that, well, maybe it was because she had you on the side. Just maybe."

"And not because she caught you with Sami's tit in your hand?"

"I screwed up. I screwed up bad. Shelley and me, we'd been fighting some, and Sami—" He broke off, shrugged. "She'd been coming on to me awhile, and that day, she says how I should come on into the back and help her with something. Then she's rubbing against me, and she's got a lot to rub against a man. She's got her shirt undone. Hell, Fox, her tit was right *there*. I screwed up bad."

"Yeah, you did."

"I don't want a divorce. I wanna go home, Fox, you know?" Misery coated the man-to-man appeal. "Shelley won't even talk to me. I just wanna fix it, and she's talking around town about how you're going to skin my ass for her in court, and shit like that."

"Pissed you off," Fox prompted as Block frowned down at his boots.

"Jesus, Fox, it steamed me up, sure, then Napper's trash talk on top. But I've never gone after somebody like that. I've never beat on a man when he's done that way." Block's head lifted, and the confusion covered his face again. "It was like being crazy or something. I couldn't stop. I thought maybe I'd killed you. I don't know how I'd live with that."

"Lucky for both of us you won't have to."

"Damn, Fox. I mean *damn*. You're a friend of mine. We go back. I don't know what . . . I guess I went crazy or something."

Fox thought of the boy laughing, swallowing itself. "I'm not going to press charges, Block. We never had any problems, you and me."

"We get along okay."

"As far as I'm concerned, we don't have any problems now. As for Shelley, I'm her lawyer, and that's it. I can't tell you what to do about the state of your marriage. If you were to tell me that you want to try marriage counseling, I could pass that on to my client. I might be able to give her my opinion, as her lawyer and her friend, that she try that route before going any further with the divorce proceedings."

"I'll do anything she wants." Block's Adam's apple rippled as he took a hard swallow. "I owe you, Fox."

"No, you don't. I'm Shelley's lawyer, not yours. I want

you to promise me that when Chief Hawbaker lets you out, you go home. Watch some NASCAR. Gotta be a race on today."

"Staying at my ma's. Yeah, I'll go on home. You got my word."

Fox went back out to Wayne. "I'm not filing charges." He ignored Gage's muttered curse. "Obviously I'm not hurt. We had an altercation that looked more serious than it was, and is now resolved to the satisfaction of both parties."

"If that's the way you want it, Fox."

"That's the way it is. I'm grateful you came along when you did." Fox held out a hand.

Outside, Gage cursed again. "For a lawyer, you've sure got a bleeding heart."

"You'd have done the same. Exactly the same," he said before Gage could object. "He wasn't responsible."

"We'd have done the same," Cal affirmed. "And have. Why don't you come up to the center and watch the game?"

"Tempting, but I'll pass. I've got a lot of reading to do."

"I'll drive you home," Gage told him.

But for a few moments the three of them stood, just stood outside the station house looking over the town that was already under a cloud.

Eleven

~⁊~

FOX SPENT A LONG TIME READING, MAKING HIS own notes, checking back over specific passages Quinn had marked in the journal.

He juggled and mulled, and read more.

No guardian ever had succeeded in destroying the Dark. Some gave their lives in the attempt. Giles prepared to give his, as no other had before him.

No precedent for whatever mumbo-jumbo Dent had used that night in the woods, Fox considered. Which meant he couldn't have been sure it would work. But he was willing to risk his life, his existence. Hell of a gamble, even considering he'd sent Ann, and the lives in her to safety first.

He has gone beyond what has been done, what was deemed could be done. The blood of the innocent is shed, and so it will be, my love believes, dark against dark. And it will be my love who pays the price for this sin. It will be blood and fire, and it will be sacrifice and loss. Death on death before there is life, before there is hope.

Ritual magic, Fox decided, and used laundry and house-keeping chores as he had juggling. Blood magic. He glanced at the scar on his wrist. Then, and three hundred years later. Blood and fire at the Pagan Stone in Dent's time, and blood, in a boyhood ritual in theirs. A campfire, the words he and Cal and Gage had written down to say together when Cal made the cuts.

Young boys—the blood of the innocent.

He toyed with various ideas and strategies as he thought of them. He climbed into bed late, on righteously clean sheets, to let himself sleep on it.

It came to him in the morning, while he was shaving. He hated shaving, and as he did many mornings, considered growing a beard. But every time he attempted one, it itched, and it looked stupid. Talk about pagan rituals, he mused as he drew blade through lather and over skin. Every freaking morning unless a guy wanted the hairy face, he had to scrape some sharp implement over his throat until—shit.

He nicked himself, as he nearly always did, pressed a finger to the wound that would close again almost before it bled. The sting came and went, and still he scowled in disgust at his blood-smeared fingertip.

Then stared.

Life and death, he thought. Blood was life, blood was death.

Dull horror embedded in his brain, in his heart. Had to be wrong, he told himself. Yet it made terrible sense. It was a hell of a strategy, if you're willing to shed innocent blood.

What did it mean? he asked himself. What did it make Dent, if this had been his sacrifice?

What did it make all of them?

He twisted and turned it in his head as he made himself finish shaving, as he dressed and readied for the workday. He had the Town Council breakfast meeting, and as town lawyer, he couldn't get out of it. Probably for the best, he decided as he grabbed his jacket, his briefcase. It was probably best to let this stew. Probably best to wait, think, before he broached the idea to the others. Even to Cal and Gage.

He ordered himself to put his head into the meeting, and though painting Town Hall and new plantings at the Square weren't high on his current list of priorities, he thought he'd done a good job of it.

But Cal was on him the minute they walked out of Ma's. "What's going on?"

"I think Town Hall needs a new coat of paint, and damn the expense."

"Cut it out. You left half your breakfast on your plate. When you don't eat, something's up."

"I'm working on something, but I need to fine-tune it, to look at it some more before I talk about it. Plus, Sage is in town. I'm meeting her and the family for lunch at Sparrow's, ergo, my appetite's already dead."

"Walk up to the center with me, run it by me."

"Not now. I've got stuff anyway. I've got to digest this, which is an easier proposition than the lentils I'll probably get stuck with at lunch. We'll roll it over tonight."

"All right. You know where I am if you want to roll it sooner."

They separated. Fox pulled out his cell phone to contact Shelley. There, at least, he'd worked out his approach. As he talked to her about coming into the office, listened to her latest idea of retribution on Block, Derrick Napper passed by in his cruiser. Napper slowed, grinned, and lifted his middle finger from the steering wheel.

Fox thought, Asshole, and kept walking. He closed the phone as he reached his office door.

"Morning, Mrs. H."

"Good morning. How was the meeting?"

"I suggested the image of a naked Jessica Simpson as the new town symbol. It's currently under consideration."

"That ought to get the Hollow some attention. I'm only in for an hour this morning. I called Layla, and she's fine coming in early."

"Oh."

"I have an appointment with our real estate agent. We sold the house."

"You—when?"

"Saturday. A lot to do," she said briskly. "You'll handle the settlement for us, won't you?"

"Sure, of course." Too fast, he thought. This was happening too fast.

"Fox, I won't be coming in after today. Layla can handle everything now."

"But—" But what, he thought. He'd known this was coming.

"We've decided to drive out to Minneapolis, and take our time. We've got most everything packed up, and ready to ship out. Our girl's found a condo she thinks we'll like, only a few miles from her. I've drawn up a limited power of attorney for you, so you can handle the settlement. We won't be here for it."

"I'll look it over. I have to run upstairs. I'll be back in a minute."

"Your first appointment's in fifteen minutes," she called after him.

"I'll be back in one."

He was true to his word, and walked straight to her desk. He put a wrapped box in front of her. "It's not a going-away present. I'm too mad at you for leaving me to give you a present for that. It's for everything else."

"Well." She sniffled a little as she unwrapped the box, and made him smile at the way she preserved the paper, folded it neatly before opening the lid.

They were pearls, as dignified and traditional as she was. The clasp was fashioned as a jeweled bouquet of roses. "I know how you are about flowers," he began when she said nothing. "So these caught my eye."

"They're absolutely beautiful. Absolutely—" Her voice cracked. "They're too expensive."

"I'm still the boss around here." He took them out, put them around her neck himself. "And you're part of the reason I can afford them." His credit card had let out a single short scream on being swiped, but the look on her face made it all worthwhile. "They look nice on you, Mrs. H."

She brushed her fingertips over the strand. "I'm so proud of you." Rising, she put her arms around him. "You're such a good boy. I'll think of you. I'll pray for you." She sighed, stepped back. "And I'll miss you. Thank you, Fox."

"Go ahead. You know you want to."

She managed a watery laugh and rushed to a decorative wall mirror. "Oh my goodness! I feel like a queen." In the glass her eyes met his. "Thank you, Fox, for everything."

When the door opened, she bustled back to her desk to log in his first appointment. By the time he escorted the client out again, she was gone.

"Alice said you and she had said your good-byes." Understanding shone in Layla's eyes. "And she showed off her pearls. You did good there. They couldn't have been more perfect."

"Stick around a few years, you may cop some." He rolled his shoulders. "Gotta shake it off, I know. Listen, Shelley's coming in—a quick squeeze-in."

"Are you going to tell her about what happened with Block?"

"Why would I?"

"Why would you?" Layla murmured. "I'll pull her file."

"No, I'm hoping we won't need it. Let me ask you something. If you loved a guy enough to marry him, and he screwed up big time, would that just be it? Say you still love him. One of the reasons you fell in the first place was because he wasn't altogether bright, but pretty affable, and he loved you back. Or would you give him another chance?"

"You want Shelley to give him another chance."

"I'm Shelley's lawyer, so I want what she wants, within reason. Maybe what she wants is marriage counseling."

"You asked her to come in so you can *suggest* she might want to try counseling." Studying him, Layla nodded slowly. "After he beat the crap out of you?"

"Extenuating circumstances there. She doesn't want the divorce, Layla. She just wants him to feel as crappy as she does and more so. I'm just going to give her another option. The rest is up to her. So, would you give him another chance?"

"I believe in second chances, but it would depend. How much did I love him, how much did I make him pay before giving him that second chance. Both would have to be a lot."

"That's what I figured. Just send her back when she gets here."

Layla sat where she was. She thought of Alice's damp eyes and beautiful pearls. She thought of Fox bleeding in the kitchen, and the pain that leeched every drop of color from his face. She thought of him playing guitar in a noisy bar, and running toward a burning house to save the dogs.

When Shelley came in, eyes glittering with fury and misery, Layla sent her back. She thought a great deal more as she answered the phone, as she finished the Monday morning business Alice had begun.

When Shelley came out again, she was weeping a little, but there was something in her eyes that hadn't been in them when she'd come in. And that was hope.

"I want to ask you something."

Here, Layla thought, we go again. "What is it?"

"Would I be a complete fool if I called this number?" She held out a business card. "If I made an appointment with this marriage counselor Fox said is really good? If I gave that idiot Block a chance and see if maybe we could fix things between us?"

"I think you'd be a complete fool if you didn't do whatever it takes to get what you want most."

"I don't know why I want that man." Shelley looked down at the card in her hand. "But I guess maybe this could help me find out. Thanks, Layla."

"Good luck, Shelley."

What was the point in being a complete fool? Layla asked herself. Before she bogged down in what-ifs and maybes, she pushed back from her desk and marched straight back to Fox's office.

He hammered at the keyboard, brows knitted. He barely gave her a grunt as she stepped to his desk.

"All right," she said. "I'll sleep with you."

His fingers paused. He cocked his head up, aimed his eyes to hers. "This is excellent news." Swiveling, he faced her more fully. "Right now?"

"This is so easy for you, isn't it?"

"Actually—"

"Just 'sure, let's go.'"

"I feel, under the circumstances, I shouldn't have to point out that, yes, I am a guy."

"It's not just that." She threw out her arms as she whirled into a pace. "I bet you were raised to think of sex as a natural act, as a basic form of human expression, even a physical celebration between two consenting adults."

He waited a beat. "Isn't it?"

Stopping, facing him, she made a helpless gesture with her hands. "I was raised to think of it as an enormous and weighty step. One that carries responsibility, that has repercussions. That because sex and intimacy are synonymous, you don't just go around jumping into bed because you want an itch scratched."

"But you're going to sleep with me anyway."

"I said I was, didn't I?"

"Why?"

"Because Shelley's calling a marriage counselor." And now, Layla sighed. "Because you play the damn guitar, and I know without counting that there's another dollar in that stupid jar even though Alice is gone, because you said fuck. Because Cal told Quinn you wouldn't press charges against Block."

"All of those sound like fairly good reasons to be pals," Fox considered. "They don't sound like reasons to have sex."

"I can have any reasons I like to have sex with you," she said, just prissily enough to make him fight off a grin. "Including the fact that you've got a great ass, that you can look at me and make me feel like you've already got your hands on me. And just because I want to. So I'm going to have sex with you."

"As I said, this is excellent news. Hey, Sage, how's it going?"

"Really good. Sorry to interrupt."

With her stomach already sinking to her knees, Layla turned. The woman who stood in the doorway had a big O'Dell grin on her face. Her hair was a short sweep of fiery red around a pretty face made compelling by a pair of golden brown eyes.

"Layla, this is my sister Sage. Sage, Layla."

"Nice to meet you." In snug jeans tucked into stylish boots, Sage stepped forward to offer a hand.

"Yes. Well. I'm just going to go out to reception and beat my head against the wall for a few minutes. Excuse me."

Sage watched her walk away, then turned back to her brother. "Very nice package."

"Cut it out. It's too weird to have you checking out the same woman I am. Besides, you're married."

"Marriage doesn't pluck out the eyes. Hey." She spread her arms.

He rose, walked into them, and banding her with his, lifted her off her feet for a quick swing. "I thought I was meeting you at Sparrow's."

"You are, but I wanted to drop by."

"Where's Paula?"

"She's taking the meeting that gave us the excuse to come East. In D.C. She'll be up later. Let me look at you, Foxy Loxy."

"Looking back at you, Parsley Sage."

"Still enjoying small-town law?"

"Still a lesbian?"

She laughed. "Okay, enough of that. I guess I should come back later, when you're not having sex with your office manager."

"I think that's been postponed due to acute embarrassment."

"I hope I didn't screw it up."

"I'll fix it. Mom said you weren't clear about how long you're staying."

"I guess we weren't. It sort of depends." She blew out a breath. "It sort of depends on you."

"You and Paula want to practice small-town lesbian law, and want to go into partnership with me in the Hollow." He got them a couple of Cokes.

"No. Partnership might be a factor, depending on your definition."

He handed her the Coke. "What's up, Sage?"

"If you're busy, we can talk about this tonight. Maybe have a drink."

She was nervous, Fox noted, and Sage was rarely nervous. "I've got time."

"Well, the thing is, Fox." She tapped her fingers on the can as she wandered around the room. "The thing is, Paula and I have decided to have a baby."

"That's great. That's terrific. How do you guys do that? Do you call Rent-a-Penis? Sperm R Us?"

"Don't be an ass."

"Sorry, there are jokes here waiting to happen."

"Ha ha. We've thought about it a lot, talked it through. We actually think we'll want a couple of kids. And we decided, for the first one, Paula will get pregnant. I'll, you know, take round two."

"You'll be great parents." Reaching out, he gave her hair a quick tug. "The kids'll be lucky to have both of you."

"We want to be. We're sure as hell going to try to be. To take the first step, we need a donor." She turned back, faced him. "We want it to be you."

"Sorry, what? What?" The Coke, fortunately not yet opened, slipped right out of his hands.

"I know it's big, and strange." Smoothly, she bent to retrieve his Coke and hand it to him while he simply goggled at her. "And we won't hold it against you if you say no."

"Why? I mean, lame jokes aside, there are, like banks for this kind of thing. You can make a withdrawal."

"And there are very good places, where donors are very well screened, and you can select specific qualities. That's an option, but far from our first. You and I are the same blood, Fox, the same gene pool. The baby, the baby would be more ours because of that."

"Um, Ridge? He's already proven himself in this department."

"Which is one of the reasons I don't feel right asking him. And, while I love him like crazy, both Paula and I zeroed in on you. Our Ridge is a dreamer, an artist, a beautiful soul. You're a doer, Fox. You're always going to try to do the right thing, but you get things done. And you and I are closer personality-wise, physically, too. Same coloring." She tugged on her hair herself now. "I went red, but under the dye, my hair's the same color as yours."

He was, he realized, still stuck back on the term *donor*. "I'm a little weirded out here, Sage."

"I bet. I'm going to ask you to think about it. Don't say

yes or no yet because it's a lot to think about. After you do, if it's no, we'll understand. I haven't said anything to anyone else in the family, so there's no pressure there."

"Appreciate it. Listen, I'm oddly flattered that you and Paula would, ah . . . want me to sub for you. I'll think about it."

"Thanks." She pressed her cheek to his. "I'll see you at lunch."

When she left he stared down at the Coke in his hand, then crossed over and put it back in his little fridge. He didn't think he needed any more stimulation. One thing at a time, he decided, and went out to Layla.

"Okay," he said.

"Your sister was very friendly, positively breezy. She behaved as if she hadn't heard me announce I was going to have sex with her brother."

"It's probably that natural act, celebration of human expression thing. And she had stuff on her mind."

"I'm a grown woman. I'm a single, healthy adult." In a gesture that smacked of defiance, she shook back her hair. "So I'm telling myself there's absolutely no cause for me to be embarrassed because . . . Is something wrong?"

"No. I don't know. It's been a really strange morning. It turns out . . ." How did he put this? "I told you my sister's gay, right?"

"It was mentioned."

"She and Paula, they've been together some years now. They're good together, really good together. And . . ." He paced to the window, back. "They want a baby."

"That's nice."

"They want me to provide the Y chromosome."

"Oh. *Oh.*" Layla pursed her lips. "I guess you have had a strange morning. What did you say?"

"I don't remember, exactly, with all the going blind and deaf. I'm supposed to think about it. Which, of course, I'd have a hard time not."

"They both must think a great deal of you. Since you didn't say no, straight off, you must think a great deal of them."

"Right this minute, I can't think at all. Can we close the office and go have sex?"

"No."

"I was afraid of that."

"Your last appointment is at four thirty. We can go have sex after that."

He stared at her. "It continues to be a really strange day."

"Your schedule on this strange day says that I'm to make a conference call for you on the Benedict case. Here's the file."

"Go ahead on that. Do you want to come to lunch with me, over to Sparrow's with the family?"

"Not for a million dollars."

He couldn't blame her, all things considered. Still it was an easy hour for him with his brother and Ridge's wife and little boy, with his sisters, his parents, filling Sparrow's little restaurant.

Layla went to lunch when he returned, and that gave him room to think. He tried not to watch the clock while he worked, but he'd never, at any time in his life, wished quite so much for time to fly.

Naturally, his last client of the day was chatty, and didn't seem the least bit concerned about billable hours, or the fact that it was now ten minutes after five. The price of small-town law, Fox thought as he fought the urge to check his watch, again. People wanted to shoot the breeze, before, during, and after business. Any other time, he'd have been perfectly happy to kick back and talk about preseason baseball, the O's chances this year, and thc rookie infielder who showed such potential.

But he had a woman waiting, and his own engine was revving.

He didn't precisely drag his client to the door and give him a boot to the sidewalk for good measure. But he didn't linger.

"I thought he'd never shut up," Fox said as he locked the door behind him. "We're closed. Shut down, don't answer the phone. And come with me."

"Actually, I was thinking maybe we should consider."

"No, no thinking, no considering. Don't make me beg." He solved the matter by grabbing her hand and pulling her toward the stairs. "Marriage counseling, burning buildings, nice ass—in no particular order—just to refresh your memory."

"I haven't forgotten, I just—when did you clean?" she asked when he drew her into the apartment.

"Yesterday. It was an ugly business, but fortuitous."

"In that case I have the name of a cleaning woman, Marcia Biggons."

"I went to school with her sister."

"So I'm told. She'll give you a chance. Call her."

"First thing tomorrow. Now." He leaned in, took her mouth while his hands skimmed down from her shoulders to her wrist. "We're going to have some wine."

Her eyes blinked open. "Wine?"

"I'm going to put on some music, we're going to have some wine. We're going to sit down in my fairly clean living room and relax."

She let out a breathless laugh. "You've just added one to the list of why I'm here. I'd love some wine, thanks."

He opened the bottle of Shiraz a client had given him at Christmas, put on Clapton—it just seemed right—and poured two glasses.

"Your artwork shows off better without the mountain of clutter. Mmm, this is nice," she said after the first sip when he joined her on the couch. "I wasn't sure what I'd get, seeing as you're more of a beer guy."

"I have deep wells."

"Yes, you do." And gorgeous, thick brown hair, wonderful tiger's eyes. "I didn't get a chance to ask if you'd read our notes, or the marked—" She swallowed the rest of the words when his mouth met hers again.

"Here's what we're not going to talk about. Office work and missions from gods. Tell me what you did in New York for fun."

Okay, she thought, small talk would be good. She could talk small with the best of them. "Clubs, because I like music. Galleries because I like art. But my job was fun, too. I guess it's always fun to do what you're good at."

"Your parents owned a dress shop."

"I loved working there, too. Well, playing there when I was a kid. All the colors and textures. I liked putting things together. This jacket with this skirt, this coat with this bag. We thought I'd take over one day, but it just got to be too much for them."

"So you went to New York, left Philly behind."

"I thought I'd go where fashion rules, on this side of the Atlantic anyway." The wine was lovely, just slid over her tongue. "I'd get some polish, some more experience in a more specialized arena, then open my own place."

"In New York?"

"I flirted with that for about five minutes. I was never going to be able to afford the rent in the city. I thought maybe the suburbs, maybe one day. Then one day became next year, and so on. Plus I liked managing the boutique, and there wasn't any risk. I stopped taking risks."

"Until recently."

She met his eyes. "Apparently."

He smiled, topped off their wine. "The Hollow doesn't have a dress shop, or fashion boutique, or whatever you'd call that kind of thing."

"At the moment, I'm gainfully employed and no longer thinking about opening a boutique. My risk quota's been reached."

"What kind of music? Do you like to listen to?" he added when she frowned at him.

"Oh, I'm pretty open there."

He reached down, slipped off her shoes, then brought her feet up into his lap. "How about art?"

"There, too. I think . . ." Her whole body sighed when he began rubbing the balls of her feet. "Any art, or music, that gives you pleasure, or makes you think—or better makes you wonder; it's—it's what makes us human. The need to create it, to have it."

"I grew up soaked in it, various forms. Nothing was out of bounds." His thumb, just rough enough to thrill, ran down her arch, back again. "Anything out of bounds for you?"

He wasn't talking about art or music now. Her stomach jittered with lust, fear, anticipation. "I don't know."

"You can tell me if I hit any boundaries." His hand went to work on her calf muscles. "Tell me what you like."

Flustered, she stared.

"That's okay. I'll figure it out. I like the shape of you. The high arch of your feet, the muscles in your calves. They draw my eye especially when you're wearing heels."

"That's the point of heels." Her throat was dry; her pulses skipping.

"I like the line of your neck and shoulders. I'm planning on spending some time on those later. I like your knees, your thighs." His hand slid up slowly, barely touching, then again, just a little higher until he found the lacy top of her stocking. "I like this," he murmured, "this little surprise under a black skirt." He hooked a finger under the top, eased it down.

"Oh, God."

"I plan on going slow." He watched her as he worked the stocking down her leg. "But if you want to me stop—I hope you won't—just say so."

His fingers skimmed over the back of her knee, down her calf, her ankle, until her leg was bare, and her skin humming. "I don't want you to stop."

"Have some more wine," he suggested. "This is going to take a while."

Twelve

~∿~

SHE ALREADY FELT DRUNK, AND THOUGH SHE considered herself fairly adept, Layla didn't think she was quite adept enough to casually sip wine while he undressed her. By the time he slipped off the second stocking it was all she could do to set the glass aside without spilling it.

He smiled, and pressed his lips to the arch of her foot. Excitement shot straight up to her belly, and pulsed there like a second agitated heart. He took his time, stirring and seducing, kindling little fires under her skin, exploiting odd and wondrous points of pleasure. When he gripped her ankles, slid her toward him in one smooth motion, she let out a sound of surprise and gratitude.

Now their faces were close, so close the rich, golden brown of his irises mesmerized her. His hand—calloused fingertips—glided up her legs, under her rucked-up skirt. Slowly, slowly. And down again while his mouth toyed with hers. A brush, a taste, a bare whisper of torturous contact even when her arms locked around his neck, even when her needy body pressed to his. Once again, the easy touch, the easy taste, left her drained and dazzled.

His hands cupped her hips, lifted her. The quick shock had her gasping, instinct had her wrapping her legs around his waist as he rose with her. This time the kiss was deep and seeking as he stood with her eagerly twined around him.

"My head's actually spinning," she managed as he began to walk.

"I plan on keeping it that way awhile." In the bedroom, he sat on the side of the bed with her straddling him. "I figured candlelight for the first time, but we'll have to save that."

He trailed his fingers over her shoulders, over the soft wool of the pretty blue sweater, along the tiny pearl buttons down the front. "You always look just right." He drew it down her arms to her elbows, left it there. "You've got a knack for it."

With her arms roped in cashmere, he pressed his lips, just a light hint of teeth, to the side of her neck, down her skin to the edge of the little sweater she wore beneath.

He loved the light tremor that ran through her, the sound of her breath quickening, thickening. And the look of her, flushed, just a little anxious. He ran his hands down her arms until both his fingers and the cashmere cuffed her wrists. Then he took her mouth, ravishing it, saturating himself with the taste of her, devouring the quick, helpless sounds she made while her pulse thundered under his hands.

He eased back, a whisper back, and smiled into her dazed eyes. "We'll save this one for later, too," he said and released her hands.

He watched her face as he drew the little sweater up and away; he watched her face as he played his fingertips over her warm, bare skin. Then he pleased himself, looked down at breasts clothed in a fancy bra of blue lace. "Yeah, you always look just right."

Reaching behind her, he eased down the zipper of her skirt.

She felt as if she moved through water, warm, softened with fragrance. Her heart thudded, slow and hard as she unbuttoned his shirt, as she found the hard muscles of his shoulders, his chest, his back. When he kissed her again, when he lowered her to her back, she was the water. Warm, soft, and fluid. His hands, his lips played over her, tirelessly, relentlessly. She had no defense against them, against her own need, and wanted none. When he freed her breasts, she arched to him. Thrilled to the steady greed of his lips, of his tongue.

He worked down her, coating her with pleasure until he drew the matching lace away and exposed her.

Then came the whirlpool. She was caught in it, a mad spin that dragged her under to where the water whirled hot and fast. She cried out, shocked, her hands fisting in the sheets for purchase as the orgasm ripped through her. Even when she sobbed out his name, he didn't stop. When she came again, it was like going mad.

Her body quivered and writhed under him, clawing at what was left of his control. She sprawled over the tangled sheets in absolute surrender while the dim light of the dying evening spilled over her and sheened her in gold. Once more he cupped her hips, lifted them. Once more his eyes met hers, held hers as he filled her. As he trapped himself inside her. He watched her eyes as he thrust deep. Watched them as he took her, and as she wrapped tight to take him.

Watched until they closed on the peak of her pleasure, and until his own needs swallowed him whole.

SHE WASN'T SURE SHE COULD MOVE, OR THAT THE bones in her body would ever solidify again and hold her upright.

She wasn't sure she cared.

He sprawled on top of her, dead weight, and that didn't seem to matter either. She liked his weight, his warmth, liked feeling the thunder of his heartbeat so she knew she hadn't been the only one to fly.

She'd known he'd be gentle, and that he'd be fun. But she hadn't known he'd be . . . astonishing.

"Want me to move?" His voice was thick, just a little sleepy.

"Not especially."

"Good, 'cause I like it here. I'll get the wine and maybe order us some dinner at some point."

"No hurry."

"Got a question." He brushed his lips over her cheek as he lifted his head. "Do you always match your underwear to your clothes?"

"Not always. But often. I'm a little obsessive."

"Really worked for me." He toyed with the glittery chain she wore around her neck. "So does this, or the fact that this and earrings are all you're wearing." He lowered his head again to kiss her, and while he lingered over it, released the chain to rub his thumbs over her nipples. His lips curved to hers when she let out a little moan.

"I was hoping you'd say that," he murmured and slipped inside her again, hard as steel.

Her eyes went wide. "How can you—don't you have to . . . Oh God. Oh God."

"You're all soft now. Wet and soft and even more sensitive than the first time." He moved in her, long, long, slow thrusts, leaving her shuddering on each stroke. "I'll take you deeper this time. Close your eyes, Layla. Let yourself take what I'm giving you."

She had no choice; she was beyond will. Her body was so heavy, while inside it a thousand small eruptions burst. He touched her, his hands alighting needs she thought had gone quiet.

So she went deeper, into pleasure both intense and foreign.

"Don't stop. Don't."

"Not until you get there."

When she did, it was like plummeting out of the sky, a tumbling free fall that stole the breath.

SHE WAS STILL LIMP WHEN HE BROUGHT HER A glass of wine. "I ordered pizza. That okay?"

She managed a nod. "How do you . . . Can you always recover that quickly?"

"One of the perks." He sat cross-legged on the bed with his own glass of wine, and cocked his head. "Hasn't Quinn mentioned it? Come on, I know your breed talks about sex."

"Mentioned . . . Well, she said it's the best sex of her life, if that's what you mean. And that he's . . ." She felt very strange, talking about their friends this way. "Well, he's got amazing staying power."

"You know how we heal fast, since that night? Sort of the same thing here."

"Oh." She drew the word out, and slaked her thirst with wine. "That is a very fine perk."

"It's a particular favorite of mine." He rose, walked around the room lighting candles.

Yes, yes, she thought, that was a *very* nice ass. His hair tumbled messily around that sharp-featured face. Those gilded eyes were satisfied, and just a little sleepy.

She wanted to lap him up like melted chocolate.

"What's your record?"

He glanced back and grinned. "What time frame? An evening, an overnight, a lost weekend?"

Over the rim of her glass her eyes challenged him. "We'll start with an evening, and I bet we can beat it."

They ate pizza in bed. The pie was cold by the time they got to it, but they were both too ravenous to care. The music changed to B. B. King, and the candles wafted out lovely light and fragrance.

"My mother makes them," he told her when she commented.

"Your mother makes candles—gorgeous, fragrant candles—throws pots, and does watercolors."

"And weaves. Does other needlework when the mood strikes." He licked sauce off his thumb. "Now if only she'd cook real food, she'd be perfect."

"Are you the only carnivore in the family?"

"My father sneaks a Big Mac now and then, and Sage fell off the veggie wagon, too." He contemplated another slice of pizza. "I decided to do it."

"To do what?"

"To, ah, give Sage—or I guess it would be give Paula—the magic elixir."

"The . . . Oh." She angled her head. "What made you decide?"

"I just figured I'm not doing anything with it, right at the moment. And they're family. If I can help make them happy, help give them a family, why wouldn't I?"

"Why wouldn't you?" she repeated quietly, then took his face in her hands to kiss him. "You're one in a million."

"Let's hope I've got one or two in a million that'll get the job done for them. I know it's a strange thing to bring up under the current conditions, but I thought you should know. Some women might find it a little weird, or offputting. I'm not getting that you do."

"I think it's loving, and lovely." She kissed him again, just before the phone rang.

"Hold that thought." He scooted back to answer the bedside phone. "Hey. Oh yeah." He tipped the phone to address

Layla. "It's Cal. No, we'll get to that tomorrow. It can wait until tomorrow. Because I'm with Layla," he said. He hung up the phone, looked at her. "I'm with Layla."

SHE HADN'T MEANT TO SPEND THE NIGHT, AND was vaguely surprised by the sun streaming through the windows. "Oh my God. What time is it?"

She started to roll out of bed, was rolled right back and under Fox. "It's morning, it's early. What's the rush?"

"I have to get home, change. Fox!" Amusement, arousal, and sheer bafflement warred inside her as his hands got busy under the covers. "Stop."

"That's not what you said last night. How many times was that?" He laughed as his mouth covered hers. "Relax. So you'll be a little late. I can guarantee your boss won't mind."

Later, a great deal later while she hunted up her second stocking, he offered her a can of Coke. "Sorry, it's the only caffeine on the premises."

She winced at it, then shrugged. "It'll have to do. It's a good thing you don't have an appointment until ten thirty, because I'm barely going to make it into the office by ten."

He watched her slip her foot into the hose. "Maybe I should help you with that."

"Stay away from me." She laughed, but pointed a finger at him. "I mean it. It's almost business hours." She drew up the stocking, slipped on her shoes. "I'll be in the office as soon as I can manage it."

"I'll drive you home."

"Thanks, but I'll walk. I think I need some air." She stood, pointed at him again. "Hands up." When he grinned, held up his hands, she leaned in to kiss him.

Then she escaped before she could change her mind.

Her hopes to dash straight upstairs when she got home

were scotched as Cybil stood on the bottom landing, leaning on the banister. "Ah, look who's doing the Walk of Shame. Hey, Q, baby sister's home."

"I've got to change and get to work. Talk later."

She made the dash, but Cybil was right behind her. "Oh no, you don't. Talk while you change."

Since Quinn swung out of the office and into Layla's bedroom with Cybil, Layla gave up.

"Obviously, I spent the night with Fox."

"Playing chess?" Quinn grinned as Layla stripped on her way to the shower. "Isn't that his game?"

"We never got to that. Maybe next time."

"From the smile on your face, it's obvious he has a few other games," Cybil commented.

"I feel . . ." She jumped into the shower. "Used and energized, amazed and stupefied." She whipped the shower curtain back an inch. "Why didn't you tell me about the perk?" she demanded. "About how they recover, sexually, the same way they heal?"

"Didn't I mention that?"

"No." It was Cybil who answered, giving Quinn a hard poke.

"Speaking of energy, the Energizer Bunny is a worn-out, sluggish rabbit comparatively." Quinn gave Cybil a sympathetic hug. "I didn't want to make you feel sad and deprived, Cyb."

Cybil just narrowed her eyes. "How many times? And don't try to tell me you didn't count," she added as she pulled the shower curtain open.

Layla pulled it back, then stuck out a hand, five fingers spread.

"Five?"

Then put the tips of her pinky and thumb together to add another three.

"*Eight?* Holy Mother of God."

Layla switched off the shower, grabbed a towel. "That's not counting twice this morning. I have to admit, I'm a little tired, and I'm starving. And I'd *kill* for coffee."

"You know what?" Cybil said after a moment. "I'm going to go down and scramble you some eggs, pour you a giant cup of coffee. Because right at the moment, you're my hero."

Quinn stayed behind as Layla, wrapped in the towel, rubbed lotion on her arms and legs. "He's a sweetie."

"I know he is."

"Are you going to be able to work together, sleep together, and fight the forces of evil together?"

"You're managing it with Cal."

"Which is why I ask, because the combination can have its moments. I guess I wanted to say that if you run into one of those moments, you can talk to me."

"I've been able to talk to you from the first. I guess that's one of our perks." Because it was true, Layla considered as she drew on her robe. "My feelings for him, for just about everything right now, are tangled and confused. And for just about the first time in my life, confusion isn't such a bad thing."

"Good enough. Well, try not to work too hard today because we're having a summit meeting tonight. Cal wants to know what Fox came up with."

"About what?"

"I don't know." Quinn pursed her lips. "He didn't mention anything to you? A theory."

"No. No, he didn't."

"Maybe he's still working it out. In any case, we'll talk about whatever we talk about tonight."

By the time Layla got to the office, Fox was already in and on the phone. With his next client due in shortly after, it wasn't the time, in her opinion, to pin him down about their other collaboration and theories.

She checked his schedule, hunting for a reasonable span

of free time, then stewed while she worried about why he hadn't mentioned anything about it to her.

When Sage came in just as Layla was about to take advantage of a lull, Layla decided she was outnumbered for the workday.

"Fox gave me a call, asked me to come by. Is he free now?"

"As a bird."

"I'll just go on back."

Thirty minutes passed before Sage came out again. It was obvious she'd been crying even when she sent Layla a brilliant smile. "Just in case you're not aware, you're working for the most amazing, most beautiful, most incredible man in the entire universe. Just in case you didn't know," she added, and ran out.

With a sigh, Layla tried to bury her own questions—and the annoyance that had been working up through them— and went back to see how Fox had weathered what must have been an emotional half hour.

He sat at his desk with the look of a man who was seriously worn at the edges. "She cried," he said immediately. "Sage, she's not much of a crier, but she sure cut loose. Then she called Paula, and Paula cried. I'm feeling a little overwhelmed, so if crying's on your agenda, could we get a continuance?"

Saying nothing, Layla walked to his fridge, got him a Coke.

"Thanks. I've got an appointment to . . . Since I just had a physical a few months ago, they're sending my records to the place where they do it. Sage, she's got a friend in Hagerstown who's her doctor. So I've got—we've got—an appointment day after tomorrow, and the day after, since Paula's going to be . . ."

"Ovulating?"

He winced. "Even with my upbringing, I'm not completely at ease with all this. So day after tomorrow. Eight.

I've got court, so I'll just go there after." He rose, put a dollar in the jar. "This is fucking bizarre. There, that's better. So what's up next?"

"I am. Quinn told me you were supposed to meet with Cal and Gage last night, and that you wanted to meet with them to tell them about a theory you have."

"Yeah, then I got a better offer, so . . ." He trailed off. He knew that look in her eyes. "That pisses you off?"

"I don't know. It depends. But it certainly baffles me that you have an idea you think worth discussing with your *men* friends, and not with me."

"I would have discussed it with you, but I was busy enjoying mutual multiple orgasms."

True, she had to admit. But not altogether the point. "I was with you all day in this office, all night in bed. I think there was time in that frame to bring this up."

"Sure. But I didn't want to bring it up."

"Because you wanted to talk to Cal and Gage first."

"Partly, because I've always talked to Cal and Gage first. A thirty-year habit doesn't change overnight." The first hint of annoyance danced around the edges of his voice. "And mostly because I wasn't thinking about anything but you. I didn't want to think about anything but you. And I'm damn well entitled to take time for that. I didn't consider my idea about Giles Dent as foreplay, and I sure as hell didn't consider talk about human sacrifice as postcoital conversation. Hang me."

"You should've . . . Human sacrifice? What are you talking about? What do you mean?"

The phone rang, and cursing, Layla reached across his desk to answer. "Good afternoon, Fox B. O'Dell's office. I'm sorry, Mr. O'Dell's with a client. May I take a message?" She scribbled a name and number on Fox's memo pad. "Yes, of course, I'll see he gets it. Thank you."

She hung up. "You can call them back when we're done here. I need to know what you're talking about."

"A possibility. Ann wrote that Dent intended to do something no guardian had done, and that there'd be a price. The guardians are the good guys, right? That's how we've always looked at them, at Dent. The white hats. But even white hats can step into the gray. Or past the gray. I see it all the time in my line of work. What people do if they're desperate enough, if they feel justified, if they stop believing they have another choice. Blood sacrifice. That's the province of the other side. Usually."

"The deer, the one Quinn saw in her dream last winter, lying across the path in the woods with its throat slit. The blood of the innocent. It's in the notes. We speculated that Dent did that, that he sacrificed the fawn. But you said human."

"Do you think that sacrificing Bambi could have given Dent the power he needed to hold Twisse for three hundred years? The power to pass what he did to me, Cal, and Gage when the time came? That's what I asked myself, Layla. And I don't think it could've been enough."

He paused, because even now it left him slightly ill to consider it. "He told Hester to run. On the night of July seventh, sixteen fifty-two, after she'd condemned him as a witch, he told her to run. That came from you."

"Yes, he told her to run."

"He knew what was about to happen. Not just that he'd pull Twisse into some other dimension for a few centuries, but what it would cost to do it."

She put a fist to her heart, rubbed it there as she stared at Fox. "The people who were at the Pagan Stone."

"About a dozen of them, as far as we can tell. That's a lot of blood. That's a major sacrifice."

"You think he used them." Slowly, carefully, she lowered to a chair. "You think he killed them. Not Twisse, but Dent."

"I think he let them die, which being a lawyer I could argue isn't the same by law. Depraved indifference we could call it, except for the little matter of intent. He used their deaths." Fox's voice was heavy on the words. "I think he used the fire—the torches they carried, and the fire he made, to engulf them, to scorch the ground, to draw from that act—one no guardian had ever committed, the power to do what he'd decided had to be done."

The color died out of her face, leaving her eyes eerily green. "If it's true, what does that make him? What does that make any of us?"

"I don't know. Damned maybe, if you subscribe to damnation. I've been a subscriber for nearly twenty-one years now."

"We thought, we assumed, it was Twisse who caused the deaths of all those people that night."

"Maybe it was. In part, even if my idea's crap, it was. How many of them would have gone to the Pagan Stone, looking to kill Giles Dent and Ann Hawkins if they hadn't been under Twisse's influence? But if we tip that to the side, and we look at the grays, isn't it possible Dent used Twisse? He knew what was coming, according to the journals, he knew. He sent Ann away to protect her and his sons. He gave his life—white hat time. But if he took the others, that put a lot of bloodstains on the white."

"It makes horrible sense. It makes sickening sense."

"We need to look at it, and maybe when we do, we'll know better what has to be done." He studied her face, the shock that covered it. "Pack it in, go on home."

"It's barely two. I have work."

"I can handle the phones for the next couple of hours. Take a walk, get some air. Take a nap, a bubble bath, whatever."

Bracing a hand on the arm of the chair, she got slowly to her feet. "Is that what you think of me? That I crumble at the first ugly slap? That I can't or won't stand up to it? It took me a while to get my feet when I came to the Hollow—hang *me*—but I've got them now. I don't need a goddamn bubble bath to soothe my sensibilities."

"My mistake."

"Don't underestimate me, Fox. However diluted, I have that bastard's blood in me. It could be, in the long run, I can handle the dark better than you."

"Maybe. But don't expect me to want that for you, or you overestimate me. Now you might have a better idea why I didn't bring this up yesterday, or you might just want to stay pissed about it."

She closed her eyes and steadied herself. "No, I don't want to be mad about it, and yes, I have a better idea." She also had a much better idea what Quinn had meant by her warning. Working, sleeping with, fighting beside. It was a lot to ask of a relationship.

"It's hard to separate the different things we are to each other," she said carefully. "And when the lines get blurred, it's harder yet. You said, when I came in, you were feeling overwhelmed. You overwhelm me, Fox, on a lot of levels. So I keep losing my balance."

"I haven't had mine since I met you. I'll try to catch you when you stumble if you do the same for me."

And didn't that say it all. She glanced at her watch. "Oh, look at that. I nearly missed my afternoon break. Only a couple minutes left. Well, I'd better put them to good use."

She walked around the desk, leaned down. "You're on break, too, by the way, so this office is closed for the next thirty seconds." She laid her lips on his, brushing her fingertips over his face, back into his hair.

And there, she thought, as strange as it was, she found her balance again.

Straightening, she took his hand between both of hers for the last few seconds, then letting it go, stepped back. "Mrs. Mullendore would like to speak with you. Her number's on your desk."

"Layla," he said when she reached the doorway. "I'm going to have to give you longer breaks."

She smiled over her shoulder as she continued out. Alone, Fox sat quietly at his desk another moment, and thought of what a good man, even the best of men, might do if all he loved was threatened.

WHEN THE SIX OF THEM WERE TOGETHER THAT evening in the sparsely furnished living room of the rental house, Fox read the passages from Ann's journal that had flicked the switch for him. He laid out his theory, as he had for Layla.

"Jesus, Fox. Guardian." Cal's resistance to the idea was palpable. "It means he protected. He'd dedicated his life to that purpose, and all the lives he remembered before the last. I've felt some of what he felt, I've seen some of what he saw."

"But not all." Gage paced in front of the window as he often did during discussions. "Bits and pieces, Cal, and that's it. If it went down this way, I'd say that these particular bits and pieces would be ones Dent would do his best to keep hidden, for as long as he could."

"Then why let Hester go?" Cal demanded. "Wasn't she both the most innocent there, and the most dangerous to him?"

"Because we had to be." Cybil looked at Quinn, at Layla. "We three had to become, and Hester's child had to survive for that to happen. It's a matter of power. The guardian, lifetime after lifetime, played by the rules—as far as we know—and could never win. He could never completely stop his foe."

"And becoming more human," Layla added. "I was thinking that through today. Every generation, wouldn't he have become more human, with all the frailties? But Twisse remained as ever. How much longer could Dent have fought? How many more lifetimes did he have?"

"So he made a choice." Fox nodded. "And used the kind of weaponry Twisse had always used."

"And killed innocent people so he could buy time? So he could wait for us?"

"It's horrible." Quinn reached for Cal's hand. "It's horrible to think about it, to consider it. But I guess we have to."

"So if we go with this, you're descendents of a demon, and we're descendents of a mass murderer." Cal shook his head. "That's a hell of a mix."

"We are what we make ourselves." There was a whiff of heat in Cybil's words. "We use what we have and we decide what we are. Was what he did right, was it justified? I don't know. I'm not going to judge him."

Gage turned from the window. "And what do we have?"

"We have words on a page, a stone broken in three equal parts, a place of power in the woods. We have brains and guts," Cybil continued. "And a hell of a lot of work to do, I'd say, before we put everything together and kill the bastard."

Thirteen

THERE WERE TIMES, TO FOX'S WAY OF THINKING, when a man just needed to be around guys. Things had been quiet since Block had pounded him into the sidewalk, and that gave him thinking time. Of course, one of his thoughts had been Giles Dent killing a dozen people in a fiery blaze, and that one wasn't sitting well with anyone.

They were in the process of reading the second journal now. Though there'd been no stunning revelations so far, he kept his own notes. He knew it wasn't always what a person said, or wrote, but what they were thinking when they said or wrote it.

It was telling to him that while she wrote about the kindness of her cousin, the movements in her womb, even the weather, the daily chores, Ann Hawkins wrote nothing of Giles or the night at the Pagan Stone for weeks after the events.

So he spent some time turning over in his mind what she hadn't written.

He sat with his feet on Cal's coffee table, a Coke in his hand, and chips within easy reach. The basketball game was on TV, but he couldn't concentrate on it. He had a big day tomorrow, he mused, and a lot on his mind. The trip to the doctor's office would be pretty quick, all in all. There wasn't that much for him to do, really. And it wasn't anything he hadn't done before. A man of thirty knew how to—ha—handle the job.

He was prepared for court. The docket gave them two days, but he thought they'd wrap it up in one. After that, they'd all meet. They'd read, they'd discuss. And they'd wait.

What he should do was go home, get out Cybil's notes, his own, Quinn's transcriptions. He should take a harder, closer look at Layla's charts and graphs. Somewhere in there was another piece of the whole. It needed to be shaken out and studied.

Instead he sat where he was, took another swallow of Coke. And said what was on his mind.

"I'm going into the doctor's tomorrow with Sage and Paula to donate sperm so they can have a kid."

There was a very long stretch of silence into which Cal finally said, "Huh."

"Sage asked me, and I thought about it, and I figured sure, why not? They're good together, Sage and Paula. It's just strange to know that I'm going to try to get somebody pregnant tomorrow, by remote."

"You're giving your sister a shot at a family," Cal pointed out. "Not so strange."

Just that one remark made Fox feel considerably better. "I'm going to bunk here tonight. If I go home, I'm going to be tempted to go by and see Layla. If I see Layla, I'm going to want to get her naked."

"And you want to go in tomorrow fully loaded," Gage concluded.

"Yeah. Stupid and superstitious probably, but yeah."

"You've got the couch," Cal told him. "Especially since I know you won't be jacking off on it."

Yes, Fox thought, there were times a man just needed to be around other guys.

THE LATE MARCH SNOWSTORM WAS ANNOYING. IT would've been less so if he'd bothered to listen to the weather before leaving the house that morning. Then he'd have had his winter coat, since winter decided to make the return trip. A thin, chilly white coated the early yellow haze of forsythia. Wouldn't hurt them, Fox thought as he drove back toward the Hollow. Those heralding spring bloomers were hardy, and used to the caprices, even the downright nastiness, of nature.

He was sick of winter. Even though spring was the gateway to summer, and this summer the portal to the Seven, he wished the door would hit winter in the ass on its way out. The problem was there'd been a couple of nice days before this season-straddling storm blew in. Nature held those warm, sunny days like a bright carrot on a frozen stick, teasing.

The snow would melt, he reminded himself. It was better to remember he'd had a pretty good day. He'd done his duty by his sister, and by his client. Now he was going home, getting out of the suit, having a nice cold beer. He was going to see Layla. And after tonight's session, he would do his best to talk himself into her bed, or talk her into his.

As he turned onto Main, Fox spotted Jim Hawkins outside the gift shop. He stood, hands on his hips, studying the building. Fox pulled over to the curb, hit the button to lower the window. "Hey!"

Jim turned. He was a tall man with thoughtful eyes, a steady hand. He walked to the truck, leaned on the open window. "How you doing, Fox?"

"Doing good. It's cold out there. Do you want a ride?"

"No, just taking a walk around." He looked back toward the shop. "I'm sorry Lorrie and John are closing down, leaving town." When he looked back at Fox, his eyes were somber, and another layer of worry weighed in his voice. "I'm sorry the town has to lose anyone."

"I know. They took a hard hit."

"I heard you did, too. I heard what happened with Block."

"I'm all right."

"At times like this, when I see the signs—all the signs, Fox—I wish there was more I could do than call your father and have him fix broken windows."

"We're going to do more than get through this time, Mr. Hawkins. We're going to stop it this time."

"Cal believes that, too. I'm trying to believe it. Well." He let out a sigh. "I'll be calling your father shortly, have him take a look at this place. He'll fix it up, spruce it here and there. And I'll look for somebody who wants to start a business on Main Street."

Fox frowned at the building. "I might have an idea on that."

"Oh?"

"I have to think about it, see if . . . See. Maybe you could let me know before you start looking, or before you decide on a new tenant."

"I'm happy to do that. The Hollow needs ideas. It needs businesses on Main Street."

"And people who care enough to fix what's broken," Fox said, thinking of Layla's words. "I'll get back to you on it."

Fox drove on. He had something new to turn over in his mind now, something interesting. And something, for him, that symbolized hope.

He parked in front of his office, stepped out into the cold, wet snow, and noticed his office lights glinting against the windows. When he walked in, Layla glanced up from her keyboard.

"I told you that you didn't have to come in today."

"I had busywork." She stopped typing to swivel toward him. "I rearranged the storage closet so it works better for me. And the kitchen, and some of the files. Then . . . Is it still snowing?"

"Yeah." He shrugged out of his light jacket. "It's after five, Layla." And he didn't like the idea of her being alone in the building for hours at a time.

"I got caught up. We've been so focused on the journal entries, we've let some of the other areas go. Cybil's hunted up all the newspaper reports on anything related to the Seven, the anecdotal evidence, specifics we've gleaned from you guys, coordinating passages from some of the books on the Hollow. I've been putting them together in various files. Chronologically, geographically, type of incident, and so on."

"Twenty years of that. It'll take a while."

"I do better when I have a system, have order. Plus, we all know that considering the amount of time, the amount of damage, the actual reports are scarce." She brushed back her hair, cocked her head. "How did it go in court?"

"Good."

"Should I ask how things went before court?"

"I did my part. They said I could just, ah, pass off the . . . second round to Sage for transport in the morning. Then I guess we wait and see if any soldier makes a landing."

"You don't have to wait long these days."

He shrugged, slipped his hands into his pockets. "I didn't think of you."

"Sorry?"

"I mean, you know, when I . . . donated. I didn't think of you because it seemed rude."

Layla's lips twitched. "I see. Who did you think of?"

"They provide visual stimulation in the form of skin mags. I didn't actually catch her name."

"Men."

"I'm thinking of you now."

Her brows lifted when he walked back, locked the door. "Are you?"

"And I'm thinking I need you to come back to my office." He came over, took her hand. "And put in a little overtime."

"Why, Mr. O'Dell. If only I'd put my hair in a bun and worn glasses."

He grinned as he drew her across the room, down the hall. "If only. But . . ." He let go of her hands to unbutton her crisp white shirt. "Let's see what's under here today."

"I thought you wanted me to take a letter."

"To whom it may concern, frilly white bras with—oh yeah—front hooks are now standard office attire."

"I don't think this one will fit you," she said, then surprised him by tugging on his tie. "Let's see what's under here. I've thought about you, Mr. O'Dell." She slid the tie off, tossed it aside. "About your hands, your mouth, about how many ways you used them on me." She unhooked his belt as she backed him into his office. "About how many ways you might use them on me again."

Like the tie, she whipped off the belt, let it fall. She shoved his suit jacket off his shoulders, tugged it away. "Start now."

"You're pretty bossy for a secretary."

"Office manager."

"Either way." He bit her bottom lip. "I like it."

"Then you're going to love this." She pushed him down into his desk chair, pointed a finger to keep him in place. Then with her eyes on his, wiggled out of her panties.

"Oh. Boy."

After tossing them aside, she straddled him.

He'd been thinking couch, maybe the floor, but at the moment, with her mouth like a fever on his, the chair seemed perfect. He yanked at her shirt, closed his mouth over her lace-covered breast. This wasn't a woman looking for slow seduction, but for fire and speed. So he used his hands, his mouth, and let her set the pace.

"As soon as you walked in, I wanted this." She fumbled between them, dragged down the zipper of his trousers. "As soon as you walked in, Fox."

She closed around him the moment he was inside her. Tightened as her head fell back, as she gasped. Then her lips were on his throat, on his face, were clashing against his in desperation as her hips pumped.

She took him over with her urgency, her sudden, fierce greed. He let himself be taken, be ruled. Unable to resist, he let himself be filled, and let himself empty. When he came, when his mind was still dazzled by his body's race, she caught his face in her hands and rode him ruthlessly to her own end.

He continued to sit, bemused, after they'd gotten their breath back, even after she rose and started to step back into her panties.

"Wait. I think those are mine now."

When she laughed, he solved the matter by getting up and snatching them out of her hand.

"Give me those. I can't walk around without—"

"You and I will be the only ones who know. It's already driving me crazy. I need to go up, change out of this suit. Come on up, then I'll drive you home."

"I'll wait here, because if I go up there, you'll get me into bed. Fox, I need those panties. They match the bra."

He only smiled as he strolled out. He intended to get the bra later. And was considering having them preserved in Lucite, along with his desk chair.

ALL GOOD THINGS MUST COME TO AN END, FOX thought, as they spent the next few hours picking through the second journal, turning Ann's ordinary words to every possible angle looking for hidden meanings. Once again, Gage's demand to skip the hell ahead was outvoted.

"Same reasons against apply," Cybil pointed out, taking advantage of the break to roll tension out of her neck and shoulders. "We have to consider the fact that she's lost the man she loved, a traumatic event. That she's about to give birth to triplets. And if that isn't a traumatic event I don't know what would be. This is her lull. She needs to steady herself and gear up at the same time. I think we have to respect that."

"I think it's more." Layla reached out to touch the book Quinn had set down. "I think she's writing about sewing, about cooking, about the heat because she needs some distance. She doesn't write about Giles, about the deaths, what was done. She doesn't write about what she thinks or fears about what's going to happen. It's all the moment."

She looked at Fox, and he nodded.

"I've been leaning that way. It's what she's not writing about. Every day she gets through is an effort. She fills them with routines. But I can't believe that she's not thinking about before and after. Not feeling all of that. It's not a lull so much as . . . She wanted us to find the journals, even this one that seems to be so full of daily debris. To me it says—she's saying—that after great loss, personal sacrifice, horror, put a name on it. After that, before and after a new beginning, the births, there's still life. That it's still important to live, to go about your business. Isn't that what we do, seven years at a time? We live, and that's important."

"And what the hell does that tell us?" Gage demanded.

"That part of the process is just living. That's giving Twisse the finger, every day. Does it know? In whatever hellhole Dent took it to, does it know? I think it does, and I think it burns its ass that we get up every morning and do what we do."

"I like it." Quinn tapped a finger on her lips. "Maybe it

even sucks on its power. It thrives on violent emotions, violent acts. When it's able, it feeds on them, creates them and feeds. Wouldn't the opposite be true? That ordinary emotions and acts, or loving ones starve it?"

"Sweetheart dance." Layla straightened in her chair. "Ordinary, fun, happy. It came there to ruin that."

"And before, in the dining room of the hotel. Sure it wanted to scare us off," Quinn said to Layla. "But its choice of time and place may be a factor. There was a couple celebrating, flirting over candlelight and wine."

"What do you do when a bee stings you?" Cybil asked. "You swat at it. Maybe we're giving him a few stings. We'll take a closer look at the known incidents, known sightings. And this idea rolls into another for me. Writing something down gives it power, especially names. It's possible she wanted to wait, or needed to wait until some time had passed. Until she felt more secure."

"We wrote down the words," Cal murmured. "We wrote down the words we said that night at the stone, for the blood brothers ritual."

"Adding to their power," Quinn agreed. "Writing, it's another answer. We're writing everything down. While that may be giving him more power—bringing him earlier—it's giving him more stings."

"When we know what we have to do, when we think we know what it's going to take," Fox continued, "we have to write it down. Like Ann did, like we did that night."

"Signed in blood at the dark of the moon."

Amused, Cybil glanced over at Gage. "I wouldn't discount that."

Gage rose to go to the kitchen. He wanted more coffee. He wanted, more than the coffee, a few minutes without the chatter. At this point, and as far as he could see for the next several points, it was all talk, no action. He was a patient man, had to be, but he was starting to itch for action.

When Cybil came in he ignored her. It took some doing. She wasn't a woman fashioned to be ignored, but he'd been working on it.

"Being irritable and negative doesn't add much."

He leaned back against the counter with his coffee. "That's why I left."

After a moment's consideration, she opted for wine over tea. "You're a little bored, too. But your way hasn't finished the job. New days, new ways." She mirrored his pose, leaning against the other counter with her wine. "It's harder for people like you and me."

"You and me?"

"We're plagued with glimpses of what might come, and sometimes does. How do we know what to do, or if we should do anything, to stop it, or change it. If we do, will it be worse?"

"Everything's a risk. That doesn't worry me."

"Annoys you though." She sipped. "You're annoyed right now because of the way things are shaping up."

"How are things shaping up?"

"Our little group's paired off. Q and Cal, Layla and Fox. That leaves you and me, big guy. So you're annoyed, and I can't blame you. Just FYI, I'm no happier than you are with the idea that some hand of fate might be moving you and me together like chess pieces."

"Chess is Fox's game."

She drew in a breath. "Dealing us into the same hand then."

His brows rose in acknowledgment. "That's why there's a discard pile. No offense."

"None taken."

"You're just not my type."

When she smiled, just that way, a man heard siren songs. "Believe me, if I aimed at you, you wouldn't have any other type. But that's neither here nor there. I came in to propose a kind of alliance, a bargain, a deal. However it suits you."

"What's the deal?"

"That you and I will work together, we'll fight together if it comes to it. We'll join our particular talents when and if necessary. And I won't seduce you or pretend to let you seduce me."

"You wouldn't be pretending."

"There, we've each gotten a shot in. Score's even. You're here because you love your friends, however else you feel about this place, about some of the people in it, you love your friends and are absolutely loyal to them. I respect that, Gage, and I understand it. I love my friends, and I'm loyal to them. That's why I'm here."

Glancing toward the doorway, she took a slow sip of wine. "This town isn't mine, but those people in the other room are. I'll do whatever I need to do for them. So will you.

"So, do we have a deal?"

He pushed away from the counter, crossed to her. He stood close, his eyes on hers. She smelled, he thought, of mysteries that were exclusively female. "Tell me something. Do you believe we're going to come out on the other side of this, throwing the confetti and popping the champagne?"

"They do. That's almost enough for me. The rest is possibility."

"I like probabilities better. But . . ." He held out a hand, taking hers when she offered it. "Deal."

"Good. Then—" She started to step away, but he held her hand firm in his.

"What if I'd said no?"

"Then, I suppose I'd have been forced to seduce you and make you my love puppy to keep you in line."

His grin spread, full of appreciation. "Love puppy my ass."

"You'd be surprised. Or would if we didn't have a deal."
She put down her wine to pat his hand before pulling hers
free. Picking up her wine again, she started to walk out,
then stopped, turned back. The amusement was gone.
"He's in love with her."

Fox, Gage realized. Cal was already a given. "Yeah, I
know."

"I don't know if he does, certainly Layla doesn't. Yet. It
makes them stronger, and it makes it all more difficult for
them."

"Fox especially. That's his story," Gage said, with final-
ity, when her eyes asked how.

"All right. They're going to need more of us soon, more
from us. You're not going to have the luxury of being bored
much longer."

"Did you see something?"

"I dreamed they were all dead, piled like offerings on
the Pagan Stone. And my hands were red with their blood.
Fire crawled up the stone, over the stone, and consumed
them while I watched. While I did nothing. When it came
out of the dark, it smiled at me. It called me daughter, and
it embraced me. Then you leaped out of the shadows and
killed us both."

"That's a nightmare, not a vision."

"I hope to God you're right. Either way, it tells me you
and I have to start to work together soon. I won't have their
blood on my hands." Her fingers tightened on the stem of
her glass. "Whatever has to be done, I won't have that."

When she left, he stayed, and he wondered how much
she would be willing to do to save the people they both
loved.

NO TRACE OF SNOW REMAINED WHEN FOX LEFT
his office in the morning. The sun beamed out of a rich
blue sky that seemed to laugh at the mere idea of winter.

On the trees the leaves of summer were in tight buds of anticipation. Pansies rioted in the tub in front of the flower shop.

He peeled off his coat—really had to start listening to the weather—and strolled as others did along the wide bricked sidewalks. He smelled spring, the freshness of it, felt it in the balm of the air on his face. It was too nice a day to huddle inside an office. It was a day for the park, or porch sitting.

He should take Layla to the park, hold her hand and stroll over the bridge, talk her into letting him push her on one of the swings. Push her high, hear her laugh.

He should buy her flowers. Something simple and springlike. The idea had him backtracking, checking traffic, then dashing across the street. Daffodils, he thought as he pulled open the door of the shop.

"Hi, Fox." Amy sent him a cheery wave as she came in from the back. She'd run the Flower Pot for years, and to Fox's mind never tired of flowers. "Terrific day, huh?"

"And then some. That's what I'm after." He gestured to the daffodils, bright as butter in the glass refrigerated display.

"Pretty as a picture." She turned, and in the glass, the dim reflection of her face grinned back at his with sharply pointed teeth in a face that ran with blood. Even as he took a step back, she turned around, smiling her familiar and pretty smile. "Who doesn't love daffodils?" she said cheerfully as she wrapped them. "Are they for your girl?"

"Yeah." I'm jumpy, he realized. Just jumpy. Too much in my head. As he got out his wallet to pay, he caught a scent under the sweet fragrance of blooms. A swampy odor, as if some of the flowers had rotted in water.

"Here you go! She's going to love them."

"Thanks, Amy." He paid, took the flowers.

"See you later. Tell Carly I said hi."

He stopped dead, spun around. "What? What did you say?"

"I said tell Layla I said hi." Her eyes shone with puzzled concern. "Are you all right, Fox?"

"Yeah. Yeah." He pushed through the door, grateful to be back outside.

As traffic was light, he walked across the street in the middle of the block. The light changed as a cloud rolled over the sun, and he felt a prickle of cold against his skin— the breath of winter out of a springtime sky. His hand tightened on the stems of the flowers as he whirled around, expected to see it, in whatever form it chose to take. But there was nothing, no boy, no dog, no man or dark shadow.

Then he heard her call his name. This time the cold washed over him, into him, through his bones, at the fear in her voice. She called out again as he ran, as he followed her terror to the old library. He rushed through the open door that slammed like death behind him.

Where there should have been empty space, some tables, folding chairs for what was now the community center, the room was as it had been years before. Books in stacks, the scent of them, the desks, the carts.

He ordered himself to steady. It wasn't real. It was making him see what was not. But she screamed, and Fox ran for the steps, taking them two and three at a time. He ran on legs that trembled, that remembered running this way before. Up the stairs, up past the attic, to heave himself against the door leading out to the roof. When his body hurtled through, the early spring day had died into a hot summer night.

Sweat ran down his skin like water, and fear twisted tearing claws in his belly.

She stood on the ledge of the turret above his head. Even in the dark he could see the blood on her hands, on the stone that had torn at them when she climbed.

Carly. Her name pounded in his head. Carly, don't. Don't move. I'm coming up to get you.

But it was Layla who looked down at him. Layla's tears spilling onto pale cheeks. It was Layla who said his name once, desperately. Layla who looked into his eyes and said, "Help me. Please help me."

And Layla who dived off the ledge to die on the street below.

Fourteen

~⌇~

HE WOKE IN A COLD SWEAT WITH LAYLA SAYING
his name over and over. The urgency in her voice, the solid
grip of her hands on his shoulders pulled him out of the
dream and back to the now.

But the terror came with him, riding on the raw and
wrenching grief. He locked himself around her, the shape of
her, the scent, the rapid beat of her heart. Alive. He hadn't
been too late, not for her. She was alive. She was here.

"Just hold on." A shudder ripped through him, an echo
of that stupefying fear. "Just hold on."

"I am. I will. You had a nightmare." While she murmured to him, her hands soothed at the knotted muscles of
his back. "You're awake now. It's all right."

Was it? he wondered. Would it ever be?

"You're so cold. Fox, you're so cold. Let me get the
blanket. I'm right here, just let me get the blanket. You're
shaking."

She pulled back, yanked up the blanket, then positioned

herself so she could rub the warmth back into his arms. In the dim light, her eyes never left his face. "Better? Is that better? I'm going to get you some water."

"Yeah, okay. Yeah, thanks."

She scrambled out of bed, darted out of the room. And Fox put his head in his hands. He needed a minute to pull himself together, to push the rest away. The dream had him twisted up, mixing his memories, tying in his fears, his loss.

He'd been too late on that ugly summer night, too busy being the hero. He'd screwed it up, and Carly died. He should have kept her safe. He should've made sure of it, should have protected her, above all else. She'd been his, and he hadn't helped her.

Layla hurried back, knelt on the bed as she pressed the water into his hand. "Are you warm enough now? Do you want another blanket?"

"No. No, I'm good. Sorry about that."

"You were like ice, and you were calling out." Gently, she brushed the hair back from his face. "I couldn't wake you up, not at first. What was it, Fox? What did you dream?"

"I don't—" He started to tell her he didn't remember, but the lie stuck bitterly in the back of his throat. He'd lied to Carly, and Carly was dead. "I can't talk about it." That wasn't quite the truth either. "I don't want to talk about it now."

He felt her hesitation, her *need* to press. And ignored it.

Saying nothing, she took the empty glass from him, set it on the nightstand. Then she drew him back, cradling his head on her breast. "It's all right now." Her murmur was as soft as the hand that stroked his hair. "It's all right. Sleep awhile longer."

And her comfort chased his demons away so he could.

IN THE MORNING, SHE EASED OUT OF BED LIKE A thief out of a second-story window. He looked exhausted, she thought, and still very pale. All she could hope was some of the sorrow she'd felt from him in the night had softened with sleep. She could find its source; he couldn't block her now. If she knew the root, she might help him dig it out, help heal whatever hurt his heart.

And while that was true enough, it was only part of what tempted her. The rest was selfish, even petty. He'd called out her name in the grip of the nightmare, called in terror and despair. But not only hers, Layla remembered. He'd called out another's.

Carly.

No, looking into his mind and heart while he slept, whether the motive was selfless or selfish, was a violation. The worst kind. A breach of trust and intimacy.

She'd let him sleep, and if she had to breach something, she'd breach his kitchen and find something reasonably sane to fix him for breakfast.

She slipped on his discarded shirt and out of the room.

In the kitchen, she got a quick jolt. Not from piles of dirty dishes and scattered newspaper. The room was what she thought of as man-clean. A few dishes in the sink, some unopened mail on the table, counters hastily wiped around countertop appliances.

The jolt came from the addition of a shiny new countertop coffeemaker.

Everything in her went soft toward the point of gooey. He never drank coffee, but he'd gone out and bought a coffeemaker for her—one that had a fresh bean grinder. And when she opened the cupboard overhead, she found the bag of beans.

Could he *be* sweeter?

She was holding the brown bag, smiling at the appliance when Fox walked in. "You bought a coffeemaker."

"Yeah. I figured you ought to be able to get your morning fix."

When she turned, his head was already in the fridge. "Thank you. And just for that I'm going to cook you breakfast. You must have something in here I can morph into actual food."

She came around the refrigerator door to poke her own head in. When he straightened, stepped back, she saw his face.

"Oh, Fox." Instinctively she lifted a hand to his cheek. "You don't look well. You should go back to bed. You've got a light schedule today anyway. I can cancel—"

"I'm fine. We don't get sick, remember?"

Not in body, she thought, but heart and mind were different matters. "You get tired. You're tired now, and you need a day off."

"What I need is a shower. Look, I appreciate the breakfast offer, but I don't have much of an appetite this morning. Go ahead and make your coffee, if you can figure that thing out."

Whose voice was that? Layla asked herself as he walked away. That cool and distant voice? With careful movements, she put the beans away, quietly closed the cupboard door. Walking back to the bedroom, she began to dress while the sound of the water striking tile in the bathroom drummed in her ears.

A woman knew when a man wanted her gone, and a woman with any pride obliged him. She'd shower at home, dress for the workday at home, have her coffee at home. The man wanted space, she'd damn well give him space.

When the phone rang, she ignored it. Then, cursing, gave in. It could be important, she thought, an emergency. Then she winced when Fox's mother gave her a cheery good morning and addressed her by name.

In the shower, Fox let the hot water pound over him while he gulped down his cold caffeine. The combination dulled some of the sharp edges, but there were plenty more where they came from. He felt hungover, headachy, queasy.

It would pass. It always passed. But a nightmare could give him a rougher morning-after than any drunken spree.

He'd probably chased Layla off, snapping at her that way. Which, he admitted, had been the purpose. He didn't want her hovering, stroking, and soothing, watching him with that worry in her eyes. He wanted to be alone so he could wallow and brood.

As was his damn right.

He turned off the shower, whipped a towel around his waist. When he walked into the bedroom, trailing drips, there she was.

"I was just leaving," she began in the frosty tone that told him he'd done his job very well. "But your mother called."

"Oh. Okay, I'll get back to her."

"Actually, I'm to tell you that since Sage and Paula have to be in D.C. on Monday, and may have to head back to Seattle from there, she's having everyone over for dinner tomorrow."

He pressed his fingers to his eyes. Probably no way out of that one. "Okay."

"She expects me to come. Me—all of us. I'm supposed to help you spread the word. You probably know she's impossible to say no to, but you can make excuses for me tomorrow."

"Why would I do that? Why wouldn't you go? Why should you get out of eating stuffed artichokes?" Since she didn't smile, he shoved at his dripping hair. "Look, I'm feeling a little rugged this morning. Maybe you could cut me a very narrow break."

"Believe me, I already have. I'm trying to cut it even wider by convincing myself you're being moody and secretive because you're an ass, not because you don't trust me. But it's tricky because while you may be an ass, you're not a big enough one to hold back the details of a major trauma like the one you went through last night just to be stupid. So

I circle right back to the matter of trust. I let you inside me, I took you inside me in that bed, but you won't let me inside you. You won't tell me what hurt and scared you."

"You need to back off, Layla. This just isn't the time."

"You get to choose the time? Well, that's fine. Just let me know when it's convenient for you, and I'll pencil me in."

She started out, and he did nothing to stop her. Then she stopped, looked dead into his eyes. "Who's Carly?"

When he said nothing, when his eyes went blank, she walked away and left him alone.

HE DIDN'T EXPECT HER TO COME INTO THE OF-fice, actively hoped she wouldn't. But while he was in his law library trying to concentrate on research, he heard her come in. There was no mistaking it for anyone else. Fox knew the way she moved, even her morning routine.

Open the door of the foyer closet, hang up coat, close the door. Cross to the desk, open the bottom right-hand drawer, stow purse. Boot up the computer.

He heard all the busy little sounds. They made him feel guilty, and the guilt annoyed him. They'd ignore each other for a few hours, he decided. Until she calmed down and he settled down.

Then, they'd just move past it.

Ignoring and avoidance worked well enough for most of the morning. Every time the phone rang, he braced for her voice to come snipping over the intercom. But she never buzzed him.

He told himself he didn't sneak from the library to his office. He simply walked very, very quietly.

When he heard her go out to lunch, he strolled out to reception, took a casual scan of her desk. He noted the short stack of while-you-were-outs for him. So she wasn't passing the calls through, he mused. No problem, that worked.

He'd do the callbacks later, he decided. Because if he took the messages into his office, it would become obvious he'd been out there poking around her desk.

Now he felt stupid. Stupid, tired, beleaguered, and a little pissed off. Stuffing his hands in his pockets, he started back to his office and jolted when the door opened. Relief came when he saw Shelley walk in rather than Layla.

"Hi. I was hoping I could talk to you for a minute. I just saw Layla outside, and she said you were in, probably not real busy."

"Sure. You want to come back?"

"No." She walked to him, and just put her arms around him. "Thanks. I just wanted to say thanks."

"You're welcome. What for?"

"Block and I had our first counseling session last night." She gave a sigh, stepped back. "It was kind of intense and it got pretty emotional, I guess. I don't know how it's all going to end up, but I think it helped. I think it's better to try, to talk, even if we're yelling, than to just say screw you, you bastard. If I end up saying that, at least I'll know I gave it a good shot first. I don't know if I would have if you hadn't been looking out for me."

"I want you to get what you want, whatever that is. And to be happy when you get it."

She nodded, dabbed at her eyes with a tissue. "I know Block went after you, and you didn't press charges. He's feeling, I guess the word's *chastised*. I wanted to thank you for that, too, for not pressing charges."

"It wasn't all his fault."

"Oh, it was, too." But she laughed a little. "He's got some making up to do, but he knows it. He's got a black eye. I don't give a rat's ass if it's small of me, but I appreciate that, too."

"No charge."

She laughed a little. "Anyway. We're going to keep going, see what happens. I get to go alone next, and I am *so* unloading." Now she grinned. "Already feels good. I gotta get back to work."

He went back to his office, worked and brooded. He heard Layla come back in. Closet, coat, desk, drawer, purse. He went out the kitchen door, making just enough noise to let her know he'd headed out.

The sun was brilliant in a ripe blue sky. Though the air was warm enough to keep him comfortable in his light jacket, the chill shot up his spine.

The afternoon mirrored his dream.

He forced himself to round the building to Main. Pansies rioted in the tub in front of the flower shop. People strolled, some in shirtsleeves, as if sucking down this taste of spring after the last gulp of winter. He curled his hands into fists, and followed the steps.

He waited for a break in traffic, crossed the street.

Amy came out of the back of the flower shop. "Hey, Fox. How you doing? Fabulous day, isn't it? About time, too."

Close enough, he thought, keeping his eyes on her face. "Yeah. How've you been?"

"No complaints. Are you looking for something for the office? Mrs. Hawbaker usually picked out an arrangement on Mondays. You don't want to buy office flowers on a Friday, Fox."

"No." Though some of the knots in his belly loosened— not the same—they tightened again when he glanced over and saw the daffodils. "It's personal. Those are what I'm after."

"Aren't they sweet? All cheerful and hopeful." She turned, and he stared at the faint reflection of her face in the glass. She smiled, but it was Amy's smile, as cheerful as the flowers.

She chattered as she prepared them, wrapped them, but the words slipped in and out of his mind as he searched the air for the scent of something rotting. And found nothing but fresh and floral.

"Are they for your girl?"

He gave her a quick, sharp look. "Yeah. Yeah, they're for my girl."

Her smile only went brighter as they exchanged money for blooms. "She'll love them. If you want something for the office, I'll have a nice arrangement for you Monday."

"Okay, thanks." He turned to go.

"Say hi to Layla for me."

He closed his eyes, relief, guilt, gratitude rushing through him. "I will. See you later."

Maybe he was a little dizzy when he stepped outside, a little shaky in the knees, but when he made himself look, the door of the old library was closed. His gaze traveled up, up, but no one he loved stood poised for death on the narrow ledge of the turret.

He crossed the street again. She was at her desk when he came in the front door. She flicked him a glance, then looked deliberately away.

"There are messages on your desk. Your two o'clock called to reschedule for next week."

He walked to her, held out the flowers. "I'm sorry."

"They're very nice. I'll go put them in water."

"I'm sorry," he repeated when she rose and made to brush by him.

She paused, just two beats. "All right." And taking the flowers, walked away.

He wanted to let it go. What was the point in dredging it all up? What could possibly be the point? It wasn't about trust, it was about pain. Wasn't he entitled to his own pain? Hurting, he strode back to the kitchen where she filled a vase with water.

"Listen, are we supposed to turn ourselves inside out, show off our guts? Is that what it takes?"

"No."

"We don't have to know every damn detail about each other."

"No, we don't." She began to slip the tender green stems into the water, one by one.

"I had a nightmare. I've had nightmares almost as long as I can remember. We've all had them now."

"I know."

"Is that your way of dragging it out of me? To agree with everything I say?"

"It's my way of controlling myself so I don't kick your ass and step over it on my way out."

"I don't want to fight."

"Yes, you do. That's exactly what you want, and I'm not going to give you what you want. You don't deserve it."

"Jesus Christ." He stormed around the little room and in a rare show of violence kicked at the cabinets. "She's dead. Carly's dead. I didn't save her, and she died."

Layla turned away from the sunbeams in the bright blue vase. "I'm so sorry, Fox."

"Don't." He pressed his fingers to his eyes. "Just don't."

"Don't be sorry because you lost someone who must have mattered a great deal to you? Don't be sorry because you're hurting? What do you expect from me?"

"Right now, I don't have the first clue." He dropped his hands. "We met the spring before my twenty-third birthday, when I was in New York, in law school. She was a medical student. She wanted to work in emergency medicine. We met at a party. We started seeing each other. Casually. Casually at first, for a while. We were both studying, crazy schedules. She stayed in New York during the summer break, and I came home. But I went up a few times because things were getting more serious."

When he sat at the kitchen table, Layla opened the refrigerator. Instead of his usual Coke, she brought him a bottle of water, and one for herself.

"We moved in together that fall. Crappy place, the kind of crappy place you expect a couple of students to be able to afford in New York. We loved it. She loved it," he cor-

rected. "I was always a little out of step in New York, a little on edge. But she loved it, so I did because I loved her. I
loved her, Layla."

"I know. I can hear it in your voice."

"We made plans. Long-range, colorful plans, the way
you do. I never told her about the Hollow, not what was under it. I told myself we'd stopped it, during the last Seven.
We'd ended it, so I didn't need to tell her. I knew it was a
lie. I was sure it was a lie when the dreams came back. Cal
called. I still had weeks to go in the semester, my job as a
law clerk. I had Carly. But I had to come back. So I lied to
her, made excuses that were lies. Family emergency."

Not really a lie, he told himself now, as he'd told himself then. The Hollow was his family.

"I went back and forth, back and forth, for those weeks
between New York and the Hollow. And I piled lie on top
of lie. And I used my *gift* to read her so I could tell what
sort of lie would work best."

"Why didn't you tell her, Fox?"

"She'd never have believed me. There wasn't a fanciful
bone in her body. Carly was all about science. Maybe that
was part of the attraction. None of this would or could be
real for her, I told myself. But that was only part of the reason, maybe that was just another lie."

He paused, pinching the bridge of his nose to relieve
tension. "I wanted something that wasn't part of this. I
wanted the reality of her, of what we had away from here.
So when summer came and I knew I had to be here, I made
more excuses, told more lies. I picked fights with her. It
was better if she was pissed at me than that any part of this
touch her. I told her we needed to take a break, that I was
going home for a few weeks. Needed some space. I hurt
her, and justified it as protecting her."

He took a long, slow drink of water. "Things got ugly
before the seventh day of the seventh month. Fights and
fires, vandalism. We were busy, me and Cal and Gage. I

called her. I shouldn't have called her, but I did, to tell her
I missed her, that I'd be back in a couple of weeks. If I
hadn't wanted to hear her voice . . ."

"She came," Layla said. "She came to Hawkins Hollow."

"The day before our birthday, she drove down from
New York. She got directions to the farm, and showed up
on the doorstep. I wasn't there. Cal had an apartment in
town back then, and we were staying there. Carly called
from the kitchen of the farmhouse. Didn't think she'd miss
my birthday, did I?

"I was terrified. She didn't belong here, wasn't supposed to come here. When I got to the farm, nothing I said
would budge her. We were going to have this out, that was
her stand. Whatever was wrong, we were going to have it
out. What could I tell her?"

"What did you tell her?"

"Too much, not enough. She didn't believe me. Why
would she? She thought I was overstressed. She wanted me
to come back to New York for tests. I walked over, turned
on the burner on the stove, and stuck my hand on it."

He did the same now, in the little office kitchen, but
stopped short of holding his hand to the burner. What
would be the point now? "She had the expected reaction,
human and medical," he added, switching the burner off.
"Then she saw my hand healing. She was full of questions
then, more insistent that I go in for tests. I agreed to everything, anything, on the condition that she go back to New
York. She wouldn't, not unless I went with her, so we compromised. She promised she'd stay at the farm, day and
night, until I could go with her.

"She stayed that night, the next day, the next night. But
the night after . . ."

He walked to the sink, leaned against it as he looked out
the window to the neighboring houses and lawns beyond.
"Things were insane in town, and in the middle of it, my
mother called. She woke up when a car started outside, and

she'd gone running. Carly was gone. She'd driven off in the car she'd borrowed from a friend to drive down from New York. I was frantic, more frantic when Mom told me she'd been gone twenty minutes, maybe a little more. She hadn't been able to reach me, just got static when she tried."

When he broke off, when he came back to sit, Layla simply reached across the table to take his hand.

"There was a house on fire over on Mill. Cal got burned pretty bad when we got the kids out. Three kids. Jack Proctor, he ran the hardware store, had a shotgun. He was just walking along, shooting at anything that moved. One barrel, second barrel, reload. A couple of teenagers were raping a woman right on Main Street, right in front of the Methodist Church. There was more. No point going into it. I couldn't find her. I tried to find her thoughts, but there was so much interference. Like the static on the line. Then I heard her calling for me."

He didn't see the houses and lawns now. He saw the fire and the blood. "I ran, and Napper was there, blocking the sidewalk. He had his car pulled across it. Had a ball bat, and came at me with it, swinging. I wouldn't have gotten past him if Gage hadn't taken him down, and Cal right behind with his burns still healing. I climbed over the car and kept running, because I heard her calling me. The door to the library, the old library, was open. I could feel her now, how afraid she was. I went up the steps, yelling for her, so she'd know I was coming. Carts hurtling at me, books flying."

Because it was as real as yesterday, he squeezed his eyes shut, scrubbed his hands over his face. "I went down a couple of times, maybe more. I don't know, it's a blur. I got out on the roof. It was like a hurricane out there. Carly was on the ledge above, standing on that spit of stone. Her hands were bleeding; the stone was stained with it. I told her not to move. Don't move. Oh God, don't move. I'm coming up to get you. She looked at me, and she was in there, for an instant it let her come all the way out so she could look at me with all that fear. She said, 'Help me. Please, God, help me.' Then she went off."

Layla moved her chair beside his, and as she had the night before, drew his head down to her breast.

"I didn't get there in time."

"Not your fault."

"Every choice I made with her was the wrong one. All those wrong choices killed her."

"No. It killed her."

"She wasn't part of this. She'd never have been part of this except for me." He drew back, drew away so he could finish. "Last night, I dreamed," he began, and told her.

"I don't know what to say to you," Layla told him. "I don't know what I should say to you. But . . ." She took his hand, pressed it between her breasts. "My heart aches. I can't imagine what you feel if my heart aches. Others who know what happened, who know you, have told you it wasn't your fault. You'll accept that or you won't. If Carly loved you, she'd want you to accept it. I don't know if you were wrong to lie to her. And I don't know if I could accept as truth everything I know if I hadn't seen and experienced it myself. You wanted to keep her separate from this, to keep what you had, who you were, who she was apart from what you have, who you are here. I know what that's like, the wanting to keep everything in its proper place. But your worlds collided, Fox, and it was out of your control."

"If I'd made different choices."

"You might have changed it," she agreed. "Or it all would have taken a different route to the same end. How can you know? I'm not Carly, Fox. And like it or not, we share what's happening in the Hollow. They aren't all your choices now."

"I've seen too much death, Layla. Too much blood and pain. I know more's coming, and I know we'll all do whatever we can, whatever we have to do. But I don't know if I can survive if I lose you."

It was his sadness that lay on her heart now. The unbearable weight of his sorrow. "We'll find a way. You've always believed that. You've made me believe it. Come on. You're going upstairs to lie down. No arguments."

She cajoled, bullied, and nagged him upstairs. By the time she got him into bed, he was too exhausted to argue, or make suggestive jokes when she undressed him and tucked him in. When she was sure he was asleep, she ran down to close the office, then back up again to call Cal and ask him to come.

Layla put her finger to her lips when he came in the back way. "He's sleeping. He had a rough night, and a rough day. A nightmare," she added, gesturing him into the kitchen. "One that blurred me and Carly together."

"Oh. Shit."

She poured coffee without asking if he wanted it. "He told me about her, not without considerable struggle, and considerable pain. He's worn out now."

"Better he told you though. Fox doesn't do well holding stuff in." He started to drink, lowered the mug and frowned. "How did coffee get in here?"

"He bought me a coffeemaker."

Cal let out a half laugh. "He'll be all right, Layla. It hits him sometimes. Not often, but when it does, it hits hard."

"He blames himself, and that's stupid," she said so briskly, Cal lifted his brows. "But he loved her so he can't do anything else. He told me as soon as he knew she'd left the farm, he tried to find her. You were burned getting people out of a house—kids out—some guy was shooting up the town, that son of a bitch Napper came at him with a baseball bat, and he's sick because he couldn't stop her from jumping."

"Here's what he probably didn't tell you, stop me if I'm wrong. He was burned, too, not as bad as I was, that time, but bad enough. When the call came through, he took off ahead of me and Gage. On the way he kicked Proctor—that was the guy with the shotgun—square in the nuts,

tossed Gage the gun, and kept going. He punched out one
of two boys tearing into a woman on the sidewalk. I got the
other one, but it slowed me down. And there was Napper.
He got a good swing in with that bat. Broke Fox's arm."

"My God."

"Gage went in like a battering ram, and Fox took off
again. It took both of us to take Napper out. Fox was already
running up the stairs when we got inside the old library. And
it was hell in there. We were too late, too. She was jumping,
hell, she was diving off that ledge when we ran out on the
roof. I thought he was going to go over after her. He was
bloody from fights, from being rammed by books that flew
around like missiles, and God knew what else. There was
nothing he could do. He knows it. But once in a while it
takes ahold of him and gives him a good, hard squeeze."

"If she'd believed him, believed in him and done what
he asked—what she promised him—she'd be alive."

Cal kept his calm gray eyes even with hers. "That's
right. Exactly right."

"But he won't blame her."

"It's harder to blame the dead."

"Not for me, not at the moment. If she'd loved him
enough, believed in him enough to keep her promise—
only that, to keep her promise—he wouldn't have had to
risk his life to try to save her. I didn't say that to him, and
I'm going to try very hard not to. But I feel better now that
I've said it out loud."

"I've said it out loud, and to his face. I felt better, too,
but it didn't seem to do the same for him."

Layla nodded. "There's something else. Why Carly?
She wasn't part of the town, but she was infected, apparently, in minutes. So strongly that she committed suicide."

"It's happened before. It's mostly people who live in the
Hollow, but outsiders can get caught up."

"I bet most of them get caught up as victims of someone
who's infected. But here she is, the woman one of you

loves, and she's *caught up* immediately. I wonder about that, Cal, and I wonder how it was he heard her calling, that she was able to call him, that she was able to wait until he ran out on the roof so he had to watch her jump."

"Where are you going with this?"

"I'm not sure. But it might be worthwhile to have Cybil do a search on her, a genealogy. What if she's connected? What if Carly was on one of our twisted family trees?"

"And Fox just happened to fall in love with her?"

"That's the point. I don't think any of this just happened. Cal, have you ever been in love—really in love—with anyone before Quinn?"

"No." He answered without hesitation, then took another contemplative sip of coffee. "I can tell you Gage hasn't either."

"It uses emotions," she pointed out. "What better way to cause pain than to use love against one of you? To twist it like a knife in the heart? I don't think she was just infected, Cal. I think she was chosen."

Fifteen

~⟊~

THAT NIGHT, THEY READ, AND FOR THE FIRST time in many pages, the first in the many months that had passed for Ann, she wrote of Giles and Twisse.

It is a new year. What was has passed into what is, and what may be. Giles asked that I wait until the new to make record of what came to be in the old. Do such turnings of time truly form shields to block the dark?

He sent me away before I ever had birth pangs. He could not do what he had determined to do with me beside him. It shames me that I wept, even begged, that I would hurt him with my tears and my pleas. He would not be swayed, nor would he send me from him weeping. He dried my tears with his fingers, and pledged that if the gods were willing, we would find each other again.

At that moment, what did I care for gods, with their demands, their fickle natures and cold hearts? Yet my beloved had pledged to them before ever to me, and so I was no match for gods. He had his work, his war, he told me, and I—and he put his hands on my belly and the lives growing in them—had mine. Without me, his work would be nothing, and his war would be lost.

I did not leave him weeping, but with a kiss as our sons squirmed between us. I went with the husband of my cousin, away from my love, the cabin, the stone. I went away on a soft night in June, and as I did, he called these words to me.

It is not death.

There was kindness in my cousin's house, such kindness I have written on other pages. They took me in, kept my secret even when it came. Bestia, *the Dark.* Twisse. *I lay in fear and in pain on the cot in the small loft of their little house. It came in the lie of a man while my sons began their struggle toward life.*

I felt its weight on my heart. I felt its fingers gliding through the air, seeking me, like the hawk seeks the rabbit. But it did not find me. When my cousin's husband would not go with him, would not join him with torch and hate on the journey to my love, to the cabin, to the stone, I felt its fury. I think I felt its confusion. It had no power here.

And Fletcher, dear Fletcher, would be spared what would come to the Pagan Stone.

It would be tonight. I knew it at the first pain. An end that was not an end, and this beginning. These tied together as Giles wished it, as he willed it. Let the demon believe it was his work, his will, but it was Giles who turned the key. Giles who would pay for opening the lock.

My sweet cousin bathed my face. We could not call for the midwife, or for my mother, whom I longed for. It was not my beloved who paced the room below, but

Fletcher, so steady, so true. As the pain built until I could no longer hold back my cries, I saw my love standing by the stone. I saw the torches lighting the dark. I saw all that happened there.

Was this the delirium of birthing, or my small power? I think it was both, the first strengthening the other. He knew I was there. I pray this is not merely the wish of an aching heart, but truth. He knew I was with him, for I heard his thoughts reach for mine, and meet for one blessed moment.

Love, be safe, be strong.

He wore the bloodstone amulet, and those red drops gleamed in his fire, and in the torches they carried toward him.

I remembered his words to me when he spelled the stone.

Our blood, its blood, their blood. One for three. Three into one.

Now I pushed, pushed, through the pain, through the blood, fighting my war for life. I saw the faces of those who'd come for him. And grieved for what had been done to them, what would be done to them. I heard young Hester Deale condemn him, and me. And still I pushed, and pushed. Sweat and blood and half mad from it all. I watched her run as Giles freed her.

I saw the demon in the eyes of a man, and the hate in the men and the women who carried its curse like a plague.

It came in fire, my beloved's power. His sacrifice came in fire and in light, and in the blood that boiled around the stone. Our first son was born while that light blinded me. While my screams rose with the screams of the damned.

As the fire blazed, as it scorched the earth, my son loosed his first cry. In it, and in the cries of his brothers as they left my womb, I heard hope. I heard love.

"It confirms a lot of what we knew," Cal said when Quinn closed the book. "Adds more questions. It can't be a coincidence that Ann gave birth as Dent confronted Twisse."

"The power of life. Innocent life." Cybil ticked points off on her fingers. "Mystical life. Pain and blood—Ann's, Dent's, the demon's—the people Twisse brought with him. Interesting, too, that Twisse came to the house where Ann was hidden, and got nothing. Even then, he couldn't infect the people in that house, or on that land."

"Dent would have made sure of it, wouldn't he?" Layla suggested. "He wouldn't have sent Ann away without knowing she was safe. Ann, and their sons." She glanced at Fox. "And those who came after."

"She knew what was coming." As he had no taste for beer or wine, even Coke, Fox drank water. "She knew anyone there when Dent made his move was dead. Sacrificed."

"Who gets the blame?" Gage demanded. "They wouldn't have been there if Twisse hadn't brought them. And if Dent hadn't made his move, they'd have torched him."

"They were still human, still innocent. But," Cybil continued before he could argue. "I agree with you, for the most part. We can add that if Giles had done nothing, or whatever he'd done hadn't worked, the infection would only have grown until they ended up killing each other and feeding the beast. Ann accepted that. Apparently, I do, too."

"She mentioned the bloodstone." Quinn picked up her neglected wine. "Three into one, one into three, all that's easy enough to get. Three pieces of the stone, to each of you. The trick is making one again out of three."

"Blood." Cybil scanned the faces of the three men. "He told her blood. Have you tried using your blood? Your mixed blood?"

"We're not stupid." Gage slumped in his chair. "We've tried that more than once."

"We haven't." Layla raised her shoulders. "Its, ours, theirs. We—Quinn, Cybil, and I—have its blood. Fox, Cal,

Gage, that's the 'our blood' portion. It seems if you add them all, you get the theirs."

"Logical, smart, a little disgusting," Quinn decided. "Let's try it."

"Not tonight." Cybil waved Quinn back to her chair. "You don't just jump into bloodletting. Even at ten, these three knew such things required ritual. Let me do a little research. If I'm going to bleed, I don't want to waste it—or worse, call up the wrong side."

"Good point." Quinn settled back. "Pretty good point. But Jesus, it's hard not to just *do* something. It's been five days since the Big Evil Bastard has come out to play."

"Not so long," Gage said dryly, "when you've done a couple seven-year waits."

"It used a lot of juice—the fire at the farm, infecting Block." Cal glanced toward the front window, and the dark beyond it. "So it's juicing back up. The longer it takes, the harder it's going to come back at us."

"On that happy note, I'm heading out." Gage pushed to his feet. "Somebody let me know when I need to slash my wrist again."

"I'll send you a memo." Cybil rose as well. "Research time. I'll see all you handsome men at the O'Dells' tomorrow. I'm looking forward to it," she added, and gave Fox a brush on the shoulder as she passed.

"Cal, I need you to look at the toaster."

Cal's brows drew together as he glanced at Quinn. "The toaster? Why?"

"There's this thing." She wondered how an intelligent man could be so dense. Didn't he see it was time to clear the room and give Layla and Fox a minute alone? She grabbed his hand, tugged, rolled her eyes. "Come take a look at the thing."

"I guess I'd better get going, too," Fox said when they were alone.

"Why don't you stay? We don't have to . . . We can just sleep."

"Do I look that bad?"

"You look a little tired yet."

"Too much sleep does that, too."

And sad, she thought. Even when he smiled, she could see the shadow in his eyes. "We could go out. I know this nice little bar across the river."

He framed her face, touched his lips to hers. "I'm lousy company tonight, Layla, even for myself. I'm going to go home, and do some research. Of the kind that pays the bills. But I appreciate the offer. I'll come by, pick you up tomorrow."

"If you change your mind, just call."

But he didn't call, and she spent a restless night worrying about him, second-guessing herself. What if he had another nightmare and she wasn't there to help him through it?

And somehow he'd managed to get through much worse than nightmares for the last twenty years without her.

But he wasn't himself. She rolled in bed to stare at the ceiling. He wasn't Fox. The dream, the memories, the telling her about Carly—all of that had just snuffed out the light inside him. Comfort, anger, understanding, rest. None of those had brought the light back. When it came back, because she had to believe it would, would she put it out again if she told him her thoughts about Carly's connection? If her thoughts proved to be fact, would it be worse for him?

Because the thoughts and worries wouldn't stop circling, she got out of bed. Downstairs, she brewed herself a cup of Cybil's tea, carried it up to the office. While the house slept, she selected the correct color index cards to note down the key words and phrases she remembered from the reading. She studied the charts, the graphs, the map, willing for something new and illuminating to jump out at her.

She frowned over Cybil's notepads, but even after the

weeks of working together she couldn't decipher the odd shorthand Quinn often called Cybilquick. Though she'd already told both her friends the details, she sat now and typed up a report on Fox's dream, another, longer one of Carly's death.

For a time, she simply watched out the window, but the night was empty. When she returned to bed, when she finally slept, so were her dreams.

FOX KNEW HOW TO FEEL ONE THING AND PRO-ject another. His profession, after all, wasn't so different from Gage's. Law and gambling had a lot in common. Many times he had to show a certain face to a judge, a jury, a client, opposing counsel that might not reflect what he had in his heart, his head, his gut.

When he arrived with Layla, his brother, Ridge, and his family were already there, as was Sparrow and her guy. With so many people in the house, it was easy to deflect attention.

So he introduced Layla around, tickled his nephew. He teased Sparrow and hunkered down with her live-in, who was a vegan, played the concertina, and had a passion for baseball.

Because Layla seemed occupied, and he could *feel* her trying to scope out his mood, Fox slipped off to the kitchen. "Mmm, smell that tofu." He came up behind his mother at the stove, gave her a hug. "What else is on the menu?"

"All your favorites."

"Don't be a smart-ass."

"If I wasn't, how could I have passed the quality on to you?" She turned, started to give him her ritual four kisses, then frowned into his eyes. "What's wrong?"

"Nothing. Worked late, that's all."

Someone had talked Sparrow into picking up the fiddle

from the music room, so Fox used the music as an excuse to dance his mother around the room. He wouldn't fool her, he knew, but she'd leave it alone. "Where's Dad?"

"In the wine cellar." It was a highfalutin name for the section in the basement where they stored homemade wine. "I made deviled eggs."

"All is not lost."

He lowered his mother into a dip as Layla came in. "I thought I'd see if there was something I could do to help."

"Absolutely." Jo straightened, patted Fox's cheek. "What do you know about artichokes?" she asked Layla.

"They're a vegetable."

Jo smiled slyly, crooked her finger. "Come into my parlor."

Layla did better when put to work, and felt very at home when Brian O'Dell handed her a glass of apple wine, and added a kiss on the cheek.

People came in and out of the room. Cybil arrived with a miniature shamrock plant, Cal with a six-pack of Brian's favored beer. There was a lot of conversation in the kitchen, a lot of music outside of it. She saw Sparrow, who lived up to her name with her sweet, airy looks, walking her nephew outside so he could chase the chickens. And there was Ridge with his dreamy eyes and big hands tossing the boy in the air.

It was a happy house, Layla thought as she heard the boy's laughs and shouts through the windows. Even Ann had found some happiness here.

"Do you know what's wrong with Fox?" Jo kept her voice quiet as she and Layla worked side by side.

"Yes."

"Can you tell me?"

Layla glanced around. Fox had gone out again. He wasn't able to settle, she thought. Just wasn't able to settle quite yet. "He told me about Carly. Something happened to remind him and upset him, so he told me."

Saying nothing, Jo nodded and continued to prepare her vegetables. "He loved her very much."

"Yes. I know."

"It's good that you do, that you understand that. It's good that he told you, that he could tell you. She made him happy, then she broke his heart. If she'd lived, she'd have broken his heart in a different way."

"I don't know what you mean."

Jo looked at her. "She would never, never have seen him, not the whole of him, not everything he is. She would never have accepted the whole of him. Can you?"

Before Layla could answer, Fox shoved in the kitchen door with his nephew clinging like a monkey to his back. "Somebody get this thing off me!"

More bodies pressed into the kitchen, more drinks were poured. Hands grabbed at the finger food spread on platters on the sturdy kitchen table. Into the noise, Sage walked, holding the hand of a pretty brunette with clear hazel eyes who could only be Paula.

"I'll have some of that." Sage picked up the wine bottle and poured a large glass. "Paula won't." Sage let out a breathless, giddy laugh. "We're having a baby."

She was still laughing as she turned to Paula, as Paula touched her face. They kissed in the old farmhouse kitchen while shouts of congratulations rang around them.

"We're having a baby," Sage said again, then turned to Fox. "Good job." And threw herself into his arms. "Mom." She swung from Fox to her mother, to her father, her siblings while Fox stood, a dazed expression on his face.

What Layla saw was Paula stepping through the excitement. As she had with Sage, Paula touched Fox's face. "Thank you." And she pressed her cheek to his. "Thank you, Fox."

What Layla saw was the light come back into his eyes. She saw the sadness drop away, and the joy leap into its place. Her own eyes went damp as she watched him kiss

Paula, and wrap his arm around his sister so that the three of them stood for a moment as a unit.

Then Jo moved into her vision, stopped in front of her. She kissed Layla on the forehead, on one cheek, the other, then lightly on the lips. "You've just answered my question."

THE WEEKEND SLID INTO THE WORKWEEK, AND still the Hollow stayed quiet. Rain dogged the sky, keeping the temperatures lower than most hoped for in April. But farmers tilled their fields, and bulbs burst into bloom. Pink cups covered the tulip magnolia behind Fox's offices, and spears that would open into tulips of butter yellow and scarlet waved in the easy breeze. Along High Street, the Bradford pears gleamed with bud and bloom. Windows gleamed as well, as merchants and homeowners scrubbed away the winter dull. When the rains passed, the town Fox loved shone like a jewel beneath the mountains.

He'd wanted a sunny day for it. Taking advantage of it, he pulled Layla up from her desk. "We're going out."

"I was just—"

"You can just when we get back. I checked the calendar, and we're clear. Do you see that out there? The strange, unfamiliar light? It's called the sun. Let's go get us a little."

He solved the matter by pulling her to the door, outside, then locking up himself.

"What's gotten into you?"

"Sex and baseball. The young man's fancies of spring."

The ends of her hair danced in the breeze as she narrowed her eyes at him. "We're not having sex and/or playing baseball at noon on a Wednesday afternoon."

"Then I guess I have to settle for a walk. We'll be able to do some real gardening in a couple more weeks."

"You garden?"

"You can take the boy off the farm. I do some containers

for the front of the office. I'd plant and Mrs. H would kibitz."

"I'm sure I can kibitz."

"Counting on it. You girls could put in a nice little vegetable and herb patch in back of your house, some flower beds street side."

"Could we?"

He took her hand, swung it lightly as they walked. "Don't like to get your hands dirty?"

"I might. I don't have any real gardening experience. My mother puttered around a little, and I had a couple of houseplants in my apartment."

"You'd be good at it. Color, shapes, tones, textures. You like doing what you're good at." He turned off the sidewalk toward the building that had housed the gift shop. Its display window was empty now. Depressingly so.

"It looks forlorn," Layla decided.

"Yeah, it does. But it doesn't have to stay that way."

Her eyes widened when he pulled out keys and unlocked the front door. "What are you doing?"

"Showing you possibilities." He stepped in, flipped on the lights.

Like many of the businesses on Main, it had been a home first. The entrance was wide, the old wood floors clean and bare. On the side, a stairway curved up with its sturdy banister smooth from the slide of generations of hands. Straight back an open doorway led to three more rooms, stacked side by side. The middle one held the back entrance, and its tidy covered porch that opened to its narrow strip of yard where a lilac waited to bloom.

"You would hardly know it was ever here." Layla brushed her fingertips over the stair rail. "The gift shop. Nothing left of it but some shelves, some marks on the wall where things were hung."

"I like empty buildings, for their potential. This one has plenty. Solid foundation, good plumbing—both that and the electric are up to code—location, light, conscientious landlord. Roomy, too. The gift shop used the second floor for storage and office space. Probably a good plan. If you have customers going up and down steps, you're just asking one to trip and sue you."

"So speaks the lawyer."

"It needs the nail holes plugged, fresh paint. The woodwork's nice." He skimmed a hand over some trim. "Original. Somebody made this a couple hundred years ago. Adds character, respects the history. What do you think of it?"

"The woodwork? It's gorgeous."

"The whole place."

"Well." She wandered, walking slowly as people did in empty buildings. "It's bright, spacious, well kept, with just enough creak in the floors to add to that character you spoke of."

"You could do a lot with this place."

She swung back to him. "I could?"

"The rent's reasonable. The location's prime. Plenty of space. Enough to curtain off an area in the back for a couple of dressing rooms. You'd need shelves, displays, racks, I guess, to hang clothes." As he looked around, he hooked his thumbs in his front pockets. "I happen to know a couple of guys very handy with tools."

"You're suggesting I open a shop here?"

"Doing what you're good at. There's nothing like that in town. Nothing like it for miles. You could make something here, Layla."

"Fox, that's just . . . out of the question."

"Why?"

"Because I . . ." Let me count the ways, she thought. "I could never afford it, even if—"

"That's why they have business loans."

"I haven't given any serious thought to opening my own place in, well, in years, really. I don't know where I'd begin even if I was sure I wanted to open my own place. For God's sake, Fox, I don't know what's going to happen tomorrow much less a month from now. Six months from now."

"But what do you want today?" He moved toward her. "I know what I want. I want you. I want you to be happy. I want you to be happy here, with me. Jim Hawkins will rent it to you, and you won't have any trouble getting a start-up loan. I talked to Joe at the bank—"

"You talked to them, about this? About me?"

"Not specifics. Just general information. Ballparking what you'd need to start up, what you'd need to qualify, the cost of licensing. I've got a file. You like files, so I put together a file."

"Without consulting me."

"I put together the file so I could consult you and you'd have something tangible to look over when you thought about it."

She walked away from him. "You shouldn't have done all that."

"It's the sort of thing I do. This—" he swept his arm in the air "—is the sort of thing you do. You're not going to tell me you're going to be happy doing office work the rest of your life."

"No, I'm not going to tell you that." She turned back. "I'm not going to tell you I'm going to dive headfirst into starting a business that I'm not sure I want in the first place, in a town that may not exist in a few months. And if I want my own business, I haven't thought about having it here. If I want my own, how can I *think* about all the details involved when all this madness is going on?"

He was silent a moment, so silent she swore she heard the old house breathing.

"It seems to me it's most important to go after what you want when there's madness going on. I'm asking you to think about it. More, I guess I'm asking you to think about something you haven't yet. Staying. Open the shop, manage my office, found a nudist colony, or take up macrame,

I don't care as long as it makes you happy. But I want you to think about staying, Layla, not just to destroy ancient fucking evil, but to live. To have a life, with me."

As she stared at him, he stepped closer. "Put this in one of your slots. I'm in love with you. Completely, absolutely, no-turning-back in love with you. We could build something good, and solid, and real. Something that makes every day count. That's what I want. So you think about it, and when you know, you tell me what you want."

He walked back to the door, opened it, and waited for her.

"Fox—"

"I don't want to hear you don't know. I've already got that. Let me know when you do. You're upset and a little ticked off, I get that, too," he said as he locked up. "Take the rest of the day off."

She started to object, he saw it on her face. Then she changed her mind. "All right. There are some things I need to do."

"I'll see you later then." He stepped back, stopped. "The building's not the only thing with potential," he told her. And he turned, walked away down the bricked sidewalk in the April sunshine.

Sixteen

~⟟~

HE THOUGHT ABOUT GETTING DRUNK. HE COULD call Gage, who'd sit and drink coffee or club soda, bitching only for form, and spend the evening in some bar getting steadily shit-faced. Cal would go, too; he had only to ask. That's what friends were for, being the company misery loved.

Or he could just pick up the beer—maybe a bottle of Jack for a change of pace—take it to Cal's and get his drunk on there.

But he knew he wouldn't do either of those things. Planning to get drunk took all the fun out of it. He preferred it to be a happy accident. Work, Fox decided, was a better option than getting deliberately trashed.

He had enough to keep him occupied for the rest of the day, particularly at the easy pace he liked to work. Handling the office on his own for an afternoon added the perk of giving him time and space to brood. Fox considered brooding an inalienable human right, unless it dragged out more than three hours, at which point it became childish indulgence.

Did she really think he'd crossed some line and gone behind her back? That he tried to manipulate, bully, or pressure? Manipulation wasn't beyond him, he admitted, but that just hadn't been the case with this. Knowing her, he'd believed she'd appreciate having some facts, projected figures, the steps, stages compiled in an orderly fashion. He'd equated handing them to her on the same level as handing her a bouquet of daffodils.

Just a little something he'd picked up because he was thinking about her.

He stood in the center of his office, juggling the three balls as he walked back over it all in his mind. He'd wanted to show her the building, the space, the possibilities. And yeah, he'd wanted to see her eyes light up as she saw them, as she opened herself to them. That had been strategy, not manipulation. Jesus, it wasn't like he'd signed a lease for her, or applied for a loan, a business license. He'd just taken the time to find out what it would take for her to do those things.

But there was one thing he hadn't factored into that strategy. He'd never considered that *she* wasn't considering staying in the Hollow. Staying with him.

He dropped one of the balls, managed to snag it on the bounce. Setting himself, he started the circle again.

If he'd made a mistake it was in assuming she loved him, that she intended to stay. He'd never questioned, not seriously—her conviction matched his—that there would be something to stay for, something to build on, after the week of July seventh. He believed he'd felt those things from her, but he had to accept now those feelings and needs were just a reflection of his own.

That wasn't just a bitter pill to swallow, but the kind that caught in your throat and choked you for a while before you managed to work it down. But like it or not, he thought, a guy had to take his medicine.

She wasn't required to feel what he felt or want what he wanted. God knew he'd been raised to respect, even require, individuality. It was better to know if she didn't share his feelings, his wants, better to deal with the reality rather than the fantasy. That was another nasty pill, as he'd had a beauty of a fantasy going.

Her smart, fashionable shop a couple blocks up from his office, Fox mused as he dropped the balls back in his drawer. Maybe grabbing lunch together a couple times a week. Scouting for a house in town, like that old place on the corner of Main and Redbud. Or a place a little ways out, if she liked that better. But an old house they could put their mark on together. Something with a yard for kids and dogs and a garden.

Something in a town that was safe and whole, and no longer threatened. A porch swing—he had a fondness for them.

And that was the problem, wasn't it? he admitted, walking to the window to study the distant roll of the mountains. All that was what he wanted, what he hoped for. All that couldn't be if it didn't mesh with her wants and hopes and visions.

So he'd swallow that, too. They had today to get through, and all the others until Hawkins Hollow was clean. Futures were just that—the tomorrow. Maybe the foundation for them couldn't and shouldn't be built when the ground was still unsettled.

Priorities, O'Dell, he reminded himself, and sat back at his desk. He pulled up his own files on the journals to begin picking through his notes.

And the first spider crawled out of his keyboard.

It bit the back of his hand, striking quickly before he could jerk back. The pain was instant and amazing, a vicious ice-pick jab that dug fire under the skin. As he shoved away, they poured out like black water, from the keys, from the drawers.

And they grew.

LAYLA WALKED INTO THE HOUSE WITH HER SYStem still reeling. Escape, that's what she'd done. Fox had given her the out, and she leaped at it. Walk away, don't deal with this now.

He loved her. Had she known it? Had she slipped that knowledge into a neat file, tucked it away until it was more convenient or more sensible to examine it?

He loved her. He wanted her to stay. More, he wanted her to commit to him, to the town. To herself, Layla admitted. In his Fox-like way, he'd laid it all out for her, presented it to her in a way he'd believed she'd appreciate.

What he'd done, Layla thought, was scare her to death.

Her own shop? That was just one of the airy little dreams she'd enjoyed playing with years before. One she'd let go—almost. Hawkins Hollow? Her commitment there was to save it, and to—even though it sounded pretentious—fulfill her destiny. Anything beyond that was too hard to see. And Fox?

He was the most beautiful man she'd ever known.

Hardly a wonder she was reeling.

She stepped into the office where Quinn and Cybil worked on dueling keyboards.

"Fox is in love with me."

Her fingers still flying, Quinn didn't bother to look up. "Bulletin!"

"If you knew, why didn't I?" Layla demanded.

"Because you've been too worried about being in love with him." Cybil's fingers paused after another click of the mouse. "But the rest of us have been watching the little hearts circling over your heads for weeks. Aren't you home early?"

"Yeah. I think we had a fight." Layla leaned against the doorjamb, rubbed her shoulder as if it ached.

Something ached, she realized, but it was too deep to reach.

"It didn't seem like a fight, except I was annoyed, among other things. He took me up to the building where the gift shop used to be. It's cleared out now. Then he started talking about potential, how I should open a boutique there, and—"

"What a great idea." Quinn stopped now, beamed enthusiasm over Layla like sunbeams over a meadow. "Speaking as someone who's going to be living here, I'll be your best customer. Urban fashion in small-town America. I'm already there."

"I can't open a shop here."

"Why?"

"Because . . . Do you have any idea what's involved in starting up a business, opening a retail store, even a small one?"

"No." Quinn replied. "You would, and I imagine Fox does, on the legal front. I'd help. I love a project. Would there be buying trips? Can you get it for me wholesale?"

"Q, take a breath," Cybil advised. "The big hurdle isn't the logistics, is it, Layla?"

"They're a hurdle, a big one. But . . . God, can we be realistic, just the three of us, right now? There might not be a town after July. Or there might be a town that, after a week of violence and destruction and death, settles down for the next seven years. If I could even think about starting my own business with everything else we have to think about, I'd have to be out of my mind to consider having one here at Demon Central."

"Cal has one. He's not out of his mind."

"I'm sorry, Quinn, I didn't mean—"

"No, that's okay. I'm pointing that out because people do have businesses here, and homes here. Otherwise, there's no real point to any of what we're doing. But if it's not right for you, then it's not."

Layla threw out her arms. "How can I know? Oh, he apparently thinks he knows. He's already talked to Jim Hawkins about renting me the building, talked to the bank about a start-up loan."

"Oops," Cybil murmured.

"He has a *file* for me on it. And okay, okay, to be fair, he didn't go to Mr. Hawkins or the bank about me, specifically. He just got basic information and figures. Projections."

"I take back the oops. Sorry, sweetie, that sounds like a man who just wanted to give you the answers to questions you'd have if this was appealing to you." Considering, Cybil tucked her legs up in the lotus position. "I'll happily reinstate the oops, even add a 'screw him' if you tell me he tried to shove it down your throat and got pissy about it."

"No." Trapped by logic, Layla let out a huge sigh. "I guess I was the one who got pissy, but it all just blindsided me. He said he was in love with me, and he wanted me to be happy, to have what I wanted. He thought my own place was something I wanted. That he was, that a life with him was."

"If it's not, if he's not, you have to tell him straight," Quinn said after a long moment. "Or I'll be forced to aim Cybil's 'screw you' in your direction. He doesn't deserve to be left dangling."

"How can I tell him what I don't know?" Layla stepped out, walked to her own room and closed the door.

"Tougher for her than you," Cybil commented. "You always made up your heart in a snap, Q. Or your mind. Sometimes both agreed. If not, you bounced. That's your way. With you and Cal, it all clicked. The idea of marrying the guy, staying here, it's a pretty easy slide for you."

"I love the guy. Where we live isn't as important to me as living together."

"And your keyboard fits anywhere. If you need to pop off somewhere for a story, Cal's going to be easy with that. The big change here for you, Quinn, is being in love and settling down. Those aren't the only big changes for Layla."

"Yeah, yeah, yeah. I'd like—and it's not just because I've got stars in my eyes—I'd like to see the two of them work it out. And for purely selfish reasons, I'd love to have Layla stay. But if she decided it's not for her, then it's not. I should go get ice cream."

"Of course you should."

"No, seriously. She's bummed out. She needs girl-friends and ice cream. As soon as I finish this up, I'm going to walk over and buy some. No, I'll go now, and walk around the block a few times first so I can eat my share without guilt."

"Get some pistachio," Cybil called out as Quinn left the room.

Quinn stopped by Layla's room, tapped on the door, eased it open. "Sorry if I was harsh."

"You weren't. You gave me more to think about."

"While you're thinking, I'm going out for some exercise. On the way back, I'm picking up ice cream. Cybil wants pistachio. What's your poison?"

"Cookie dough."

"Got you covered."

When the door closed, Layla pushed at her hair. A little caloric bliss was just the ticket. Ice cream and friends. She might as well complete the trio of comfort with a hot shower and cozy clothes.

She undressed, then chose cotton pants and her softest sweatshirt. In her robe, she decided what the hell, and opted to give herself a facial before the shower.

How many women in town would actually shop in a place stocked as she'd want to stock a boutique? How many, she thought as she cleansed, exfoliated, would really support that sort of business, instead of heading straight out to the mall? Even if the Hollow was just a normal small town, how could she afford to invest so much—time, money, emotion, hope—into something logic told her would probably fail within two years?

Applying the mask, she toyed with the idea of colors, layout. Curtained off dressing rooms? Absolutely not. It was just like a man to suggest that women felt comfortable stripping down behind a sheet of fabric in a public place.

Walls and doors. Had to be secure, private, and something the customer could lock from the inside.

And damn him for making her speculate about dressing rooms.

I'm completely in love with you.

Layla closed her eyes. Even now, hearing him say those words in her head made her heart do a long, slow roll.

But she hadn't been able to say the words back to him, hadn't been able to respond. Because they hadn't been standing in an old building full of character in a normal small town. They'd been standing in one that had been battered and bruised, in a town that was cursed. Wasn't that the word for it? And at any time, it all could go up in flames.

Better to take one cautious step at a time, to tell him it would be best for both of them—for all of them—to go on just as they were. It was, most essentially, a matter of getting through.

In the shower, she let the water soothe. She'd make it up to him. Maybe she wasn't sure what she wanted, or what she dared to wish for. But she knew she loved him. Maybe that could be enough to get them through.

As she lifted her face to the spray, the snake began its silent slither out of the drain.

QUINN STARTED OFF WITH A POWER WALK BEcause it made her feel righteous. It wasn't a hardship to do the extra stint of exercise—not with ice cream at the end of it—and with spring stirring all around. Daffodils and hyacinths, she thought, swinging her arms to kick up her heart rate. Blooming trees and grass starting to green up.

It was a damn pretty town, and Cybil was right. It had been easy for her to slide into the idea of living there. She liked the old houses, the covered porches, the sloping lawns as the ground rose. She liked, being a sociable sort, coming to know so many people by name.

She turned at a corner, kept up the steady pace. Pistachio and cookie dough, she thought. And she might go for the fudge ripple, and screw the healthy, balanced dinner idea. Her friend needed ice cream and girl vibes. Who was she to count the calories?

She paused a moment, frowned at the houses on the corners. Hadn't she already passed this corner? She could've sworn . . . shaking her head, she picked up her pace again, turned, and in moments found herself back at the exact same spot.

A trickle of fear worked down her spine. Deliberately, she turned the opposite way, kicked up to a jog. There was the same corner, the same houses. She ran straight, only to arrive at the same spot, as if the street itself shifted its position to taunt her. Even when she tried to run to one of the houses, call for help, her feet were somehow back on the sidewalk again, back on that same corner.

When the dark dropped on her, she ran full out, chased by her own panic.

IN THE BOWLING CENTER, CAL STOOD BESIDE HIS father, hands on hips as they watched the new (reconditioned) automatic scoring systems being installed.

"It's going to be great."

"Hope you're right." Jim puffed out his cheeks. "Big expense."

"Gotta spend it to make it."

They'd had to close the lanes for the day, but the arcade

and the grill were both open. Cal's idea there had been to have anyone who came in get a look at the process—the progress.

"Computers run everything. I know how that sounds," Jim muttered before Cal could speak. "It sounds like my old man crabbing when I finally talked him into going with automatic pin setters instead of having a couple guys back there putting it up by hand."

"You were right."

"Yeah, I was right. I couldn't help but be right." Jim tucked his hands into the pockets of his traditional khakis. "I guess you're feeling the same way about this."

"It's going to streamline the business, and increase it. It's going to pay for itself in the long run."

"Well, we're in it now, so we'll see how it goes. And damn it, that sounds like my old man, too."

With a laugh, Cal patted Jim's shoulder. "I've got to take Lump out for a walk, Grandpa. You want to come along?"

"No. I'll stay here, scowl some and complain about newfangled ways."

"I'll be back in a few minutes."

Amused, Cal went up to get Lump. The dog enjoyed going out when they were in town, but was filled with sorrow at the sight of the leash. It gleamed out of his eyes as Cal clipped it to his collar.

"Don't be such a baby. It's the law, pal. I know and you know you're not going to do anything stupid, but the law's the law. Or do you want me to have to come up to the pen and bail you out?"

Lump walked, head lowered like a prisoner of war, as they went down the back stairs, and out. Since they'd had this routine for a while, Cal knew the dog would perk up, as much as Lump ever perked, after the first few minutes.

He kept his eyes on the dog, waiting for the moment of acceptance as they started around the building. Unless they were walking to Quinn's, Lump preferred his leg-stretching along Main Street, where Larry at the barbershop would wander out as they passed, and give Lump a biscuit and a rub.

Cal waited patiently while Lump lifted his leg and peed lavishly on the trunk of the big oak between the buildings, then let the dog lead him out to the sidewalk on Main.

There, Cal's heart slammed into his throat.

Scarred and broken asphalt marred the street; charred bricks heaved out of the sidewalk. The rest of the town was gone, leveled into rubble. And the rubble still smoked. Blackened, splintered trees lay like maimed soldiers on jagged shards of glass and blood-smeared stone. Scorched to ruin, the grass of the Square and its cheerful spring plantings steamed. Bodies, or the horrible remnants of them, scattered over the ground, hung obscenely from the torn trees.

Beside him, Lump quivered, then sat on his haunches, lifted his head, and howled. Still holding the leash, Cal ran to the entrance of the bowling center, yanked at the door. But the door refused him. There was no sound, within or without, but his pounding fists and frantic calls.

When his hands were bloody from the beating, he ran, the dog galloping beside him. He had to get to Quinn.

GAGE WASN'T SURE WHY HE'D COME BY. HE'D BEEN itchy at home—well, at Cal's. Home was wherever he stayed long enough to bother to unpack his bag. He started to knock, then shrugging, just opened the unlocked door of the rental house. His concession to the inhabitants was to call out.

"Anybody home?"

He heard the footsteps, knew they were Cybil's before she appeared at the top of the stairs. "I'm anybody." She started down. "What brings you by before happy hour?"

She had her hair scooped back at the nape—all that thick, curling black—as she was prone to do when working. Her feet were bare. Even wearing faded jeans and a sweater, she managed to look like stylish royalty.

It was a hell of a knack, in Gage's opinion. "I had a conversation with Professor Litz, the demon expert in Europe. I told him about the idea of a blood ritual. He's against it."

"Sounds like a sensible man." She angled her head. "Come on back. You can have what's probably your tenth cup of coffee of the day, and I'll have some tea while you tell me his very sensible reasons."

"His first, and most emphatic echoed something you said." Gage followed her into the kitchen. "We could let something out we aren't prepared for. Something worse, or stronger, simply because of the ritual."

"I agree." She put the kettle on, and while it heated, started to measure for a fresh pot of coffee. "Which makes it essential not to rush into it. To gather all information possible first, and to proceed with great care."

"So you're voting to do it."

"I am, or I'm leaning that way, once we're as protected as possible. Aren't you?"

"I figure the odds at fifty-fifty, and that's good enough."

"Maybe, but I'm hoping to weigh them a little heavier in our favor first." She lifted a hand, pressed it against her eye. "I've been . . ."

"What is it?"

"Maybe I've been at the monitor too long today. My eyes are tired." She reached up to open the cupboard for cups, missed the handle by inches. "My eyes are . . . Oh God. I can't see. I can't see."

"Hold on. Here, let me look." When he took her shoulders to turn her, she gripped his arm.

"I can't see anything. It's all gray. Everything's gray."

He turned her around, bit off his own sharp intake of breath. Her eyes, those exotic gypsy eyes, were filmed over white.

"Let's sit you down. It's a trick. It's just another trick. It's not real, Cybil."

But as she clung to him, shuddering, he felt himself fade away.

He stood in the dull and dingy apartment he'd once shared with his father over the bowling alley. The smells struck him with violent memory. Whiskey, tobacco, sweat, unwashed sheets, and dishes.

There was the old couch with the frayed arms, and the folding chair with the duct-taped X over the torn seat. The lamp was on, the pole lamp beside the couch. But that had been broken, Gage thought. Years ago, that had been broken when he'd shoved his father back. When he'd finally been big enough, strong enough to use his fists.

No, Gage thought. No, I won't be here again. He walked to the door, grabbed the knob. It wouldn't budge, no matter how he turned, how he pulled. And in shock he looked at the hand on the knob, and saw the hand of a child.

Out the window then, he told himself as sweat slid down his back. It wouldn't be the first time he'd escaped that way. Fighting the urge to run, he went into his old room—unmade bed, a scatter of school books, single dresser, single lamp. Nothing showing. Any treasures—comics, candy, toys—he'd hid away, out of sight.

The window refused to open. When he was desperate enough to try, the glass in it wouldn't break. Whirling around, he looked for escape, and saw himself in the mirror over the dresser. Small, dark, thin as a rail. And terrified.

A lie. Another lie. He wasn't that boy now, he told himself. Wasn't that helpless boy of seven or eight. He was a man, full grown.

But when he heard the door slam open, when he heard the stumbling tread of his drunken father, it was the boy who trembled.

FOX BEAT AND KICKED AT THE SPIDERS. THEY covered his desk now, spilled in a waterfall from the edge to the floor. They leaped on him, hungrily bit. Where they bit, their poison burned, and the flesh swelled and broke like rotted fruit.

His mind couldn't cool, couldn't steady, not with dozens of them crawling up his legs, down his shirt. He stomped them into the floor, into the rug, while his breath whistled out between gritted teeth. The pocket doors he'd left open slammed shut. As he backed against them, the windows ran black with spiders.

He shook like a man in a fever, but he shut his eyes, ordered himself to control his breathing. As they crawled and clawed and bit, as they covered him he wanted to give in and scream.

I've seen worse than this, he told himself. His heart pounded, hammer to anvil, as he struggled for some level of calm. Sure, I've seen worse. I've had worse, you fucker. Just a bunch of spiders. I'd call the exterminator tomorrow except *they're not real*, you asshole. I can wait you out. I can wait till you run out of juice.

The sheer rage inside him won over the fear and disgust until he could bring his heart rate down. "Play all the games you want, you bastard. We won't be playing when we come for you. This time, we'll *end* you."

He felt the rush of cold that burned as bright as the bites. *You will die screaming.*

Don't count on it, Fox thought, gathering himself. Don't you fucking count on it. He grabbed one of the spiders on his arm, crushed it in his fist. Let the blood and puss run like fire through his fingers.

They dropped from him, first one, then another. It was they who screamed as they died. With his swollen hands, Fox pushed open the doors. And now he ran. Not for himself, but for Layla. One of the screams inside his head was hers.

As he ran, he bled; as he bled, he healed.

He cut through buildings, leaped fences, sprinted across yards. He saw Quinn standing in the middle of the street, shaking.

"I'm lost. I'm lost. I don't know what to do. I can't get home."

He grabbed her hand, dragged her with him.

"It's the same place. It's always the same place. I can't—"

"Shut it down," he snapped at her. "Shut everything down."

"I don't know how long. I don't even know how long I've been . . . Cal!"

She jerked away from Fox, and whatever she had left, she pulled into her, and ran to where Cal stood with his howling dog.

"It's gone, it's all gone." He caught Quinn in his arms, pressed his face to her neck. "I thought you were gone. I couldn't find you."

"It's lies." Fox shoved Cal back. "It's lies. My God, can't you hear her screaming?"

He hurtled across the street, up it, then burst into the rental house. Charging up the stairs he felt his fear tearing at him as the spiders had torn at his flesh. Her screaming stopped. But its echo led him to her, had him shoving open the bathroom door where she lay naked and unconscious on the floor.

In the kitchen, Cybil cried out when she heard the front door slam open. She threw her arms up, took a blind step forward. The gray wavered, thinned. And she sobbed as her vision cleared. She saw Gage, only Gage, pale as a sheet, staring back at her. When she threw herself into his arms, he caught her, and held her as much for himself as for her.

Seventeen

◦⟋◦

SHE WAS WET AND COLD, SO FOX CARRIED LAYLA to the bed, wrapped the blanket around her. A bruising scrape marred her temple, and would undoubtedly ache when she came to. No blood, no breaks as far as he could see on a quick and cursory look. Getting her warm and dry were priorities, he thought. Then he'd make certain, then he'd look closer, look deeper. He'd barely had time to check her pulse before Quinn and Cal rushed in.

"Is Layla— Oh, God."

"Fainted, I think. I think she just fainted," Fox told Quinn when she dropped down beside him. "Maybe hit her head. Something happened when she was in the shower. I don't think there's anything there now, but Cal—"

"I'll check."

"You said . . . Sorry." Quinn mopped at her own tears. "Really bad day. You said you heard her screaming."

"Yeah, I heard her." Her terror had been so huge, he thought as he pushed her wet hair away from her face. It had reached out and gripped him by the throat, had filled his head with her screams. "I heard all of you."

"What?"

"I guess our Bat Signal worked. It was jumbled, but I heard all of you. She needs a towel. Her hair's wet."

"Here." Cal handed him one. "Bathroom's clear."

"Cybil, Gage?"

Cal squeezed the hand Quinn held out to him. "I'll go check on them. Stay here."

"What happened to you?"

Fox shook his head. "Later." He lifted Layla's head to spread the towel under her hair. "She's coming around. Layla." Relief gushed through him when her eyelids fluttered. "Come on back, Layla. It's all right. It's over."

She surfaced with a wheezing gasp, with her hands slapping wildly, her eyes wide with horror.

"Stop. Stop." He did all he could think to do. He wrapped himself around her, pushed calm into her mind. "It's over. I've got you."

"In the shower."

"Gone. They're gone." But he could see in her mind how they'd come out of the drain, slid across the tiles.

"I couldn't get out. The door wouldn't open. They were everywhere, they were all over me." Shuddering, shuddering, she burrowed against him. "They're gone? You're sure?"

"I'm sure. Are you hurt? Let me see."

"No, I don't think . . . My head a little. And—" She focused on him. "Your face! Oh God, your hand. It's swollen."

"It's healing. It's okay." And the healing pain was nothing against the overwhelming relief. "It looks like Twisse took a shot at all of us at once."

Quinn nodded. "He hit me and Cal. Grand slam."

"More a clean sweep," Cybil said from the doorway. "He hit me and Gage, too. Six for six. Fox, why don't you go on downstairs? Your pals are still pretty shaken. We'll help Layla get dressed, then we'll be down in a few."

She was ice pale, he noted. It was the first time he'd seen Cybil that far off her stride in the months he'd known her. Quinn was already rising, going to her. Because the room became essentially and completely female again, Fox decided it was probably best for each sector to retreat to its particular corner, take a deep breath before mixing again.

"All right." But he touched Layla's face, kissed her gently. "I'll be right downstairs."

Times like these, fox thought, called for whiskey. He found the single, unopened bottle of Jameson among the wine, and figured it had been Cal's contribution to the liquor supply. He got glasses, ice, and poured a generous two fingers in each.

"Good thinking." Cal downed half of his in one swallow, and still his eyes remained haunted. "You healed up. You looked bad when I saw you outside."

"Spiders. Lots of them. Big bastards."

"Where?"

"My office."

"The town was gone for me." Cal studied the whiskey, swirled it. "I came out of the center with Lump, and it was gone. Like a bomb had gone off. Buildings leveled, fire and smoke. Bodies. Jesus, pieces of them everywhere." He took another, slower sip. "We'll need to write this down, get everybody's deal."

"Oh yeah, that'll help." Gage downed a single, bitter swallow. "It got us, big-time. Now we're going to take minutes of the meeting."

"You got better?" Cal shot back. "You got the final solution, bro? Because if you do, don't hold back."

"I know we're not going to talk it to death. And sitting

around taking notes doesn't mean dick unless you're writing a book. That's your lady's business, not mine."

"So what are you going to do? Take a walk? You're good at that. Are you just going to catch a plane to wherever the hell and come back for the finale? Or do you want to just skip that part this year?"

"I come back to this hellhole because I swore on it." Rage whirling around him like wind, Gage moved in on Cal. "If I hadn't, it could blow to hell as far as I'm concerned. It doesn't mean a damn to me."

"Not much does."

"Stop!" Fox's voice snapped out as he wedged between them. "It doesn't do any good to start swiping at each other."

"Maybe we should make peace signs and daisy chains."

"Look, Gage. If you want out, there's the goddamn door. And if all you can do is kick him while he's down," Fox added, swinging around to Cal, "don't let the same goddamn door hit you on the ass on your way out."

"I'm not kicking anyone, and who the hell asked you?"

Raised voices had Cybil quickening her steps. She took stock of the scene in the kitchen quickly, and stepped into it before someone threw a punch. "Well, this is productive."

She walked right in the middle of three furious men, snatched the glass out of Gage's hand, drank. And her voice held the faintest edge of boredom. "At least someone had the good sense to get out the whiskey before the testosterone attack. If you boys want to fight, go outside and beat on each other. You'll heal quickly enough, but the furniture in here won't."

Fox settled down first. He set the whiskey he no longer wanted aside, gave a sheepish shrug. "They started it."

Appreciating him, Cybil cocked a brow. "And do you do everything they do? Jump off bridges, play with matches? Let's try this instead. I'm going to put food and drink together to address that basic human need. The comfort it brings should help us get through telling each other what happened."

"Gage doesn't want to talk," Cal said.

"Neither do I." She looked at Gage as she spoke. "But I'm going to. It's another basic human need, and shows us we've got that all over the Big Evil Bastard." Smiling with lips she'd painted a defiant coral before coming down, she shook back her hair. "Why doesn't somebody order pizza?"

IT LACKED EFFICIENCY, BUT THERE WAS SOME-thing more comforting about gathering in the living room rather than sitting at the dining room table like sensible adults. Cybil set out a platter of antipasto while they waited for pizza.

Fox sat on the floor at Layla's feet. "Ladies first," he suggested. "Quinn?"

"I went out for ice cream, and since I was going to eat ice cream, I went for the power walk first." Her fingers twisted the chunky silver chain around her neck. "But I kept ending up in the same place, on the same corner. It didn't matter which direction I took. I couldn't find my way, couldn't get home." She gripped Cal's hand, pressed her forehead to his shoulder. "I couldn't find you. It went pitch dark. There was no one, and I couldn't get back."

"Everything was gone for me." Sliding an arm around her shoulders, Cal gathered her close. "The town was destroyed, everyone dead, blown to pieces. I ran here, but there was nothing. Just a smoking hole in the ground. I don't know where I was going. Looking for you. Because I couldn't, I wouldn't believe . . . Then I saw you, and Fox."

"I saw you first," Quinn said to Fox. "It was like you came through a wall of water. You were blurred at first, and your footsteps—you were running—but the sound was smothered. Then it all cleared. You grabbed my hand, and it all cleared.

"That has to mean something, don't you think?" She glanced around as she asked. "I was heading for hysterical. I think I'd been there and back at least once already, and was making the return trip. Then I saw Fox, and when he took my hand everything went back the way it's meant to be. Then Cal was coming."

"You weren't there, either of you. Nothing was. Then you were." Cal shook his head. "It was almost like switching a channel. Like a click. You were bleeding," he said to Fox.

"Spiders," Fox said and told them. "I didn't notice anything off about the town when I got out. I saw you on the corner, Quinn. Looking lost, I guess. I'd heard you—sensed you, and the others. Like a bad connection, fuzzy and weak. But I could hear Layla screaming. I heard that loud and clear."

"You were two blocks away," Quinn pointed out.

"I could hear her screaming," he repeated. "Right up until I got into the house. Then it stopped. It must've been when you passed out."

"It was after Quinn went out. She went for ice cream because I was upset." Her gaze flicked to Fox, then back to the fingers linked in her lap. "I decided to take a shower while she was gone. I felt it first, sliding over my foot. They were coming out of the drain. Snakes. With the screams I let out, I'm surprised they didn't hear me in the next county."

"I didn't hear you," Cybil told her. "I was right downstairs and I didn't hear a thing."

"They kept coming." When her breath wanted to snag, Layla eased it out slowly, deliberately. "I got out of the shower, but they were on the floor, too. Coming up out of the sink. Not real, that's what I kept trying to tell myself, but I couldn't—I didn't keep my head. When the door wouldn't open, I went a little crazy, beating at them with a towel, with my hands. The window was too small, and it wouldn't open anyway. I must've fainted, because I don't remember anything else until Fox was there. I was in bed, and Fox and Quinn were there."

"Your passing out might be part of the reason it stopped," Cybil speculated. "There's no maintaining an illusion when you're unconscious."

"What happened to you?" Layla asked her.

"I couldn't see. Gage and I were in the kitchen, and my eyes stung for a minute, then went blurry. Then everything went gray. I went blind."

"Oh, Cyb."

She smiled at Quinn. "Q knows that's a small, personal terror of mine. My father lost his sight in an accident. He was never able to adjust, accept. Two years later he killed himself. So blindness holds a particular terror for me. You were there," she said to Gage, "then you weren't. I couldn't hear you, and I asked you to help me, but you didn't. I guess you couldn't."

She paused, but he said nothing. "I heard the front door slam open. I heard Fox. My vision started to clear, and then . . . you were there again." He'd held her, she thought. They'd held each other. "Where did you go, Gage? We need to know what happened to each one of us."

"I didn't go far. Back to the apartment where I used to live. Above the bowling alley."

At the knock on the door, Cal rose, but he kept his eyes on Gage's face. "I'll get that."

"There was a physical thing with you," Gage went on. "With your eyes. The irises, the pupils were covered, the whole of your eyes were white. And no, I couldn't help. I stepped toward you, and right into the apartment."

Cal came back, set the pizza boxes on the table. "Were you alone?"

"At first. I couldn't get the door open, the windows. That seems to be a recurring theme."

"Trapped," Layla murmured. "Everyone's afraid of being trapped, being locked in."

"I heard him coming. I knew—I know the sound of his feet on the stairs, when he's drunk, when he's not. He was, and he was coming. Then I was back in the kitchen."

"There's more. Why are you holding back?" Cybil demanded. "We all went through something."

"When I reached for the doorknob, it wasn't my hand. Not this hand." Gage held his up, turned it, studied it. "I saw myself in the mirror. I was about seven, maybe eight. Before that night at the Pagan Stone, younger than that. Before things changed. Before we changed. And he was drunk, and he was coming. Clear enough?"

In the silence, Quinn reached down for her tape recorder, ejected the tape, put in a fresh one. "This hasn't happened before, am I right on that? That all of you were affected at the same time, that so many were affected?"

"Dreams," Cal said. "The three of us have dreams, usually on the same night, not always about the same thing. That can happen weeks, even months before the Seven. But something like this, no. Not outside of those seven days."

"It went to a lot of trouble to get to us," Fox commented, "to cherry-pick our particular and specific fears."

"Why were you the only one who was hurt?" Layla demanded. "I felt them bite me, but I didn't have any bites when I came out of it. But you did. They're healed now, but you did."

"Maybe I let it in too far, and my own ability worked against me. Made my fear more real, more tangible. I don't know."

"It's possible." Quinn considered. "Could it have started with you? Given the timing, it could have started with you first. Used more, well, juice. Fed off that for the rest. Not just your fear, but your pain, too. It used the connections.

You to Cal or me—one of us was probably next. Then Layla, then Cybil, and rounding it up with Gage."

"Like a current. The energy." Layla nodded. "Moving from one to the other. Fox weakened the current when he broke free. And back down the line. If that's the way it happened, it could be a kind of defense, couldn't it? Something we could use."

"Our energy against its energy." Quinn gave in and flipped open the pizza box. "Positive against negative."

"I think we'll need to do more than think of raindrops on roses." Cybil slid a slice out for herself. "And whiskers on kittens."

"While I doubt we're going to hear the guys do a chorus of 'Do-Re-Mi,' even if lives depend on it, roses and kittens are a springboard." Considering big trauma, Quinn treated herself to an entire slice. "If each of us has personal fears, don't we all have personal joys? Yes, yes, hokey, but not really over the top. Oh God, this is good. See, personal joy. Pepperoni pizza."

"That's not how Fox broke its hold," Layla pointed out. "I don't think he mentioned focusing on pizza or rainbows."

"Not entirely true." Because Lump's eyes filled with love, Fox peeled a piece of pepperoni off his slice, fed it to the dog. "I thought about how what was happening was bullshit. Not easy when hungry mutant spiders are crawling all over you."

"Eating here," Cal reminded him.

"But I thought more about how we were going to kick the Big Evil Bastard's ass. How we were going to end him. I kept thinking that, like I was telling him. Trash talking, lots of very foul language. That's a personal pleasure, on a very real level. And when those things started falling off me, thumping on the ground, I started feeling fairly perky. Not, the hills are alive, spinning around like a lunatic perky. But not half bad, considering."

"It's always worked that way for you. Once you figured it out," Cal added. "And it's worked for me, for Gage. We've been able to break down the illusions—when they are illusions. But I tried, and I couldn't this time."

"So you bought it."

"I—"

"You bought it, at least for a few minutes. Because it was too much, Cal. Everything that matters to you gone. Quinn, your family, us, the town. And just you left. You didn't stop it, so everyone and everything was gone, killed, destroyed. But you. It was too damn much," Fox repeated. "Those spiders weren't real, not all the way real. But I saw my hand after they had at me, and it was swollen to the size of a cantaloupe, and bleeding. The wounds were real, so I'm saying Twisse put a hell of a lot into this one."

"It's been over a week since the last incident. Also starting with you, Fox." Cybil laid a slice on a plate, walked it over to Gage. "It used Block's jealousy, his anger, maybe his guilt, fed off that, used that to infect him enough to have him attack you."

"So where did it get the extra amps for this?" Gage shrugged. "If that's the question, there are plenty of negative emotions running around this town, just like any place else."

"It's specific," Cal disagreed. "It was specific to Block. This was specific to us."

Cybil slid a glance toward Layla, but said nothing as she took her seat again.

"I was upset, and angry. So were you," Layla said to Fox. "We had . . . a disagreement."

"If it can cook up something like that every time one of us gets pissed off, we're toast," Gage decided.

"They were both upset." Quinn considered how best to phrase it. "With each other. That could factor. And it may be that when the emotions involved are particularly intense, when there's sexuality involved, it's more potent."

Gage lifted his beer. "Again. Toast."

"I happen to think intense human emotion, emotion that draws from a well of affection," Cybil added, "and good healthy sex, is a hell of a lot more potent than anything the son of a bitch can throw at us. That's not spinning in circles on a mountaintop naïveté. It comes from studying human relationships and their power, and this particular situation specifically—and how it's come to us. How many times have the three of you had a scene like you did before in the kitchen?"

"What scene?" Quinn wanted to know.

"It was nothing," Cal muttered.

"You were in each other's faces, shouting obscenities, and about to come to blows. It was . . ." Cybil's smile was sly and just a little feline. "Stimulating. Countless times, I wager—want to take the bet?" she asked Gage. "Countless times, and I up my bet to wager several of them have resulted in fists in faces. But here you are. Here you are because at the core, you love each other. That's the base, and nothing changes it. It can't shake that base. It must beat its fists—if fists it has—at the barrier it can't pass. We're going to need that base, and we're going to need all those intense human emotions, especially if we're going to do the incredibly foolish and attempt a blood ritual."

"You've got something," Quinn stated.

"I think I do. I want to wait to hear back from a couple more sources. But yeah, I think I do."

"Spill!"

"For one thing, it means all six of us, and we'll have to go back to the source."

"The Pagan Stone," Fox said.

"Where else?"

LATER, CAL GRABBED A MOMENT ALONE WITH Quinn. He drew her into her bedroom, and with his arms around her, just breathed her in. "It was worse," he said quietly, "worse than it's ever been because for a while I thought I might have lost you."

"It was worse, because I couldn't find you." She tipped her head back, sank into the kiss with him. "It's harder when you love someone. It's better and it's harder, and it's pretty much everything."

"I want to ask you a favor. I want you to go away, just for a few days," he continued, talking fast. "A week, maybe two. I know you've got other writing projects you're squeezing in. Take a break, maybe go back home to—"

"This is my home now."

"You know what I mean, Quinn."

"Sure. And no problem." Her smile was sunny as June. "As long as you come with me. We'll have ourselves a little holiday. How's that?"

"I'm serious."

"So am I. I'll go if you go. Otherwise, you're going to want to drop this. Don't even think about picking a fight," she warned him. "I can practically see you trying it out in your head, calculating if you got me mad enough I'd walk. You can't. I won't." For emphasis, she put her hands on his cheeks, squeezed. "You're scared for me. So am I, just like I'm scared for you. It's all part of the package now."

"You could go buy a wedding dress."

"Now that's fighting dirty." But she laughed, kissed him hard. "I've already got some lines on that, thank you very much. Your mother and mine are bonding like Super Glue and . . . more Super Glue over wedding plans. Everything's under control. We had a bad day, Cal, but we came through it."

He drew her back, breathed her in once more. "I need to take a walk around town. I need to . . . I need to see it."

"Okay."

"I need to take a walk with Gage and Fox."

"I get it. Go on. Just come back to me."
"Every day," he told her.

WHEN HE GOT THEM OUTSIDE, CAL WALKED THE neighborhood first. The light was soft, easing in on evening. There were the houses he knew, the yards, the sidewalks. He walked by his great-grandmother's house, where his cousin's car sat in the drive, and flowers budded and bloomed along the walk.

There was the house of the girl he'd been crazy about when he'd been sixteen. Where was she now? Columbus? Cleveland? He couldn't quite remember where she'd gone, only that she'd moved away with her family in the fall of the year he'd turned seventeen.

After that Seven, when her father had tried to hang himself from the black walnut tree in their backyard. Cal remembered cutting the man down himself, and having no time for more, tying him to the tree with the hanging rope to hold him until the rage passed.

"You never did score with Melissa Eggart, did you, hotshot?"

How like Gage to remember and to turn the memory into something normal. "I doubled. Was working my way up to stealing third. Then things got busy."

"Yeah." Gage slid his hands into his pockets. "Things got busy."

"I'm sorry about before. And you were right," he added to Fox. "It's stupid to swipe at each other."

"Forget it," Gage told him. "I've thought about walking plenty of times."

"Thinking and doing got miles between them." They turned, headed toward Main. "I wanted to punch something, and you were handy."

"O'Dell's handier, and he's used to getting punched."

When there was no sarcastic rejoinder from Fox, Gage eyed him. He thought of the ways he could handle Fox's mood, and opted for what he did best. Needling him. "Are you having intense human emotions?"

"Oh, suck off."

"There he is." Gage swung an arm over Fox's shoulders.

"Punching you still isn't out of the question."

"If she was pissed at you," Cal said helpfully, "she's not now. Not after your white-charger routine."

"It's not about that. About being pissed, about saving the girl. It's about wanting and needing different things. Look, I'm heading home from here. I didn't shut anything down, lock anything up."

"We'll go with you, check it out."

"No, I got it. I've got some actual work to do. If anything else needs going over tonight, I'll crib off your notes. See you later."

"He's got it bad," Gage commented as they watched Fox head down Main. "Real bad."

"Maybe we should go with him anyway."

"No. We're not what he wants right now."

They turned, walking the opposite way as night crept closer.

Eighteen

ᴄᴏᴜɴᴛɪɴɢ ᴏɴ ᴘᴀᴘᴇʀᴡᴏʀᴋ ᴛᴏ ᴋᴇᴇᴘ ʜɪᴍ ʙᴜsʏ and distracted, Fox settled down in his home office. Flipping his CD player to shuffle for the variety and surprise factors, he prepared to make up for the fractured workday with a couple of hours at his desk.

He drafted some court petitions on an estate case he hoped to wrap up within another ninety days, shifted to fine-tune a letter of response to opposing counsel on a personal injury matter, then moved on to adjusting the language in a partnership agreement.

He loved the law, the curves and angles of it, its flourishes and hard lines. But at the moment, he was forced to admit, the work couldn't light a spark in him. He'd be better off cruising ESPN.

The file he'd put together for Layla still sat on his desk. Because it annoyed him, Fox dropped it in a drawer. Stupid, he thought. Stupid to think he understood her simply because he usually understood people. Stupid to think he knew what she wanted because it was what *he* wanted.

Love, he had good reason to know, didn't always do the job.

Better to stay in the moment, he reminded himself. He was good at that, had always been good at that. Much better to focus on the now than to push himself, and Layla, toward some blurry and nebulous tomorrow. She had a point about there being no clear future for the town. Who the hell wanted to set up shop in a place that might not exist in a few months? Why should anyone invest the time and the energy, plant the roots, sweat it out, and hope the good guys won in the end? They'd all gotten today's ugly memo that the clock was ticking down for the Hollow, and for the six of them.

And that was bullshit. Annoyed, he shoved away from the desk. That was absolute bullshit. If people thought that way why did they bother to get the hell out of bed in the morning? Why did most of them at least try to do the right thing, or at least their version of it? Why buy a house or have kids, or hell, buy season tickets if tomorrow was so damn uncertain?

Maybe he'd been stupid to assume where Layla was concerned—he'd cop to that. But she was just as stupid to back away from what they could make together because tomorrow wasn't lined up in neat columns. What he needed was a different approach, he realized. For Christ's sake, he was a lawyer, he knew how to change angles, detour around obstacles and reroute to the goal. He knew about compromise and negotiation and finding that middle ground.

So what was the goal? he asked himself as he wandered to the window.

Saving the town and the people in it, destroying the evil that wanted to suck it dry. Those were the bigs ones, but if he set those life-and-death matters aside, what was Fox B. O'Dell's goal?

Layla. A life with Layla. Everything else was just details. He'd fumbled the ball on the way to the goal because he'd gotten bogged down with details. The first thing to do was carve them away. Once he did, what was left was a guy and a girl. It was as simple and as complex as that.

He turned back to his desk. He'd toss the file, it was just a symbol of those details. As he reached for the drawer, the knock at the door had him frowning. It had to be Gage or Cal, he thought as he walked out of the office to answer. He didn't have time to hang out. He needed to work on his more simplified, whittled-down approach to winning the woman he loved.

When he opened the door, the woman he loved stood on the other side.

"Hey, I was just . . . Are you alone?" His tone changed from flustered surprise to irritation as he grabbed her hand and pulled her inside. "What are you thinking, wandering around town at night alone?"

"Don't start on me. Twisse will go under after a day like this, and I wasn't wandering. I came straight here. You didn't come back."

"We don't know what the hell Twisse might be able to do after a day like this. And I didn't come back because I figured you'd want to get some sleep. Besides, before this afternoon's performance, you weren't real happy with me."

"Which is exactly why I thought you'd come back, so we could talk about it." She poked a finger at his chest. "You don't get to be mad at me over this."

"Excuse me?"

"You heard me. You don't get to be mad because I didn't jump headfirst into plans you made without consulting me."

"Wait a damn minute."

"No, I will not wait a damn minute. You decided what I should do for the rest of my life, where I should live, how I should make my living. You made a *file*." Indignation flashed from her eyes, her voice. From where he was standing, it all but flashed out of her fingertips. "I wouldn't be surprised if it includes paint chips and possible names for this imaginary boutique."

"I was thinking puce, color-wise. I don't think puce gets enough play. As for names, topping my list right now is Get a Fucking Grip—but it probably needs work."

"Don't curse at me, or try to make this a joke."

"If those are your two requirements, you're in the wrong place with the wrong guy. I'll drive you home."

"You will not." Feet planted, she folded her arms. "I'll walk when I'm ready to go, and I'm not ready. Don't even think about kicking me out or I'll—"

"What?" How could he help but make it a joke? It was ludicrous. He lifted his fists in a boxing pose. "Think you can take me?"

The temper that gushed out of her was hot enough to boil the air. "Don't tempt me. You sprang this on me. Out of the blue, then when I don't do a happy dance and fling myself into the program, you walk away. You tell me you love me, and you walk away."

"Sorry, I guess I needed a little alone time after realizing the woman I'm in love with isn't interested in building a life with me."

"I didn't say—I never meant . . . Hell." Layla covered her face with her hands, took several deep breaths. The anger evaporated as she lowered her hands. "I told you once you scare me. You don't understand that. You're not easily scared."

"That's not true."

"Oh, yes, yes, it is. You've lived with this threat too long to be easily scared. You face things. Some of it's circumstance, some of it's just your nature, but you face what comes at you. I haven't had to do a lot of that. Things were pretty ordinary for me, right up until February. No big bumps in my road, no particularly big moments. All in all,

I think I'm doing reasonably well. All in all," she repeated on a sigh as she began to wander the room.

"You're doing fine."

"I'm scared of what's here, of what's coming, what may happen. I don't have Quinn's energy or Cybil's . . . savoir faire," she decided. "I do have persistence, once I commit to something I do my best to see it through, and I have a way of putting the big picture into components that I can reason out. So that's something. It's not as overwhelming, not as frightening when you have those smaller pieces to work with. But I can't seem to reason things out with you and me, Fox. And that scares me."

She turned back to him. "It scares me that I've never felt for anyone what I feel for you. And I told myself it was okay, it was all right to have all these feelings rush in and grab me. Because everything's crazy. But the fact is, it's all crazy, but it's all real. What's happening around us, what's happening inside me, it's all real. I just don't know what to do about it."

"And I added to the mix with the idea of starting a business here, making it more complicated and scary. Understood. We'll take it off the table. I didn't look into it to put pressure on you. We've all got enough of that as it is."

"I wanted to be mad, because it's easier to be mad than scared. I don't want to be at odds with you, Fox. Everything that happened today . . . you were there. I woke up from that nightmare, and you were right there. Then you didn't come back." She closed her eyes. "You didn't come back."

"I didn't go far."

Emotion swam into her eyes when she opened them. "I thought you might have. And that scared me more than anything else."

"I love you," he said simply. "Where would I go?"

She launched herself into his arms. "Don't go far." Her mouth found his. "Don't kick me out. Let me be with you."

"Layla." He took her face in his hands, easing her back until their eyes met. "All I want at the end of the day is for you to be with me."

"I'm here. It's the end of the day, and I'm here. That's where I want to be."

Her lips were so soft, so giving. Her sigh, as her body molded to his, like music. Her hands brushed his face, through his hair as he circled her toward the bedroom. And in the dark, they lowered to the bed. She reached out, their legs tangling as they lay facing each other. As they stirred each other with long, lingering kisses, he could see the gleam of her eyes in the dark, the curve of her cheek, feel the shape of her lips and the beat of her heart against his.

She shifted, kneeling to unbutton his shirt. Then her body bowed down as she pressed her lips to his heart. Lightly, her fingertips grazed down his sides as her mouth brushed, her tongue slicked along his skin. She felt his muscles quiver as she trailed those slow openmouthed kisses over his belly, as she flipped open the button of his jeans.

She wanted him to quiver.

She eased the zipper down, a slick hiss of sound in the dark, and drew denim down those narrow hips where the skin was warm. He groaned as she pleasured him.

She ruled his body. Her mouth and hands guided him slowly, inexorably into the rocking sea of heat until he was drenched in it. And when the blood began to burn under his skin, she shifted again. He heard the soft rustle as she undressed.

"I want to ask you for something." She came toward him across the bed on her hands and knees and his mouth went dry as dust.

"If you want a favor, this is probably a good time to ask for it."

Teasing, she lowered her lips to his, brushed, retreated. When he cupped the back of her head to bring her mouth to his again, she took it, brought it to her breast.

"When you touch me, when you make love with me, when you're inside me, can you feel what I feel? Can I feel what you feel? I want that with you. I want to know what it's like to be together that way, when we're like this."

A gift, he thought, of complete trust, on both sides. He sat up, looked into her eyes. "Open," he murmured, and rubbed his lips to hers. "Just open."

He felt her nerves, her needs, and the thoughts that came and went in her head like soft shimmers. To be wanted, to be touched. By him. When her hands ran up his back, he knew both her pleasure and her approval. He knew the press of their bodies, the beats of their hearts.

Then easing her down, he deepened the kiss. And opened himself to her.

At first it was like a sigh, through her body, through her mind. She thought: Lovely. It's lovely. Anticipation built. She turned her head to give him the pulse in her throat when she felt his need to taste there.

Her breath caught, a quick little shock when his mouth took her breast. So much to feel, to know, she trembled with each new sensation that slipped and slid inside her, around her. His hands, her skin, his lips, her taste. Her needs tied, tangled with his on a free-falling leap.

Greed—was it hers or his that had her rolling over the bed with him, desperate for more, and the more only unleashed new, wild cravings. His hands used her, rougher than before, answering her unspoken demands. Take, take, take. Pleasure swelled, unfurled, then burst with shock after radiant shock.

Her nails bit, his teeth nipped. And when he drove into her she thought she'd go mad from the force of mingled power.

"Stay with me, stay with me." Desperate, delirious, she wrapped her legs around him like chains when she sensed him start to close off. Pleasure, a two-edged sword, was brutally keen. She gripped it with him.

She held his body, his thoughts, his heart, until neither could hold any longer.

He sprawled facedown on the bed, head swimming, lungs laboring. He didn't have the strength, as yet, to ask her if she was all right, much less to try to link to make sure for himself.

She'd taken him apart, and he wasn't quite capable of putting himself back together. None of his thoughts would coalesce. He wasn't quite sure if there weren't still echoes of hers inside him.

Still, after a few minutes, he realized he might die of thirst if he didn't crawl off for water.

"Water." He croaked it out.

"God. Please."

He started to roll, bumped her where she'd flung herself crossways on the bed. "Sorry."

He only grunted as he got his feet on the floor, then stumbled his way to the kitchen. The light in the refrigerator branded his eyes like the blaze of the sun. With one hand pressed over them, Fox felt his way over the shelves for a bottle of water.

He drank half of it where he stood, naked in front of the open refrigerator, his eyes slammed shut against any source of light. Steadier, he opened his eyes to slits, grabbed a second bottle and took it into the bedroom.

She hadn't moved a muscle.

"Are you all right? Did I—"

"Water." Her hand flayed in the air. "Water."

He opened the bottle, then slid an arm under her to prop her up. Leaning back against his arm she drank with the same urgent gusto as he had.

"Are your ears ringing?" she asked him. "My ears are ringing. And I think I may be blind."

He hauled her around so she was propped against the pillows instead of his arm, then he switched on the bedside light.

She screamed and slapped a hand over her eyes. "Okay, I wasn't blind, but now I may be." Cautiously she peeked out between two spread fingers. "Have you ever . . ."

"No. That was the first." Because his legs were still a little weak, he sat down beside her. Which was too bad, he mused, because he'd liked the full-length view. "Intense."

"*Intense* is too mild a word. There isn't a word. They need to invent one. I guess that's not something we could handle every time."

"Save it for special occasions."

She smiled and stirred up the energy to sit up, rest her head on his shoulder. "Arbor Day's coming up, I think. That's pretty special."

He laughed, turned his head to rub his cheek against her hair. I love you, he thought, but kept the words to himself this time.

SINCE FOX HAD OUTSIDE MEETINGS, LAYLA TOOK advantage of a slow afternoon to read over portions of Ann Hawkins's third journal. There was not, as they'd hoped, a spell, a formula, step-by-step directions on how to kill a centuries-old demon. It led Layla to believe Giles Dent hadn't told his lover the answers. Cybil's take was more mystical, Layla supposed. If Ann knew, she also knew that whatever needed to be done to end Twisse would be diluted, even invalidated if the answers were simply handed over.

That seemed too cryptic and irritating to Layla, so she spent considerable time trying to read between the lines. And came away from it frustrated and headachy. Why couldn't people just be straightforward. She *liked* step-by-step directions. And she was sure as hell going to record them, if they ever found them, used them, and were successful, on the off-chance some future generation had a similar problem.

"Why don't you come back here?" Layla muttered. "Come on back and talk to me, Ann. Just spell it out. Then we'll all go about our normal lives."

Even as she said it, Layla heard the front door creak open. She bulleted to her feet. Brian O'Dell sauntered in.

"Hey, Layla. Sorry, did I startle you?"

"No. A little. I wasn't expecting anyone. Fox is out of the office this afternoon."

"Oh. Well." Brian dipped his hands in his pockets, rocked back on his heels. "I was in town, thought I'd drop in."

"He probably won't be back until after six. If you want to leave a message—"

"No. No big. You know, since I'm here, maybe I'll just go back." He pulled a hand free to gesture with his thumb. "Fox is talking about new flooring in the kitchen, and a couple of things. I'll just go measure. Want any coffee or anything?"

Layla tilted her head. "How are you going to measure without a measuring tape?"

"Right. Right. I'll get one out of the truck."

"Mr. O'Dell, did Fox ask you to come in this afternoon?"

"Ah. He's not here."

"Exactly." Like the son, Layla thought, the father was a poor liar. "So he asked if you'd come in, check on me. Which I might not have copped to except that your wife dropped in about an hour ago, with a dozen eggs. Putting that together with this, I smell babysitters."

Brian grinned, scratched his head. "Busted. He doesn't like you being here alone. I can't say I blame him." He strolled over, dropped into one of the visitors' chairs. "I hope you're not going to give him a hard time about it."

"No." She sighed, sat herself. "I guess, one way or another, we all worry about each other. But I've got my cell in my pocket, and everyone I know on speed dial. Mr. O'Dell—"

"Brian."

"Brian. How do you handle it? Knowing what's happening, what may happen to Fox?"

"You know, I was nineteen when Sage was born." In the language of a man settling in for a spell, he propped one work-booted foot on his knee. "Jo was eighteen. Couple of kids who thought we knew it all, had it all covered. Then, you have a kid of your own, and the whole world shifts. There's a part of me that's been worried for thirty-one years now." He smiled as he said it. "I guess there's just more parts of me worried when it comes to Fox. And truth? It pisses me off that he had his childhood, his innocence stolen from him. He came home that day, his tenth birthday, and he was never a little boy, not in the same way, again."

"Did he tell you what happened? The morning he came back from the Pagan Stone?"

"I like to think we got a lot right with our kids, but one thing I know we got right. They know they can tell us anything. He'd spun that one about camping out in Cal's backyard, but Jo and I saw through that."

"You knew he was going to spend the night in the woods?"

"We knew he was taking an adventure, and we gave him the room. If we hadn't, he'd've found a way around it. Birds have to fledge. You can't stop it, no matter how much you want to keep them safe in the nest."

He paused a moment, and Layla could see him looking back, wondered what it was like to look back over the course of another's lifetime. Someone you loved.

"He had Gage with him when he came home," Brian continued. "You could see, in both of them, something had changed. Then they told us, and everything changed. We talked about leaving. Jo and I talked about selling the farm and moving on. But he needed to be here. After the week was up, we all thought it was over. But more than that, we knew Fox needed to be here, with Cal and Gage."

"You've seen him face this three times before, and now he's facing it again. I think it must take tremendous courage to accept what he's doing. Not to try to stop him."

The smile was easy, the smile clear. "It's not courage, it's faith. I have complete faith in Fox. He's the best man I know."

Brian stayed until she closed the office, then insisted on driving her home. The best man I know, she mused as she walked in the house. Was there a higher tribute from father to son? She walked upstairs to take the journal back to the home office.

Quinn sat at her desk, scowling at her monitor.

"How's it going?"

"Crappy. I'm on deadline with the article, and I can't keep my head in the game."

"Sorry. I'll go down, give you the room."

"No. Shit." She shoved away. "I shouldn't have said I'd write the stupid article except, hello, money. But we've been pushing on this idea of the blood ritual, and clever words to go with it, and Cybil's snarly."

"Where is she?"

"Working in her room because apparently I think too loud." Quinn waved it away. "We get like this with each other if we work on a project for any serious length of time. Only *she* gets like this more. I wish I had a cookie." Quinn propped her chin on her hand. "I wish I had a bag of Milano's. Crap." She picked up the apple from the desk, bit in. "What are you smiling at, size freaking two?"

"Four, and I'm smiling because it's reassuring to come home and find you in this lousy mood wishing for cookies, and Cybil holed up in her room. It's so normal."

With something between a grunt and a snort, Quinn

took another bite of apple. "My mother sent a swatch for bridesmaids' gowns. It's fuchsia. How's that for normal, Sunny Jane?"

"I could wear fuchsia if I had to. Please don't make me."

Blue eyes wickedly amused, Quinn chewed and smiled. "Cyb would look horrible in fuchsia. If she keeps crabbing at me, I'll make her wear it. You know what? We need to get out of here for a while. All work, no play. We're taking tomorrow off and shopping for my wedding dress."

"Seriously?"

"Seriously."

"I thought you'd never ask. I've been *dying* to do this. Where—"

Layla turned as Cybil's door opened. "We're going shopping. For Quinn's wedding gown."

"Good, that's good." At the doorway, Cybil leaned on the jamb, studied both her friends. "That's what we could call a ritual—a white one, a female one. Unless we want to take a closer look at the symbolism. White equals virginal, veil equals submission—"

"We don't," Quinn interrupted. "I will, without shame, toss my feminist principles to the wind for the perfect wedding dress. I'll live with it."

"Right. Well, anyway . . ." Absently, Cybil shoved back her mass of hair. "It's still a female ritual. Maybe it'll balance out what we'll be doing in another two weeks. Blood magic."

FOX DROVE STRAIGHT TO LAYLA'S AFTER HIS AP-pointments. She opened the door as he started up the walk, her hair swinging, her lips curved in a welcoming smile. Could he help it if that was exactly what he hoped to come home to every night?

"Hey." He leaned down to kiss her, leaned up and cocked

his head at the absent response. "Why don't we try that again?"

"Sorry. I'm distracted." She took the lapels of his jacket in her hands, and put herself into the kiss.

"That's what I'm talking about." But he saw now there was no reflection of that smile of greeting in her eyes. "What's the matter?"

"Did you get my voice mail?"

"Meeting here, as soon as I could make it. I made it."

"We're in the living room. It's—Cybil thinks she's nailed down the blood ritual."

"Fun and games for all." Concerned, he brushed his thumb over her cheekbone. "What's the problem?"

"She— She's waiting until you get here to explain it to the three of you."

"Whatever she explained to you didn't put roses in your cheeks."

"Some of the variables on the potential outcome aren't rosy." She took his hand. "You'd better hear it for yourself. But before . . . I have to tell you something else."

"Okay."

"Fox . . ." Her fingers tightened on his, as if in comfort. "Can we just sit here a minute?"

They sat on the porch steps, looking out at the quiet street. Her hands clasped on her knee, one of her signs— Gage would call it a tell—of nerves. "How bad is it?" Fox asked her.

"I don't know. I don't know how you'll feel about it." She pressed her lips together once, hard. "I'm going to say it straight out, then you can take whatever time you need to, well, absorb it. Carly was connected. To this. She was a descendent of Hester Deale's."

It hit him, a hard, fast punch to the solar plexus. His thoughts spun, so he asked the first question that popped. "How do you know?"

"I asked Cybil—" She broke off, shifted to face him,

started again. "It seemed that there had to be a reason for what happened, Fox, a reason she was infected so quickly, so . . . fatally. So I asked Cybil to look into it, and she has been."

"Why didn't you say anything to me?"

"I wasn't sure, and if I'd been wrong, I'd have upset you for nothing. And . . . I should've told you," she amended. "I'm sorry."

"No." The spinning stopped; the ache just under his heart eased. She'd wanted to shield him until supposition became fact and he'd have done exactly the same. "No, I get it. Cybil climbed Carly's family tree?"

"Yes. Tonight she told me she'd found the connection. She has the details of the genealogy if you want to see them."

When he only shook his head, she went on. "I don't know if this makes it better for you, or worse, or if it changes nothing. But I thought you should know."

"She was part of it," he said quietly. "All along."

"Twisse used that, and you, and her. I'm sorry. I'm so sorry, but nothing you did, nothing you didn't do would have changed that."

"I don't know if that's true, but there's nothing I can do now to change it. Maybe we found each other, Carly and me, because of this. But then we made choices, both of us, that led to the end of it. Different choices, maybe a different result. No way to know."

After a moment, he laid his hand over hers. "There's always going to be guilt, and grief, when I think of her. But now, I know at least part of the why. I never understood why, Layla, and that twisted me up."

"Twisse took her to hurt you. And was able to take her, the way he did, because she was of his bloodline. And because . . ."

"Keep going," he told her when she trailed off.

"I think because she didn't believe, not really. She didn't

believe enough to be afraid, or to fight, even to run. That's just speculation, and I might be overstepping, but—"

"No." He said it quietly. "No, you're exactly right. She didn't believe, even when she saw with her own eyes." He lifted his free hand, studied the unmarred palm. "She told me what she thought I wanted to hear, promised to stay at the farm that night without ever intending to keep the promise. She was built skeptical, she couldn't help it."

He closed his hand into a loose fist, lowered it. And for the first time in nearly seven years, he let it go. "I never thought of a connection. That was smart. And you were right to tell me." He lifted their hands, slid his fingers between hers. "Being up-front with each other, even when it's hard, that's the best choice for us."

"I want to say this one thing more before we go in. If I promise you something—if you ask me to do something, or not to, and I give you my promise, I'll keep it."

Understanding, he brought their joined hands to his lips. "And I'll believe what you tell me. Let's go inside."

He couldn't change the past, Fox thought. He could only prepare for the future. But he could prize and hold the now. Layla was his now. The people in this house were his as well. They needed him, and he needed them. That was enough for any man.

He settled into his usual spot on the floor with Lump. Whatever was in the air, Fox thought, was something between nerves and fear. That was from the women. From Cal and Gage he sensed both interest and impatience.

"What's going on? And whatever it is, let's get on with it."

Cybil took the stage.

"I've talked with a number of people I know and, for the most part, trust, regarding performing a blood ritual, the object being to re-form the three pieces of Dent's blood-stone into one. We're assuming that's something we need to do. There are a lot of assumptions here based on bits and pieces of information, on speculation."

"The three separate pieces haven't done us much good up till now," Gage pointed out.

"Well, you don't know that, do you?" Cybil tossed back. "It's very possible that those individual pieces are what's given you your gifts—your sight, your healing. Once whole, you might lose that. And without those gifts in your arsenal, you'll be all the more vulnerable to Twisse."

"If you don't put them back together," Cal pointed out, "they're just three pieces of stone we don't understand. We agreed to try. We *have* tried. If you've found another way, that's what we'll try next."

"Blood rites are powerful and dangerous magicks. We're dealing with a powerful and dangerous force already. You need to know all the possible consequences. All of us need to know. And all of us have to agree because all of us need to be part of it for the ritual to have any chance of working. I'm not going to agree until everyone understands."

"We get it." Gage shrugged. "Cal may need to dig out his glasses, and the three of us will be susceptible to the common cold."

"Don't make light of this." Cybil turned to him. "You could lose what you have, and more. It could all blow up in our faces. You've seen that possibility. The mix of blood and fire, the stone on the stone. Every living thing consumed. It was your blood that let the demon out. We need to consider that performing this rite could loose something worse."

"You have to play to win."

"He's right." Fox nodded at Gage. "We risk it, or we do nothing. We believe Ann Hawkins or we don't. This was the time, that's what she told Cal. This Seven is the all or nothing, and the stone—whole—is a potential weapon. I believe her. She sacrificed her life with Dent, and that sacrifice led to us. One into three, three into one. If there's a way, we go."

"There's another three. Q, Layla, and me. Our blood, tainted if you will, with that of the demon."

"And carrying that of the innocent." Layla sat with her

hands folded, as if she held something delicate inside them. "Hester Deale wasn't evil. Innocent blood, you said, Cybil, innocent blood is a powerful element in ritual."

"So I'm told." Cybil let out a sigh. "I was also warned that the innocent can be used to give the demon strain more power. That a ritual such as we're suggesting could be an invitation. Three young boys were changed by a blood rite on that ground. It could happen again, with us." She looked at Layla, at Quinn. "And what's diluted, or dormant, or just outweighed in us by who we are, could rise."

"Not going to happen." Quinn spoke briskly. "Not only because I don't consider horns and cloven feet a fashion statement but—" she ignored Cybil's annoyed oath "—because we won't let it. Cyb, you're too goddamn hardheaded to let a little demon DNA run your show. And you're not responsible. Don't even," Quinn ordered when Cybil started to speak. "Nobody knows you like I do. If we vote go, we're all in it, we're all making the choice. And whatever happens, thumbs-up or -down, it's not on you. You're just the messenger."

"Understand if it goes wrong, it could go seriously and violently wrong."

"If it goes right," Fox reminded Cybil, "it's a step toward saving lives. Toward ending this."

"More likely we'll lose a little blood and not a damn thing will change. Any way you look at it, it's a long shot," Gage added. "I like a long shot. I'm in."

"Anyone not?" Quinn scanned the room. "That's a big go."

"Let's get started."

"Not so fast, big guy," Cybil said to Gage. "While the ritual's pretty straightforward, there are details and procedure. It requires the six of us—boy-girl, boy-girl—like any good dinner party, in the standard ritual circle. On the ritual ground at the Pagan Stone. Cal, I don't suppose you have the knife you used before?"

"My Boy Scout knife? Sure I do."

"Sure he does." Charmed, Quinn leaned over to kiss his cheek.

"We'll need that. I have a list of what we'll need. And we'll work out the wording of the incantation. We have to wait for the night of the full moon, and begin in the half hour before midnight, finish before the half hour after."

"Oh, for Christ's sake."

"Ritual requires ritual," she snapped at Gage. "And respect, and a hell of a lot of faith. The full moon gives us light, literally and magickally. The half hour before midnight is the time of good, and the half hour after, evil. That's the time, that's the place, and that's our best shot of making it work. Think of it as stacking the odds in our favor. We've got two weeks to fine-tune it, work out the kinks—or to call off the whole deal and go to St. Barts. Meanwhile . . ." She looked into her empty glass. "I'm out of wine."

As the discussion started immediately, Gage slipped off to follow Cybil into the kitchen. "What's got you spooked?"

"Oh, I don't know." She poured herself a generous glass of cabernet. "Must be the death and damnation."

"You don't spook easy, so spill."

She took a small sip as she turned to him. "You're not the only one who gets previews of coming attractions."

"What did you see this time?"

"I saw my best friend die, and the death of the woman I've come to love and respect. I saw the men who love them die trying to save them. I saw your death in blood and fire. And I lived. Why is that worse? That I saw everyone die, and I lived."

"Sounds more like nerves and guilt than a premonition."

"I don't do guilty, as a rule. On the plus side, in my dream it worked. I saw the bloodstone whole, resting on the Pagan Stone under the light of the full moon. And for a moment, it was brighter than the sun."

She took a long, quiet breath. "I don't want to walk out of the clearing alone, so do me a favor. Don't die."

"I'll see what I can do."

Nineteen

~⌒~

OUTSIDE, UNDER THE DIM LIGHT OF THE WAXING moon, Layla kissed Fox good night. And that brush of lips slid into a second, soft and seductive as the night air. "I just think I need to stay here tonight." But she melted into him for another. "Cybil's edgy, Quinn's distracted. And they've been poking at each other. They need a referee."

"I could stay." Gently, he grazed his teeth over her bottom lip. "Back you up."

"Then I'd be distracted. I'm already distracted." With a little groan, she eased away. "Besides, I have a feeling you'll be going to Cal's. The three of you are going to want to talk this over."

"It's a lot." He ran his hands down her arms. "You're up for it."

"That wasn't a question."

"No. I could see it. I can see it now."

Very little could have pleased her more than that single,

almost casual, vote of confidence. "Time to take the next step. And by the way, I need tomorrow off."

"Okay."

"Just okay?" She shook her head. "No what for, or who the hell's going to run the office?"

"Three or four times a year—that was the limit—we could take a day off school. We just said, I don't want to go to school tomorrow, and that was okay. Never had to fake sick or sneak a hook day in. I figure the same applies to work."

She leaned into him, arms around his waist, hands linked together. "I've got a terrific boss. He even sends his parents in to check on me when he's out of the office."

Fox winced. "I may have mentioned that—"

"It's all right. In fact, it's better than all right. I had a nice chat with your mother, then one with your dad—who dazzles me a little because you look so much like him when you smile."

"Number One O'Dell Charm Tool. Never fails."

She laughed, leaned back. "There's something I should tell you before you go. I've been working it out in my head for a while now, then today, when I was talking to your father, something occurred to me. Why was I working on it so much? Why couldn't it just be? Because, well, it is."

"What is?"

"I'm in love with you." She let out a half laugh. "I love you, Fox. You're the best man I know."

He couldn't find words, not with so much blowing through him. I love you, she said, with a smile that made the words sparkle in the dark. So he lowered his brow to hers, closed his eyes, and gave himself to the moment. Here she was, he thought. Everything else was details.

Then tipping her head back, he kissed her brow, her cheeks before laying his lips on hers. "You're telling me this, then sending me home?"

She laughed again. "Afraid so."

"Maybe you could just come over for an hour. Make it

two." He kissed her again, deeper, and deeper. "Let's go for three."

"I want to, but . . ."

Even as she started to yield—what was an hour or two when you were in love—Gage came out of the front door. "Sorry." He glanced at Fox, cocked his head. Fox nodded.

"How do the two of you manage to have a conversation without speaking?" Layla wondered as Gage strode down to his car.

"Probably has something to do with knowing each other since birth. I'm going to ride with him." Fox caught her face in his hands. "Tomorrow night."

"Yes. Tomorrow night."

"I love you." He kissed her again. "Damn it, I've gotta go." And again. "Tomorrow."

When he walked to the car, his mind was too full of her for him to notice the dark cloud that smothered the moon.

LEAVE IT TO QUINN, LAYLA THOUGHT, TO FIND the perfect bridal boutique. Every minute of the two-and-a-half-hour drive had been worth it once they'd arrived at the charming three-story Victorian house with its stunning gardens. Layla's retailer's eye noted the details—the color schemes, the decor, the fussily female sitting areas, the oh-so-flattering lighting.

And the stock. Displays of gowns, shoes, headdresses, underpinnings, all so creatively contrived, made Layla feel as if she wandered along a wedding cake, with all its froth and elegance.

"Too many choices. Too many. I'm going to choke." Quinn gripped Cybil's arm.

"You're not. We've got all day. God, have you ever seen so much white? It's a blizzard of tulle, a winter forest of shantung."

"Well, there's white, and ivory, cream, champagne, ecru,"

Layla began. "I'd go for the white with your coloring, Quinn. You can pull it off."

"You pick one. That's what you do—did—right?" Quinn rubbed a hand over her throat. "Why am I so nervous?"

"Because you only get married the first time once."

Quinn poked at Cybil and laughed. "Shut up. Okay." She took a steadying breath. "Natalie's setting up the dressing room," she said, referring to the shop's manager. "I'll try on what she's picked out. But we're all going to pick at least one gown each. And we have to vow to be honest. If the gown sucks on me, we say so. Everybody, spread out. Dressing room, twenty minutes."

"You'll know yours when you see yourself in it. That's the way it works." But Layla wandered off.

She looked at lace, silk, satin, beads. She studied lines and trains and necklines. As she stood, eyeing a gown, visualizing Quinn in it, Natalie bustled over.

Her cap of salt-and-pepper hair suited her gamine face. Small, black-framed glasses set it off. She was tiny and trim in a dark suit Layla imagined she chose to contrast rather than blend with the gowns.

"Quinn's ready, but doesn't want to start without you. We've got six gowns to start."

"I wonder if we can add this one."

"Of course, I'll take care of it."

"How long have you been in business?"

"My partner and I opened four years ago. I managed a bridal boutique in New York for several years before relocating."

"Really? Where?"

"I Do, Upper East Side."

"Terrific place. A friend of mine bought her gown there just a few years ago. I live—lived—" Which was it? Layla wondered. "Um, in New York. I managed a boutique downtown. Urbania."

"I know that store." Natalie beamed. "Small world."

"It is. Can I ask what made you leave I Do and New York, open here?"

"Oh, Julie and I talked about it endlessly over the years. We've been friends since our college days. She found this place, called me and said, 'Nat, this is it.' She was right. I thought she was crazy. I thought *I* was crazy, but she was right." Natalie angled her head. "Do you know what it's like when you find the customer exactly what she wants—exactly what's right. The look on her face, the tone in her voice?"

"Yes, I do."

"Triple it when it's your own place. Should I take you to the dressing room?"

"Yes, thanks."

There was tea in delicate china cups in a spacious room with a tall triple mirror and chairs with needlepoint cushions. Paper-thin cookies waited on a silver tray while blush pink lilies and white roses scented the air.

Layla sat, sipped, while Quinn worked her way through the selections.

"It doesn't suck." Cybil pursed her lips as Quinn turned in front of the mirror. "But it's too fussy for you. Too much . . ." She circled her hand. "Poof," she decided.

"I like the beadwork. It's all sparkly."

"No," was all Layla said, and Quinn sighed.

"Next."

"Better," Cybil decided. "And I'm not just saying that because it's the one I picked out. But if we're considering this the most important dress of your life, it's still not ringing the bell. I think it's too dignified—not quite enough fun."

"But I look so elegant." Quinn turned, her eyes shining as she watched herself in the triple glass. "Almost, I don't know, regal. Layla?"

"You can carry it with your height and build, and the lines are classic. No."

"But—" Quinn blew out a breath that vibrated her lips.

After two more tries and rejections, Quinn took a tea break in her bra and panties. "Maybe we should elope. We could go to Vegas, have an Elvis impersonator marry us. That could be fun."

"Your mother would kill you," Cybil reminded her as she broke one of the delicate cookies in two and offered Quinn half. "So would Frannie," she added, referring to Cal's mother.

"Maybe I'm just not built for the gown kind of thing. Maybe a cocktail dress is a better idea. We don't have to go so formal and fussy," she said as she set down the tea and picked another gown at random. "This skirt is probably going to make my ass look ten feet square." Her glance at Layla was apologetic. "Sorry, this one's your pick."

"It's your pick that counts. It's ruching—called a pickup skirt," Layla explained.

"Or we could just go for completely casual, a backyard wedding and reception. All this is just trappings." She spoke to Cybil as Layla helped her into the dress. "I love Cal. I want to marry Cal. I want the day to be a celebration of that, of what we are to each other, and to what the six of us have accomplished. I want it to symbolize our commitment, and our happiness, with a kick-ass party. I mean, for God's sake, with all we've faced, and are going to face, one stupid dress doesn't mean a thing."

As Layla stepped back, Quinn turned around. "Oh my God." Breathless, she stared at herself. The heart-shaped bodice of the strapless gown showed off strong, toned shoulders and arms, and glittered with a sprinkle of cut-glass beads. The skirt fell from a trim waist in soft ruches of taffeta accented with pearls.

With her fingertips, Quinn touched the skirt very lightly "Cyb?"

"Well, God." Cybil knuckled a tear away. "I didn't expect to react this way. Jesus, Q, it's perfect. You're perfect."

"Please tell me it doesn't make my ass look ten feet square. Lie if you must."

"Your ass looks great. Damn, I need a tissue."

"Remember everything I just said about the dress and the trappings not being important? Now forget I said any of that. Layla." Quinn closed her eyes, crossed her fingers. "What do you think?"

"I don't have to tell you. You know it's yours."

SPRING BROUGHT COLOR TO THE HOLLOW WITH greening willows reflected in the pond at the park, with the redbuds and wild dogwoods blooming in the woods, along the roadsides. The days lengthened and warmed in a teasing preview of the summer to come.

With spring, porches gleamed with fresh paint and gardens shot out a riot of blooms. Lawnmowers hummed and buzzed until the smell of freshly cut grass sweetened the air. Kids played baseball, and men cleaned their barbecue grills.

And with spring, the dreams came harder.

Fox woke in a cold sweat. He could still smell the blood, the hellsmoke, the charred bodies of the doomed and damned. His throat throbbed from the shouts that had ripped out of him in dreams. Running, he thought, he'd been running. His lungs still burned from the effort, and his heart still drummed. He'd been running through the deserted streets of the Hollow, flaming buildings around him, as he tried to reach Layla before she . . .

He reached over; found her gone.

He leaped out of bed, snagging a pair of boxers on the run. He called out for her, but he knew—before he saw the door standing open, he knew where her own dream lured her.

He was out the door, into the cool spring night, and running, just as he'd run in the dream. Bare feet slapping in a wild tattoo on brick, asphalt, grass. Fetid smoke hazed the deserted streets, stinging his eyes, scoring his throat. All around him, buildings roared with flame. Not real, he told himself. The fires were lies, but the danger was real. Even as the heat scorched his skin, as it seemed to burn up through the bricks to sear his feet, he ran.

His heart hammered even when he saw her, walking through the false flames. She glided through the smoke, like a wraith, the mad lights from the fires rippling over her body. He called, but she didn't turn, didn't stop. When he caught her, yanked her around to face him, her eyes were blind.

"Layla." He shook her. "Wake up. What are you doing?"

"I am damned." She almost sang it, and her smile was tortured. "We are all of us damned."

"Come on. Come home."

"No. No. I am the Mother of Death."

"Layla. You're Layla." He tried to push himself into the haze of her mind, and found only Hester's madness. "Come back." Chaining down his own panic, he tightened his grip. "Layla, come back." As she fought to break free, he simply locked his arms around her. "I love you. Layla, I love you." Holding tight, he drowned everything else, fear, rage, pain, with love.

In his arms, she went limp, then began to shudder. "Fox."

"It's okay. It's not real. I've got you. I'm real. Do you understand?"

"Yes. I can't think. Are we dreaming?"

"Not anymore. We're going to go back. We're going to get inside." He kept an arm firmly around her waist as he turned.

The boy skimmed along the fire. He rode it as a human child might a skateboard, with glee and delight while his dark hair flew in the wild wind. As the rage rolled into Fox, he poised to spring.

"Don't." Her voice was thick with exhaustion as Layla

leaned her weight against Fox. "It wants you to, it wants to separate us. I think we're stronger together, holding on to each other."

Death for one, life for the other. I'll drink your blood, boy, then plant my young in your human bitch.

"Don't!" This time Layla had to lock her arms around Fox's neck to keep him from rushing forward. She pushed her thoughts into his head. *We can't win here. Stay with me. You have to stay with me.* "Don't leave me," she said aloud.

It was brutal, walking away, struggling to ignore the filth the thing hurled at them. To continue to walk as the boy whipped around them in circles, taunting, howling as it flew on its skate of flame. But as they walked, the fires sputtered. By the time they climbed the steps to his apartment, the night was clear and cool again, and carried only the dying hint of brimstone.

"You're cold. Let's get back in bed."

"I just need to sit." She lowered to a chair, and helpless to do otherwise, let the trembling take her. "How did you find me?"

"I dreamed it. Running across town, the fire, all of it." To warm her, he grabbed the throw his mother had made him off the couch, spread it over Layla's bare legs. "To the park, to the pond. But in the dream, I was too late. You were dead when I pulled you out of the water."

She reached for his hands, found them as icy as hers. "I need to tell you. It was like back in New York, when I dreamed it raped me. When I dreamed I was Hester, and how it raped me. I wanted it to stop, to end. I was going to kill myself, drown myself. She was, too. I couldn't stop her. It had my mind."

"It doesn't have it now."

"It's stronger. You felt that. You know that. Fox, it nearly made me kill myself. If it's strong enough to do that, if we're not immune—Quinn, Cybil, and I—it could make us hurt you. It could make me kill you."

"No."

"Damn it, what if he had made me go into the kitchen, get a knife, and stab it into your heart? If it can take us over when we sleep then—"

"If it could have infected you that way, to kill me, it would have. Offing me or Cal or Gage, that's its number one. You come from it and Hester, so it used Hester against you. Otherwise, I'd be dead with a knife in my heart, and you'd be going under for the third time in the pond. You've got a logical mind, Layla. That's logical."

She nodded, and though she struggled, the first tears escaped. "It raped me. I know it wasn't me, I know it wasn't real, but I *felt* it. Clawing at me. Ramming inside me. Fox."

As she broke, he gathered her in, gathered her up. There was no hell dark enough, he thought, cradling her in his lap, rocking her as she sobbed.

"I couldn't scream," she managed, and pressed her face to the plane of his shoulder. "I couldn't stop it. Then I didn't care, or couldn't. It was Hester. She just wanted to end it."

"Do you want me to call Quinn and Cybil? Would you rather—"

"No. No."

"It used that. The shock, the trauma, to push your will down." He brushed at her hair. "We won't let it happen again. I won't let him touch you again." He lifted her face, brushed at her tears with his thumbs. "I swear to you, Layla, whatever has to be done, he won't touch you again."

"You found me, before I found myself." She laid her head on his shoulder, closed her eyes. "We won't let it happen again."

"In a few days, we'll take the next step. We're not going through this to lose. And when we end this thing, you'll be part of that. You'll be part of what ends it."

"I want it to hurt." On that realization, her voice strengthened. "I want it to scream, the way I was screaming in my head." When she opened her eyes again, they were clear. "I wish there was a way we could lock him out of our heads. Like garlic with vampires. That sounds stupid."

"It sounds good to me. Maybe our research ace can come up with something."

"Maybe. I need to take a shower. That sounds stupid, too, but—"

"No, it doesn't."

"Will you talk to me while I do? Just talk?"

"Sure."

She left the door open, and he stood leaning against the jamb. "Pretty close to morning," he commented. "I've got some farm fresh eggs, courtesy of my mother." Switch to normal, he told himself. That's what they both needed. "I can scramble some up. I haven't cooked for you yet."

"I think you opened a couple of soup cans during the blizzard when we stayed at Cal's."

"Oh, well, then I have cooked. I'll still scramble some eggs. Bonus feature."

"When we went to the Pagan Stone before, it wasn't as strong as it is now."

"No."

"It'll get stronger."

"So will we. I can't love you this much—scrambling eggs much—and not get stronger than I was before you."

Under the hot spray, she closed her eyes. It wasn't the soap and water making her feel clean. It was Fox. "No one's ever loved me scrambling eggs much. I like it."

"Play your cards right, and that might bump up one day to my regionally famous BLT."

She turned off the water, stepped out for a towel. "I'm not sure I'm worthy."

"Oh." He grinned as he trailed his gaze over her. "Believe me. I can also toast a bagel, if I have the incentive."

She stopped in the doorway. "Got a bagel?"

"Not at the moment, but the bakery'll be open in about an hour."

She laughed—God what a relief to laugh—and moved by him to get the robe she stashed in his closet.

"Lots of excellent bakeries in New York," he commented. "The city of bagels. So, I've been thinking, as I like a good bakery, and a good bagel, after this summer I could look into taking the bar up there."

She turned back as she belted the robe. "The bar?"

"Most law firms are fussy about hiring on associates unless they pass their particular bar. The sublet on your apartment runs through August. Maybe you'd want to hang here until after Cal and Quinn get married in September anyway. Or you might want to find a new place up there. Plenty of time to decide."

She stood where she was, studying his face. "You're talking about moving to New York."

"I'm talking about being with you. It doesn't matter where."

"This is your home. Your practice is here."

"I love you. We covered that, didn't we?" He stepped to her. "We covered the part about you loving me back, right?"

"Yes."

"People in love generally want to be together. You want to be with me, Layla?"

"Yes. Yes, I want to be with you."

"Okay then." He kissed her lightly. "I'll go break some eggs."

LATER THAT MORNING, FOX SAT IN CAL'S OFFICE, rubbing a foot over Lump's hindquarters. Gage paced. He hated being here, Fox knew, but it couldn't be helped. It was private, and it was convenient. Most of all, Fox had taken a personal vow to stay within hailing distance of Layla until the full moon.

"There has to be a reason it targets her, specifically, for this. Fucking rapist."

"And if we knew the reason, we could stop it." Cal nodded. "It could be that she's the loosest link. Meaning, the three of us go back all the way. Quinn and Cybil since college. None of us knew Layla until February."

"Or the evil bastard could've just rolled the dice." Gage stopped by the window, saw nothing of interest, moved on. "None of the others have shown any signs of infection."

"It's different. It's not like what happens to people during the Seven. It's only happened, the rape, when she's asleep. And it was a kind of sleepwalking after. Following the same pattern as Hester Deale. Lots of ways to kill yourself, and we've seen plenty. But it was going to be drowning, in an outdoor body of water. Same as Hester. Maybe it had to be."

"One of us stays at the house at night until this is over," Cal decided. "Even if Layla's at your place, Fox, none of them are left alone at night from here on."

"That's where I was heading. Once we've done our full-moon dance, we should look into this angle more. We need to find a way to stop this, to protect her—all of them."

"Day after tomorrow," Gage muttered. "Thank Christ. Has anybody been able to squeeze more details out of Madam Voltar?"

Cal's lips twitched. "Not really. If Quinn knows, she's got it zipped, too. All she'll say is Cybil's fine-tuning. Then, she distracts me with her body, which isn't hard to do."

"She writes the script." Fox lifted his hands at Gage's snort. "Look, we tried it our way, various ways, and managed dick. Let the lady have a shot at it."

"The lady's worried we're all going to die. Or five out of six of us."

"Better worried than too cocky," Fox decided. "She'll

cross all her t's. That's one smart skirt. Added to, she loves Quinn. Layla, too, but she and Quinn are as tight as it gets."

Fox pushed to his feet. "I've got to get back to the office. Speaking of which, I'm thinking I'll probably be moving to New York after you and Quinn get married."

"God, another with a hook in his mouth." Gage shook his head. "Or maybe it's a ring through the nose."

"Bite me. I haven't said anything to my family yet. I'm going to ease into that by degrees." Fox studied Cal's face as he spoke. "But I thought I'd give you a heads-up. I'm figuring I'll wait until after the Seven to put the building on the market. I've got some decent equity in it, and the market's pretty stable, so—"

"Eternally the optimist. Brother, for all you know that place'll be rubble come July fourteenth."

This time Fox simply shot Gage his middle finger. "Anyway. I thought you or your father might be interested in it. If you are, we'll kick around some figures at some point."

"It's a big step, Fox," Cal said slowly. "You're established here, not just personally, but with your practice."

"Not everybody can stay. You won't," Fox said to Gage.

"No, I won't."

"But you come back, and you'll keep coming back. So will I." Fox turned his wrist up, and that scar that ran across it. "Nothing erases this. Nothing can. And hell, New York's only a few hours away. I zipped up and down Ninety-five the whole time I was in law school. It's . . ."

"When you were with Carly."

"Yeah." He nodded at Cal. "It's different now. I've still got a few lines up there, so I'll put some feelers out, see what comes. But right now I've got some town lawyer business to take care of. I can take a shift at the house tonight," he added as he started for the door. "But I still say those women *have* to get ESPN."

Gage sat on the corner of Cal's desk when Fox left.

"He'll hate it."

"Yeah, he will."

"He'll do it anyway, and he'll find a way to make it work. Because that's what O'Dell's about. Making it work."

"He'd have tried with Carly. I don't know if he could've pulled it off, but he'd have tried. But he's right. It's different with Layla. He'll make it work, and I'm the one who's going to hate it. Not being able to see his stupid face every damn day."

"Cheer up. Five out of six of us could be dead in a couple days."

"Thanks. That helps."

"Anything I can do." Gage straightened. "I've got some business of my own. Catch you later."

He was nearly to the door when his father stepped up to it. They both stopped as if they'd walked into a wall. Helplessly, Cal got to his feet.

"Ah . . . Bill, why don't you check the exhaust fan on the grill? I'll be down in a minute. I'm nearly done here."

As the pink the climb up had put in his cheeks faded, Bill stared at his son. "Gage—"

"No." It was an empty word in an empty voice as Gage walked out. "We are done."

At his desk, Cal rubbed at the fresh tension in his neck as Bill turned shamed eyes on him. "Um . . . What'd you want me to check?"

"The grill exhaust. It's running a little rough. Take your time."

Alone, Cal lowered to his chair, pressed his fingers to his eyes. His friends, his brothers, he thought, had both chosen rocky roads. There was nothing he could do but go with them, as far as it took.

Twenty

~⁓~

SOME PEOPLE MIGHT THINK IT WAS A LITTLE ODD
to get up in the morning, go to work as usual when the evening plans included blood rituals. But Fox figured it was
pretty much standard operating procedure for him and his
friends.

Layla, who in straight managerial areas could make the
beloved Alice Hawbaker look like a slacker, had squeezed
and manipulated his schedule to ensure the office closed
promptly at three on the big day. He'd already packed his
kit. Most might not know what to take along on an early
evening hike through the woods by a haunted pool toward a
mystical clearing ruled by an ancient altar stone, but Fox
had that down. For once, he'd even remembered to check
the forecast.

Clear skies—that was a plus—with temps sliding from
a balmy seventy to the cool but pleasant midfifties.

Layers were the key to comfort.

In his pocket was his third of the bloodstone. He hoped it would prove to be another key.

While Layla changed, he added some essentials to his cooler. He glanced around when she came in, and he broke into a smile. "You look like the cover for *Hiking Style*—if there is such a thing."

"I actually debated with myself over earrings." She surveyed his cooler and open pack. Coke, Little Debbies, Nutter Butters. "I guess it's like you say, we all do what we do."

"These particular provisions are a time-honored tradition."

"At least the sugar rush is guaranteed. God, Fox, are we crazy?"

"It's the times that are crazy. We're just in them."

"Is that a knife?" She gaped at the sheath on his belt. "You're taking a knife? I didn't know you had a knife."

"It's actually a gardening saw. Japanese sickle knife. It's a nice one."

"And what?" She put a hand to the side of her head as if the pressure would help her mind make sense of it all. "You're planning on doing a little pruning while we're there?"

"You never know, do you?"

She put a hand on his arm as he closed his pack. "Fox."

"Odds are Twisse is going to take an interest in what we're doing tonight. It can be hurt. Cal did some damage with his handy Boy Scout knife the last time we were there. You can bet Gage is bringing that damn gun. I'm not going in there with just my Nutter Butters."

She started to argue—he saw it in her eyes—then something else came into them. "Have you got a spare?"

Saying nothing, he went to the utility closet, rooted around. "It's called a froe." He showed her the long, flat blade. "It's good for splitting wooden pins in joinery work.

Or taking a slice out of a demon. Keep it in the scabbard," he added, sliding it into the leather. "It's sharp."

"Okay."

"Don't take this the wrong way." He laid his hands on her shoulders. "Remember I'm a strong proponent of equality, of women's rights. I'm going to protect you, Layla."

"Don't take this the wrong way. I'm going to protect you, too."

He brushed his lips to hers. "I guess we're set then."

THEY MET AT CAL'S TO BEGIN THE HIKE ON THE path near his home. The woods had changed, Layla thought, since her previous trip. There had been snow then, pooled in pockets of shade, and the trail had been slick with mud, the trees barren and stark. Now, leaves were tender on the branches, and the soft white of the wild dogwoods shimmered in the slanting sun.

Now, she had a knife in a leather scabbard bumping against her hip.

She'd walked here before, toward the unknown, with five other people and Cal's affable dog. This time, she knew what might be waiting, and she went toward it as part of a team. She went toward it beside the man she loved. Because of that, this time she had more to lose.

Quinn slowed, pointed at the scabbard. "Is that a knife?"

"Actually, it's a froe."

"What the hell's a froe?"

"It's a tool." Cybil reached out from behind Layla to test the weight of the scabbard. "Used for cutting wood by splitting it along the grain. Safer than an ax. This one, by its size and shape, is probably a bamboo froe, and it's used for splitting out the bamboo pins used in Japanese joinery."

"What she said," Layla agreed.

"Well, I want a froe, or something. I want a sheath. No," Quinn decided. "I want a machete. Nice long handle, wicked curved blade. I need to buy a machete."

"You can use mine next time," Cal told her.

"You have a machete? Gosh, my man is full of hidden pockets. Why do you have a machete?"

"For whacking at weeds and brush. Maybe it's more of a scythe."

"What's the difference? No." Quinn held up her hand before Cybil could speak. "Never mind."

"Then I'll just say you probably want the scythe, as, traditionally, it has a long handle. However . . ." Cybil trailed off. "The trees are bleeding."

"It happens," Gage told her. "Puts off the tourists."

The thick red ran in rivulets down bark to spread over the carpeting leaves. The air stank of burnt copper as they followed the path to Hester's Pool.

There they stopped beside the brown water, and there the brown water began to bubble and redden.

"Does it know we're here?" Layla spoke quietly. "Or is this the demon version of a security system? Can it think this kind of thing scares us at this point, or is it what Gage said? A show for the tourists?"

"Maybe it's some of both." Fox offered her a Coke, but she shook her head. "Security systems send out an alert. So if the Big Evil Bastard doesn't know when we head in, it knows when we reach certain points."

"And this is a cold spot—in paranormal speak," Quinn explained. "A place of import and power. When we . . . Oh, Jesus."

She wrinkled her nose as something bobbed to the surface.

"Dead rabbit." Cal put a hand on her shoulder, then tightened his grip when other corpses rose to the bubbling surface.

Birds, squirrels, foxes. Quinn made a sound of distress,

but she lifted her camera and began to document. Death
smeared its stench on the air.

"It's been busy in here," Gage mumbled.

As he spoke, the bloated body of a doe floated up.

"That's enough, Quinn," Cal murmured.

"It's not." But she lowered the camera. Her voice was
raw, her eyes fierce. "It's not enough. They were harmless,
and this is *their* world. And I know, I know it's stupid to get
so upset about . . . fauna when human lives are at stake,
but—"

"Come on, Q." Cybil draped an arm around her, turned
Quinn away. "There's nothing to be done."

"We need to get them out." Fox stared at the obscenity,
made himself see it, made himself harden. "Not now, but
we'll have to come back, get them out. Burn the corpses. It's
not just their world, it's ours, too. We can't leave it like this."

With a sick rage lodged in his gut, he turned away. "It's
here." He said it almost casually. "It's watching." And it's
waiting, he thought, as he moved up to take point on the
path to the Pagan Stone.

The cold rolled in. It didn't matter that the cold was a
lie, it still chilled the bones. Fox zipped up his hooded
jacket, and kept the pace steady. He took Layla's hand to
warm it in his.

"It just wants to give us grief."

"I know."

His mind tracked toward the sounds of rustling, of
growling. Keeping pace, he thought. Knows where we're
going, but not what we plan to do when we get there.

Thunder rumbled across a clear sky, and the rain pelted
down from it to stab and pinch the skin like needles. Fox
flipped up his hood as Layla did the same. Next roared the
wind in frigid, sweeping gusts that bent trees and tore new
leaves from their branches. He wrapped an arm around her
waist for support, hunched his shoulders, and plowed
through it.

Raindrops on roses, my ass, he thought, but kept his mind calm.

"All right back there?" He'd already looked with his mind, but was reassured by the affirming shouts. "We're going to do a chain," he told Layla. "Get behind me, get a good hold on my belt. Cal knows what to do. He'll hook to you, pass it back."

"Sing something," she shouted.

"What?"

"Sing, something we all know the words to. Make a goddamn joyful noise."

He grinned through the teeth of the storm. "I'm in love with a brilliant woman." Songs everyone knew, he thought as Layla got behind him, gripped his belt. That was easy.

He launched with Nirvana, calculating that none of the six could've gotten through high school without picking up the lyrics from "Smells Like Teen Spirit." The chorus of *Hello!* rang out defiantly while the diamond-sharp rain slashed. He tossed in some Smashing Pumpkins, a little Springsteen (he was the Boss for a reason), swung into Pearl Jam, sweetened it up with Sheryl Crow.

For the next twenty minutes, they trudged, one combative step at a time through the lashing storm, singing Fox's version of Demon Rock.

It eased by degrees until it was no more than a chilly breeze stirring a weak drizzle. As one, they dropped onto the sodden ground to catch their breath and rest aching muscles.

"Is that the best it's got?" Quinn's hands trembled as she passed around a thermos of coffee. "Because—"

"It's not," Fox interrupted. "It's just playing with us. But damned if we didn't play right back. Wood's going to be wet. We may have some trouble starting a fire." He met Cal's eyes as Cal unhooked Lump's leash from his belt.

"I got that handled. We'd better get moving. I'll take point for a while."

A dog leaped onto the path. Huge and black, fangs gleaming, it snarled out threats. Even as Fox reached for his sheath, Cybil pushed to her feet. She drew a revolver from under her jacket, and coolly fired six shots.

The dog howled in pain and in fury; its blood smoked and sizzled on the ground. With one wild leap, it vanished into the swirling air.

"That's for ruining my hair." Cybil shook back the curling mess of it as she unzipped a pocket in her jacket for a box of ammo.

"Nice." On his feet as well, Gage held out a hand. He examined the revolver—a trim .22 with a polished pearl handle. Ordinarily, he'd have smirked at that sort of weapon, but she'd handled it like a pro.

"Just something I picked up, through *legal* channels." She took the gun back, competently reloaded.

"Wow." Fox hated guns—it was knee-jerk. But he had to admire the . . . pizzazz. "That's given the Big Evil Bastard something to think about."

She slid it into the holster under her jacket. "Well, it's no froe, but it has its merits."

The air warmed again, and the evening sun sparkled on young leaves as they hiked the rest of the way to the Pagan Stone.

It rose from the burned ground in a clearing that formed a near-perfect circle. What every test had deemed ordinary limestone speared up, then spread altarlike in the quieting light of the spring evening.

"Fire first," Cal decided, dragging off his pack. "Before we lose the light." Opening the pack, he pulled out two Dura-Logs.

After the miserable journey there, Fox's laughter was like a balm. "Only you, Hawkins."

"Be prepared. We start one of these, tent wood around it, the flames should dry out the wet wood. Should do the job."

"Isn't he cute?" Quinn demanded, wrapping her arms around Cal for a cheerful snuggle. "Seriously."

They gathered stones and branches, stripped off wet jackets to hang on the poles Fox fashioned in hopes the fire would dry them. They roasted Quinn's contribution of turkey dogs on sharpened sticks, passed out Cybil's brie and Layla's sliced apples and ate like the starving.

As darkness settled, Fox broke out the Little Debbies while Cal checked the flashlights. "Go ahead," he told Quinn as she gave the snack cakes a wistful look. "Indulge."

"They go straight to my ass. If we live, I have to fit into my absolutely spectacular wedding dress." She took one, broke it prudently in half. "I think we're going to live, and half a Little Debbie doesn't count."

"You're going to look amazing." Layla smiled at her. "And the shoes we found? So exactly right. Plus, Cybil and I aren't going to look shabby. I love the dresses we found. The idea of the plum with the orchid's just—"

"I feel an irresistible urge to talk about baseball," Fox said, and got an elbow jab from Layla.

Conversation trailed off until there was only the crackle of wood, the lonely hoot of an owl. So they sat in silence as the fat moon glowed like a white torch in a star-struck sky. Fox pushed to his feet to gather trash. Busy hands packed away food or added wood to the fire.

At a signal from Cybil, the women unpacked what Layla thought of as the ritual bag. A small copper bowl, a bag of sea salt, fresh herbs, candles, springwater.

As instructed, Fox poured the salt in a wide circle around the Pagan Stone.

"Well." Cybil stepped back, studied the arrangement of supplies on the stone. "I don't know how much of this is visual aids, but all my research recommended these elements. The salt's for protection against evil, a kind of barrier. We're to stand inside the circle Fox made. There are six white candles. Each of us lights one, in turn. But first, the springwater goes into the bowl, then the herbs, then the three pieces of stone—in turn. Q?"

"I printed out six copies of the words we need to say." Quinn took the file out of her pack. "We do that one at a time, around the circle, as each one of us draws his or her own blood with Cal's knife."

"Over the bowl," Cybil reminded her.

"Yeah, over the bowl. When the last one's done that, we join hands, and repeat the words together six times."

"It should be seven," Layla said. "I know there are six of us, but seven is the key number. Maybe the seventh is for the guardian, or symbolizes the innocent, the sacrifice. I don't know, but it should be seven times."

"And seven candles," Fox realized. "A seventh candle we all light. Shit, why didn't we think of this?"

"A little late now." Gage shrugged. "We got six, we go with six."

"We can do seven." Cal held out a hand to Layla. "Can I borrow your froe?"

"Wait. I got you." Fox pulled out his knife. "This'll work better. Let me see." He picked up one of the thick, white columns. "Beeswax—good. I spent a lot of time working with beeswax and wicks growing up." After he'd laid it on its side, he glanced at Cybil. "Any reason for the dimensions of these? The height?"

"No, but my sources said six." She looked at Layla, nodded. "Screw the sources. Make us another candle."

He set to work. The wax was going to do a number on his blade, he thought, but all things being right in the world, he'd be able to clean and sharpen it when he got home. It took time, enough that he wondered why the hell Cybil hadn't picked up a half dozen tapers. But he cut off three inches, then took Layla's tool to dig a well for the wick.

"Not my best work," he decided, "but it'll burn."

"We light it last." Layla scanned the other faces. "Light it together." She had to take a breath to keep her voice steady. "It's almost time."

"We need the stones," Cybil began, "and the ritual Boy Scout knife," she added with a faint smile.

The boy came out of the woods, executing cheerful handsprings. The claws on his hands, his feet, dug grooves in the ground, and the grooves welled with blood.

"You should know we've used salt before." Gage drew his Lugar from the small of his back. "Didn't do squat." His brows lifted as the boy's hand brushed the salt. It squealed in pain, leaped back. "Must be a different brand." Even as Gage aimed, the boy hissed and vanished.

"We need to start." With a steady hand, Cybil poured the water into the bowl, then sprinkled the herbs. "Now the stones. Cal, Fox, Gage."

Thunder boomed, and with a flash of lightning, bloody rain gushed from the sky. The burned ground drank it, and steamed.

"It's holding." Layla looked up. "It's not coming inside the circle."

Fox held the stone inside his fist. He'd carried it with him like hope for nearly twenty-one years. And with that hope, he slipped it into the water after Cal's. Outside the circle, the world went mad. The ground shook, and blood swam across it to lap and burn at the barrier of salt.

It's eating it away, Fox thought, burning and eating away the barrier. He set his candle to flame, passed the lighter to Layla.

In the light of six candles, they laid hand over hand, fired the seventh.

"Hurry," Fox ordered. "It's coming back, and it's pissed."

Cal held his hand over the bowl, drew the knife across his palm as he read the words. As did Quinn, then Fox.

"My blood, their blood. Our blood, its blood. One into

three, three into one. Dark with the light. We make this sac-rifice, we take this oath."

Screams, ululations neither human nor animal rolled through the dark. Tethered to the base of the stone, Lump lifted his big head to howl.

Layla took the knife, hissing against the quick pain as she read the words. Then her mind flew to Fox's while Gage took his turn. *The cold! It's nearly through!*

As the ground quivered underfoot, he clasped her bloodied hand with his.

The wind tore in. He couldn't hear the others, not with his ears or his mind, but shouted the words, prayed they were with him. On the Pagan Stone, the seven candles burned with unwavering flame, and in the bowl, reddened water bubbled. The ground heaved, ramming him into the table of the stone with enough force to knock his breath away. Something like claws raked at his back. He felt him-self spinning, impossibly. In desperation, his mind reached out for Layla's. Then the blast of light and heat flung him blindly into the black.

He crawled, dragging himself over the ground toward the faint echo of her. He yanked his knife free, pulled him-self over the bucking ground.

She crawled toward him, and the worst of his fears broke away when he found her hand. When their fingers linked, the light burst again with a sound terrible as a scream. Fire engulfed the Pagan Stone, sheathed it as leather sheathed a blade. In a deafening roar the flame gey-sered up toward the cold, watching moon. And it *flew* to ring the clearing in a writhing curtain of fire. In its savage light, Fox saw the others, sprawled on, kneeling on the ground.

All of them, all of them trapped inside a circling wall of flame while in its center, the Pagan Stone spewed more.

Together, he thought as the vicious heat slicked his skin with sweat. Live or die, it would be together. With his hand locked on Layla's, he pulled them both across the clearing. Then her arm was around him, and they were pulling each other. Cal gripped his forearm, dragged him forward. He met Gage's eyes. With the air burning, they once again clasped hands.

Together, Fox thought, as the deadly walls of fire edged closer. "For the innocent," Fox gasped out against the smoke coating his throat. The fire, blinding bright, ate across the ground. There was nowhere to go, and he knew, only moments left. He pressed his cheek to Layla's. "What we did, we did for the innocent, for each other, and fucking A, we'd do it again."

Cal managed an exhausted laugh, brought Quinn's hand to his lips. "Fucking A."

"Fucking A," Gage agreed. "Might as well go out with a bang." He jerked Cybil against him, covered her mouth with his.

"Well, hell, we might as well try to get through it." Fox blinked his stinging eyes. "No point in just sitting here getting toasted when we could . . . It's dying back."

"Busy here." Gage lifted his head, scanned the clearing. His smile was both grim and satisfied. "I'm a hell of a good kisser."

"Idiot." Cybil shoved him back, pushed up to her knees. Flames retreated toward the stone, began to slide up it. "It didn't kill us."

"Whatever we did must've been right." With dazzled eyes, Layla stared as the fire poured itself back into the bowl, shimmered gold. "I think what we did here, especially, finding each other, staying together."

"We didn't run." Quinn rubbed her filthy cheek against Cal's shoulder. "Any sensible person would have, but we didn't run. I'm not sure we could have."

"I heard you," Layla said to Fox. "Live or die, it was going to be together."

"We swore an oath. Me, Cal, Gage when we were ten. The

six of us tonight. We swore an oath. The fire's out." He managed to gain his feet. "I guess we'd better go take a look." When he turned to the stone, he was struck speechless.

The candles were gone, as was the bowl. The Pagan Stone stood in the moonlight, unmarred. In its center the bloodstone lay, whole.

"Jesus Christ." Cybil choked the words out. "It worked. I can't believe it worked."

"Your eyes." Fox whipped around to Cal, waved a hand in front of his face. "How's the vision?"

"Cut it out." Cal slapped the hand aside. "It's fine. It's just fine, good enough to see three's back into one. Nice job, Cybil."

They walked toward it, and much as they had during the ritual, formed a circle around the stone on the stone.

"Okay, well." Quinn moistened her lips. "Somebody's got to pick it up—meaning one of the guys because it's theirs."

Before he could lift his hand to point at Cal, both Cal and Gage pointed at Fox. "Damn it." He rubbed his hands on his jeans, rolled his shoulders, reached out.

His head fell back, his body convulsed. And as Layla grabbed him, he laughed like a loon. "Just kidding."

"God*damn* it, Fox!"

"A little levity, that's all." He scooped the stone into his hand. "It's warm. Maybe from the scary magic fire, or maybe it just is. Is it glowing? Are the red splotches glowing?"

"They are now," Layla murmured.

"It . . . it doesn't understand this. It doesn't know this. I can't see . . ." Fox swayed, the world rocked around him. Then Layla gripped his hand, and it steadied again. "I'm holding its death."

Nudging by Gage, Cybil edged closer. "How, Fox? How is that stone its death?"

"I don't know. It holds all of us now. You know, from

what we did. Our blood is what fused it. And this is part of what can—will—end it. We have the power to do that. We had it all along."

"But it was in pieces," Layla finished. "Until now. Until us—all of us."

"We did what we came to do." Reaching out, Quinn brushed her fingertips over the stone. "And we lived. Now we have a new weapon."

"Which we don't know how to use," Gage pointed out.

"Let's just get it home, find the safest place to keep it." Cal looked around the clearing. "I hope nobody had anything important in their pack, because they're incinerated. Coolers, too."

"There go my Nutter Butters." Fox took Layla's hand, kissed the wounded palm. "Wanna take a walk in the moonlight?"

"I'd love to." Could there be a better time, she thought. Could there be a more perfect time? "Good thing I left my purse at Cal's. Which reminds me. Cal, I've got the keys in there, but I'd like to hang on to them if it's okay with you and your father."

"No problem."

"What keys?" Fox asked as he rubbed some soot off her face.

"To the shop on Main Street. I needed them so Quinn and Cybil could look it over with me. It's all fine for you to look at the space with carpenter eyes, or lawyer eyes, whichever, but if I'm going to open a boutique for women, I wanted women's eyes."

"You're—what?"

"But I am going to need you, and hopefully your father, to go through it with me. And I'm going to charm your father into an I'm-in-love-with your-son discount. Hopefully a deep discount because of deep love." Fussily, she brushed at the dirt coating his shirt. "And the fact that even with the loan—and I'm counting on you to put in a really good word for me at the bank—I'm going to be on a very tight budget."

"You said you didn't want it."

"I said I didn't know what I wanted. Now I do." Clear, green, amused, her eyes met his. "Did I forget to mention it?"

"Yeah, pretty much altogether."

"Well." She gave him a shoulder bump. "I've had a lot on my mind lately."

"Layla."

"I want my own." She tipped her head to his shoulder as they walked. "I'm ready to go after what I want. After all, *Jesus*, if not now, when? By the way, consider this my two-weeks' notice."

He stopped, took her face in his hands as the others trudged and limped by them. "Are you sure?"

"I'm going to be too busy supervising the remodeling, buying stock, fighting demons to manage your office. You'll just have to deal with it."

He touched his lips to her forehead, her cheeks, her mouth, then grinned at her. "Okay."

Exhausted, content, he walked with her behind the others on a path spattered with moonlight. They'd made magic tonight, he thought. They'd chosen their path, and found their way.

The rest was just details.

Turn the page for a look at

THE PAGAN STONE

The final book in the
Sign of Seven Trilogy

Out now from Piatkus

April 2001
Mazatlán, Mexico

SUN STREAKED PEARLY PINK ACROSS THE SKY, splashed onto blue, blue water that rolled against white sand as Gage Turner walked the beach. He carried his shoes—the tattered laces of the ancient Nikes tied to hang on his shoulder. The hems of his jeans were frayed, and the jeans themselves had long since faded to white at the stress points. The tropical breeze tugged at hair that hadn't seen a barber in more than three months.

At the moment, he supposed he looked no more kempt than the scattering of beach bums still snoring away on the sand. He'd bunked on beaches a time or two when his luck was down, and knew someone would come along soon to shoo them off before the paying tourists woke for their room-service coffee.

At the moment, despite the need for a shower and a shave, his luck was up. Nicely up. With his night's winnings hot in his pocket, he considered upgrading his ocean-view room for a suite.

Grab it while you can, he thought, because tomorrow could suck you dry.

Time was already running out; it spilled like that white, sun-kissed sand held in a closed fist. His twenty-fourth birthday was less than three months away, and the dreams crawled back into his head. Blood and death, fire and madness. All of that and Hawkins Hollow seemed a world away from this soft tropical dawn.

But it lived in him.

He unlocked the wide glass door of his room, stepped in, tossed aside his shoes. After flipping on the lights, closing the drapes, he took his winnings from his pocket, gave the bills a careless flip. With the current rate of exchange, he was up about six thousand USD. Not a bad night, not bad at all. In the bathroom, he popped off the bottom of a can of shaving cream, tucked the bills inside the hollow tube.

He protected what was his. He'd learned to do so from childhood, secreting small treasures away so his father couldn't find and destroy them on a drunken whim. He might've flipped off any notion of a college education, but Gage figured he'd learned quite a bit in his not-quite twenty-four years.

He'd left Hawkins Hollow the summer he'd graduated from high school. Just packed up what was his, stuck out his thumb, and booked.

Escaped, Gage thought as he stripped for a shower. There'd been plenty of work—he'd been young, strong, healthy, and not particular. But he'd learned a vital lesson while digging ditches, hauling lumber, and most especially during the months he'd sweated on an offshore rig. He could make more money at cards than he could with his back.

And a gambler didn't need a home. All he needed was a game.

He stepped into the shower, turned the water hot. It sluiced over tanned skin, lean muscles, through thick black hair in need of a trim. He thought idly about ordering some coffee, some food, then decided he'd catch a few hours' sleep first. Another advantage of his profession, in Gage's mind. He came and went as he pleased, ate when he was hungry, slept when he was tired. He set his own rules, broke them whenever it suited him.

Nobody had any hold over him.

Not true, Gage admitted as he studied the white scar across his wrist. Not altogether true. A man's friends, his true friends, always had a hold over him. There were no truer friends than Caleb Hawkins and Fox O'Dell.

Blood brothers.

They'd been born the same day, the same year, even—as far as anyone could tell—at the same moment. He couldn't remember a time when the three of them hadn't been . . . a unit, he supposed. The middle-class boy, the hippie kid, and the son of an abusive drunk. Probably shouldn't have had a thing in common, Gage mused as a smile curved his mouth, warmed the green of his eyes. But they'd been family, they'd been brothers long before Cal had cut their wrists with his Boy Scout knife to ritualize the pact.

And that had changed everything. Or had it? Gage wondered. Had it just opened what was always there, waiting?

He could remember it all vividly, every step, every detail. It had started as an adventure—three boys on the eve of their tenth birthday hiking through the woods. Loaded down with skin mags, beer, smokes—his contribution— with junk food and Cokes from Fox, and the picnic basket of sandwiches and lemonade Cal's mother had packed. Not that Frannie Hawkins would've packed a picnic if she'd known her son planned to camp the night at the Pagan Stone in Hawkins Wood.

All that wet heat, Gage remembered, and the music on the boom box, and the complete innocence they'd carried along with the Little Debbies and Nutter Butters they would lose before they hiked out in the morning.

Gage stepped out, rubbed his dripping hair with a towel.

His back had ached from the beating his father had given him the night before. As they'd sat around the campfire in the clearing those welts had throbbed. He remembered that, as he remembered how the light had flickered and floated over the gray table of the Pagan Stone.

He remembered the words they'd written down, the words they'd spoken as Cal made them blood brothers. He remembered the quick pain of the knife across his flesh, the feel of Cal's wrist, of Fox's as they'd mixed their blood.

And the explosion, the heat and cold, the force and fear when that mixed blood hit the scarred ground of the clearing.

He remembered what came out of the ground, the black mass of it, and the blinding light that followed. The pure evil of the black, the stunning brilliance of the white.

When it was over, there'd been no welts on his back, no pain, and in his hand lay one third of a bloodstone. He carried it still, as he knew Cal and Fox carried theirs. Three pieces of one whole. He supposed they were the same.

Madness came to the Hollow that week, and raged through it like a plague, infecting, driving good and ordinary people to do the horrible. And for seven days every seven years, it came back.

So did he, Gage thought. What choice did he have?

Naked, still damp from the shower, he stretched out on the bed. There was time yet, still some time for a few more games, for hot beaches and swaying palms. The green woods and blue mountains of Hawkins Hollow were thousands of miles away, until July.

He closed his eyes, and as he'd trained himself, dropped almost instantly into sleep.

In sleep came the screams, and the weeping, and the fire that ate so joyfully at wood and cloth and flesh. Blood ran warm over his hands as he dragged wounded to safety. For how long? he wondered. Where was safe? And who could say when and if the victim would turn and become attacker?

Madness ruled the streets of the Hollow.

In the dream he stood with his friends on the south end of Main Street, across from the Qwik Mart and its four gas pumps. Coach Moser, who'd guided the Hawkins Hollow Bucks to a championship football season Gage's senior year, gibbered with laughter as he soaked himself, the ground, the buildings with the flood of gas from the pumps.

They ran toward him, the three of them, even as Moser held up his lighter like a trophy, as he splashed in the pools of gas like a boy in rain puddles. They ran even as he flicked the lighter.

It was flash and boom, searing the eyes, bursting the ears. The force of heat and air flung him back so he landed in a bone-shattering heap. Fire, blinding clouds of it, spewed skyward as hunks of wood and concrete, shards of glass, burning twists of metal flew.

Gage felt his broken arm try to knit, his shattered knee struggle to heal with pain worse than the wound itself. Gritting his teeth, he rolled, and what he saw stopped his heart in his chest.

Cal lay in the street, burning like a torch.

No, no, no, no! He crawled, shouting, gasping for oxygen in the tainted air. There was Fox, facedown in a widening pool of blood.

It came, a black smear on that burning air that formed into a man. The demon smiled. *You don't heal from death, do you, boy?*

Gage woke, sheathed in sweat and shaking. He woke with the stench of burning gas scoring his throat.

Time's up, he thought.

He got up, got dressed. Once dressed, he began to pack for the trip back to Hawkins Hollow.